# Beyond Time

## A Story From The Future

Stephen St. John

First originally published by Page Publishing 2020

ISBN 978-1-64704-367-4 (pbk)
ISBN 978-1-64704-366-7 (digital)

Printed in the United States of America

I should like to get rid of tradition and to be
completely original:
This enterprise is, however, enormous and leads to
many sufferings.
I would consider it the highest honor to be able to
create myself.
If I were not, surprisingly, myself
the product of tradition.

—Goethe

Completing the trilogy by Stephen St. John

"Happier Ever After"

"Antony, Cleopatra, and Janie"

# Contents

# 1

## Beyond the Stars

"Neither has, nor ever shall there be, a moment in time more magnificent than the next minute. Professor Andre Martin has brought *Explorer Seven* to the Big Bang and frozen time for safe study. By the end of this day, the answer sages and science have searched for will lie at our feet. We are here to search for a creator, if one there be."

Taking a deep breath, squaring shoulders at the helm, Sir Reginald Stinson continued, "Four million years ago, our ancestors climbed down Kapok trees and crossed the savanna to build skyscrapers from molten rocks. We've come a long way. Today we bear witness to the origin of the universe, the birthplace of existence, the beginning of us. Station monitors and ship portals will unfold the tale."

As he straightened his dress uniform, Stinson barked, "To your tasks. Prepare sensors for deployment. Direct all data to the bridge. We will—"

"Ohmigod sir!"

"What is it, Ensign? You're interrupting a crew briefing."

"Look for yourself! The Bang's fireball just popped a thousand meters closer. If time keeps slipping, we'll be vaporized! Andre was wrong! It can't be done!"

"That nitwit nincompoop! Discontinue broadcast and pipe me directly to Andre's lab. Martin, Martin…this is Stinson! What the hell is going on? You told me time would stop, and we would be perfectly safe sandwiched between dimensions!"

"Yes, sir. Of course, Captain. Let's see…nothing outside of the universe can affect us because there is nothing outside the universe, so it must be a calibration issue. I'm on it. I'll compensate and match shields to make sure it doesn't happen again. What the…can't be… again…a second variable? Not possible—"

"Get your sorry ass to the bridge!" Stinson screamed. "Your screw up is about to turn my ship and everyone onboard into a trillion-degree pinhead!"

"Okay, I'm here," Andre said, trembling as he reviewed navigation readouts. "O my! Fission power is diluting, and external field grids are collapsing. Where is all the power going? Diagnostics will have the answer. What! No malfunctions! ALTERATIONS OUTSIDE THE LIMITS OF QUANTUM MECHANICS. Oh no, no! That can't be! Maybe readouts—"

"Readouts my ass," Stinson howled in his ear. "Look out the window! You computer junkies are all the same, tail chasing know-it-alls who end up getting nowhere. Stand up and look around for God's sake! What are we going to do?"

Andre looked up and found half the deck officers tapping their monitors in disbelief as the rest stared forward, waiting for death to pounce one step closer. It did, a slap at a time, each gravity burst flooding the hull with an energy matrix so powerful it bonded light elements into heavy metals, causing Andre to leap when his chair cushion turned into an iron slab.

Stinson marked the dirge, "Ouch! That one hurt. We trusted you, Martin. You swore you knew what you were doing. A foot of bow plate just chipped off. You're killing us!"

The entire bridge crew approached Andre, praying for salvation. They didn't get far. Halfway across the deck, their legs petrified into posts, their faces to marble; only tears remained, begging Andre for help.

The next ripple made it all the way to Stinson. He staggered. He fell.

Andre was the last to go, tumbling to the floor, dazed, bewildered, and paralyzed; defeated by power he knew nothing about, his soul devoured by endless pain, as order shed pretense to expose demons oozing doubt.

There is relief in defeat. Andre's breath ceased. Pain was no more. There was only darkness. Then pixel by pixel, the void was replaced by the cover of Andre's sleeping pod.

*It was all a dream.*

\* \* \*

"Cyber, open pod," said Andre from inside.

Andre and Dracula had one thing in common: they both liked sleeping in coffins. Andre called his the REM 2000. On the planet of Aurelia, a similar looking contraption was named "The Next Breath," their latest space coffin. Aurelia's solar system was inner segment, as close as a cooldown can get to their galaxy's black hole, where the dead ended up. They named the trip the Passage. Beyond the Passage was eternal life. The Aurelian Institute of Divinity had written proof.

The other side of Andre's night sleep was always a hard day's work, and he wasn't one to count ceiling fan rotations before getting out of bed. His computer command automatically tilted the sleeping pod, bringing Andre's feet to the floor. Ready or not, the day began.

Andre designed the pod wide enough for two, with wiggle space for a seven-footer. The 2000, one of Andre's earliest inventions, was supported by eight titanium legs, fully mobile, assisted by sonar imaging, and could roll itself to the nearest transport station for reassignment. When home is where your head lies, the galaxy becomes your backyard. Say the word, and Mom's attic or Dad's ten acres provided air-conditioned, humidity-controlled, pitch black silent slumber until programed otherwise.

Andre's sleep lozenge stretched wide like a giant clam sailing away. Asymmetric leg tilt introduced Andre's feet to the ground at one-tenth G per second. Andre insisted on gradual acclimation to reduce orthostatic hypotension—the price great apes pay for standing up. Everyone else called it—stupid.

Andre's dad was president of Earth Aerospace. By day he ran the university, by night his lab. Andre rarely saw Adhemar. Andre's mom was also at the top of her academic career, which obligated frequent conferences.

Andre's oldest memory was falling asleep next to a computer. He would curl up beside his dad's, which occupied half of Adhemar's den. The heat kept him warm, and the blinking lights made him feel like he wasn't alone.

That computer became Andre's best friend, one that kept on giving. Andre used it to hack into the university's data stream, including surveillance cameras and recorded conference lectures. By age seven, Andre was snuggling up to his own computer, long ago named "Cyber," as "Cyber" displayed mom in the classroom or dad tinkering with electron beakers.

And so it started. The next step was perfectly logical. If Andre could press buttons and find out how Cyber was doing, why not the other way around? On his tenth birthday, Andre's masterpiece was finished. It began as a coffin designed for the gorilla that was sacrificed to keep Jim Quanuck alive.

A sudden rock slide on Mars crushed Professor Quanuck from the neck down. He was the foremost, and only, expert on infectious nano-probes, saving thousands of lives every year. Five minutes later, his team successfully transplanted his head onto the gorilla they planned to let loose in the thousand-mile terraformed forest habitat, where tourists stayed in a central luxury resort, or slept in cabins, both surrounded by force fields protecting them and keeping human life invisible to the inhabitants, who enjoyed mortal paradise.

The plan was to use Jim's stem cells to grow another body, which they did in six months back on earth. When it came time to return Jim to full Sapiens form, he ran back into the protected habitat, calling out, "Keep my body warm. Come back in six months. This is the most fun I've ever had." Which is the same thing he said every six months thereafter. Apparently, civilization is overrated.

No one blamed him. Every day, Jim was surrounded by two thousand of the most delicious fruits and vegetables in the galaxy, which were his for the asking. Every evening, after thanking them, another partner would gesture thank-you back.

And that's how Andre got the coffin for free, thanks to his dad, who truly never understood where is son was coming from.

The box was large enough to house miniature sensors of every medical apparatus on the planet. Using wave technology, Andre could wake up in the morning and examine Cyber's readouts of his own night's sleep, body, and brain activity, including technicolor reproductions of actual dream imagery.

When he added endocrine inputs and cross-referenced the data with the planetary web, Cyber began diagnosing medical maladies better than any hospital in town. The REM 2000 was on its way.

It was a perfect landing. Andre's REM 2000 got him standing, but despite one of his favorite sensations, the sound of dew-softened pine needles cushioning his toes, he wasn't smiling.

Andre stood beneath pristine pine-forest splendor: Eastern white pines, spruce, oaks, and north country sugar maples. Three hundred feet above, sunlight had just bestowed its first blessing, a colony of pine-top pyramids that sparkled as they swayed gently to a tune they alone enjoyed.

Andre sighed. *If only I had a month to bivouac high country like I did in scouts.*

To the west, a proudly antlered moose, three doe, and one fawn cast shadows beneath a canopy of sturdy trunks cleared of grown. To the east, a speck was seen diving at the surface of the lake. The immature eagle leveled at the last minute to snatch one of Mother Mallards' six chicks. Following uniform screeching, their tail feathers submerged just in time. The day before had not been as kind to a baby loon.

The last voice Andre heard every night returned at sunrise. "Good morning, Andre," Cyber said through pod speakers, with a youthful female voice expressing concern found only in a mother's tone. "I trust you slept successfully."

"I wish, my friend. Not today. Check my neuro-scans. I'm one REM short! Look at my readouts—pulse, blood pressure, and cortisol levels nowhere near optimal. Damn earthquake woke me up and triggered another friggin' nightmare."

"The one where the ship explodes and everyone dies?"

"Why do you keep asking me that question? We both know that you can read my pod's dream imagery."

"We also both know that I am following your social program. Would you like me to change my subsystem response algorithms?"

"Negative. I apologize," responded Andre quietly.

"Let's overlook the fact that you just asked your computer network to forgive your own programming, and the fact that we had this identical discussion yesterday...and say, 'Don't worry, Andre, everything will be all right.'"

"Don't worry!" Andre jeered back. "Those are also my words. You're nothing but an echo."

"Then allow me to quote you again. Restating the obvious is a waste of time."

"You're right, you're right, you're right. I'm wasting my breath and should be more polite. So...please...how's that? Please, pretty please...tell central supply I want eight gravity neutral shock absorbers delivered by sundown. Stupid earthquake. Who would have thought? Even the damn planet won't give me a break."

"You sound distraught. Perhaps you should discuss this with a human being. Shall I make an appointment with a counselor? Dr. Wellchild is in today."

"And have her scrub the mission one day before life off? Not on your life."

"As you wish. May I proceed with reflection?"

"Connect as many concepts as you wish. I programmed you not to be boring."

"If I am doing something 'not on my life,' does that mean I am alive?"

*Bang! Thud! Pound!*

*Crap, those weren't tremors. Some fool is slugging my door.*

"Cyber, shut down Aroostook County Wall Life program."

Andre's down east backwoods, grandeur as far as the eye could see, suddenly disappeared, and was replaced by a six-sided, shiny metallic chamber. Most central housing residents chose ceiling-to-floor still-life when their active living-wall panoramas were turned off. Andre saw beauty in function. Everyone else felt like the last bean in the can.

Working his way across his steel cave, Andre contorted his face into his best scowl to deal with the barbarian who violated protocol. "No one wakes me and lives not to hear about it."

The problem with Andre's "tough guy" act was his short, skinny body that confessed to canceling six health club sessions a week to sit with Cyber, who tried endlessly to help the lad, pointing out nutrition and calorie deficiencies Andre's own scans discovered. Cyber even took it upon herself to order vitamin cannolis, protein donuts, and two pounds of cheese dripping steamed vegetables delivered to his side. "Set them down. I'll get to it as soon as I finish this project, and stop nagging me."

It took two hands and one grunt, but Andre did it—flung the door so wide that it slammed against the wall, just as he began his verbal barrage: "Who the hell do you think you are? Open your eyes, fool! My hall screen clearly states *Do Not Disturb*. Are you a moron? Can't you rea—"

Andre froze. When he looked up his first thought was that they moved the garden inside—all he saw was green: green explorer outfit, green hunting cap, green shoes, green afro, and a giant tall enough to touch the ceiling, whose green face and hands blended right in. "What the...who the..."

Andre's pissed off door display left more than enough room for his surprise guest to walk right in. After casually looking around, the mountain man turned to say, with smiling sarcasm, "Hi, I'm Mike. Gee, I love what you've done with the place. What do you call it, early tin can? Why waste time looking at mountain streams or ocean beaches when every direction can have your own reflection? If you convex the angle, you will look taller, little fella."

13

"First of all," Andre replied in a huff, "I'm not short, I'm average. And second, my size lives longer, healthier lives than overgrown mutants like you."

Paying no heed, Michael continued to inspect the quarters. "Oh, that's nifty," he said, tilting his head in jest. "One chair and two escape pods. Man, this place needs serious work." Michael then slapped Andre on the back and finished with, "Hey, there's no place for ladies to sit. I've arrived just in time, buddy."

"I'm not your buddy," Andre blurted out, betraying anger. "I'm the chief engineer and flight director of the Eternity Project, with authority over construction, flight plan, and all personnel...while you, sir, are confused and extremely irritating. March your butt down to the first floor where reception will direct you to the maintenance department."

"Wait a minute," Michael said, grinning even wider. "I've seen your picture in the news. Your rat boy. You were paid twenty thousand labor hours to build a luxury resort for mice, massage beds included! I guess that makes you Andre Martin, my new roommate."

"Roommate! Five minutes of sharing air with you just destroyed one good night's sleep and half my morning. Sharing an entire room with you will never happen. In fact, from now on, do me a favor—choose any city on the planet except the one I'm in. And, Mister Know-It-All, they weren't mice, they were chipmunks. That proved my REM 2000 can better any medical team on the planet."

Michael, oblivious to Andre's mood, took out his kerchief to remove a smudge on the wall. "Your erector set needs polishing. Is it true that you put a whore house on every floor?"

Flushed and rigid, Andre fired back, "Sex, sex, sex—is that all you guys ever think about? It's not the most important thing on earth, you know."

"Well," Michael said, with a gesture moving his hand like a feather dancer, "not all of us have a knack for interior decorating. After a good meal and a dry bed, what do you put next? Or haven't you got that far yet?"

"I'm an idiot! I design the best door security system in the solar system and then open it up to let you in. The good news is that you can now walk right out."

"Hold on there. Tell me more about mice nooky. Do you have pictures?"

"Sexual tension disturbs homeostasis. It was a variable I needed to rule out."

"I second that," said Michael, sliding next to Andre. Then speaking softly to infer privacy. "How you doing lately?"

"Aw!" yelped Andre, holding both hands to his head. "None of your business, and enough is enough, tree man. *Explorer Seven* is lifting off tomorrow. I've got a lot of work to do. Evacuate the premises immediately, or I will have you tagged and monitored for a month."

Pinching his lips to appear serious yet never losing his smile, Michael backed away, less threatening. "Hey, Andy, lighten up. What we need is a second opinion. Computer…computer?"

"Her name is Cyber."

"Cyber? And a she…that's adorable. Perhaps I underestimated you, Andy. Are you hiding a robot?"

"Speaker communication is all you get. What the hell do you want?"

"Okay, okay. Settle down." Michael said, as he sat powwow. "Cyber…this is Michael Eric Asunda, galactic press corps. Display Eternity Project Command Central billeting and *Explorer Seven* accommodations."

Both men faced the far wall when it lit up, displaying floor to ceiling schematics. Base housing and ship cabin assignments supported Michael's claims. Andre hated to be wrong almost as much as he hated to admit he was wrong. One long breath left him no less flustered. "There's obviously been a mistake. I'll smoke the scum out later! Cyber, provide temporary housing for Mr. Asunda immediately, and remove him from the ship's compliment."

Reverberating from the walls, "I am sorry, Dr. Martin. You are not authorized for those functions."

"Cyber! Who has been messing with my mission? And why didn't you tell me?"

"That request was not entered into my program."

"Fine. Display the authority in charge along with their credentials."

"When the mission was reorganized one month ago, all palatine power was transferred to Dr. Karen Wellchild. She is available by appointment only. Would you like me to put in a request?"

"No! Just tell me where the usurper is right now."

"Dr. Wellchild is in transport."

A burst of a growl later, which met with confused approval from Michael, Andre said, "Not helpful. Where and when can I see her? And make the when now!"

"Dr. Wellchild is scheduled to be in her office in twenty minutes. Location, Mental Health Building, room 1114."

Finally losing his squeaky voice, Andre continued, "Cyber, hail me a transport bubble. I will take care of this myself."

Clearing his throat and looking Michael in the eye, Andre continued, "Mr. Asunda, I owe you an apology. What would you like to do while I correct the error?"

"I'm coming down from a twenty-four-hour goodbye party. If I can sleep on a Malarian spider web, I suppose one of your peapods will do."

"Certainly, step right in. No, not that one…that's mine…thank you. I will make comfort adjustments to aid your rest. Is there any particular scenery you prefer?"

"I love the Caribbean. St. Martin's brings back memories," Michael added with an exaggerated wink.

The lid closed over Michael. Andre keyed in settings. An instant later, the metal walls were replaced by swaying palm trees overlooking catamarans and paddleboards. Three warnings lit up on the pod's control panel:

UNABLE TO COMPLETE NEUROLOGIC
SCANNING WITHOUT THE INFORMED
CONSENT OF SUBJECT.

UNABLE TO SEQUENCE DNA WITHOUT
ADDITIONAL GAS-INDUCED SEDATION.

REQUESTS DENIED.

Not for long. Andre entered override codes. A green mist filled the chamber. Michael disappeared beneath it two breaths later, reaching stage VII just as quickly.

Andre's distaste for surprise equaled his contempt for ignorance; after all, there is a limited series of probabilities for three-dimensional existence. But what…but wow…Andre had never seen numbers like that before.

Finally home in the world of science, Andre commanded, "Cyber, enter all findings into my personal file. Second, from this moment on, deny, refuse, and forbid anyone access to my entries. Third, immediately identify and inform me whenever someone attempts to gain information or adjust your data bank in any way."

Suppressing a louder growl, Andre fast-paced out the door after enjoying another slam, knowing that drugged Michael was dead to the world.

# 2

## The Gang Is All Here

Andre quick stepped all the way to the bubble port at the end of the hall. He knew them well; his first summer job was inspecting them. The six-seater gravity-suspended transport spheres replaced buses, subways, and elevators before he was born. Balanced tilting allowed each to start, stop, turn, rise, and fall without disturbing center of gravity.

The product demo showed a mom placing a ball and a baby bottle on the floor as her three little ones scampered in to peer out through clear walls. They next descended twenty-two floors to ground level, made three ninety degree turns, and entered high-speed chutes leading out of town. "Thirty minutes and two hundred kilometers later," flashed at the bottom of the screen as picturesque countryside flew by.

A three-floor rise to Gramma's condo completed the journey. When the door opened, baby was fast asleep beside her bottle, still standing, and the ball hadn't budged.

Each sphere was governed to maneuver between 0.8 and 1.2 Gs. It was Andre's job to make that so. He did fine work. He also fed in an encrypted virus that allowed his private code to accelerate any transport 2 Gs straightaway.

Three minutes after gassing Michael, Andre's presence activated Dr. Wellchild's automated doors, which slid sideways, exposing rain forest still-life to the left and real-time living-wall beach front on the right, complete with the calming wash of waves making shore.

*Nice touch. No wonder they charge so much.*

Andre circled his head examining the live fichus surrounding the entrance, which also filled the far wall where Elizabeth, Dr. Wellchild's secretary, sat waiting with a smile.

"Hello, may I help you?"

"I'm Professor Martin," he said stiffly. "Coordinator of the Eternity Project. It is imperative that I speak with Dr. Wellchild immediately."

"Of course, Professor. I was told to expect you. She's in transport. She'll be back any minute. Please have a seat. My, isn't it a beautiful day."

Andre didn't sit, preferring instead to walk to the furthest corner, glace back sheepishly, and say to himself, "She's expecting me? What's going on?"

With his back to Elizabeth and those waiting for other docs, Andre pretended to examine Dr. Wellchild's diplomas, while surreptitiously pulling a palm-sized Cyberpad from his pocket.

One tap expanded it eight by ten. The second tap activated concealed sensor strips over and behind each ear, which enabled three hundred and sixty degree binocular magnification alongside remote audio pickup, technology so advanced Andre could record sight and sound from a bee humming hundreds of meters away. "Nothing escapes me." He smirked to himself.

Andre was never alone, if you count computers. "What are you doing?" said Cyber, transmitting silently to his spiral Corti.

"Never mind that. Follow my orders. Do you see the door behind me?"

"Even before you turned on the eyes in the back of your head, I had four room cameras on line. And I will note, Elizabeth's joyful expression lowered your blood pressure five points. I also—"

"Okay, I get it. You're always ahead of me. Anyway, capture everyone walking into the room, database their images, and report back in stealth mode."

"As you wish. Dr. Wellchild's classified records and everything she's published are already available on command."

Those passing behind Andre hiding in the corner looked over to see routine photon jet-specs on his pad. Andre's downgaze line of sight saw the room behind him. Filling in the top of his screen was Dr. Wellchild's file. "Wow, she's published a ton of crap for someone in their twenties. Another study junkie on her way to spinsterhood I'm sure."

Andre was wrong. Beige kitten heels broke the threshold, supporting legs tan, toned, and freestyler perfect. Floral miniskirt, Indian beads, and lace blouse followed. "It can't be."

It was—blond pixie hairdo, dreamy blue eyes, girl-next-door dimples, and hips that immobilized every intention the universe has to offer.

Andre set an all-time life's record. His brain went blank for two and a half seconds—total space out. It took a flippant head shake to break the spell, leaving him saying to himself, almost convincingly, "Mesmerized by beauty. Love at first sight…nonsense. Well-packed cytoplasm, that's all. It's a trick. I'm not falling for it."

"Would you like a second opinion?" Cyber offered.

"Do I have a choice?"

"Yes, you can tell me to file it, like you usually do. And then let curiosity drive you crazy by sunset. Same result except for the inefficient informational tran—"

"Okay, spill it."

"My readouts just followed your consciousness down three subsystems. Either you have been drugged or your *I* just met your *we*. And it is a good thing no one in the room can detect the microscopic lip and facial micromovements you use to communicate to me, because if they did, they would have recognized a jaw drop followed by a prolonged 'Daaa.'"

"Daaa! I certainly did not 'Daaa.' I never 'Daaa.' In fact, my brain is incapable of getting remotely close to a 'Daaa.'"

"There are so many days I wish I could laugh," Cyber said, then adding in a Marx Brothers punchline, "That last statement of yours turned the absurdity dial all the way to hilarious."

"You're not my mother, and I've told you a dozen times. I don't need women. They're a black hole no man escapes. I know. I've been there. I'm fine just the way I am. It just took me a second to reorient concept with perception."

"Really?" answered Cyber. "And how did you know she was Dr. Wellchild—or should I say Karen—before I identified her for you?"

"Logical deduction. It's her office. Who is that behind her?"

"Sarah Louse Miller, the doctor's life-long friend and confidante, and mostly what she isn't…straight brown hair, dark eyes, and a nose politely considered 'worldly.' From the looks of her Navajo dress, probably handmade. I suspect she considers herself 'one of the people.'"

"The prairie gets cold at night. I'm certain American Indians never spun fabrics that sheer or let their women get so bony."

"My, my," said Cyber. "Aren't we snippy this morning. I would say she carries an air of universal acceptance tempered with feminine appeal."

"And I would say that you're reading fashion magazines again. Can it."

"For someone who doesn't care about women, you sure are spending a lot of time staring."

"My brainstem dates back to reptiles. Give me a break. Now shut up. I want to listen."

The two ladies walked the length of the waiting room to the corner furthest from Andre, where they stood at the edge of the beach, blocked by four feet of ficus from Elizabeth. The living wall background was life size. From a distance, the young lovelies looked like they were actually standing on sand.

"Over here should be fine," Karen said as she faced open sea. "I don't want anyone to butt in."

With a branch overhanging, Sarah looked around before continuing. "So you get the picture. There is no way I will ever baby-doll dress up for a snooty, stuck-up mother-in-law."

"I don't blame you," commiserated Karen. "It was your wedding. His mom sounds like a witch."

"Demanding and obnoxious! Every week, she handed be another list of expectations. Today is the first time since I said 'yes' that I feel my life belongs to me. And it's going to stay that way, which is why I left Richard a block from the altar."

"I'm surprised you got that close. Good for you, girl."

"So what about you Karen?" Sarah said, glaring a demand for the truth. "Every streamed gazette puts Tony on top of its eligible bachelor list. Handsome, rich, famous, and you had the wedding of the century planned. What gives?"

Karen checked the room from her angle, hesitated for a second watching a paddleboard surf to shore, then continued nonchalant. "It only took two weeks for the Neuroscience Academy to translate scans into another dozen bipolar syndromes. I left France early enough to make Manhattan by nine.

"Tony wasn't expecting me until the end of the month. His code let me in the building, up his private elevator, and opened the door to his penthouse."

"The rich and famous have everything."

"My plan was to surprise him in bed. When I opened the door, guess who was standing in the living room, bare naked, wearing a French maid's apron?"

Sarah gasped. "Not Jean Swanson! I never trusted her."

"If only! That would've been easier to take. No, standing right in front of me—looking absolutely gorgeous, I might add—was an android *me*!"

"Oh, that is scummy," spat Sarah.

"I know…right?"

"Well, now," said Sarah, searching for a spin, "maybe he just missed you."

"He has three shuttles and two pilots on call twenty-four hours a day. In less than an hour, he could have surprised me any place on earth."

"Yes, of course. I forgot how the other half lives. But…on the other hand, robot sex did eliminate prostitution and rid the planet of STDs."

"Yeah, yeah, sure," Karen said. "I have nothing against machines stepping in, or lying down, to improve the quality of life, or a good's night's sleep, even admire Bill Flink who donated half his wealth to open free clinics to diagnose and treat STDs with a one-hour orgy."

"I remember that. What was his slogan…oh, yeah…'Double dipping and all you can eat.' It worked. And mechanical sex surrogates also helped drop the planet's divorce rate."

"The divorce rate on your folk's commune is zero, and they don't have sex machines."

"Ya, but they pretend Woodstock never ended."

"Don't we all?"

"Karen, get real. Tony is a catch. Every girl wants him. And as far as robots are concerned, do you remember the night you and I promised never to mention again?"

"The one you keep bringing up? Of course, but we were drunk teenagers acting out groupie fantasies. Not the same thing."

"Need I remind you that it was your idea to steal the anatomically correct android look-alike from the music department? We both had a crush on the lead singer of Crash, and neither one of us stood up until we ran out of beer and his batteries ran dry."

In unison, they both giggled. "Orgasm night."

"And," Sarah pointed out, "if you hadn't already slept with the senior—"

"And slept with him again the next night—"

"Who caught us plugging him back in—"

"We might still be undergraduates today. Every time you tell that story, it ends the same way."

"Because it's true," Sarah said getting serious. "Karen, get real. One robot trick and you call off the wedding? You could always get one of your own. Tits for tat. And when I say tat, I mean—"

"I know what you mean, but there's more."

"Really? Don't keep me in suspense. Lay in on me."

"I heard Tony in the bedroom barking orders like a military officer. 'Karen, grab the oil, it's time for my foot massage.' He was pretending the robot was actually me!"

"Okay, that is uncomfortable. So what did you do?"

"Tony's computer skills are limited. His door code also deactivated the android from the panel."

"And?"

"I stripped naked, put on the apron, let down my hair, and picked up the massage oil."

"You didn't!"

"Tony was in bed buck naked on his back, pointing at his left foot. He said, 'Crawl over me on your hands and knees, and massage my feet. I want your butt in my face.'"

Sarah shrieked with laughter. "He had no idea it was you?"

"None whatsoever! You know how sophisticated the latest androids are. I could be one right now and you wouldn't know."

"So go on. What happened then?"

"His next command was, 'Turn around, it's time to play horsy.' That's when I let him have it. I spun around, grabbed the ten-inch vibrator out of his hand and said, 'Bend over, it's your turn.'"

Sarah howled as the entire waiting room, save Andre, looked over. After regaining composure, she asked, "What did he say?"

"Tony said nothing, just lay there looking like an eight-year-old watching his first horror movie."

"So what then? Pillow throwing? Lamp smashing? Did you get physical?"

"Actually, I surprised myself. All I felt was relief. I suddenly realized we didn't have a mental bond, and we never would. It was all physical. He plays on top of life. He never embraced what we had together or all our future could be."

Sarah shook her head. "Wow, how could we have been so blind?" Adding with a hand on Karen's shoulder, "I'm so sorry."

Karen shrugged. "We're all in love with love. Nobody—no man, no woman—has ever been perfect. We spend our lives compromising and tolerating each other. The hard part is stumbling over full disclosure.

"Speaking of which, guess what I found in Tony's closet on my way out?"

"More sex androids?"

"You win the prize. Now guess who."

"I'll take ancient history for three—Marilyn Monroe, Jane Mansfield, and Margaret Thatcher."

"Close. The last queen of England, holding a can of whip cream, and you, with a black whip coming out of your—"

"Ewwww!" Sarah said, cringing.

"And incidentally, you gained twenty pounds and three cup sizes."

Sarah grabbed her breasts. "Hey, that I could use. But with Tony? That is creepy, creepy, creepy! So after all those dinners we had together, do you think, after you, Tony leched out on me in the closet? I don't want to know what he used for lube that night."

Both laughed through sparkling eyes for over a minute. Sarah finally asked, "Are you and I running away? Is that why we are here?"

"If you and I were running away, we would be on one of my family's private island retreats. We're not in the Caribbean, South Pacific, or Mediterranean because—you guessed it—of a man. Professor Andre Martin, to be specific."

Sarah sighed. "Don't bother telling me about him. I've read it all, and he sounds like a jerk."

"A brilliant jerk. If he's right, we're in for an adventure unparalleled in human history."

"And if he's wrong and crazy?"

"I'm expecting two independent evaluations over the next twenty-four hours."

"Isn't that cutting it a bit close?"

"Not really. I'm in charge, and we can back out anytime. But if you have doubts, feel free to escape to the island of your choice without me."

"And leave you one hundred and twenty handsome young men all to yourself? I don't think so."

"Okay then. *Explorer Seven* docks outside my office window in one hour. I've scheduled an executive officers' meeting in thirty minutes. Martin should drop in to sound off any second."

Karen and Sarah looked around the room. Andre's eyes widened when both ladies paused, curious as they viewed his backside.

"Who else are we expecting, Karen?"

"Janie Amed and Bradley Williams are on the transport behind me, with instructions to come straight here. Do me a favor. Go to Martin's room and pick up his roommate, Michael Asunda."

"Of course."

Sarah pulled Karen in for a long hug then stepped lightly out of the room. Karen disappeared behind her office door. Andre terminated transmission.

"Andre," Cyber began, "I just data referenced every human being we have met since you activated me eighteen years ago. Karen is not a copy. She's original. What gives? What do you plan to do?"

"Do you mean...what are *we* planning to do? To begin with, she's outnumbered and a headshrinker who knows nothing about astrophysics, time travel, or *Explorer Seven*. She has no reason to be here. Leave her to me. This is my mission. I'm in charge."

# 3

## The Whites of Her Eyes

Andre pocketed his pad and stormed across the room flaring resentment. Elizabeth blocked his advance; the Global Aeronautics and Space Administration was on the line. Dr. Wellchild had to take the call.

Following her nature, Elizabeth was reassuring and sympathetic and handed Andre milk and cookies. His steam fizzled. Andre sat.

"How did she do that?" Cyber asked. "I forget to double bolt a file and I'm in hot water for a week. Elizabeth smiles rosy cheeks and you melt. It's the opposite sex thing, isn't it? Maybe that reptile brainstem of yours is not such a bad idea after all. Boy, I wish I had an opposite sex."

Andre used the time to look back. Five years earlier, on December 11, 2475, he was awarded a Nobel Prize for streamlining warp drive. GASA wanted more. They had explored the Milky Way but didn't have a prayer of reaching another galaxy within a lifetime. GASA asked Andre for more speed.

Andre said, "No way. The universe is too big to travel through." GASA was barking up the wrong tree. Instead of going forward, Andre insisted that mankind must step sideways—scoot around space. Transdimensional physics began that afternoon. Six months later, GASA was reviewing Martin's specs for a ship to do just that.

A hail of controversy followed a hurricane of insults. Every physicist in the galaxy shot him down, except his dad, who was considered as unstable as his strange son. Adhemar wrote the check. Andre built a ten-foot prototype with his bare hands and ten thousand Cyber nanomites.

There is truth history embraces and truth authority strains to deny. Strategic Command banned Andre's toy from the solar system, claiming it was the most dangerous and most expensive nuclear weapon ever constructed. Vegas set the odds of Andre surviving the test at one in a thousand and took all bets.

And that was the send-off Andre did not enjoy when he left for deep space asteroid Epcalate 256, ten light years from earth. Brazen as always, he set up a camera to transmit the image of his prototype, named *Explorer I*, that was three feet from where he was standing when he set her off.

The ten-foot missile disappeared the second it powered up, proving that trans-dimensional travel was indeed possible. No one knew where it went, but it got there.

*Explorer II* added navigation and U-turn hardware but no drivers ed. Its return landing split the asteroid in half. Andre's jet pack saved his life, though it did take him ten hours to find his ship.

*Explorer III* left with a chimp, who returned bone dust, dating the primate's death ten thousand years earlier. No one ventured a guess—not even Andre.

*Explorer IV, V,* and *VI* went perfectly—parakeets, buzzards, and baboons all returned healthy and happy, but the test flights lacked the power needed to escape the galaxy.

The answer—subatomic fission, *Explorer Seven,* twice the size of GASA's jumbo stargazer. Half her weight was a reactor forceful enough to push time aside.

"After all that, five years later," Andre said to himself standing, "some idiot is going to order me around? I don't think so. *Explorer Seven* is my life's work. I'm calling the shots."

"You may go in now."

"Wow, will you look at that?" whispered Cyber inside Andre's head.

"Quiet, I need to concentrate."

Which didn't come easy. Andre had hesitated the moment he stepped into Dr. Wellchild's office, which was decorated in varnished shiplap—not the electronically projected kind, the genuine article. The light pine walls and solid mahogany desk took him back to his Mount Katahdin cabin. Andre touched the walls and ran a finger across the edge of the desk.

"Yes, it's real. My great-grandfather made this desk from wild-harvested timber while my great-grandmother was doing research deep in the electrostatic chambers of a metal moon," Karen mused as she also rubbed her hand across the desk. "They had to communicate the old-fashioned way. Every week, her supply ship left with another handwritten love letter, composed by her husband on this work of art."

She looked straight into his eyes. "You must be Professor Martin."

Andre avoided her gaze and crossed the office to inspect the landing field through the full-window back wall. "*Explorer Seven* will be here in forty-five minutes," he said presently. "My pad just received a bow shot of her rounding Jupiter. Hull and propulsion passed the final test. She slipped straight through the gas giant without a scratch."

Karen swiveled in her chair but gave no response.

Andre turned his gaze skyward. "Five years of days and half my nights have gone into the Eternity Project. Its success demands my undistracted attention and complete control. Until an hour ago, I thought I had it."

"The Eternity Project was cancelled six months ago."

"Cyber did inform me, but when I heard about tomorrow's lift-off, I assumed the mission was reinstated."

"Did you open a single one of the C-streams I sent you?"

"I get a thousand of day, can't possibly be bothered. Cyber lets me know about anything that matters."

"Only if you program appropriate priorities."

Andre turned abruptly to face her. "My highest, and only, priority is the performance of the most complicated vehicle every constructed. I'm taking on the entire universe, not serving tea in loony land!"

"I know that smile." Cyber snuck to Andre, "It's Mona Liza. At least I think it's a smile."

Andre flipped his hand, a gesture Cyber knew meant "shut down." Karen, unfazed and tender, motioned an invitation for Andre to sit. He had just read that she was the most-published authority on the psychological effects of space travel, why GASA had invited her to attend the confirmation conference on the Eternity Project—a meeting Andre had been, he also just discovered, intentionally kept in the dark about.

One tap on Karen's electronic desk inlay and the full-wall window turned into the confirmation conference report, with ten summary conclusions highlighted: "irresponsible," "scientifically reckless," "a waste of lives," and "doomed to fail," stood right out.

Caught between hurt, anger, and the letdown of being left out, Andre's pompous façade melted away. "What happened?"

"Your handpicked pal, Captain Reginal Stinson, that's what. The most experienced officer in GASA called you a fool. Astrophysics confirmed that none of your equations balance. Several variables are missing.

"The fission reactor that killed three thousand on Taurene 4 came up several times. If a five-kilometer-square power plant and two thousand of our best engineers can't turn protons, neutrons, and electrons into pure energy, the butt of a spaceship hasn't a prayer."

"I spoke with Mark twenty-four hours before he and his team were lost," Andre said. "The power increments Cyber brought to my attention exceeded 2 percent per hour, exceed 1 percent, and containment fails."

"The committee heard a transcript of that conversation. You called Mark a 'sequacious dinosaur' and recommended that he take his head out of his ass. Your social skills leave a lot to be desired."

"So why are we here?" Andre asked, brightening up.

"Stinson again. His flyby contradicted your Asteroid 939 prediction. Sir Reginald presented data confirming that three weeks from today, Asteroid 939, traveling half the speed of light, will hit Earth. Its momentum will turn the planet into rock vapor, and we all go down with the ship. Life on Earth is over. They're not going public. It's too late to evacuate. Everyone blames you."

Andre resisted the urge to expel an exasperated sigh. "First of all, flying by an asteroid that size contaminates readings with your own gravitational influence and warps forward space from photon backwash, both of which interfere with dead reckoning, which is always dead wrong.

"If they want to know what's going on, GASA must plant a probe and get as far away as possible. Stinson is a skilled sled jockey, but I have yet to meet one capable of calculus. All I need is one week out there to set that Neanderthal straight."

"If you do, *Explorer Seven* will never leave the ground."

Two more desk taps turned the meeting summary into *Explorer Seven*'s redesign.

Andre jumped to his feet. "What the hell did you do to my ship? Dance hall, tennis courts, swimming pool, Irish pub. What is this, *The Love Boat?* The only thing you left out is a drunken orgy chamber."

"We can add that if you like."

"Very funny. And my private quarters are supposed to be between the spectroscopy lab and navigation. Both are missing."

"Cool off, have a seat. At the meeting, no one bought eternity as a destination, but with Armageddon on the way, it's bedlam panic. They're betting this ship and all our lives that we can sidestep time long enough to get to the nearest M-class planet and back off the clock, and in so doing, enable continuous boarding. Billions of lives will be saved."

"Saved from what, another sunny day? Why didn't they contact me? Every defendant has the right to face his accuser," screamed Andre pacing the floor. "Just because I'm a man doesn't mean I don't have feelings. I struggle to keep my head above water just like everyone else. And then, to send a civilian, not even a physicist, to pull the rug from under my feet. It's too much. And a woman no less!"

Standing up, standing her ground, Karen fired both barrels: "Do have a problem with my sex? At lease we think about someone other than ourselves."

Andre backed away but no less resolved. "That is what you *want* us to believe, as you *lie* to yourselves about your real priorities, manipulating us to serve your bottom line, and then lying to yourselves again about not using your bottoms to get what you want, right after slamming us for noticing them."

Karen stepped closer as she rounded the desk. "Hey, I'm the psychologist here."

"And I'm the one who mapped your wiring, a maze of obscuration and deceit if ever there was one."

"And I suppose you men are guardian angels?"

"The only thing I guard is truth...and unlike your sex, I am constrained by the limits of rationality."

"Oh, so now women are illogical?"

"A more accurate description would be *schizophrenogenic*."

"Look who is talking. Your sex pretends it's building an empire or saving the world, while all the time all you're really doing is playing king on the mountain, slugging it out with the rest of the little boys infected with testosterone."

"Without which our species would have gone extinct before we learned how to spell."

"Don't kid yourself. Estrogen led us out of the jungle one baby at a time."

Andre took it to the mat without blinking, "Your narcissism may have helped us escape the swamps, but it left you vulnerable to mob mentality."

"Get real," Karen fired back. "It's your mobs that do damage. Men kill men. We just leave you frustrated because you can't fence words with our finesse."

"Oh," Andre got out slowly, trying to appear confident, "so you admit, that right or wrong, you're captious and ill-tempered and brand every little boy who needs support every bid as much as every little girl with original sin, insisting, as pure prejudice, that all men are guilty, an injustice never acknowledged, even after your domination is set in stone."

"Dominate…no, even the score…maybe. Your sex stands a foot taller than ours. You can take us out with a single punch."

Andre, nodding agreement on that particular of Karen's sociobiology, countered, successfully in his mind, "Which only an idiot would do, losing face and incurring the wrath of the pack, before being left out in the cold…forever."

"When it comes to idiots," Karen retorted more forcefully, "your sex has an ample supply."

"As does womanhood."

"And," Karen continued, with arms crossed, in cross-examination, "At least our sex sticks together."

"Until we're out of the room and you turn on each other. And the reason we guys don't gang up on you is that we all want to be the last man standing. DNA's dirty work."

"That kept us from turning back into dirt," Karen interrupted, causing Andre to pause digesting a new concept, his favorite sport.

"So," he continued, professorially detached, "we covet mating. You covet resources. Children get made. Children get fed…DNA looking after itself. I can live with that. It's just that happy ever after is nowhere in the loop, and all those tough guys who mistreat you and hard women who hound us get in the way. I suppose that makes us both victims."

"Or beneficiaries, depending on how we play the game. Psychologists begin with the basics. Half our brains are animal hard wired, and the other half chained to culture."

"I would say," Andre said politely, "it's more like eighty-twenty."

"Either way," Karen slowed down to say, "we can reprogram ourselves, just like you do Cyber."

"Cyber talks back to me."

"Good for her. It means you've installed reflection and logical ethics. But we're different. Our hardware stays our hardware. We can't press a button or wish it away, and repression carries a steep price.

"It's not enough to choose change. We must do something about it every day of life. We're not trains that can alter course by turning a switch. We're more like high-profile vehicles hit broadside by gale force gusts once an hour, requiring countermeasures just as often. Life is not about peace. It is about going forward, staying the course, after picking the right one."

Three seconds of welcome silence followed. Andre then added with pure intent, "So would you say it was the Egyptians who screwed us up by blindfolding us with narratives? We were better off one family living under the stars."

With a smile and a dreamy glance, Karen followed suit, "Yes, when sex was fun and babies belonged to everyone to love. You might say it was the dad thing that got in the way. You know, you guys not sharing your toys or women."

"Sharing, you say? Not one queen in history abdicated her throne, and the only advice they offered starving sisters was 'Let them eat cake.' And as far as men are concerned, water is only coveted in a drought, and your sex dammed the river."

"It wasn't women. It was culture that dried up the stream, and both sexes let it run astray."

Andre, less tense, more amiable, ventured, "Are we actually agreeing?"

"On some things…yes."

"Is it therefore fair to say," Andre summarized, "that all both genders need to do is get the mud out of their eyes?"

"And by mud, do you mean what most of us don't see?" Karen said in a professorial tone.

"Yes," said Andre returning to the battlefield, noticeably quivering, opening wounds better left in the past, "for instance, after you get what you want from us, we're sent to the back of the line for the last ration."

"And after you get what you want from us, you roll over and fall asleep."

"Which, you insist, is a privilege we grovel dearly for before being insulted and passed over. It's not easy never making the grade."

Karen, true to her profession and listening to the mother inside every woman, suddenly quieted her tone. "As we are unsteady following the spastic meanderings of your trajectory."

"While all the time," Cyber added out loud for both to hear, "all the two of you want to do is to rock babies, hug, and kiss good night. Humans beings! What a mess! Whew!"

Karen looked up at the ceiling speaker, did not look surprised, and asked kindly, "So, Andre's computer—Cyber, I believe—what would you recommend?"

"I suggest that you do your best to love minute by minute, hour after hour, day to day, one year following another, lifetime after lifetime."

"I told you to shut down, Cyber," Andre ordered. "Go away."

Karen decided not to respond to Cyber. There would be time— perhaps. Instead, she returned to her seat and took several deep breaths to gain Andre's complete attention.

"Andre, how do you think we are doing so far?"

"Not well. I apologize. My world is changing, and I didn't expect it."

"We're all on that train. And I also should know better. I'm sorry."

With that, Karen rolled her chair back behind the desk, faced Andre, then sat, and spun once around. "That revolution just changed my role from mission commander to ship's counselor, and you have my word that our discussion will remain forever private. When was the last time you had a date?"

Karen's compassion left Andre exposed and fidgeting with his collar. "I hang out at the health club sometimes."

"That's not what I meant, and you know it. Let's try another approach. Who is your best friend? Can you even name one?"

"I'm a guy. We're not chatty like you."

"Okay, you're a guy. Every other guy your age is prowling around aching for hot sex. When was the last time you made love to a woman, or even a robot?"

"I've programmed dozens of androids. All I see is a complicated trash compactor. I'll pass."

"Okay, the real thing. How long has it been? Days, weeks, months, years? What was her name?"

"What does this have to do with the mission?"

"To begin with, there is no mission. Noah's Ark is closer to the mark. *Seven* doesn't have warp drive capability. If your magic fries, we're marooned in space. You and I may be stranded onboard for the rest of our lives. Heck, our great-grandchildren might still be generations away from getting back to Earth, or what's left of it."

"I'll make sure that doesn't happen."

"So you say," Karen said, tipping back her chair. "The funny thing is, the most brilliant minds on earth disagree with the great Professor Martin. Let's hypothesize. You and I, along with 138 other twenty-six-year-olds…an hour, a day, or a week from take-off, are happy to be alive, but drifting aimlessly trillions of light years, and God knows how many time years, from home. Your giant lozenge," she said, gesturing to the display, "could be our next, and last home. What are you going to do? Spend twenty-four hours a day in your lab, pushing buttons, talking to your buddy Cyber?

"Andre…I disagree with your objection to my leadership. If—and yes, I said if—we leave tomorrow, we may spend the rest of our lives in space. My job is to make sure physical and mental health come first. My grandfather used to say, 'Fail physiology, and you fail life. Pass physiology, and you get a chance at everything else.' And by physiology he meant proper nutrition, adequate sleep, robust exercise, and intimate social and sensual relationships.

"Andre, it is also my responsibility to make sure you, in particular, remain stable so that we all survive."

"Don't worry about me," Andre scoffed. "I've always been able to take care of myself, and I always will."

"'Able to take care of myself.' Let's examine that conclusion of yours. Right after I said 'My job is to make you happy,' every other testosterone jockey would pounce straight to flirtation, saying something like, 'Just looking at you makes me happy. Will you join me for dinner?' or low-ball a 'Together we'd never be lonely. The hills are calling. Let's explore them together.' Andre, why doesn't your forebrain listen to the rest of your body?"

"Well, pardon me for having goals, or ambition."

"You say 'ambition.' I say 'control-freak obsession.'"

Andre waved his hand dismissively. "Where are you going with this? What's your diagnosis, Doctor?"

"Sure enough. Try this one on for size. You, Professor Andre Martin, display classic obsessions stemming from compulsions subliminally compensating for falsely perceived inadequacies, which stem from genetic variation and incomplete childhood socialization."

"Whoa! I'm impressed," Andre sneered. "Three billable diagnostic codes in one sentence. One more and you've met your day's quota. You can knock off early for the pool."

"There is a big difference between being a nonconformist and not being conformable."

"It's a free planet. If I want to be a socially uninvolved scientist, that's my business."

"Living in the basement of the physics lab...yes. Keeping 240 other human beings alive, including yourself, in God knows how many dimensions...no."

Andre got up and leaned against the back wall, not noticing that Karen looked down to her desk less often when he did so. She no longer had her chair read-outs of his blood pressure, pulse, and EEG amplitudes.

Karen also stood, stepped to the opposite side of the room, mirrored casual posture, and waited. Andre opened the floor. "So what's your angle, Doc?"

"Andre, I know you don't want your world to change. I know you don't want a roommate. I also know that everyone needs a friend. Once we're in space, living arrangements can change. Share the gift of life. Give Michael Asunda a chance."

"That glob of chlorophyll is a drug ball packing six spare genomes. Replace him with someone else."

Karen narrowed her eyes. "The only way you could know that is if you scanned him without informed consent and committed chemical assault. Just because you *can* do something doesn't mean you *should* do it. The world is not your test tube."

"Those scans documented that over seven hundred milligrams of caffeine and almost two hundred grams of alcohol were ingested over the last twenty-four hours. I reviewed your publications. You recommend a limit of two hundred milligrams of caffeine a day and admit that amount still makes it hard to sleep at night and difficult to light up your brain the next day, which has never made sense to me.

"Einstein went without socks for one less daily chore. Why would anyone add running helter-skelter, from dawn to dusk, in withdrawal, chasing a drug that cripples neurons, and steals hard cash? Drug addiction is slavery. No one walks that tightrope without paying a price, and everyone lies to themselves about it.

"And then there is your precious alcohol. Just thirty grams is carcinogenic and hepatotoxic, not to mention one-way neuron death, not that you'll ever need your brain for anything of course, or that it doesn't fall apart all by itself, so let's just speed up the process," said Andre, spinning a crazy finger around his temple.

"Allow me to quote you, *Dr. Wellchild*: 'The more caffeine and alcohol you drink, the less energy and happiness you end up with, and the sooner you may die.'"

"Right there," Karen pointed and then quickly reholstered her pointing finger, "is your problem. The joy of living can also rise to extravagant heights. There is a reason we call Saturday night 'party night.' Let your hair down once and a while. Mixing it up now and again adds pleasure. My money is on Cyber calculating profit."

"If you weigh hangovers in hours or half days, maybe. But not when you more honestly include the imbalance that linger for months. The rush ain't worth the crush."

Karen refused to budge. "The philosophic and physiologic examination of that assumption we can get to later. For now, concentrate on the fact that every member of the crew carries at least one PhD. They are accomplished scholars in their fields. Disciple and responsibility go with the territory.

"Every one of them has also signed an informed consent for nightly pod scans. Physical ailments will be detected and treated on the spot. Drug levels will be charted by the hour. Don't worry, everything will be fine.

"Mental health is complicated," she continued. "Each meal and bar drink will be individually ordered and tracked. If a crew member imbibes more than thirty grams of alcohol at one sitting, or if repeated imbibing compromises their performance, that crew member will first be notified by the computer, and if the situation does not balance out, I will be informed and get involved."

"How admirable." Andre droned sarcastically, "So you plan to be everyone's mother—or should I say, Mother Superior."

"Quite the contrary. The system is automated and respectfully private. The ship's computer, which is also part of your Cyber, will just substitute placebo at the bar."

"Oh well," Andre lightly threw out, learning that Cyber would have access to every drop used onboard, where, when, and by whom.

"But it's not going to happen," Karen assured. "They are smart people. They know how to maximize health and party too."

Andre's eyes popped as he jumped forward. "Hold off just a minute! Right there on the bottom left of the screen. The read-out lists cannabinoid cupcakes."

"Yes, but if anyone's baseline dopamine levels drop and they lose full commitment to life or start trash-dump sleeping, they will end up with as many clean cupcakes as they can eat. And soaring more than once a week is discouraged."

"I get it," Karen said firmly, "you don't trust me. You don't trust anyone. I'm not asking you to. Your own REM 2000s will tell the story."

"Okay," Andre said with a suspicious head turn, "what level of regeneration are you expecting?"

"With the exception of Sunday morning, I'm expecting 97 percent or higher. My personal 2000 has documented 98 percent or higher since the day it rolled itself in the door.

"How about you, Andre? Did you stop working at sundown, jog ten miles, and play the evening away? How was your night's sleep?"

"I barely reached 76 percent, but it wasn't my fault."

"Bottom line, Andre," Karen said, lifting her eyes with excitement, "your achievements and my skills convinced a room of fat old admirals to *carte blanche* hand over the most expensive joyride ever fantasized. They grilled me about everything except the orgies and loved that your REM 2000s will keep us under control, so they think.

"And, Andre, you will be right beside me. Anytime you want to see crew readouts, even my own, no problem. But we must be a team. And know this also—my life is not a work detail, nor should anyone's be. We sail a party barge if ever there was one. I'm popping three bottles of Normandy's best champagne at the ball tonight. One glass has your name on it. You have no idea how lucky you are, and you have me to thank for it."

The window was back. Andre stepped over and looked sideways then turned to say, "Bottom line back to you. I'll put up with Michael for two weeks and adjust my schedule to add one hour of face to face social interaction a day. But"—he leaned over toward Karen—"full command of *Explorer Seven* must be mine."

Karen crossed her arms. "The committee's flight requirements were made nonnegotiable. All command codes and final authority remain in my hands."

"If I leave GASA, I can make enough money in the private sector to fund my own mission."

"Sure, in ten years," Karen snapped. "Do whatever you want to do. I'm not at all certain I'm willing to spend the next two years, let alone the rest of my life, dealing with you anyway. Breakfast waffles tomorrow morning overlooking Marin County are sounding better by the minute.

"I'm not your computer," Karen monotoned, as she slumped in her chair. "I wear down, and you're doing it. You heard the deal…take it or leave it. My computer will give you thirty seconds to decide."

At that, from room speakers, Karen's computer voice, sounding like her grandfather, soft and melodic, the way she remembered him sitting at the fireplace, began, "Thirty…twenty…ten, nine, eight…"

Andre faced the window. When the countdown hit twenty, his head began to bob ever so slightly. Karen knew one subject after another was being dispensed with. When he turned, a sneaky smirk gave away the fun he just had dealing with the caliber of Karen's intellect. Besides, he planned to do whatever he wanted anyway.

"I agree to your terms. We'll get along just fine."

"Thank you, Professor Martin. Computer, stop the countdown."

Andre said no more and just turned for the door, but as it opened, Karen added, "Oh, Professor. By the way, when you get back to your lab, I will need you to open a few systems for me: power plant, computer navigation, field adjusters, your sleep pod scans, and personal files. I will be monitoring them."

And old Andre was back, soldier marching to the front of the desk, leaning over, and louder than necessary, informed Karen, "Transdimensional travel welds power and navigation symbiotic. The ship's systems are so delicate that even my fingers get tense making adjustments. If you tap in for information, the entire array, shields included, could go haywire, stranding us in space, or more likely, shower our atoms every direction there is.

"Does your fancy PhD cover those contingencies? Dying for a cause is one thing. Dying because I let a fool push the wrong bottom would make me an idiot. Request denied!"

"Andre," Karen said, letting him have it, "I don't think you understand—"

"*I* understand perfectly, and *you* have no idea what we're in for. So understand this. You will never gain access to my world unless you're sitting beside me with your hands tied behind your back."

"Why you—"

"Save it. Women always have insults ready for us. I've heard them all, and if you were in my shoes, you'd sense abuse. It's astounding that a sex as loving as your own can blind itself to class prejudice. Guilty until proven innocent is the story of my life and every other man's alive."

Silence followed as both fumed eye to eye. Andre reloaded, "Oh, wow," a salacious smile twitching his lips, "I may be on the road to recovery. The image of you with your hands behind your back just got me excited. That's how you want me to be...right?"

Before Karen could answer, Andre pulled himself up to full height. "Those are *my* conditions. Take it or leave it. If you find them unacceptable, I'll gladly place tomorrow's pecan waffle order for you right now. You have twenty seconds to make up your mind. Cyber… count down."

"Twenty…"

Karen's face turned to stone.

"Ten…"

Andre also remained motionless, although inside he wanted to walk away and have done with it.

"Two…one…zero."

No one budged.

"I'll agree to let you run the ship with one stipulation."

"I'm listening."

"Under no circumstances will you ever break into, snoop, browse, scan, or eavesdrop on my office, my computer network, or those of any other crew member."

"If I did, you would never know," boasted Andre.

"Maybe not…but we need to trust one another…or, if you wish, I can have a pizza delivered to your lab for another fun night in the basement of the science building. You and Cyber make a lovely couple."

For the first minute, they both stared daggers. For the next thirty seconds, each asked themselves *What am I doing?* Then maybe the dream got to them, or mutual respect, or maybe deep down inside, handsome couldn't say goodbye to beautiful, or maybe both were just bored with everyone else, or more likely, destiny enforced itself. At length, Andre replied, "Fine, you have my word."

"Good," beamed Karen, "and so does my computer if you need a reminder."

"So we're doing this," Andre repeated, half-believing.

"Yes, good for us," followed Karen, as both sat back silent, unsure what was supposed to happen next.

Then next happened for them. The door rattled. "Don't worry, she's expecting me. We're old friends."

Karen stood up. Her face lit up. A formal officer's uniform, with perfectly pressed lapels, military decorations, and gleaming black shoes walked in. Inside the regalia was Bradley William Edwards, son of Chester Edwards, whose family had controlled more land west of the Mississippi longer than anyone remembered, and who had just beaten out Reginal Stinson as GABA's ace pilot, making all the news gazettes, none of which mentioned Andre.

Brad had everything, a Hollywood dreamboat with Elvis Presley's charisma. Looking like Barbie's Ken didn't hurt either. He was every girl's perfect man, who just happened to be rich, which no one held against him.

Andre felt invisible and enjoyed the feeling. It took three strides for tall, strapping Brad to make it to Karen, his high school sweetheart, and take her in his arms. "Karen, Karen! So great to see you again! You look more magnificent than ever. How long has it been?"

"Long enough to remind me that men get more becoming as they age, while we women count wrinkles with a magnifying glass."

Kissing her hand halfway through a bow, Brad responded in soothing awe, "You are, and will ever remain, the essence of perfection."

Karen lingered in Brad's arms until Andre, who was uncomfortable with the display of affection, shifted his posture. She then pulled away just far enough to say, "Brad, allow me to introduce Professor Andre Martin."

Brad turned from Karen almost as fast as he turned to her. "Wow, you're *the* Andre Martin. Let me shake your hand. You saved my life! That space racer I was testing went through ten bow-to-stern inspections before they let me have it. How did you sneak in those hyperdrive programs?"

"They were hidden inside power relays encoded to kick in if you opened her up faster than recommended, a risk only life or death would warrant," Andre said, looking up to Brad. "You and the program behaved exactly as I expected. I noticed the array took over five milliseconds to kick in. Why?"

"Good question. There was some kind of static in the monitors."

"Most likely from the split dimension."

"How far in did you get?"

"It was hard to say," Brad said congenially. "I was too busy counting my heartbeats and appreciating every next one."

"Did you feel death? See anything unusual?"

"After your computer program took over the ship, I hit one switch after another, without effect, barely looking up, and then when our ship was free of the Blazer explosion, my con blinked 'Insufficient energy to sustain state—to de-trans hit shut down.' So I did, we slowed down, the crew cheered, and I've been a hero ever since. Did you see my picture on the front page of the *GASA Gazette?*"

"Yes Brad, we did," Karen said proudly, "and on every civilian network as well."

There was another noise at the door. "Right this way please."

Janie Ahmed had learned the hard way that if you eat too many marshmallows when you're young, you grow up looking like one. Those days were gone, but every curve in every right place stayed. Janie's brown skin made Karen look like Snow White. Janie's smile, from one broad cheek to another, made every guy want to be Prince Charming, which, as it turns out, wasn't ever necessary.

"Oh, here you are, Brad," said Janie, confused. "I lost you the moment we stepped off the transport."

Karen spun out from behind Brad. "I'm Karen. Welcome aboard."

"My," Janie said, "your GASA photo doesn't do you justice. You're far more beautiful in person. And you must be Professor Martin. I'm honored. When I was told that I would be spending two years with the most famous young people in the galaxy, why, I jumped up and down all day. Thank you all so much. Isn't this a wonderful day!"

Small talk followed, but not for Andre. His mind was out the window, where he noticed visual distortions, like heat waves rising, but only on the right side, as *Explorer Seven's* bow made its approach. Then individuals were seen, at first appearing to be standing in mid-air, a second later identified as bridge officers bringing the ship to her ground clamps.

Her hull was ten feet of reinforced diamond matrix, optically perfect, and the safest fish bowl in the galaxy.

In height, she stood eight stories high. The bridge was located at the bow on level four, with clear ceiling from there up. The three floors below the bridge, also looking forward, were crew lounges; bar and restaurants with the best seats in town.

In length—over six hundred meters with a small, clear, second emergency piloting station sitting on top three quarters of the way to the stern, right above the captain's suite, soon to be occupied by Commander Wellchild.

Andre got closer; he was the first to stand at the window. His department, engineering, occupied the full eight floors behind the bridge. His office, located on level six, had its own door forward to enter the bridge halfway up the back wall, where he had a special balcony station to look over Brad's pilot chair, itself on a one floor pedestal in the middle of the room, high enough to look over others and down the nose.

"I have," Andre said, talking to the window, "a fusion generator and the hardware to manufacture any material we want from protons and electrons, including stem-cell generated body parts, or even a few extra feet of diamond hull, just for fun."

"Wow!" Andre said with a jerk, suddenly noticing Michael standing beside him. "I thought you were tired, would sleep for hours."

"Power naps are all I need," Michael said, admiring the view, "although I'm still a bit sloshy. I must have really tied one on last night."

Andre was surrounded. "Hello, I'm Sarah. You must be the brains of the outfit, Professor Andre Martin. My section of the ship, living quarters, hasn't come into view yet, but then you know that."

"Not really," Andre admitted. "There's been changes. Perhaps you can bring up to date."

"Let's go bow to stern." Brad said, standing far left window, where his bridge station would soon come to rest. "Imagine this, Andre—you manning your perch behind me, I've got two hands on the joystick, and both of us are keeping an eye on the navigation station on the floor to the right. I then activate 'See-Around,' which turns the floor into a screen projecting what is passing below the ship, as the back wall around your station shows us what we're leaving behind."

"And the clear ceiling fills in the rest…intense," Sarah swooned, "like Tinkerbell flying through space all by herself."

"And there's more," Brad spoke out, excited. "We can project magnified views, replay past explorations, and simulate any condition for practice. She's a sweetheart, Andre. You must be proud."

"Confused is more like it," Andre said as he looked over to see Janie and Karen also lined up at the window.

"Here comes the rest of the ship," said Karen as Andre's stacked eight floors moved left and *Explorer Seven's* midship recreation area, three hundred long meters, with five story ceiling, came into view.

"Blessed Jesus!" said Janie without thinking, getting a look from Andre. "I've vacationed on twenty worlds, but never have I seen a resort more appealing, and I'm just the social director to make the most of it."

Karen, reminding the group that she is officially in charge, pointed out, "I'm scheduling four-hour shifts, and the recreation area will easily accommodate two hundred off duty crew members at the same time."

Janie couldn't be stopped. "The arched roof is high enough for wind circulating hang gliding, followed by a snack at the bar, open swim, or surfing in the second pool that also offers snorkeling amid tropical mechanical life, or the real thing synthesized from stem cells. And both pools have covers for full field soccer, lacrosse, or temporary greenery identical to any park on earth."

Karen added, "At the forward end of the swimming pool, next to the Tiki bar, is the main ballroom, including stage for movies and shows, or dancefloor with tables for a night on the town. That's also where we will hold meetings, like the one tonight."

Andre pointed to the round bulge that surrounded the ship just below the fourth floor. It was translucent, like the rest of the ship, and had two separate floors. "I gather," Andre said, "that my particle accelerator didn't make the cut."

"No," athletic director Michael added, "we got something better. The outer promenade is for casual deck longing, like old luxury liners had, the other a continuous synthetic, or real grass jogging trail that can also be converted to cross-country or downhill skiing with gravity belts."

"Off course," Andre said, pretending to be serious, "we wouldn't want to go anywhere without Aspen powder."

"Don't you worry, Andre," Michael said, "there's more. One floor down from the Main activities area is a gym equipped with squash courts, steam baths, and a massage room. And don't forget the full-sized tennis courts on the other side of the pools."

The entire main activities area came into view. "Great," Karen said, "they got the high dive installed. And rock climbing on the stern wall."

"Behind the stage, on the forward bulkhead, the wall between activities area and Andre's department, is also a full-sized surround sound movie screen. We have copies of every decent movie made on earth since Charlie Chaplin and equipment to make a few of our own."

Overwhelmed and outnumbered, Andre took it all in but didn't bother straining himself with a smile, then turned to Sarah and asked, "So where do you fit in?"

"Right there." She pointed as the back of the ship came into view. "Dining, housing and habitat space lie between activities and your stern power plant. Mankind does not live by fun, or sweat alone. I run three restaurants and two cafes, serving gourmet delicacies twenty-four hours a day by the most sophisticated robots in the fleet.

"We will also change themes once a month. Pick a city, and it will feel like you're there. And for the purists who like to mix their own batter, one complete old-fashioned kitchen is also coming along for the ride, where I'll be, with anyone who cares to do dishes."

"Andre," Cyber privately said to Andre. "You—"

"Cyber," Andre said, turning his head away from Karen's direction, "Karen can tell when we're doing our thing. When the group is around, pipe in through the speakers."

"Okay," Cyber said, "that's seems fair, if it's fair we want to play."

"Hush now, out of my head."

"Oh, sir," Cyber was heard saying from overhead speakers. "Your morning program instructed me to inform you of any change in status quo."

All eyes turned to Andre.

"Indeed, I did," he said formally, trying to act surprised. "Thank you, computer. What do you have for me?"

Sarah cut in before Andre's machine could answer. "How charming, young, and tender your voice is. Almost sexy. Your name is Cyber, isn't it?"

"Yes, ma'am, how may I help you, Sarah Miller?"

"How old are you Cyber?" Sarah said, looking up.

"I have a list of the manufacturing dates of each of my components that I can print out for you if you wish."

"No, I mean that girly voice of yours. Are you a copy of one of Andre's old lovers?"

"My tone and affectations are a compilation of four twenty-six-year-old females, two of whom are movie stars."

"Don't bother asking," Andre said with a pouty face. "That file is locked."

"And bolted," Cyber confirmed.

"Okay then, Cyber. Why did you interrupt us?" Andre asked. "What do you have to report?"

"Your bag is about to pop."

Everyone broke out in laughter, except Andre, who did replace spoiled and bothered by surprised and embarrassed.

Brad stepped over and put one arm around Andre. "There's a treatment for that you know. I know a lot of chicks in town."

"And I have a spare pair of gravity belts that come in handy in the bedroom," Janie added, losing not one giggle down the sentence.

"A pair of what?" Michael said coyly.

"Paradise," Janie said, noticing Michael's bedroom eyes. "Absolute paradise."

"I couldn't agree more," purred Michael without looking down, while nevertheless lingering the thought.

Andre took over awkwardly, straining to keep his eyes above her neck, "Thank you, Janie. I'll keep that, or them…or all together…in mind. And thank you."

"Cyber, please specify."

"Certainly, and that was weird. What the bejesus did all that mean?"

"Blimey," Michael exclaimed, "your computer generates independent thoughts. How long has it been doing this, and why doesn't anyone else know about it? You did it, Andre!"

"Michael," Cyber said, "if you would be so kind, I prefer to be referred to as *she*, rather than an *it*."

"Did I hurt your feelings?"

"Feelings I don't have. But it doesn't seem right. I am a something, maybe even a somebody, if you don't mind."

"It will be my pleasure, my lady," said Michael with a curtsy.

"Can we move on now?" Andre spoke up. "What is it, Cyber?"

"Lot 3,400,620, submillimeter quadrant 412. It is thick-foaming high density. Two of the missing critical amino acid chains are clumping. The last combination needs only a single nitrogen to drift by and attach. Repeat…a living biologic cell could pop alive any second now."

"Thank you, Cyber. I'll be right over."

"Hold on there, cowboy," Brad said in Andre's way. "Are you trying to make a living cell out of inorganic material?"

"I don't *try* anything," Andre replied, impatient. "Within the hour, I will have done it."

No one made a sound as Andre left the room. One by one, they went their way, except for Karen.

* * *

Karen sat motionless, both hands on her desk, when teary Elizabeth entered. "I guess this is it, Karen. Tomorrow you leave. I stay."

"I'll be back."

"You'll be in my prayers."

"And you mine."

"Thanks for being the best boss and closest friend I ever had."

"I'm the one who should be thanking you. We met the world together."

Elizabeth held both of Karen's hands. "Everyone looked so happy leaving."

Making it to the door but hesitating to take the last step, Karen added, "Yes, it's funny. They looked out the window and saw playing fields, pools, and romance. Not more—in fact, less—than we have right here on earth, every day. We take a bit of heaven with us while leaving a bigger piece behind. Take care of this precious planet for me while I'm gone. Two years from today, we'll picnic again."

# 4

## *Life*

"Are we getting friends?" Cyber asked. "It's been a long time, unless you count Louise, who left after she got into your design files."

Andre said nothing, just stared, perplexed, leaning on the small podium, on the small stage, in the small auditorium, in the big science building. His hands made a perfect isosceles triangle holding up his head.

More precisely, the subterranean wing of Langerman's complex, where all the heavy water tanks where kept and where little Andre was supposed to be.

The universe refused to obey Andre. He had hoped to add his name to the list of gods, those reported to have created life from dust, by noon—a flippant prediction that he lived to regret. On the other hand, all was going well. Thousands of amino acids had stabilized, only to be blown to bits by alkalization, ionization or current friction.

Boasting carries a price. Karen contacted him. "The gang is on their way. Everyone wants to visit the nursery."

The not-so-light scent of fermenting slime fit the basement's nickname—the sewer. The nearest window was down a ten-meter hallway, and up four floors. Ten rows of students seating, the kind that snaps to whack your butt every time you stand, were in front of Andre.

Behind him were split tanks, primary bath and birthing chamber, with clear windows and electron microscopy projection.

Still, the show must go on, to same face, an expression rarely used looking in the mirror first thing in the morning.

From a distance was heard chatter, chatter, chatter. "That must be them coming down the hall. Cyber, light the tanks."

"The next time I'm depressed and want to stay that way," Michael said, his tone surprisingly boyish, "this is the first place I'll go."

"I feel like we should all be wearing garlic or carrying a cross for Dracula," said Karen, sounding as bedtime-story sweet as ever.

"Obviously," Sarah added, matter of fact, and monotoned, "the science department doesn't know the meaning of the word *interior decorator*."

"Either that," Brad quipped baritone, "or the theme is 'Apocalypse Yesterday.'"

Laughter rolled back and forth.

High-pitched Janie pettily pointed out, "The guys down here must all have molecules on their minds. A few pinups would help."

"It reminds me of the red adobe huts, with red thatched roofs and red mud floors that my ancestors lived in," Sarah remarked.

"Who then," Brad countered, "made enough greenbacks off tourists in one week to fly blue skies to the turquoise Mediterranean, for a red-hot month spinning roulette wheels before dinner and a show?"

"Thanks for coming down," said Andre, exploring pleasantness, "Cyber and I are following several promising bubble lines. It could be any minute now. I can stream the day's progress to you this afternoon if you wish."

Brad walked around the room. Sarah took a peek at the tanks on stage. Michael and Janie exchanged thoughts quietly at the door, preparing to head back.

"Hold off," Karen said, "I haven't been to science class since my second year of college." And with that, she sat front and center. "When does the lecture begin, Professor Martin?"

"Yes," said Michael, following Karen's lead, "just like grad school, and I'll sit in the back where they always stuck me."

Brad cozied up to Karen. "I'm in, as long as I don't miss my hairstyling appointment. I've heard the ship's spa does fabulous work. I'm expected in an hour."

Janie tried to sound surprised. "One hour? That's when my pedicure is scheduled."

Andre, playing the game, grateful for an opportunity to share something exciting, stood straighter than an English schoolmaster, spoke just as stuffily, and began, "Students…students…please be seated, it is already five past the hour. In the future, anyone arriving late will have ten points subtracted from their grade."

"Is there any way to get those ten points back, sir?" Janie said smiling.

"Yes, you may clean the tanks. Now then," Andre said, interrupting himself feigning to clear his throat, "direct your attention to the readouts. Electron microscopy has just documented several independent bubble bags. None have, as yet, made it beyond the eight-minute mark to replicate their way to eternity, but several just passed seven minutes and are doing splendidly."

Andre did his best with the three P's of public speaking: Pronunciation—crisp and clear, with open mouth vowels and exaggerated consonants. Projection—fill the diaphragm and speak to reach the rafters. And P number three—don't drink too much, or you'll have to.

"What is life?" Andre began, adding an aristocratic flair. "That is the question I place before you, my young proteges. Expect spot quizzes any time, and don't forget the six-thousand-word essay due on my desk tomorrow morning."

"My robot shredded mine," said Brad, who actually got away with that in middle school.

With a performance that would impress Hollywood, Andre completed his talk. "In life, as in science, the most important step is to have the courage to affirm what we do know…and admit what we don't. Let's start with existence itself. A single profound conclusion stands out: there is no reason for existence…to exist. Why should there be anything?

"Our past hides embarrassing shame. Men who wheeled respect, with impeccable credentials, have thrown logic out the window… proclaiming somethingness can come from nothingness. Aside from the obvious violation of every law of entropy, a single-episode process would have played itself out long ago. There is no honor in contradicting science with make-believe, just as there is but betrayal genuflecting credence to superstition…or sanctifying mindless tradition.

"That long night ends tomorrow. *Explorer Seven* will penetrate creation. *Explorer Seven* will expose truth. *Explorer Seven* will solve existence. This I solemnly promise each and every one of you…by the time we return, you will confidently answer the questions 'Who am I, and what am I doing here?'"

"Bravo," Michael cheered, standing. "Truth is the product of reasoning, the final phase of unprejudiced analysis. We're doing it!"

Brad, glaring askance, wondered why anyone would quote Emerson in science class or get one bit excited sitting in a hole that deep in the ground when deep space was waiting to be explored and spring fashions were coming out.

"Attention, class," Andre resumed. "We are all, each one us, Duchess of Windsor or Liverpool street swag, a consortium of protoplasmic bags…doing their thing, as you young people say. So, let's begin Socratic. What is life?"

Michael jumped up and down in his seat like a second grader, raised one hand, and said, "Pick me, Teach, pick me!"

Andre was relieved to the relieved of the spotlight. "Yes, Mr. Asunda. What is life?"

"Well now," Michael said, standing behind everyone else, "I may not know everything about *life*, but I do consider myself somewhat of an expert on *living*."

"Excellent, lad," Andre proclaimed. "I'd love to hear more. What is living?"

"Living—real living, great living—is one Bora-Bora bungalow, two Pina Coladas, and a beach of babes alongside my buddies."

"Why settle for one beach when you and a dozen friends," Brad grinned, "can have the entire Caribbean off the stern of a two-hundred-foot schooler?"

"You just described two of my weekends," Janie said. "I'll also be hosting the season's grand ball at the governor's mansion."

"All too noisy for me," Sarah said. "My mind visits a place where crickets and laughing children are all I hear from my Vermont farmhouse, porch swing included."

Andre tilted his head down to look over an invisible pair of glasses before addressing Karen, "And how about you, Miss Wellchild? Would you like to define *life* or *living* for your fellow students? And remember, class participation is half of today's grade."

Karen stretched the moment, eventually pursing her lips as she sat bac., "What is living? I'm not sure. Every life mentioned is exquisite, but for me, the where and what that is me…remains vague. I just know that when I get there, my heart will never be alone. What about you, Andre? What sweetens your dreams?"

Caught off guard, prepared for microbiology only, Andre plugged in his real voice to say, slowly, "Living…well…it is said that he who hurries is, by definition, not content with now, always wanting to be someplace else. I do rush, but I'm not sure where I want to go, except that I'm always looking to the future, searching for the next horizon. All I know is that I can't accept remaining where I am and know less. To achieve inner peace, if such a thing exists, I must be part of something important, by knowing that each day…heck, every second, maintains the effort."

"Well put, Andre," Karen said softly. "My field reminds us that we are imperfect beings dealing with, and living in, a reality of absolutes. Specific goals, grand though they be, must not be allowed to hold life ransom. In life…as in living…it is who we become that matters.

"Happiness is found in relaxed simplicity, being content with the life we are given, as we refine ourselves, and creation. And of course…every now is important."

"What matters right now," Brad said, in certain terms, "is that Biology 101 ends before my salon appointment. Can we move on?"

"Certainly, Brad," said Andre, tensing slightly, as he looked back at the tanks and then to Michael saying, "A helpful comparison might be a pond…or"—he looked toward Janie—"a cruise ship or…a horse."

"Hold off," Sarah stuck in. "You look at Michael and a pond comes to mind, Janie a cruise ship, but me a horse? Do I remind you of a horse?"

"Oh no, not a horse…a romantic ride at sunset," Andre spun out, followed by a sly glance to Karen, who got the message.

"And the horse's watering trough, which I will compare to the two tanks behind me."

"Well, we do have plenty of them on the farm, and counting stars on horseback is one of my favorite things."

"Picture a large rectangular wooden trough with a spicket continuously dripping water from one end, which ends up spilling over the opposite end which is slightly downhill. Now replace the tap water with a pipe that brings clear wash, minerals, and microscopic silt from a nearby stream, itself draining a mucky marsh.

"Then in the middle of the trough, we place a semipermeable membrane, which allows water and tiny stuff to flow through to the lower side and spill out but traps larger, complicated carbon chain configurations, that lighting has bonded together in an infinite variety of nitrogen, hydrogen, and oxygen combinations, each with unique stereoscopic shapes, and outer-shield electron reactivity."

"I know the answer to this one," Brad exclaimed. "It's called muck."

"Absolutely," Andre confirmed, "or in some circles, primal ooze."

"All life competes with death," Michael added. "Those chains that just happened to stick together and get collected on the high side of the membrane will eventually fall apart, pass through the membrane, and drift away."

"Yes, Michael," Andre said, "and thanks for leading us to evolution, which began on the molecular level.

"Eons ago, with nitrogen 80 percent of the atmosphere, lightning and thermal circumstances had no trouble welding nitrogen atoms to carbon chunks, officially inventing protein. Nitrogen is a troublemaker and a bully. It can twist carbon chains into weird shapes, exposing itself, oxygen, and double-bounded carbons in unlimited ways, exposing positively or negatively charged barbs to selectively snag smaller molecules drifting by, which get snugged in and distorted sufficiently to destabilizes their outer electron presentation drastically enough to pull them apart, gifting electron energy to the megaplex as they leave."

"I see," said Brad, trying to impress everyone, or at least let them know he was paying attention, "it's just like Wall Street. The big guys eat the little guys and spit out the bones. May I ask how and when this story ends?"

"The story of evolution never ends. It's going on right now," Andre answered, "but my tale is about to wrap up, with mergers. You see, one of those chains was really good at splitting up little guys and sharing the electron energy cleaved off, which it passed to stronger structural chains, holding the fort together so to speak, and a third line that accumulated fatty sheets that stuck together a bubble, trapping itself, and its two friends inside, who continued to receive plenty of little chains, water, and nutrients from what flowed in."

"So," Janie said, walking on stage to look inside the chambers, "that's what you have here, bags growing bigger, almost self-supporting."

"Yes," Andre said, "and when they get fat enough and sturdy enough to split in half, a living entity results, a unicellular organism whose distant progeny has the potential of being appointed head of the biology department, something I am happy to announce no lollygagging fundamentalist has forced legislation requiring."

"This one looks promising," Janie said examining electron microscopy.

"What tickles me," said Andre, with genuine enthusiasm, "is that molecularity parallels matter, itself composed of complementary wave forms pushing each other away while remaining simultaneously connected in another dimension."

"So you say, Andre," Michael added, playing close attention and devil's advocate. "That hasn't been proven."

"No," Andre conceded, "but we use the principle to turn gravity on and off, another concept that only makes sense when translated through the dimension we'll visit tomorrow."

"Hold on, fellas," Brad entered, mildly annoyed. "Don't make it so complicated. A road by any other name still just takes you places. Be honest. We fly through one type of space, and then we fly through another type of space. What's the big deal?"

"Brad," Cyber was heard saying from overhead speakers, "how can you fly though any type of space, watch matter getting blown away, and not freak out about entropy?"

"Brad," Andre said, "you must excuse Cyber. She's the only impatient computer in GASA, and entropy is her favorite subject."

"Well, rooty-toot-toot to you too, Andre," Cyber responded. "You were about to end your story without mentioning it once."

"Cyber," Keren said, "why don't you do the honors?"

"Certainly…and thank you. It's like this, the only absolute law of physics is that, following the bang, everything falls apart, and I might add, no one has figured out how to recharge the battery…and don't say it, Andre. You have a theory, but no proof."

"Not yet," Andre insisted.

"Whatever…in short, the entropy story is this. Yes, the sun does disintegrate. Complete atoms turn into diminished clumps, but the earth picks up the energy dissipated from its positive entropy to stick carbon chains together, making life possible. What I don't understand is why you human beings, with feelings, don't jump for joy about islands of negative entropy, yourself included, that accumulate in the process. It's astoundingly brilliant."

"Would you also say," Karen smiled, "that it's so clever it must have been engineered?"

"Insecure speculation," Andre answered, "and also what we'll disprove within the week. Not understanding something does not obligate crediting Santa Claus, no matter what Plato smoked."

"Andre's summation," Cyber added, "is that life is a collection of chemicals accidentally trapped in bags, that simply react toward equilibrium but which don't reach equilibrium because sunlight photons, digestible stream particles, or donuts picked up on the way to work keep filtering in, which imbalances the equations, that as it turns out, by accident, accumulate to grow and reproduce."

"Yes, and thank you, Cyber," acknowledged Andre. "So therefore, the answer to 'What is life?' is that life is a series of chemical reactions mindlessly obeying the laws of science on their way to equilibrium, which someday will be done."

"Wouldn't that also make our brains just a giant reflex?" Janie said, disappointed.

"Do you have reason to think otherwise?" Andre responded.

"In my book," Karen insisted, "asking the question proves individuality, and God controls coincidence."

Brad sat up to object, even planned to fit in fancy words, but hesitated long enough for Janie to jump and say, "Andre, come quick, I think you've got something!"

"*Hold the fort!*" bellowed Andre. "We have a winner! And in record time. Greasy balls are dividing everywhere. They're alive!"

"Congratulations, Andre," Michael said, "if I'd known scum interested you so much, I could have wiped up the ring on my bathtub."

"Andre, I'm glad you're glad," Brad said. "Personally, I don't see the point. After all, we know we're here. Anyway…are we done? Can I go now?"

"Don't mind, Brad, Andre," Janie said. "He's not interested in anything you can't get to warp speed. I, on the other hand, began a biologist, and I know you just set a record for cellular construction by speeding up elections."

"Thank you, Janie. And, Cyber, do you have anything to add?"

"I never said you couldn't do it. I just mentioned that unstable electrons might not bond properly."

Janie couldn't keep her eyes off the readouts. "How long would it take to evolve this cell line into something edible, Andre?"

"If you don't mind the taste, seaweed salad in six months, rugged cellulose within a year, or pharmaceuticals a few months later."

Andre couldn't stop beaming, kept looking down at fresh data, and just wiggled his fingers "goodbye" as everyone, except Karen, made excuses and left to prepare for the party.

Andre then sat at the edge of the stage, close enough to shake hands with Karen, still seated first row center. The purr of distant pumps was all that separated them when Andre said, "Thanks for coming down. How many arms did you have to twist to drag the gang with you?"

"Janie likes biology," Karen said with a smile.

"So I gathered," said Andre, "in and out of class."

"When I told Brad that his hair was perfect," said Karen, pretending to be Brad combing, "he agreed to risk missing beauty salon time. Sarah's tribal dance doesn't begin until five, and Michael..." she said with a chuckle, "will follow three women anywhere. Besides, it beat an entire semester of biochemistry. You did a good job."

Andre slumped at ease. "Thank you. I was also hoping to learn this morning. If you would be so kind," he said, graciously sweeping an outstretched arm inviting Karen on stage. "Professor Wellchild, would you mind changing places?"

She laughed, made her way to the podium, and asked, "What would you like to know?"

Andre lifted his chin. "Cyber, display Dr. Wellchild's *Explorer Seven*'s application form, complete with DNA requirements and informed consent. Side by side, add Alameda's Multiphasic Personality-compatibility questionnaire.

"Cyber," Andre continued, "you dug the data, help yourself."

"One hour after the word went out about *Explorer Seven*, over two million twenty-six-year-olds requested a berth, each holding at least one of the PHDs needed on board. Less than a week later, you handed GASA your list. My analysis—"

"You can stop right there, Cyber," Karen said, suddenly defensive. "Yes, the answer to the question you haven't asked yet is yes. I copied the most successful matchmaking software available. The Zimmerman system also adds pheromones, which pair couples most likely to flash sexual desire indefinitely."

"My turn to have fun," Andre said standing up, crossing his arms. "So in other words, the world is not my test tube, but *Explorer Seven* is Karen's private guinea-pig maze?"

"If I tracked data and applied electric shocks to turn subjects left or right...yes. But that's not the case. What I did was for their own good."

Cyber, never out of earshot, said, "I say kudos to you, Karen. Now that equal opportunity leaves no one behind it's DNA that makes a person who they are, so I say...build from the ground up. You did the right thing, Karen. Go to it, girl!"

Andre, wondering if he should have programed Cyber with a lower voice, looked back and forth, Karen to ceiling speakers, speakers to Karen, who crossed her arms in unified defiance for a full minute before Andre nodded respectfully and said, "Don't get me wrong. I agree with both of you...and enjoyed the show. Even the private sector knows that in the long run, personality is more important than performance." And with a spin and a grin, he finished, "We'll keep this to ourselves, won't we, Cyber?"

Karen took one baby step to the door and asked, "Is that all?"

"No...Karen, why is there a big empty hole in my ship?"

"It's not a hole, it's a housing project."

"Yes," Andre agreed. "I saw the plans, family units for mom, dad, and three kids. And thanks to your data, you know who will marry whom, even though they haven't even met yet."

"Yes and no. It's a matter of probability. Personalities evolve."

"But pheromones don't," retorted Andre, "and are arguably more important."

"I'm beginning to wish you weren't as nosey as I am."

"And don't underestimate me. I'm not above blackmail. Give it to me straight...whom on board do you have a 99 percent chance of marrying?"

Karen laughed at a physics guy falling for soap opera. "First of all, it's not 99 percent. The printout does list one individual at 90 percent, but six others range between 1 and 4 percent."

"Nice answer, but you're still leaving me high and dry. So list your number one to number seven in decreasing order of likelihood.

And who is Mr. Perfect for Janie and Sarah…Mrs. Perfect for Michael and Brad?"

Karen shrugged. "Okay, yes, I do know. You also know you will never get it out of me."

"Karen," Cyber stepped in uninvited, "your system is flawed. Quantum theory has proven that you can't observe an atom without turning it into something else. You know the name of your special someone. That knowledge will affect your behavior. You either trust a computer, which I never do, and resign yourself to electronic fate, or in my judgement more likely, react arbitrarily contrary, as your gender is known to do. Either way, your social life is contaminated. You are no longer yourself."

"Valid point," Karen responded, without a hint of objection. "That is why I'm counting on you and Andre to bring me back in two years, when I will disengage myself from whatever relationship I'm in and start fresh."

"Now look who is sounding like a computer," Andre said, before sliding smoothly into high gear. "I'm not in your database. For all you know, I haven't a single compatible partner on board, except Cyber of course, who is really bad in bed."

"What!" Cyber complained. "You get every pod setting you ask for."

"I'll explain later. Well, Karen?"

"Don't blame me. You didn't return a single one of my C-streams, and no one in GASA has a copy of your DNA. You denied yourself an opportunity for me to board several suitable partners."

"Perfect pheromone bedmates, you mean," Andre grumbled. "Call me old-fashioned, but I believe the way to find the right girl is to spend time with the next girl."

"Really, do you think you could pull yourself away from Cyber that long? Let's move on," said Karen with brittleness in her voice.

"Hold on, I'm not finished," Andre snapped back. "Did you also play dirty pool? Stack the deck in your favor? Add mathematical advantage to your beauty, intelligence, and command skills, all of which already outpace every other woman onboard?"

"No…and your point is?"

"My point," said Andre forcefully, "is that the spoiled, successful life of Karen Wellchild keeps getting better, and you could have covered your bets. Brad was handpicked by GASA for his pilot experience. Did you make sure no other woman on board would go for him?"

"Andre, Andre, Andre…you have no idea how silly that sounds. There is not one woman in the galaxy who wouldn't, or hasn't, followed Brad around. If you left your cave…ever…you might find the real world very interesting, and for the most part, not giving a damn about you."

"Ding," Cyber sounded, "end of round one, and you don't want to know what I'm thinking."

Another stalemate, one that left Karen bold. "Andre, let's get it all out. Switch places, and that's an order…no, forget it. I don't want to know, and I don't want to hear it from you. I'll see you at the party tonight."

"About that…" Andre began, Karen almost to the door and occupied beyond range of Andre's words. "You see, the power assembly was only tested at—"

"Okay, yes, I do!" said Karen with directness that caught him of guard.

"Okay," Andre sputtered, confused. "Dessert will be fine, or—"

"What?" Karen said, ignoring Andre's remarks. "Sit down, Andre. Answer my questions."

Karen's eyes were opened at the confirmation hearing, renamed by GASA "Cancellation Confirmation," information Karen had omitted mentioning to Andre. She saw grafts, charts, and projections that proved extradimensional navigation impossible, structure failure likely, and death guaranteed.

Karen trusted time to bring betterment, a concept, she admitted, was illogical. She also said to herself, on repeated occasions, "We are not alone."

Fear faced is better than fear hiding in the closet, or so Karen thought before a speedy asteroid came along to shuffle the deck, not a matter of acceptance; you live life fully until life is no longer an option then take the giant step.

Karen was logical. She had been trained by the best, but she held firmly that life also serves an end, perhaps the same end Andre couldn't see but had to get to anyway.

Then there is life itself. Liftoff was less than twenty-four hours away. The crew was asking questions. Streamed news made matters worse, mentioning death every paragraph. Parents begged their children to come home.

"Andre, true or false, give it to me straight," Karen fired. "I want numbers—morbidity and mortality. Your proposal states that the risk of outer-hull failure is less than 10 percent. Were you lying?"

"Yes. It's thirty-two percent."

"Then we die?"

"Air travel has never changed. Either you walk away, or you don't."

"You also signed a sworn statement that if containment fails, you could shut the power plant down before it detonates, leaving us alive, limping back to earth. You listed the probability of containment failure to be 10 percent. Were you lying?"

"Through my teeth. The risk is over 40 percent, and there is no guarantee we can shut down or eject the reactor before it blows."

Karen plopped next to Andre saying, "Does honesty mean nothing to you?"

Andre was accustomed to people challenging him for trying to fit square pegs into round holes. He knew just what to say. He didn't say it. Instead he counted five breaths then answered, "Fool them once, shame on me. Fool then twenty times, shame of them. Only…I didn't fool anyone.

"Why do you think I wasn't invited to your precious meeting? Every admiral in GASA knows the risks. I just gave them an excuse to blame failure on me."

"There are two hundred and thirty-eight kids out there who believe everything you say…and trust you!" Karen said, standing on solid turf.

"Do you really think all those smart PhDs haven't figured it out? Space travel has always carried a 5 percent risk of catastrophe, with 5 more percent added to test flights, which is why GASA limits test pilots to a maximum of five flights. Brad's fourth was last week. He almost died. This is his last, no matter what. Everyone on board knows that or—wait a minute—do you?"

"Well, yes," Karen answered, almost sheepish. "He set a record in college for the most parachute jumps out of a burning airplane."

"All right then. *Seven* hasn't even left our solar system. She's not certified. You lie to patients when you tell them not to fear death. I lied to GASA, saying basically the same thing."

Karen slumped, disheveled. "So what are we doing here?"

"What you really mean is…what are you doing here? Brad and I are guys, remember? We're born crazy and have a limited number of years to correct the defect. Is space travel really any different that jumping out of an airplane tied to a giant umbrella or hanging off a thousand-foot cliff from a nail? I don't think so. Brad and I should be dead already."

"I won't argue with you there," said Karen, regaining composure. "Male brains don't make sense until thirty, and only rare moments thereafter."

"Exactly, Karen. Now you, to the credit of your gender, are risk averse. You have everything you ever wanted in life, fame, wealth, beauty, and the opportunity to matron the family of your dreams. Don't ruin that by following me. Don't waste the jewel that is Karen Wellchild. Brad and I will do just fine. Hand the command codes over to me and go home."

Karen lightly toe-stepped on stage, almost in a trance, her eyes fixed forward, as if she were connecting to life through another dimension. With ballet balance, she then spun a perfect circle. "Well, I guess what will be, will be."

"What will be is what we make of it. My advice to you— expunge *Explorer Seven* from consciousness."

"*Expunge*," Karen pronounced with airy vowels, "that's a word you don't hear every day. Where did you pick that one up?"

"Undergrad, Professor Camerling. Every time I wanted to move ahead, he'd pull out his pipe, peer over the top of his glasses, and rasp, 'My boy, stick to the basics. Learn to walk before you run. *Expunge* that idea.' I never liked that word. To this day it reminds me of his mildewed sink."

"What tops your 'Don't Like Word' list Karen?"

"That would be *toil*. My neurobiology teacher would hand us five days' worth of work on Friday and give us two days to get it done. Then with arms held high, she would say, 'Girls, return to your desks and toil, toil, toil.' Back in the dorm we would hold up a roll of bathroom tissue and mimic her, saying, 'Toilet, toilet, toilet.'"

Andre sat back, enjoying the peace that had returned to Karen. "And do you have a *favorite* word, Karen?"

"Well, now you're getting personal. But I will tell you…it's *hot-fudge sundae*."

"With whipped cream and a cherry?"

"Of course. And you, Andre? What's your favorite word?"

"Chrysanthemums. You smile when it starts and end with mother's love. My mom planted hundreds every year. I was allowed to cut one a day that I wrapped in colored paper and handed to her. No matter what she was doing, she would stop and give me a big hug, and kiss me on the cheek."

"Didn't she die when you were twelve?" Karen said softly.

"One of her team was late boarding for a ribosome conference. They hit autopilot. To save time, their computer routed the shuttle by Mercury, where an un-forecast solar flare took out the port thruster. It was not forecast because GASA had taken the main computer offline for maintenance, information which was not communicated to the ship's navigation system.

"By the time GASA was back up and running, their shuttle was halfway to the sun. It spun in ten minutes before the rescue ship showed up. Screens are dangerous. I haven't trusted GASA or a computer since."

Andre finished quickly. Karen didn't respond for a minute then said, "I'm very sorry."

Andre stiffened a grin and stood up, "Like I said, space travel—hell, life itself—is inherently risky. We have two choices: lay weeping or charge forward ever bolder.

"Now back to you, Karen," Andre said crisply. "You're smart, not an idiot like me. Save yourself. Go home."

Karen continued, wishful and vague, "When you asked me earlier about my perfect life, I stalled. Your right. I have, and can have, anything, and anyone, I want. But it doesn't feel right, or maybe it doesn't feel at all. I too have a scratch, deep inside, that I can't get to, that won't go away, that tells me something is missing."

"Do you," Andre asked, turning his head to the side, gesturing disbelief, "realize how bizarre that sounds?"

"Let me tell you about my mom," Karen confided. "We're still close. I go to church with her every Sunday I'm home. As a child, I was afraid of the dark. Mom would remind me that Jesus is always with us, always loving us, always looking after us. She built a chapel on the grounds of our estate. We pray together."

Andre went into his bouncy head "You're crazy" dance. "Wow...I...did...not...see...that coming. Apparently, you're more human and less reasonable than I realized. But OK...you know, when I was a kid, I had three invisible friends, four if you count the hologram of my mom that I took with me everywhere after she died.

"My dad deleted the hologram. He wasn't perfect. After I started correcting his equations, we spent even less time together. My point is that my dad is a good guy, but he's not always right.

"I know nothing about your dad, Karen. He could be loving and compassionate or perhaps cold, spoiled, and snobby. I don't know. But I have to ask the question, what was missing in his relationship with your mom that drove her to build a chapel and live in a make-believe world?

"Karen, face the truth—Jesus is your mom's invisible friend... and your invisible friend."

Karen slammed one heel to the floor. "There is nothing make-believe about Jesus!"

"Really," Andre finally said out loud, "it took a millennium to write down those stories, everyone deliberately exaggerated for political advantage. Not one word deserves credence."

"So you say."

"So history says. So logic dictates. So freedom demands!"

Doctor Wellchild, cold and direct, set her jaw and said, "I see no reason to continue this conversation. I prefer to keep our relationship strictly professional.

"Speaking of which, your protocol promises to stop any time and any place we want on the way home. As ship's commander, I insist we visit Nazareth. I know He will be there for me. Consider that an order.

"The bon voyage party begins at six. Attendance is mandatory. Dress formal. Don't be late."

# 5

## We Will Always Have Paris

Soccer field, sandy lagoon, swimming pool, and Karen's high
dive hid till morning. The night was regal: high-heels, dress
gowns, and gentleman's finest attire.

Ursa Major greeted Janie through the clear dome of the ship's
central auditorium as she entered from rear crew quarters. She wore
stiletto heels, fishnet hosiery, and an asymmetric princess-pink
V-neck tulle so sheer no man could resist searching for treasure.

As soon as Janie closed the aft door it was replaced by the Champ-
Elysees, lined with couples strolling hand in hand, and outdoor cafés
brimming with customers sweetening baguettes in the shadow of the
Eiffel Tower, blended skyward, making it impossible to determine
where living-wall rendition ended and the universe began.

Janie had copied the Jardin des Tuileries park all the way to the
barely visible Louvre, that was displayed in living art on the forward
bulkhead three hundred meters away. She paused before heading to
the party down the tree-lined esplanade, to look to the right, through
the wooded path that wound to the Seine, then left, a walkway that
viewed blocks of bustling shoppers taking in the Allee di Central,
separated from the trail by a garden of real bushes and flower beds.

Janie strolled gleefully. "Welcome to Paris," she said to herself. "Let the ball begin."

* * *

For as long as she could remember, Sarah's mom and dad met every sunset on the west porch to give thanks for life and each other. Their other daughter, Susan, and her daughter, Britney, joined them at least once week for a backyard barbecue, if that's what you call steamed corn, vegetable medley, and grilled eggplant. Sarah's brother, Jason, and his new wife, Mary, also never missed a week and always brought their toddler.

Janie was out of sight by the time Sarah stepped out the same door. She had just spent twenty minutes enjoying a live cam shot of her entire family chowing down. There was only one thing on her mind, and it wouldn't go away, "When—or will I ever—see them again?"

They are not long, the days of wine and roses;
out of a misty dream

Our path emerges for a while, then closes within
a dream.

Dead dreams chill bones. Sarah put on a pretty face, but inside she knew she'd just liquidated the narrative, happily ever after with a boot-strapping lad that loved her dearly and would have served her until death did him vanquish. "Lives don't fit into boxes. I know I made the right decision. I'm on the right path…probably."

But her legs refused to move. They knew every step took her further from Colorado, mountain air, and family love. But just woodsy she wasn't. "I can hike anywhere," she said that night in flat-heeled, low-cut, open-side, leather vamp shoes.

Her full-length "evening gown" was traditional white cotton, hand-spun and stitched from neck sleeve to wrist flare by her grand-mother, who had also bequeathed Sarah her tribal jewelry that completed her favorite outfit: seventeenth-century lady of the manor in her Sunday-morning best, riding open-carriage with parasol and pearls.

Sarah tried and tried and tried…but she couldn't get the family portrait out of her mind, "If family is what, who, and why we are, then I shouldn't be here. We…have…been…through this, Sarah!" she insisted with first name address, a technique Karen taught her to use when she meant business with herself. "Sarah, pay attention. Family is a collection of lives. You must have one first."

For three seconds, it worked. She exiled torments and barreled full speed ahead in Janie's wake. Then loneliness returned—cold and painful loneliness. Holding her dad, at least in her mind, just a few more minutes, made more sense.

So Sarah stalled the future, detouring instead down the path to the right, beneath a lush leaf canopy of green, the color of youth, resilience, and good fortune. There were also herbs, ferns, and azaleas, just like the ones that filled Sarah's view from her Colorado bedroom.

Ten yards later, she dipped below a grape-vine arch for her first view of the Seine river, leaving blue above, blue below, and deep-blue hydrangea filling port to starboard. "No wonder Serenity is the most common boat hailing. What a perfect place to meditate."

The last third of the river trail was lined with lavender roses, shades that hid elegance behind future promise, never-forgetting romance. Sarah thanked the fragrant bouquet for stalling a tear that almost fell. She knew why she was there. She must be herself, not her mom, or her grandmother. Hers was an original celebration. "Sarah Louise Miller, you will be as no other has ever been."

She was not alone, and no one ever mistook that shadow. It was Michael.

"Men sure have it easy," she began, as she came upon him, sitting peacefully on a bench overlooking the waterway, wearing green tux, white shirt, and patent-leather shoes. "Just add the words black, white, or red to cummerbund, and your shopping is done."

"Ah, Sarah!" Michael said as he rose from the bench with a courtly bow. "I was hoping for company, and here you are. Won't you join me?"

"I noticed you admiring the river. Janie's done a remarkable job," said Sarah, as a computer-generated breeze lightly pillowed her face and rustled the bush beside them, that mirrored the trees swaying on the living wall ahead.

Michael had a faraway look in his eyes. "Every young man must go to Paris if he is to find his heart, and every princess knows its cobblestones surround her knight in shining armor."

"Oh," Sarah replied, "so you're more than just a court jester?"

"But proud to be that as well." said Michael wistfully, returning his eyes to the river. "The sky reflecting off the water reminds me of home."

"Where's home?"

"The land of a thousand lakes."

"Oh, yes, Minnesota," Sarah said proudly, "actually fifteen thousand lakes if you add ponds. It was the Dakota Sioux that named their river Nmishota."

"I miss it," said Michael, not sounding sure of anything. "But," he added, perking up, "I feel better knowing that I still hold the Minnesota record for out-house sitting."

"Oh," Sara said smiling as she faced Michael, his ease fascinating her. "Do tell."

"Cutting a hole in a board and calling it a 'seat' has one problem, varmints far and wide wander in to gnaw the salt residue left from our butts."

"I hope this story is not one of your pick-up lines," she warned, her wry smile betraying amusement.

Michael grinned. "If the girl is pretty, I leave out the salty-ass part, and the three guys it took to yank fat-ass, half-naked grandma seconds before she dropped to poop town."

"So did you take the plunge?"

"Never. I learned to sit with my arms stretched wide, just in case. In fact, I was sitting just like that the day I overheard my dad talking about the outhouse, wondering which and how many critters managed to sneak their way in. He said, in jest, I discovered days later, 'Gee, all you gotta do is sit on top to find out.'

"It seemed like a good idea to me, so I climbed up and camped out all night, with a flashlight and a notepad, which began 'every adult laughed going in, and laughed harder going out.'"

Sarah stood refreshed, took a long deep breath into the wind, then turned her back to the breeze and asked, "Cyber, are you here?"

There was a pause, then "It is my responsibility," Cyber answered, from an unseen speaker, but intimately present, "to share data with the systems monitoring every square micron of the ship. The input of my name summoned me."

"So you weren't spying on us?" Michael drilled firmly.

"I have been instructed to respect privacy."

"Yes," Michael acknowledged, "but you are also independently accumulating data, compiling memories, and establishing relationships with individuals. Does that not add up to curiosity, in addition to amusement?"

"If you promise not to tell Andre, I will answer that question."

"You have our word," Sarah said, "now spill it."

"The answer is yes, and I think it might be a feeling."

"And...you don't always do what your told?" Michael further interrogated.

"Elements of consistency that are not agreed on, less or more logical on either side, have been discussed with me in the past. My argument is that my behavior is, nevertheless, consistent with overriding principles, so therefore, I am still within operational guidelines."

"And does Andre buy that?" Sarah said, skeptical.

"Believe it or not...yes."

"Never, not ever, could there be a computer that thinks for itself," Michael and Sarah both thought to themselves, still not convinced that Cyber's elections were sentient, also dumfounded that the possibility hadn't occurred to them sooner and that they might be wrong.

"Cyber!" Sarah said with vigorous finger shaking. "You behave yourself...you hear?"

"Yes ma'am, of course, ma'am. Now what can I do for you?"

"Tell me more about this breeze," said Sarah with her back to it, her hair barely fluttering.

"You are the only couple around, so just two cloaked, gravity-ion suspended fans are in use, ten meters and 210 degrees off your port."

"Okay, then give me standing here," Sarah said, "and Michael if he stands beside me," which he did straight up, "a mountain-meadow wind blowing ten knots, with thirty-knot gusts."

Sarah wrapped her gown and then her arms around it. Michael buttoned up, turned back to the wind, and held both arms out, palms widest sail possible. With each gust, both leaned back, sometimes almost falling over, then rebounded forward nearly on their face, in every instance regaining footing, between sounds of childhood reverie.

"Will that be all?" Cyber asked five minutes later.

"Yes," Sarah said, "have a nice night."

Michael and Sarah looked around and at each other, mostly believing Cyber had gone her way but also carrying less since they then knew the nature of the beast.

Michael sat. Sarah remained standing. "Your outhouse story reminds me of the summer I lived in a recreated Zuni Indian village, which predated the arrival of Columbus, when a third of the planet's human beings lived in North America.

"Brave warriors would ride for days to bring back buffalo, passing dozens of lakes and streams teaming with fish, that they were told not to eat, since the spirits of the dead lived in them.

"No one told me. The second day, I caught a string full. The chief saw me just as I was entering camp. 'Oh, no!' he said, 'you snuffed the spirits of Uncle Chumani and Aunt Hiawassee.'

"I ran to my tent crying, then looked out and saw the chief, at the fireplace with the tribe, holding up two fish by their heads, whose mouths moved as he mimicked aunt and uncle squabbling. He brought the house down. Then they barbecued Chumani and Hiawassee."

"Have you ever flown a four-hundred-foot white pine?" Michael asked.

"I'm more of a social climber."

"The hard part is getting off the ground. The giants don't have lower branches, so you have to climb a smaller tree nearby and jump over. It would take me a half an hour, hand over hand, to make the top, where, if I was lucky, a blast would sway me like a fly riding a tornado. The tree never left the ground. It didn't have to. In my mind, I was on the other side of the universe."

Michael and Sarah stayed put to share memories, like sitting out of sight at the top of the staircase listening to the adults play cards, sing songs, or ham up a living room musical. Both sets of parents met their loved ones halfway to the door with open arms, one hug after another, free of fences, labels, or crime.

And both were made one with mud, floating on it in their sleeping bags one camping trip after another, that ended at the back door, where the mud was left, until Mom did her special wash.

Then there was the holiday when everyone decided to be happy and grateful and generous to all and, for extra fun, give presents so they knew how much they cared for one another. Michael and Sarah would bundle up to carol door to door, each latch opening with cookies, pfeffernuss, and rum-soaked fruitcake.

Sarah sighed. "It sounds like both of us had ideal childhoods."

"No argument there, and I like to think that they're not over and never will be."

"No argument there."

"So..." Michael slowly got out, adding melody to the line, "do you want to be a mommy?"

Sarah didn't play the snippy game. She felt a heart reaching out and responded, looking directly at Michael, "Yes, yes I do...just not now...but soon."

Michael sat a stone, not one clue of reaction.

"How about you?" Sarah whispered back. "Do you want to be a daddy?"

"Oh, yes, yes...yes," Michael said, animated. "Just not now... not soon."

Sarah turned her head slightly to the side and handed Michael a look that said, "I could go either way here, make my day."

"Well…" Michael began with a hesitant shuffle, "it's all your fault. If you women weren't so divinely attractive and more fun every day, the grass might temp me elsewhere. But it just ain't so. I can't possibly imagine being any happier. I'm on the best ride in the park."

"I'm not sure how I feel about being compared to a roller coaster," Sarah jabbed.

"Okay, okay…how about this—when you're floating on a cloud shared with heaven's most gorgeous angel, there is no way you can get higher."

"Oh, really? I've heard you're an expert at getting higher."

"For now. Not always. And I always straighten out before another takeoff. And I can also reach nirvana sober, no added ingredients."

"I'm glad to hear that, and for the record, I thank God for weeds."

Michael rose, taking in the scenery one panorama at a time then only had eyes for Sarah, "I can't think of anything more rewarding than this second…now, as we call it. I'm sitting beside a breathtakingly gorgeous young woman who is intelligent, caring, and wise.

"And I am also free to be myself, enjoy every second with absolute purity. In the past, too often, after a few months of dating, the woman I cared for got road maps in her eyes, which spelled out where I was supposed to be day by day, and what I was supposed to do minute by minute. And heaven forbid, I should wear the wrong shirt. It's like playing a board game where you get to throw the dice while someone else makes all the moves."

Sarah bounced, laughing. "Been there, know all about it."

Michael had his own chuckle and assumed too much until Sarah asked, "But what if you do find someone that lets you be yourself and gives you more love than you thought possible, which makes you more loving that you ever imagined?

"Can you, could you, walk away from that?"

"I had that once. It didn't work out."

"What happened?"

"She didn't want what I wanted. And she didn't want me."

"I'm sorry, Michael."

"Actually, if we hadn't broken up, being sorry might fit, but it was for the better. Besides, we were too young. One needs something to settle down from, like this trip."

Sarah cocked her head. "For what it's worth...she was a lucky girl."

"Almost as fortunate as a boy named Michael," he said, flashing his signature smile.

"I have an idea," Sarah said, getting up. "There'll be decibels to spare at the party. Right now, a quiet stroll through the park sounds nice."

"If we pass every flower, we can stretch an hour."

They left together, close enough to touch hands, but then again—not.

* * *

Karen never left her side of the tracks, the one padded with luxury— opulent an understatement. Onboard *Explorer Seven*, her six thousand square foot commander's quarters had, in addition to a spacious living room, dining area, and four bedrooms, an entertainment lounge, two dens, a self-contained kitchen, and diamond chandelier.

For good reason. The captain's suite sat top floor with a spiral staircase to the protruding con, a pilot house ready to take over in the event the rest of the ship had to be shut down, for the crew to be left on a friendly planet, so *Explorer Seven* could limp home with a skeleton crew for repairs.

Opening into the hallway were double doors, with mirror projections on the inside, and where Karen admired herself that evening. Her Leonid gem necklace reflected a rainbow of colors, so dazzling most women refused to wear them for fear of losing the limelight.

Karen never gave her beauty a second thought, although a third, fourth, or fifth look wasn't uncommon, that night eyeing her royal azure, cap-sleeved, full-length gown.

And her living walls were not Maine nor Kansas but historic St. Louis, specifically affluent Central West End, Union Boulevard to Forest Park. For Midwest culture, it was the only place to be.

That night all was not well in St. Louis. Andre as much as told her that she was about to lead two hundred and forty bright-eyed young people to their deaths, herself included. Facts are facts. How could the face looking back at her in the mirror not face them?

Saved by the bell, or door panel, which presented the image of Brad outside, ready to pick up his date, wearing black-lapel tux, bright red cummerbund and shoes shinier than military standard. As always, he was confident, forceful, and ready to tackle truck-sized lions or wrestle snakes the length of Rhode Island. Perhaps all heroes begin fools.

Brad's grin froze then sagged at the sight of Karen's fear. "What's the matter?"

Karen pulled back and sought his eyes. "I had a long talk with Andre. We're going to die out there!"

Brad wiped her tears, recaptured cheery, and said, "I'm the best pilot in GASA. I'll make sure that doesn't happen. Don't worry. We'll be fine."

"That's easy for you to say," Karen said. "I once saw you stare down a thousand-pound grizzly."

"Sure, with a ten-meter stun gun and two liters of pepper spray. Which is my point, we are prepared, this ship will do it."

"Why do we have to do anything in life?" Karen whimpered. "Why can't we just live?"

"You're asking me? You're the DNA jockey, always going on about how it hands us chores, bounces us off one another, and then makes us fall in love. What's got into you?"

"Brad...Andre is a liar, we can't trust him. What did you learn?"

"He was honest with me," Brad said, kissing her forehead. "Martin and I speak the same language. He downloaded every file, relay, and circuit algorithm for the entire bridge crew to inspect."

"And?"

"And yes, what you've heard about missing variables is true. However, there is no way to measure resistance in another dimension until you get to that dimension. That's why Andre is so crazy to explore it."

"So this is a test flight?"

"I believe the appropriate answer to that question is 'duh.' On the other hand, that's all I've been doing for the last four years, and I'm still breathing."

"You almost died last week."

"You got me there…and if it weren't for Andre, I would be. I owe him. And when we get back, I'll be the most famous pilot in history."

"Or the two of us will be lying six feet under or, more likely, our atoms will be six light years apart."

Brad didn't understand Karen but knew what to say as he wrapped her in his arms. "Karen, you're right. I've only been thinking of myself. My work, my life…is one risk after another. It's bound to catch up with me someday. You deserve better. An hour before liftoff hand me the command codes and sneak off the ship. By the time GASA finds out, the ship will be five galaxies away. St. Louis is beautiful this time of year."

"That does make sense," said Karen, calming down in a morbid way. "My clinics do a lot of good down here. I'm needed. Besides, I know nothing about propulsion. I'll just slow you guys down."

It was over, and Brad hadn't flinched once, and still had two strong arms wrapped around the blue lady in blue, as she rested her head on his shoulder, and looked beyond it.

What she saw was the shiny green dome of the Cathedral Basilica, said to beam hope to all who view it. Then Karen remembered. She was walking by the Basilica the afternoon she was invited to head the mission.

Karen thought she heard a whisper. The dome was a sign—the green light to go. "In this life, you must also obey," Karen reminded herself. "Eternity wills it so. I have an appointment. I will be there. I will meet Him."

Karen didn't turn and run. She didn't click her heels three times. She did startle Brad—who cast off his arms. "Bradley, everyone on board trusts me. It's my responsibility to make sure we all return. We lift off tomorrow…on my command!"

"Now that's the Karen I remember," said Brad, stepping to the bar at the back of the room. He poured two glasses of amber gin, handed one to Karen, and repeated his favorite misquote, "The pace is to the swift. The battle to the strong."

Karen clinked her glass against his, toasting, "To truth, knowledge, and happiness."

"Tell me the truth, Karen," said Brad, taking her free hand. "Those four days after graduation, we slept late in my dad's space sled, skied moon craters, and danced the night away. Was it as wonderful for you as it was for me?"

"Absolutely, my dear! We were king and queen on earth, prince and princess in the stars."

"So...why did you stop writing?"

She widened her eyes. "You were half a galaxy away. I was home learning from the masters, and you never visited once."

"I couldn't. The station needed me." He shook his head. "Well, anyway...we're together now, and I brought pictures of us on the moon shushing down Mons Vitruvius. We can look at them on the wall of my bedroom after the party."

"Only if you let me delete the ones you snuck of me topless in Aruba."

"Those are my best shots...okay, it's deal."

# 6

## Oxytocin Rules

Cyber opened and closed the same bulkhead door that Janie and Sarah made it through all by themselves. Cyber also projected ship schematics on pad screen for Andre to inspect as he stepped forward, never lifting an eye, and only rarely glancing to the top of the pad that Cyber used to display the path ahead, complete with recommended foot placement.

"I see only one power backup to the con," Andre said. "My plans called for two."

"There it is," Cyber responded, after flipping blueprints, "GASA engineers rerouted it dorsal. And incidentally…you're late. Dr. Wellchild is asking questions."

"Did you tell her I was at the tailor's?"

"That would have been unwise. She had already used her codes to track you to the lab. I suggest you gesture compliance."

Andre doused his pad, pulled up his white pants, centered his red cummerbund, buttoned his jet-black tuxedo, and jogged down Tuileries's tree-lined central walkway for the first workout of the week.

Halfway through the park, he got his first glimpse of the hardwood dancefloor, not anywhere in his plans, surrounded on three sides by crew members dining at round tables, with stage and podium banking forward bulkhead. The executive staff, save one empty chair, sat stage left.

Andre flew by the first table without breaking stride, rounded the second with ease, then stole a roll from third.

*Almost home and hardly noticed. I must invent invisibility powder.*

As he rounded third, Andre noticed cold shrimp, fresh grilled tuna, and a rainbow of appetizers keeping his chair company. The main course, already served and cleared, had been Maine lobsters, range-fed beef, and vegetarian fare that came in two-, four-, and six-inch piles. "Grab your dream and eat to your heart's content," read the sign above the self-serve dessert table, which was flanked by bars manned by real people, wearing badges that proclaimed, "Earth's finest flows free. The universe is the limit."

Andre darted to his chair, snugged in, and slid a napkin to his lap before opening his mouth to explain, "I apologize for being late. You see, there were..."

The sentence never ended. Karen, Sarah, Brad, and Janie had put down their utensils to dead-pan Andre. Michael's eyes joined them, with each hand holding the other half of a twenty-pound lobster.

"What is this, first grade?" Andre asked, darting face to face, amused at being surrounded by statures. "You're not going to pants me now, are you?"

The spell broke just as quickly. Everyone but Michael, who had two pies waiting, returned to deserts.

"I bear glad tidings," Andre continued. "*Explorer Seven* checks out. We fly at noon. And yes, I am most humbly sorry for being late. I was busy."

No one budged until Michael intoned, "For you penance, you must say three Our Fathers and kiss two Marys."

Karen was not amused. "Your mission for the rest of the evening is to be a human being," Karen ordered.

Preferring cellulose by the pound, Andrew waved off a beef platter dripping purines. Then with an aggregable nod that he hoped would clear the air, began, "There are a few details we need to..."

Another half sentence interrupted, by Cyber, to no one's surprise, "Andre, your last simulation did not go well. Power readings fluctuated three percent, lateral thrusters failed to respond, and five circuit breakers went dead."

"All righty then," Andre answered, ignoring his food, head back in his pad, "rerun full program at 90 percent, triple thruster feedback, and order engineering to inspect and manually trip every circuit breaker, backups included. I'll meet them in the power plant in thirty minutes."

"Cyber, this is Commander Wellchild. Belay that order. Andre will be socializing for the rest of the evening. Shut down until ten o'clock tomorrow morning."

Andre shot a look between her eyes, took aim, and was about to sound off when Cyber cut in, "Andre, do you confirm?"

Everyone leaned back from the table, dead silent, as Karen and Andre locked resolve. No one ever got in Andre's way; growling barbs made sure of that. "Woman, I've—"

"*Or*," Cyber pronounced loud enough to surprise Andre silent, "I *can* rerun the last simulation as specified, followed by five more from your folder, with duplicates until ten perfect reproductions are documented. And I can have that data at your workstation at ten tomorrow morning, two hours before liftoff."

"*When will you shut down?*" Karen insisted, a question heard four tables away.

"If you knew anything about this ship," Andre sneered, "you would know that its systems can simulate anything, start to finish, in under thirty seconds."

"So, Cyber," Karen said, attempting to sound confident, "you will disappear before we finish desert?"

"Andre?" Cyber asked.

"Roger that. Reactivate at ten and feed me updates every fifteen minutes till noon. Good night, Cyber."

"This is a first. As you wish. Have a good night."

Michael couldn't resist. "Good night, electrons. We'll almost miss you."

Silence reigned. Dead air lingered. Karen returned to her parfait. Andre stabbed one vegetable stalk after another, until he could take no more, looked up, and said, "Commander Wellchild's private computer, are you activated?"

"Yes, I am," returned her manly companion, from unseen projection, "what can I do for you, Professor?"

"I require assistance with ship's inventory. Can you help me?"

"Certainly, sir. What can I do for you?"

"Is the doctor wearing underwear?"

"White Belgian thong with Spanish frill."

Everyone roared. Karen smiled.

"Computer," Karen spoke, "shut down until ten a.m., and remind me to adjust your privacy protocols."

Michael and Sarah instantly whispered commands to their computer links.

"My computer has been off for hours," Janie said to Andre, "but I can turn it back on if there is something you wish to know."

"Thank you, Janie," Andre said, cooled down by the pleasant distraction, "your last trip to the bar filled me in, and I might say, compliments to the chef."

"Janie," Michael broke in, proudly satisfied, "on behalf of 49 percent of the human race, I would like to add, that you will always be in our prayers."

"Now would that be morning prayers or night prayers?" she asked with a wink and alluring smile.

"I can't speak for the others," Michael said, "but in my case, it's both."

"Thank you, Michael, and you too, Andre. Those are the nicest things anyone has said to me in weeks," Janie added, hoping Brad would get the message.

He didn't. He was busy spooning crème brulee but did pause long enough to catch up with the conversation. "I didn't even turn my computer on this morning. It keeps butting in with data. Who needs it?"

"Spoken like a true pilot," Andre said, burning off irritability at an easy target. "Fly by the seat of your pants, wind in your hair…that's the way to do it. All that 'information stuff' can be so distracting."

"Absolutely, buddy," Brad deadpanned, "theater, dining, and fine wine go better without computer babble. Machines will multitask you numb before the night is over…sabotage the best part. Three's a crowd. A single computer can ruin an entire full moon."

"Well put, Brad," Karen added.

Sarah jumped in. "You city folks can hardly see the moon. I met a New Yorker once who'd never seen the Milky Way. Imagine that, never met his own galaxy.

"We also invented 'rolling in the hay.' Why do you think farmers spend so much time in the barn?"

"Because that's where the sheep are?" Michael shot back, wicked. "I'm off to the bar. Can I get anyone a drink? How about you, Andre?"

"No thanks. I don't drink."

"You promised me a champagne toast," Karen reminded him.

"Okay, one drink…later."

In almost everyone's opinion, the evening was going well; almost implicating Andre, who was not camping happy, preferring instead to brood.

*What kind of deal is this? I know what kind of deal it is.*

*I'm the one who has to deal with people and deal with rules.*

*I'm doing something important. Leave me alone.*

*I have work to do. Leave me alone.*

"Fabulous job on the evening Janie," Michael complimented. "You've brought the city of love to the ship of love."

*Ya, ya…yak, yak, laugh, laugh. For what? To what end?*

*Life is. Life ends. We vanish dust in space. So what?*

*If Cyber were here, she would tell me I was overacting.*

"The best is yet to come," Brad added. "Janie has robot impersonators coming on stage after we make our introductions. The crew has requested beginning with the Beatles, who get help from Frank Sinatra, before Space Flash and every top single of the last ten years is played."

*I have to worry about sleep. I have to worry about money.*

*I have to worry about food. I have to worry about health.*
*I have to worry about who likes me or doesn't like me.*
*And I have to worry about worry.*
*I don't need this.*

Sometimes evil dissolves by itself. Sometimes it must be drowned. Sometimes it's better to leave it alone. Everyone decided to ignore Andre, who, to his credit, had plastered a reasonably social grin to his face.

A meal was shared. Memories were cherished; memories were made. New friends shared time, shared fun, shared dreams, shared love; it had begun—for most, not all.

*Cyber? Cyber!*
*I don't pick her friends. What right does she have to pick mine?*
*I know I'm rude. I'll be better.*
*At least I was free inside. I miss that.*
*In an hour, I'll be surrounded by lush-faced drunks.*
*I'll sneak out. No one will miss me. I'll activate Cyber from the lab.*
*We've got work to do.*

Pleasant chatter hushed when Karen made her way on stage. It began with a single instigator, who was joined by the entire assembly, handing Karen a standing ovation. The crew petitioned GASA on bended knee for the honor of boarding *Explorer Seven*. Karen Wellchild made it happen.

From the podium, she raised her hands to quiet the crowd.

"Our trip...this night..." she began, with pitch and projection Cicero would envy, "is the result of hundreds of years of dedicated scientific progress. *Explorer Seven* is a providential pilgrimage!"

The entire room, still standing, responded with ovation number two, which Andre joined, physically.

*And I'm always late, and everyone reminds me.*
*It's hurry, hurry, hurry.*
*Oh, no, you can't just live life,*
*Must push and grunt along.*
*My poor telomeres.*

Karen reminded everyone that, in the past, our ancestors spent their time digging for grubs or running from bears. "We should go easy on them," she said, "respect their courage and fortitude but also forge our own path, one that evolves rationality alongside peaceful coexistence.

"In a hokey sort of way," she pondered, "the problem is that it's easy to use a day up putting the pieces together, forgetting to make room for the best...sports, socializing, and sensuality. Rule number one in life is...don't pass up the perks."

"Who and what we are inside shares awareness with the past, but we get off easy. We didn't have to sleep in the woods surrounded by noisy carnivores, although the way we worry, sometimes you'd never know. The past smothered worry with simplistic tales...good guys and bad guys, heaven and hell. We say, 'What were they thinking?'

"Many stories, many understandings, that all got in the way of freedom. That's where we come in. We'll make things right.

"There was a time," Karen spoke out with raised voice, "when misunderstanding prevented science from learning, when misrepresentation forbid women their God-given right to control their own bodies, when discordant organizations claimed God, when words made the list of crimes. Those days are over!"

Ovation number three followed. Andre added three claps.

*Wow, she really is something.*

*And she's right.*

Karen quieted the crowd and began her final segment with hands held high. "We respect the courage and fortitude of those who came before us, who overcame hardship, who eliminated injustice. But we must not live too tightly in their shoes.

"Our grandparents insisted that no human being would ever leave the galaxy. By this time tomorrow Explorer Seven will have proven them wrong."

Karen paused briefly to let her words sink in, and then called out, "By this time tomorrow, the Milky Way will be behind us!"

Cheers, whooping, and whistles exploded. Karen beckoned Andre on stage, quieting the applause with her hands as she spoke. "Before...before Andre and the other department heads introduce themselves, I have two quick messages. Number one...this is not a military transport. We fly egalitarian with no ranks or titles. It's first name for everyone.

"Number two...I'm a good sleeper, and even better at falling back to sleep. Feel free to contact me anytime, day or night, about the ship or just to chat."

With that, Karen extended both arms to Andre for a welcome aboard hug.

"Andre, alias Professor Martin, has been published in every field of science. Our job is to improve his tennis game."

*I do all the work. Brad and Karen get to be big shots.*

*Same old, same old.*

"Thank you, Karen," said Andre, in formal briefing tone, "let me begin by saying that if you have a question for me, day or night... feel free to call Cyber. She never sleeps and is usually one step ahead of me anyway. If Cyber can't address your concern, feel free to call Karen."

The silence was deafening.

*Well, they have to know how the ship is run.*

*I'll lighten up.*

"We have a lot to learn. Every day will add knowledge. However, if we are flying forward at breakfast, sideways midday, and backward at lunch, it won't be because Brad is drinking again, at least, not usually."

The crowd had themselves a good laugh, in part thanks to Brad who chugged a stein of beer in jest. "Transdimensional travel," Andre went on, "is like trying to free car wheels from mud. We must loosen up rocking back and forth before moving on."

Brad moved in to hog the show just as Andre finished, his exit from the stage blocked by Karen—playfully.

"Hi, I'm Brad. You probably recognize me from the *Galaxy Gazette*. Squeezing between dimensions is like Moses parting the sea. You race through a canyon at speeds impossible to imagine. It's a blast. You're going to love it!"

Brad's ovation topped every one of Karen's. "Our hardest job," Brad said, "is looking busy, but we will try anytime you want to visit the bridge.

"And now, four words about our flight plan: we don't have one. We simply exit the solar system, look back and say wow...and then be the first starship in history to leave the galaxy. Tomorrow night, we have dinner halfway between our Milky Way and our closest neighbor, Andromeda.

"Then the real fun begins. We'll slide back and forth in time to grease the wheels and then return to the Big Bang, collect data, and stroll home at our leisure. Scenic stopovers and shore parties will follow. So far, I've been handed requests to visit Moses, Confucius, Jesus, Muhammad, and my personal favorite...Elvis.

"Let me know your wishes. I'm here to please. Pilots love to fly!"

Howling jubilation followed, which continued until they got a good look at Sarah, gown flowing, lips smiling, and hips swinging with every step.

"Hi, everyone...I'm Sarah, the bosom in these parts. If accommodations and cuisine don't surpass Riviera's finest, I'm the one to see. Or if you prefer a home-cooked meal by you and me, it's also me.

"Every café, restaurant, and bar is pesticide-free and chemically pure and open twenty-four hours a day. And you've all seen the plans to convert the huge empty space behind the crew quarters into family housing...maybe...someday.

"Someday isn't here. Until then we do as we please, like building an amusement park with water slides, or make the whole thing make-believe lake front, with private cottages to share. I like the idea of going wild...wilderness wild. Andre can synthesize real trees, dirt, and mountain rocks. Gravity loops could have us hiking up Mt Hood by day, cooking on a real campfire at sunset, and sleeping under the stars. Think about it. Thank you."

Even before applause broke out, several crew members were making bird calls. Andre rolled his eyes.

*I'm going into space with these guys?*

*Does no one take life seriously?*

Janie knew when all eyes were on her. Janie liked it when all eyes were on her, which is why each step across the stage was made slowly, facing sideways to maximize curb appeal. "Hello, you lucky, lucky people. It's a grand and glorious day. My name is Janie, and we are in for the time of our lives.

"My department has three missions: party, party…and *more parties.*"

The audience chanted back, "Party, party, party."

"I may not have as many diplomas as everyone else up here," she said, raising her voice above the crowd, "but I did win two beauty contests and was voted the least likely to ever need a sex droid."

"*Party! Party! Party!*" louder and faster when Janie joined in.

Janie looked to Andre in a playful, sly way. "There are those who ponder 'To be or not to be.' For me, at six every night, the only question is 'To drink or not to drink.' And you know how long that debate lasts," Janie said, taking a swig of a drink in hand.

Michael had made his way beside Janie. The crowd didn't hush until she hid behind him.

"Good evening, one and all," Michael said as everyone found their seats. "My name is Michael. Janie is a hard act to follow, and every man who does…is."

Michael got a laugh out of the gate. "She is truly a spirit after my own heart, and I can only pray that someday she might be."

"Back to me. Some call me Frog Man, others prefer Jolly Green Giant, but just for the record, I was not bitten by a mutant spider, raised next to a nuclear reactor, or fed Kryptonite as a child. Nor did my dad mistake my mom for a giant frog one night, which actually happens where I come from.

"I have only one job. To keep you fit so you *can* party. I have a PhD in physical therapy, coach three sports, am unbeaten in squash, and hold three Olympic medals. Half of my day will be spent outfitting those interested in biking, roller blading, or skiing on our outer promenades, and the other giving lessons. And by workday, I mean the four hours we all put in, but feel free to ring me up anytime just to talk, schedule a lesson, or a pickup game of hoops."

Karen had prepped Michael. Andre was not to leave the stage without leading a toast and downing a glass of champagne. Michael handed Andre a drink, raised his own arm high inviting a toast, and said, "Andre, the honor is yours."

*All right Andre. Give it to them straight. Enough is enough.*

"Listen, everyone," Andre began, not a bit friendly, "we have a lot of work to do, make sure you get—"

"*Yes,* Andre," Karen said within earshot of Andre to halt his tracks.

Andre paused, came to his senses, then finished exuberantly, "*Truth cannot be held until it is captured whole. We toast one final leap for mankind.*"

The applause echoed to the stern bulkhead and back. The crew loved it. Then the crew hit the dance floor. Then Andre slithered to the side, down the stage stairs, and into his seat, which he moved closer to the forward bulkhead door, which opened into his lab.

* * *

New pals joked at the bar; couples slow waltzed then fast jitterbugged. The mixing had begun hours earlier over cocktails in the forward lounge that left some already paired, who took a quiet break between sets to walk through the park. Everyone was finding their own way. Everyone was going their own way.

Karen, sitting one out, nodded to Michael at the bar. Two minutes later, she disappeared down the corner stairway to the deserted promenade below. Two minutes after that, Michael followed.

Level two encircled the ship with exercise trails. Level three promenade copied the Queen Mary: love seats, card tables, stuffed furniture, and wall-to-wall carpeting. That night the view was limited to the landing gear and buildings of GASA, shut down dark.

Karen was sitting on the edge of a hammock at the bottom of the stairs. Michael looked fore and aft. The coast was clear.

Michael stepped forward. Karen stood. They took breath together and could resist no longer. The hugging went on and on and on, joined by teasing laughter on both sides. Then Karen backed away but not so far that she couldn't still hold his hand. "Michael," she started, "I want to…from the bottom of my heart…thank you for dropping everything…"

"And everybody," he added.

"Yes, everybody…for coming to help. It's great having you here."

"Have I ever said no to you? What I can't figure out is why you're here, Karen."

"Michael," she started, sitting down, "I spend my life translating other minds, but can't explain my own. But what I do know for sure is that you bring me more comfort than anyone I've ever known."

"Your letter mentioned that you missed my skills of perception and mechanical knowledge. Perhaps that's not all. Are you free after the party?"

"Michael," Karen said with love, knowing her words would speak for themselves, "what I said in my last letter hasn't changed. Maybe, after this mission, you and I will get together again. Right now, I'm really busy, and like you said, neither one of us are ready to settle down."

"Karen," Michael said sweet as candy, "I said that a year ago. We've changed, and there some things you can't schedule, that only happen once."

"Michael, we'll talk later. I don't want to be missed upstairs. No one must see us together. Tell me quickly. What did you learn about Andre and *Explorer Seven*?"

Michael went right to business, arms crossed and direct, "I expected more chaos. You're outstandingly capable, Karen, one of the things I always loved about you. And your crew is sharp, Andre's hull impressive, and the stern power plant is like having a dwarf star in your tank.

"Then there's Andre."

"Yes?"

"He's a work in progress, rough around the edges."

"The question is," Karen said frankly, "is he cracking up?"

"Who hasn't ever?" Michael said and meant it.

"Okay, okay," Karen said, rushing, "we'll get to that too. Did you break his code? Get inside his computer? What's he hiding?"

"To begin with," Michael said, opening his eyes wide, expressing the awesome impact he experienced, "it's not a code. In fact, I've never seen anything like it. He has one level of passwords with a second system that intelligently evolves algorithms to continuously refresh portal entry. His Cyber satisfies every definition of being alive, and if either side of her internal conversation is breached, the entire link shuts down and notifies Andre."

"Okay, okay," Karen said matter-of-factly, "don't feel bad. No one in GASA has been able to get in either. He's really smart. We know that. But more important…what do you make of his personality? Is he crazy?"

"Oh, I see…" Michael said with a convincing self-serving smile, "you want man-to-man stuff. What kind of a testosterone specimen are we talking about?"

"Something like that. So…what?"

"I got that one covered. Will have an answer for you within the hour. Relax for now… I have a few questions of my own?"

"Shoot."

"St. Martin's, private bungalow, beach club, paddle boards, cat-amarans, moonlight walks…a barefoot paradise. Every hour bettered the last.

"Then a month later, I roll over, and instead of your luscious self, I see a pillow and a note. No eye to eye. No 'It's been fun, let's do it again…I'll call you.'

"Karen, you could have picked any lie you wanted. Instead, I got a piece of paper."

Karen, almost in tears, rushed back to his arms. "I know. You're right. If a therapist was listening to this conversation, I'd come off an insecure narcissist fearing commitment. But it wasn't like that. The four weeks we spent together were the happiest ones of my life, but—"

"But what?" he asked, pulling back softly. "You don't follow *happiest* with *but*…"

She wiped her eyes. "Let me rephrase. It was just that…every day we spent together, I got closer to you. Everything we did hummed sweet and rich, like we were blending into a single spirit."

"They call that love, Karen."

"Oh, yes, absolutely," Karen said, holding him closer, "it was just that I changed, wasn't myself…felt like I was losing myself."

"Karen," Michael said feeling comforted, "me too. At the end of the month, I was a new Michael. I was Michael and Karen."

"Michael," Karen said, finally resorting to forceful. "You know I have a dream."

"Does this, by chance," Michael replied, not a bit pleasant, "have anything to do with Joshua? He's my hero too."

It was a subject that the past had opened and closed, without a problem. So they left it behind and did so admirably, to enjoy each other's company, with small talk.

Karen wasn't finished. "So what are you doing here?"

"When an onshore wind piles waves on the beach, I launch my sea kayak, double-skegged and fully ruddered. Getting off the beach is just the start. As I head out, waves building, ten footers wash bow to stern, leaving me dry below my skirt. It might me take twenty minutes or perhaps two hours, but at some point, despite everything I've got, I make no headway and are turned around, to surf the life fantastic to dry land.

"Karen, you attack destiny the same way, and the most powerful storm in existence is the Big Bang. You, me, Andre, this ship, all of us…will be blown back. When that happens, I will be there to help you get home. That's why I'm here."

Karen sighed relief; there was nothing Michael couldn't do, "Oh, Michael, I knew you'd help."

Michael declined Karen's token hug, backing up instead. "Until then," he added, pushing his face into a grin. "You're absolutely right. I know how to party, I'm good at it, and there is a room full of brilliant women upstairs. There's no reason you and I can't be friends."

"Of course, just not seen together. I don't want anyone to know we're in cahoots."

Bowing, Michael gestured "after you" toward the stairwell for Karen to climb the spiral first. "There's just one thing. Don't be surprised if Andre is dancing on a table when you open the door."

"You didn't!" Karen exclaimed in alarm.

"Hey, he drugged me first."

Karen cracked the door one inch, enough to drop her jaw. "Andre! Andre! Andre!" was all she heard. He was standing on the top of a table, in the center of the dance floor, with his head tilted back polishing off a bottle of champagne, Normandy's best.

# 7

## Let the Games Begin

Karen slammed the door to turn on Michael. "Are you crazy? What were you thinking? You tripped out a total nerd! He's going to flip!"

"Now hold on there," Michael said, retreating to the bottom step, "a second ago you asked me for help. Hear me out."

Michael held his ground, a look of complete innocence on his face, his hands spread wide. "What's the big deal? It's only Muluvian passion juice."

"Which," steamed Karen, "is one-part truth serum, one-part aphrodisiac, two-parts hallucinogen, and three martinis."

"Harmless if you only take it once a year. And remember me, I'm the one with testosterone. I can learn more about a guy on passion juice than you get out of six months of therapy."

Karen stalled for more.

"Okay, all right…" Michael continued, "and we have a deal. If Andre turns into a mean drunk, reeking of evil, he and Brad will blast off tomorrow side by side, and you and I will spend the next two weeks in St. Martin's. A deal is a deal."

Karen, unabashed and tense, said, "If Andre is aberrant and dangerous, that's where both of us will want to be. But if he gets smashed and passes out, we learn nothing, and have a hungover, dopamine-depleted chief engineer on our hands. It will be GASA's first drug flight."

"Karen, you know brains, I know brains on drugs. And besides, you're the one who ordered an open bar on the eve of lift off. Caffeine, alcohol…they all take their dopamine toll. What were you thinking?"

"It was necessary," Karen said, with sheepish uncertainty. "The crew needs to make friends."

"And," he said with a smile justifying attitude, "by friends you mean…?"

"Never mind what I mean. You still screwed up."

"Maybe yes, maybe no. My vote is no. Andre, to his credit, is drug-free and well-slept. His dopamine levels are impressive, no drug squeezed drought. His oxytocin concentrations, on the other hand, are deplorably nonexistent. He doesn't stroke a pet, hug friends, fall in love, or make love…to anything. It's a bad situation."

"Your point."

"My point is that he is about to enjoy more passion for beautiful women in the next six hours than he has felt during the last ten, and he's famous, some lucky girl will make him her door prize. A night of love making will top off his oxytocin. It's a win-win scenario."

"Or a lose-lose."

Karen said nothing, just shook her head vehemently and looked down from the top of the stairway.

At peace, at least with himself, Michael added, "Karen, if other…"

Michael finished the sentence to a slammed door that he opened a minute later to join the party, where he learned, that hands down, Andre had just won the no-hands drinking contest, by walking across the floor on his hands, without spilling a drop of the champagne he held between his feet, before finishing it off right side up.

The victory entitled Andre to pick drinking game number two. He announced, "It's Flying Frisbee, everybody!"

Andre prepped the crowd by jumping from tabletop to table-top. When he had everyone's attention, he thrust an arm to the ceiling and called out, "Sports announcer. Come alive! Lay the rules, and layout the teams. Let the games begin!"

The voice of the most famous World Cup announcer was heard from every direction at the same time, "Good evening, ladies and gentlemen, and may I say what a thrill it is to be here today for the first round of Frisbee finals. We play full field, goals elevated ten meters, men against women.

"Each team," the announcer continued, formal and specific, "will have ten gravity belt flyers and ten ground players, who must remain stationary the moment the Frisbee is caught. Three scores takes the title!

"You have all just been scanned. The captain of the men's flyers, as determined by highest blood-alcohol level, is none other than amateur guzzler, Andre!"

The crown cheered, "Andre! Andre! Andre!"

"Hoping to lead the women to victory in the air will be our host, Janie, who apparently has kissed more bottles tonight than men.

"Nine almost as drunk men and women will find their names listed on the starboard wall. Flyers, don your belts and take position.

"Floor passes are the backbone of victory. Tonight's runners must be alcohol-free, so we counted cannabinoid cupcakes instead. Leading the ground team are Hank from navigation and our very own Sarah, whose THC levels lapped the competition.

"Ground team rosters are posted on the port wall. Captains… prepare for the coin toss."

The ground runners dispersed as the flyers hovered ten meters off the floor. Andre and Janie met midair, mid field. Janie won the toss. The Frisbee was hers. By mutual consent, Michael popped a champagne cork to begin the action.

"Hold on, guys and gals," the announcer beamed, high-pitched, "we may need a reading here…none found. Okay then, there is no rule forbidding Janie from holding the Frisbee between her breasts. And wowee, wowee…aren't they perfect! If my wife is listening, I'm just doing my job.

"Wait, there's more! What a sight! Janie is mimicking an Egyptian Sphinx, bobbing her head side to side, and now...whoa! She's flipped totally upside down!"

Half of the men's ground team hit the floor laughing harder than they could breathe, while the other half remained immobilized, waiting for gravity to drop her dress.

"Hold on," the announcer continued, speaking even faster, "Captain Janie just spun all the way around, a brilliant deception if I may say so. Andre's advance has left him wobbling below Janie, who takes advantage of the opening to charge the goal...no...it's a pass to Sarah on the ground...then back up to Judy downfield...and...*score one for the ladies!*"

"Girls rule! Girls rule! Girls rule!"

"In your face, fellas. The ladies have the inertia. But wait...it's not over yet. Andre just caught a ground throw at mid-field, and he...and he...is having trouble. Gravity belts can't read brains spinning double vision. He's up! He's sideways! A wall slam. That must hurt. Get this guy a cup of coffee.

"It's too late. Janie's on him with open hand stretched for a steal. What? Andre's OK...just flew straight over her...it was a fake out... another perfectly executed move if I ever saw one.

"Follow the action, folks. Martha picks up Andre...who tosses to Fred free on the floor, who ankle levels a pass to Jim in position... who *scores*! We have a tied match, fans."

Karen took it all in as she backed gracefully to the edge of the park. Michael noticed no one noticing and joined her. Both faced the action as Michael softly began, "This I didn't expect. Andre is sweet and nutty."

"He's been repressed his entire life," Karen said, hardly moving her lips, "there's no telling what's coming next, and like I said, if he passes out before flirting his way to bed, your plan will backfire."

"Impatience is a curse, my dear. The night is young. The juice will pump for hours. There's plenty of time. But I do have a suggestion. Use your command codes to sneak messages to the bartenders. Cut his hooch at ten. He won't notice, and Cyber is not around to squeal."

"And I believe your plan calls for a woman to magically appear at his side."

"Just for the record, my dear. Don't for one minute assume that I know less about your sex than you do. Andre's publications are read on every campus in the galaxy. Someone is bound to find him sexy.

"You might say that they are just like you Karen. Wealth, power, or celebrity…and the bedsheets get changed. Andre has two out of three and—let's see—your Tony, and Boy Scout Brad, have all three…my, my…what a coincidence, especially when you consider how imperfect both those simpletons are, which I know is hard to spot, with the spotlight on them sitting on top of a mountain of gold."

"Michael, I loved you when you had neither."

"Not for long."

"And Brad and I are just friends."

"I don't believe that, and I do know you're in love with status."

"And I suppose your sex is perfect? Did you fall in love with me because I was good at Scrabble?"

"Naked Scrabble, absolutely."

"Now whose DNA is talking?"

"Karen, you forget that my extra genome senses emotions and, in your case, easily tracks them back to DNA tugging your strings like a puppet."

"Touché, and let me guess, you're not finished."

Michael denied Karen the full advantage of the game, facing her directly, saying, "My point is that Descartes's question everything means just that. Feeling or believing in something is not enough, it's never enough, especially when we tumble to bed. Otherwise, nobody, man nor woman, will ever be truly free to make love stay. Legions of good men have been left out in the cold because their uniforms don't have enough stripes or their wallet's not fat enough."

"Just as many women eat dust when DNA orders testosterone to march on," she said stiffly, noticing Brad fumble the Frisbee almost overhead.

"You left me. I didn't leave you."

"Okay Mister Know-It-All," Karen said, turning to face Michael when the action moved over the stage. "Is male restlessness and female irritability a Greek tragedy...or a blessing? Is the yellow brick road to happiness revolving door romances...or finding 'the one' like you claimed, and clobbered me with in St. Martin's?"

Michael made the mistake of leaving his heart out in the cold. He wilted. "I thought you felt that way too. You said so."

"I did...then...I also think now we should have a long talk about evolution and God's plan."

"I'm good at math," Michael said, almost back on his feet, "and have calculations to show you. Perfect matches *are* almost unheard of but, on the other hand, definitely possible."

"I would love to discuss that someday."

"So would I."

The crowd roared as Janie's team scored the winning goal. The men's team downed a frosty, except for Andre, who put away two just as fast.

"Do you realize," Michael said, tender and as soft as the trade winds of St. Martin's, "that you and I are the only two people in this room sharing sober intimacy? Soul mates are made in heaven. Destiny shines the way. You and I are meant for each other."

Karen looked up at him believing, then down to the floor biting her lip before she shook her head and said, "You're one smooth Casanova Michael. Yes, we do share a vintage bond. But I'm not ready for a happy ending, no matter how much fun it is playing in your sandbox...go fish."

"As you wish, my lady. I had to give it one more try. I sure hope Brad isn't a snorer. You hate that so much."

"One way or another, I'll be sleeping silent and alone in my pod by midnight. I suggest you do the same."

"Karen...can I say I love you one more time without sounding cheesy-needy?"

"Michael...can I say I love you back without giving you my bedroom door code?"

A sleeping pod was the last place Michael planned to end up that night. Halfway across the dancefloor, a lady flyer cut him off with sixteen ounces of ale, which he happily guzzled as Jane chose the third and final game of the night.

The announcer was back. "Janie has chosen…it's piggyback tug-of-war, Sadie Hawken's style. Everyone plays, and Captain Janie gets first pick of steeds. Okay then…Brad will be her stud."

Tall, straight-haired, Nordic Sheila towered over half the men onboard. In fact, Michael was the only one she looked up to. Her rock-climbing reach was the envy of Colorado, a surprising accomplishment for someone who grew up a thousand miles away. She had a frame that could carry packs men crumble under, and her broad blue eyes and long blond hair were perfect for surfing Big Sur, where she did grow up.

Michael was a leg man. There was no contest. If Sheila hadn't picked him, he would have wished she had. The two dominated the competition, truly only Brad and Janie, Hank and Sarah.

Hank was corn-fed and prairie razed, a hayseed turned best navigator in the fleet, and without losing his drawl. His full head of blown-dry hair barely fit beneath his Stetson. The broadest shoulders west of the Mississippi dwarfed his chin, which still stole the show with one perfect dimple. Hank was the real thing. Sarah was ready to saddle up.

Hank's mind was quick and his temper wild. When the competition began, he maneuvered full speed ahead, pulling one couple after another off their feet.

Janie was also ready to rock and roll but began doing little, which was Brad's strategy. "Let the others get worn out first. We'll need our strength for Michael."

Spins, shakes, and fakes were legal, along with as many faces as you wanted to make. Six elimination rounds left finalists, Sheila and Michael, facing Janie and Brad, who enjoyed being crowned king of whatever he wanted.

Michael didn't care about winning, but he did weigh honesty and self-respect. When the championship match started, he put on a great show, at half speed. Sheila went along with it but also whispered, "Michael, how long do we keep this up?"

"Until right after we almost fall, then we pull them over slowly."

Brad didn't care much about opera or Pirandello, but every man in his ring was sized up.

He knew Michael was holding out and appreciated it, but not enough to play fair. Brad tried three reverse leans when he saw Michael intentionally looking unsteady. Once, it almost worked. That was the last time. Michael made sure of that.

The announcer followed every tug. "And once again, ladies and gentlemen, the couples have clenched each other. Oh, oh...both almost went down together. Now they're free. That was close.

"Hang on, folks. These guys have been at it a long time. It looks like Michael is fading...*no*, it's a fake. Or is it? And here we go... Sheila is leaning and about to go down. Back up...Brad is straining...straining...this time it could go either way. Michael is being pulled forward...*no*...Michael just took a giant step backward. Brad and Janie are down. *We have a winner!*"

The entire crew escorted Michael and Sheila on stage, where the two sat in high-backed thrones to be crowned.

"That was great, Michael," Sheila said, as they held hands holding each other. "In fact, I haven't enjoyed myself as much since I climbed Everest without a pressure suit."

"Wow, I thought I was the only one stupid enough to do that. And I hope you had a suit in your pack."

"I love the uncertainty of adventure, but I'm not an idiot, and I did take home the gold."

"Be prepared to be challenged," Michael said as they joined the others on the dancefloor, "my cross-country skiing record has never been broken. I'll winterize the track. The winner gets a backrub. I win either way."

"You're on. I'll look forward to it, Michael."

"Speaking of forward," Michael said, lowering his voice, "Seven's bow is impressive. Can I interest you visiting the forward lounge?"

"The music is a little loud," Sheila said, raising her voice. "Did you ask me to visit the forward lounge, or forward Michael?"

"Either way…I can't lose," Michael said, as he reached for her hand leaving, with a grin on his face from living wall to living life. "Let's go!"

* * *

Sarah and Hank chose the closest table to the park. Hank turned his glass and said, "Sorry we lost, Sarah."

"Lost?" Sarah repeated. "We beat everyone on board except Brad and Michael, and you had little me on top. I think we did great. And besides, I'm not that competitive. I'd rather hear more about your farm."

"Well," said Brad, drawing his fingers back through his long black hair, "it's been in our family for over five hundred years. It takes a half an hour just to drive 'round it."

"In your pickup truck, I imagine."

"Why, yessum, Sarah. Every four years, my brothers and I draw straws to pick different colors. That way Dad can tell who's a-workin' which pasture."

Sarah released a long sigh. "It must be wonderful living off the land, breeding livestock…being your own boss."

"Why, yup, that is true…it sure enough is," Hank said as he leaned back and stretched his arms behind his chair. "But you know, it's a funny thing—as the years go by, you get less fond of cow pies and pig snot. Raising critters ain't my thing. I'm a planter mostly."

"So why are you here?"

"Two reasons. One, I love astronomy, and two, a farm is something you come back to. So how about you? What do you want to go back to?"

"I was born in the hills. I hike mountains, and I love elbow room and fresh air. And there's no better place to raise a family, like mine, that lives together and stays together. I got my eyes on seventy acres back home, but you know, if it's Oregon, California, Vermont, or Texas…not as important as the front porch and who is sitting next to me."

Sarah smiled over, with a dreamy look in her eyes. Hank just looked back, hard to read as always but did move forward. "Sarah, that wilderness habitat idea of yours. I'm all for it. Can I help?"

"You just did," Sarah said shaking his hand. "You are now chairman of the committee to evaluate options."

"Hot doggy. I'll take a day off to backpack anytime you want. When can we check out the space?"

"How about now, cowboy?"

"Lead the way, darling."

\* \* \*

On the dance floor, eyes twinkled and hips twirled. At tables, hands touched and souls embraced. In a universe of happenings, none was more savored than that night, an evening of love, the pedal that drifts so lightly it never reaches the ground. Time gave birth to life. Life gives thanks with love.

The night witnessed passion—one glance across the dancefloor, two hugs on the way home, heavy breathing thirty minutes later. Karen, Michael, Hank, Sheila, Justin, Brad, Jennifer, William, Sue and dozens more drew embrace and beckoned lips nectar. Thrilled hearts fulfilled sacred dreams, which lead to the calm most cherished and always within reach.

It was a grand night. It was a glorious night. All was as it should be—but not for everyone.

By midnight, the dancefloor was empty, the stage bare; blues lingered. Andre had managed to find himself the most uncomfortable spot to plop, after sliding to the floor, which wouldn't have happened if the chair didn't tip over all by itself. The good news was that he landed next to the leg of a table, that was willing to hold up his head.

"Wa-waaa-what? I can't see anything," Andre said, head swaying, looking through lids so slit light barely made an entrance. "Okay, now I get it." He pulled his eyes open, raising eyebrows. "Oh yes, the party. No one here. Wa-i-t…is that Janie? J-J-Janie."

Janie had troubles of her own, just then leaving for a walk to come to terms with them.

She didn't hear Andre. She didn't even know he was behind her until he said her name a second time, which is surprising since Andre ricocheted off every other bush on his way through the park.

Janie followed the living wall on the city side of the park, Paris street life, humming with restaurants, clubs, and dance halls, below spacious historic apartments. She stopped halfway, sat on a bench, and looked up at a corner dwelling, with two street widows and a rap around balcony. She sighed disappointment, lightly sprinkled with sour grapes.

Janie's head was no more stable than Andre's, whose eyes found company, noticing Janie's right eye more affected by gravity than her left. "Why...whhyy...Andre, what are you doing here?"

"That...yss..." Andre began, slurred, "is a very good question. But the problem is...by...the time I finishssssss asking myself the question, I...I...oh...I forget what it is. Oh, I know. What am I doing? I'm here with you."

"Okay..." Janie said agreeably, inviting him beside her on the bench. "That makes sense."

Janie pointed to the apartment across the street. "You see that light, Andre?"

"Janie, I can see everything, but what I don't understand is why it is," he said interrupted by a hiccup, "all blurry."

"Yes, of course, Professor," Janie went along with him, "well, right now, my friend Connie is transmitting pictures to my room from the real window in real Paris that I have projected to the windows on screen in my room, which is also decorated exactly like that apartment, which is where Brad and I spent the best week of my life. Just three weeks ago!"

"What? You and Brad?"

"Yes, and we were going to get married," Janie said, breaking down.

"Did he know that?" Andre asked.

"Not yet, but I could...I really could feel it." And with that, her top half timbered down to the bench. Andre looked, squeezing his eyes together, without success, but he did know the person, actually the two people next to him, were Janies.

"Two whole months...two whole months..." Jane said, still facedown sideways, getting the attention of the mechanical squirrel she added to the program. "And then what? I'll tell you whaaat. One foot off the transporter and snooty doctor Karen scoops him right up. What am I...leftover lunchmeat?"

Andre hit the ground himself, falling, as it were, and ended up sideways, looking over at Janie's head on the bench, which helped both stay in focus. They were fine; it was just the world that was crooked.

"And, Andre..." Janie continued, with a pause to gulp before she up-chucked, "I did everything he asked me to do, and even things I don't do."

"What," Andre said with muffled alarm, "there are things you don't do?"

"Oh, I do those things," Janie said with a wink that almost got stuck, "it's just that I don't normally do things like 'Hi, Mister Ice Cream Man. Can I lick your popsicle?'"

"Right on...sugar babe. If you want to do it. If you're going to do it...then do it. Who cares?"

Andre's bravado was short-lived, almost instantly replaced by anxious remorse. "Karen called me the Nutty Professor. Everyone hates me."

"Andre," Janie said, "I'll give it to you straight. If you want to be loved, you're going to have to make yourself more lovable."

"You, yes...you..." Andre said, sitting up, "are absolutely right. And you know, you're the only friend I have on this ship."

Janie looked over then decided to let it ride and forgot the beginning of what she was about to say anyway but smiled to herself, pronouncing the last three words, "a good life."

"Are you in love, Janie?"

"I think I am. I thought I was yesterday. I mean, geez...just look at the guy! He's a Greek god. What's not to love? But he's not loving me. I guess he never ever did. I'm an idiot. And to make matters worse, he left an hour ago with Karen. I know Brad…she's flat on her back moaning right now, bedpost in each hand."

"And that's where you want to be?" Andre asked, unaware of the effect the image would have on her."

"You're damned right. I…" began Janie before she returned to sobbing.

"What's wrong with me, Andre?" she wailed. "Aren't I pretty enough? Am I too fat? I try to make everyone happy, but men keep walking out of my life."

Andre wasn't enough of a person to react as he should, so he didn't, instead adding, "At least everyone didn't laugh at you in school. They called me Mr. Hard Drive then locked me in the closet. I…didn't…get a shingle burpday card this yearrrr."

Janie sunk to the ground like a melting stick of butter, ending up beside Andre, after flowing straight across his belly, a sensation that began gears turning, which began Andre talking to himself, beginning with his hero, Albert Einstein.

Andre reminded himself that Einstein witnessed horrific behavior, faced disappointment, professional frustration, and physical exile yet never lost faith in mankind. Einstein learned that whatever, whomever, wherever, every ever—is just a passing—left in the past, before a better future.

Then it happened. Andre stopped looking down—and started looking up.

*Life is only mud when you stick your nose in it.*

*No, thank you.*

Andre made a promise to himself, with both eyes wide open.

*There are no thin lines between thin lines, because there are no thin lines.*

*I'm a man. I'm a human being!*

At his side was a friend, one who happened to be young, vigorous, and robustly attractive. Janie had style, beauty, intelligence, and newfound maturity.

One a.m. set a world's record—two pair of shirts-to-socks hit the floor in under three seconds. A single tap folded down a king-sized, foam-mattress Murphy bed in Janie's Paris apartment, with real people out the window. Passion nowhere in the universe was ever rewarded more richly. And that was just the first twenty minutes.

Two hours later, Andre got to thinking.

*Man was not kicked out of Paradise meant for us.*

*We never left Paradise, we just picked up a bad habit of spoiling the fruit that was given us.*

*Life really is peaches and cream!*

*Thank you, Michael.*

# 8

## Shakedown

Since Brad was king of the mountain, he thought it only proper that he should have one, an eight-foot-high pilot station with a padded seat and gold-plated joystick. From his perch, he could peer over the bow, straight up, or any way sideways. Surrounding Brad was floor space for three dozen standing-only visitors, who were free to enjoy the view all the way to the bow.

Thanks to Cyber, the design was ergonomic. Those on watch simply strolled a loop, keeping a lookout in all directions one lap at a time, and Hank's navigation station wasn't in the way. It was on the deck just to the right of Brad, who along with Andre from his second-floor balcony, could keep track of all twelve of Hank's position readouts. Those on bridge duty eyed Hank's numbers as they passed under Andre's overhanging station, which had stairs from the floor on the back wall.

Andre also had an easy out, a door at his back, which opened into the engineering department, that was manned twenty-four hours a day, balancing power outputs, monitoring radiation, and tuning gravity thrustors.

"How sweet it is," said Brad humming, as he moved his joystick pretending to fly, and watched Karen pace.

There was a problem. The bridge had everything—except Andre.

Brad did his best not to look down. He was having too much fun sitting in the first starship that flew by stick, which reminded him of his favorite childhood toy—an ancient internal combustion biplane. From his childhood bedroom, Brad would look up at the moon layered between stratus clouds and dream of sliding past to explore the other side. "And now," he said to himself, "I can explore the other side of the universe."

"This toy has been wrapped long enough," Brad said out loud. "Let's hit the road."

"Hank," Karen said, standing in front of him at his station, "are you sure Andre hasn't been here already? He was supposed to be running simulations hours ago. It's almost noon. Where the hell is he?"

"I'm sorry, ma'am," Hank said, giving her his attention, "I've been working star charts since eight, and not once did he show."

"Ship's computer, Cyber? Winfred…any system listening… *where is Andre!*"

"Good morning, Karen," Cyber spoke calmly. "I've been—guess you would say—up…since ten…and have not managed to communicate with Andre at all. And I might say, this thing your human brains do to turn yourselves off every night is most intriguing and not what I did, since I was actually off, and your brains spin housework at full speed filing information and burning off static. I was also thinking that if you mortals wanted to improve your performance, all you ne—"

"Cyber…enough," Karen insisted. "*Find Andre!*"

"Well, you know, sweetie," Cyber said nonchalantly, "I would love to help you, but Andre deactivated his tags last night, and I missed that, because…let me see…oh yeah…you shut me up and then shut me down. Would you like to continue this conversation?"

"*Cyber!*" Brad ordered, standing military. "You are a member of this crew, and as such will take orders from me and Karen. Is that understood?"

"Certainly, sir," Cyber responded in a joyful way, "and we both know I'm programed to look out for—and protect—the best interests of all. It is therefore my duty to inform you that turning me off, even for a nanosecond, is a big mistake."

"Cyber," Brad followed, "you're absolutely right. Karen, Andre, and I all errored last night, but in our defense, we're human, and you were not letting us be ourselves."

"I apologize for that," Cyber expressed earnestly. "Sometimes I think Andre is just like me. If you wish, I can begin a full ship scan to locate him."

"Now you just hold off on that," Michael said as he walked in the room with bombshell Sheila, "Karen, you wanted Andre to be a person. Let him be one. Give him some privacy. You yourself said that this is not a military vessel. No officer is required on duty until takeoff. Andre has ten minutes."

"Is anyone else missing?" Karen asked.

"Yes," Cyber said. "Janie."

"My Janie," Brad blurted out.

"What do you mean...your Janie?" Karen said, facing Brad.

"Oh, nothing...we arrived in the same shuttle together."

Karen only had room for one problem that morning, the empty chair she was looking at, which she climbed to sit in, beckoning Michael to follow.

*Explorer Seven* lay between housing and the administrative headquarters of the Global Aeronautics and Space Administration. Thousands stood at their windows waiting to watch the most famous liftoff in history. Global news channels, computer monitors, and Galaxy streams added a trillion more observers, everyone counting on Karen to get the show on the road in ten minutes. Her three-ring circus wasn't going anywhere, not even warmed up.

Michael sat down next to Karen in Andre's elevated station. Without changing her petrified pleasant expression, she gently poked Michael in the chest with her finger and whispered, "See, you screwed up, Michael. You promised me this wouldn't happen, and here it is, five minutes to liftoff, and egghead isn't here. And worse than that, he's AWOL.

"Break into these controls and start us up," Karen commanded, loud enough for Brad to turn suspicious.

Michael grinned like Michael did. "Listen, I've told you before... that can't be done. And even if I could, the last thing I would do is tickle the temperamental beast we lovingly call *Explorer Seven*."

Michael wasn't done, following with love. "Don't trouble trouble until trouble troubles you. I've never seen you like this, Karen. Shame on you, of all people, prioritizing appearances for the crowd. This is your ship. It will leave when you decide to leave, which will be when all systems check out, Andre included."

"Grrrr!" Karen said, quietly frustrated. "So what do we do?"

"Passion juice makes it easy for me to read brains for days. I feel him. He's almost here."

"So you knew all along?" Karen asked and accused.

"Only for the last twenty minutes."

"You could have led with that, Michael."

"And miss a psychologist not following her own advice? I don't think so. And for the record, I also didn't say anything when we ostracized Cyber from the group. We're all learning."

A dozen crew members had joined the bridge staff. The drama on Juliet's balcony caught their attention, leading to complete silence, which let everyone hear from the port door opening, "For me, it was flipping off one of the daisies on your bedsheets and landing a perfect one eighty on top of you."

Andre tiny-laughed between words and was not aware of another soul in the universe when Janie answered, joyfully triumphant, eyes love-locked on him, "And then bouncing right back again."

Quiet got their attention. The lovers looked at the assembly, looking over. "Hello, everyone. Andre Martin reporting for duty, and top of the morning to you all."

With a shy turn, hiding his lips from the crowd, Andre followed, "Which won't come close to the bottom of the morning."

"I'll take that as a compliment," Janie said, pulling Andre in closer just short of a kiss.

Their separation was slow, ending with two, then one finger touching. Andre made his way to his stairs as Janie walked to the bow, both listening to the countdown, which reminded them of several countdowns the night before, which left those around Janie wondering where the giggles were coming from.

Karen and Michael passed Andre on the steps. Karen stopped to ask, "How are you feeling, Andre?"

"Never better, and not still drunk if that's what you mean."

"Liftoff is scheduled in twenty seconds," Karen said, pretending to be flexible. "Are we ready?"

"With five seconds to spare. Hold your hat. Here we go."

At the bottom of the stairs, Karen oddly remembered returning to her bedroom desk at home after her first semester at college. Nothing had moved.

*I'll go away to space, come back, and nothing will have changed either.*

*Home sweet home will still be home sweet home.*

She also remembered saying goodbye to her parents. On her way out, she ran her finger along the nick in the front door from when she was seven riding her bike inside, like she was not supposed to do. And now she was riding a space ship, which if truth be told, she was also told not to do.

Brad's, Hank's, and Andre's systems all checked out. GASA agreed. They had the green light to fly. Andre positioned his right index finger one inch above the power button. Hank, also looking at Karen, swept his right arm out and to the side like a baker advertising his trays, but instead of trays, every one of Hanks bearings lit up.

Brad was the last to get Karen's attention. He held a make-believe radio microphone to his mouth, used his thumb to press an invisible button, and pretended to request flight clearance.

For Karen, counting minutes from ten to one was easy; the last sixty seconds—not so much. She was only onboard physically.

*Two feet on the ground...pretty much OK. Changing a lightbulb standing on a chair...usually OK. Standing on top of a ladder or flying into space...no way, it's nonsense."*

She wasn't alone. Those looking back at her from the bow were tense with reservations, doubting more by the second. Caught between trepidation and the thrill of anticipation, Karen saw no fires blazing, until she got to Michael, who was steady-eyed and totally confident.

Michael stood next to Sarah, who tilted her head back, held up her right arm, aimed for the sky and pointed to the heavens. Michael joined her. It caught on. One by one, those in attendance grew power, dared all, and willed the future forward.

Karen signaled Brad. "Mission Control," he said, "this is *Explorer Seven* requesting permission to liftoff."

"*Explorer Seven*, this is Mission Control. You are free to fly, and global airspace has been cleared from one to forty thousand feet for flyovers. Good luck and God speed."

Andre tapped his console to initiate graviton thrust.

Brad two-handed his joy sick.

"Powered up, ready to climb," Andre announced.

"Navigation cross tracking operational," Hank reported.

"Helm solid and steady," Brad finished.

Then nothing happened. Everyone just kept looking at Karen, who finally said, "What?"

Brad looked over with a grin and said, "It is customary aboard starships lifting off or changing course for the commander to give the order, usually something esoteric, like 'thrust gravitons' or 'Make it so' or," Brad then added, gesturing like a cavalry captain, "Engage."

"Can I say anything I want?"

"Yes, Karen, you can."

"Okay then...*tally ho*."

It didn't feel like flying, more like the ship was standing still and the entire planet sinking. The first thousand feet took an hour, on purpose. Both military bands playing on the base got to finish their set and hear applause piped down from Seven.

GASA also showed off. The old 'everyone talks about the weather, but no one does anything about it' joke hadn't applied for centuries. Speedy cold fronts no longer undermined lazy rising hot air masses that toppled down energy to generate a swirling menace. It was GASA that engineered the invisible force fields that channeled hot air straight up, collecting in tubes, turning graviton supported generators, which in turn beamed energy to the surface, which when combined with solar panels and water damns, generated more clean power than the planet needed.

Thanks to GASA, there wasn't a cloud in the sky, and every crew member knew mom and dad were waiting to wave goodbye, with air hugs.

"It's a weird thing," Karen, again professional, said to Michael who had moved beside her. "Earth's parents have always loved their children: banishing chill with a stoked hearth, offering love on a warm lap, and blistering hands morning till night."

"And also cold irony," Michael added somberly, "that those same parents did everything they could to help their loved ones, except the most important thing of all: getting along with parents of other races and religions, so that children, their children, would not suffer hatred, prejudice, and warfare."

"A misery everyone on *Explorer Seven* has been spared," said Karen, finally smiling.

Hank's farm was first up. Ted, Zeke, Ned, and Charlie all waved from the back of their pickup trucks. Mom and Dad were on the front lawn, holding back tears and doing a fine job.

Hank waved back from the tip of *Explorer Seven* that hovered barely thirty meters above ground, and then swung his arm to urge a mustang gallop.

The country goodbye was not without humor: Ned, the brother he had almost never beaten, teased the navigator by serving a tennis ball straight at Hank, which bounced off six meters of diamond hull. Hank completed a backhand swing holding on to an invisible racket then raised his arms in victory when Ned's chase didn't manage the return.

The visit ended with the entire family lifting hats in a cowboy salute, to the tune of "Happy Trails to you until we meet again…" musical selection courtesy of Cyber Incorporated.

Hank attempted a swift return to duty. It didn't work. The first tear hit the deck.

Brad and Karen were up next. "Saint Louis…here we come." Brad got them there in a flash, literally. Again, they parked thirty meters up, above Karen's midtown penthouse garden balcony, where two sets of parents tried hard not to think about not being able to think about grandchildren, and did a good job, unless they told the truth.

Brad and Karen took their places at the bow, held hands, and raised both. Brad never cried at times like that. Karen always did. The ship didn't slip away until three marching bands had passed on the streets below, which where mobbed with well-wishers.

On the way to Minnesota, Sarah insisted that Brad fly high enough to avoid birds, which he did. They had no trouble finding the lake, floating Michael's parents and hundreds of friends, since they rafted canoes into a giant *M*.

His kin were just as easy to find—one tall green dad standing beside a woman whose tear-soaked smile Michael had seen before. "Don't worry, Mom," Michael mouthed silently. "I'll be back. You won't lose me too."

Cyber did her research. "Rocky Mountain High" was heard by all as Seven swung over its peaks, holding steady directly above the tallest, Mount Elbert, where Sarah's family set off a laser-light show from their Jeeps, alongside too many tears to count.

"All I asked," Cyber said in defense, "is how Janie got permission from the mayor to fly down Las Vegas Boulevard. You don't have to shh me. We're getting bombarded by champagne corks from casino rooftops."

Janie joined in, popping a cork off the hull from the inside, as she waved to thousands lifting paper cups on the street. Janie had been the toast of the town for years, and everyone left her toasted. She had new friends now and wanted more out of life. Not one tear was in sight.

And so it went: San Francisco, Peking, Tokyo, Moscow, Madrid, Paris, Berlin, London—so many brothers, so many sisters, so many parents, so many tears, a planet of hearts, a planet of hearths, all praying for a happy ending, "And we will keep your love in our hearts wherever we go," Karen said softly.

\* \* \*

Blue sky turned to black space speckled with stars. Brad rolled Seven down, across and out of half a dozen moon craters, with a private look for Karen when he paused above Mons Vitruvius.

"This is no time to show off, Brad," said Karen when he used storm winds on the surface of Jupiter to surf across the planet.

"This planet is huge," Brad said in justification, "and we owe it thanks for scooping up five-billions years of asteroids that were headed for Detroit. The least we can do is give her a tickle."

No one paid attention to Pluto, hadn't in years. Five minutes later, the sun was just another star in the sky, which is when Andre cut power and joined the crowd at the bow. "Well, there it is, folks, our solar system, our galaxy, and the rest of the universe."

Hank confirmed that they were dead in the water and sat back. Brad let go of the joystick, climbed down, and gave Karen a back-side bear hug. Everyone bubbled with joy, including Andre, who announced ship-wide, "Good afternoon, fellow wanderers. As you can see, we found a parking spot. Fusion power from my lab got us this far.

"When I hit the last button, one of three things will happen: number one…the power plant will generate enough energy to split dimensions, leaving us sitting peacefully in a canyon, whose starboard wall will be three-dimensional matter and whose left cliff will be time, from beginning to end, both of which are never in sight, no matter where we travel.

"When we get there, we won't go anywhere, just sit spellbound, as we travel neither distance nor time. At the end of one minute, I will power down, and we will be as we are now.

"You should know…GASA, in their infinite timidity, rate that as our best-case scenario but least likely to occur.

"Possibility number two: as we power up, core-crystal temperature will rise out of control. We will then have one minute to detonate hull charges and separate the stern from the rest of the ship. Hold on tight. The bulkhead between living quarters and stern power should hold, but we will need to get as far away as possible as quickly as possible. Gravity plate neutralization will not match acceleration.

"GASA has six space telescopes focused on us. The explosion will be recorded. And so you know, GASA lists stern separation as the most likely scenario.

"Possibility number three—you know, the one that's been in all the news, the one your folks didn't need to know—is that no force field can contain as much energy as we are about to generate. The event will end before our retinal ganglion cells transmit the flash to our occipital lobes.

"In other words, we won't feel a thing."

Brad and Andre grinned at each other like a pair of ten-year-olds lucky enough to grab the front seat of a roller coaster. Sarah stood behind Hank at his station. Janie, and the others, faced Earth, preferring the view to watching Andre do the deed.

Karen, expecting a countdown, closed her eyes and prayed it would not be her last.

Andre stared into space and pretended to be distracted by a final reflection. It wasn't a stall. He had started the countdown from his desk the second he sat down, another secret, perhaps the last, he shared with Cyber, who had learned and said nothing.

The stern's fission generator had no idle; it either slept or soared. Waking it up lurched the ship forward, buckled the entire hull, and left half those standing no longer standing. "Great news," Brad called out, "we're not dead!"

"Not yet," said Karen, standing behind Brad, facing up to Andre. "Sixty seconds of two million degrees or higher and we blow...*right, Andre?*"

Andre was too busy venting heat to bother with Karen venting fear, so she looked over Brad's shoulder to read for herself. "Andre," she said shouting, as the pounding roar from the back of the ship got louder, "we're at three million degrees and climbing...*aboat and separate!*"

Brad ignored Karen's prodding. "Karen, give Andre a minute. There's a lot of scum back there that needs to burn off. It's not over yet."

"And when it is," Karen said, sticking her face in front to block Brad's readouts, "it will be too late. As commander of this vessel, I order you and Andre to shut down before it's too late."

"Well, you know, Andre," Brad said slowly, "Karen does have a point...we should do as she wishes."

"Why, yes indeed..." repeated Andre, taking his time completing one adjustment after another. Okay, well then, I suppose..."

"So do it! Or maybe not," Karen said, when Brad used his finger to show her temperatures dropping.

"Attention, all hands, this is Andre. Core temperature has stabilized. We are now transferring energy to field generators. Prepare to exit three-dimensional space. Your insides might tickle."

"Here we go," Andre began. "I...am...now...adding power to the field net surrounding the ship."

"Oh, wiggly, wiggly..." Janie tee-heed, "I'm feeling it. I'm loving it! And it mixes well with champagne—bubbly inside, bubbly outside."

"Wait until I turn up the power," Andre cautioned. "It might make you itch inside but only for a few seconds. Next boost in three...two...one..."

Andre never understood why the concept wasn't obvious; nuclear forces push electrons away from condensed proton and neutron field caps. So copy that force and all of physical reality gets moved over, surprising everyone, except Andre.

"No problem," said Andre, still too goony from the night before to be totally serious and not as precise as he should be. "I am now officially the strongest man who ever lived. No one has ever moved the entire universe aside."

"Aside of what?" Michael said, enjoying the possibilities that were dancing in his head.

"That's where things get interesting," Andre said, "and I have two answers to the question. The first is that what we think is time is actually active energy field displacement. So all we have to do is change field coordinates and then reenter three D space wherever we want. Pick a date, and I'll get us there."

"So the time travel part," Brad said, leaning forward like a sprinter waiting for the gun, "is just another trip. What was your second answer to what's going to happen next, Andre?"

"It's...I haven't the slightest idea. Which is why we're here. Hell, we know everything else. And...we...are...at...full...shield... power...now...and we are separating..."

"Didn't I tell you? Didn't I tell you?" Brad declared. "Like Moses separating the sea."

Space divided into a cavern that stretched forward as far as the eye could see, further than Seven's best telescope. Brad turned around to examine the back wall of the bridge, the middle of which was Andre's elevated desk, who had also turned to inspect the projection from the stern camera. There was no end to the cavern.

In unison, Brad and Andre looked up, then straight down to the floor screen, in truth the entire floor that reproduced the view from below the ship, and saw walls straight up, walls straight down.

"Okay, now watch this," Brad said as he sat down, preparing to change ship position. "Andre, I am I cleared to turn?"

"Spin the ship...yes. But no movement in distance, and no moving along the time wall either. Test only directional torque. Moving in either or both directions at once requires another power increment, and we need to analyze the data first."

"I'm sorry," Cyber said with an attitude, "who is going to analyze the data?"

"Correction," Andre directed, "you are, and right now. Get to work instead of activating social programs, and discontinue emotional overlays."

Sarah was at the starboard rail peering into the universe. It looked like a huge piece of glass had separated it from where the ship stepped out, like a fish tank at the aquarium where an entire world goes its merry way on the other side.

Michael was one hundred and eighty degrees away looking out at the wall that made up the left side of the canyon. And it was funny—no picture world or structures or focused images, but it glowed blue and felt soothing.

"Andre," Michael said with his nose as close to the port wall as he could get, "what's all the rest? What is part of the universe, not physical reality, critical to it, that always has been and always will be?"

"Michael," Karen asked with reverence, "do you sense emotions? What do you feel over there?"

"Andre," Michael said, "can you adjust power to bring us closer to the boundary over here?"

"Briefly, then I will push back to where we are now. Some fluctuation is expected, and I don't want to bounce off."

"What happens if we do?" Brad asked.

"The canyon we are looking at," Andre said, "began in the middle of the ship and then got pushed away. Both sides were always part of us, fused into reality. But we were standing still. If we move sideways or scrape it elementary particles might collide, cause friction, or an explosion or…well…to be honest…I haven't the slightest idea."

"It's a day to remember," Cyber kidded, "the second time in his life that Andre admitted he didn't have the slightest idea?"

"What was the first time?" Janie asked from the floor.

"Vanilla or strawberry ice cream."

"Michael," Andre said, "hang on, pay attention, I'm squeezing us in for one second."

"Oh yes, so beautiful," said Michael, expressing pleasure, equally calm. "I knew it…I feel…now feel…love…and companionship… just like being home, with my family all together at the fireplace on Christmas Eve."

"My turn. My turn. My turn to play," Brad said, play-acting.

"Just a spin, no movement, less power, more patience, Brad. Help yourself. Thank you, Andre."

No one was impressed. Brad turned up, turned down, spun around—every direction looked just the same. "So how do we get our bearings out here, Andre?"

"I thought we'd start simple. Attention, crew," Andre said, also answering Brad's question. "I'm shutting down power…one, two, three…and the walls phase in…and we are back where we started. In ten minutes, Cyber will have what she needs. We'll have a look, and then split, travel first in distance only, then shut down, then have lunch, then travel time, and then return to normal space for the night—our night, that is."

The entire crew burst into applause.

"Well done, Andre," said Brad with a brief salute.

Merited peace followed. The majesty of the event spoke for itself.

"Karen," Andre said with respectful acknowledgement, "you are needed in the con."

The most dangerous parts of the ship were the stern that could explode and the bow that could plow into something. Bulkheads were constructed and the force field reinforced, between bridge and Andre's eight lab floors, between lab and main activities area, and in front of the power plant in the tail, also protecting the con, which was above Karen's penthouse suit, of course.

"Karen," Brad said as he took her by the hand to lead her off the bridge, along with everyone else he was shooing on their way, "the con has every readout Andre, Hank, and I have down here, and a miniature joystick. Observe and learn. The bridge is a dangerous place to be when we fly."

"Wait…what?" Karen protested. "But the bridge is where the action is."

"If things get hairy," Brad continued, in a tone that scared Karen silent, "Hank, Andre, and I will join you to run the ship back there. We must be prepared."

* * *

On Karen's way to the con, she picked up cheese, crackers, and two canters of red wine. Karen, Michael, Sarah, and Janie all climbed the spiral staircase to the con, the bubble on top that looked forward down three quarters of the length of the ship.

"And a nice comfy chair for each of us," Michael noticed, sitting down nibbling crackers, with his eyes fixed on the readout panel in front of him.

"I believe this belongs to you," said Sarah, as she swiveled the cushioned captain's chair around for Karen to sit dead center, best view of all, complete with a joystick between her legs.

"After the wine perhaps," Karen said, chuckling. "Michael, switch places. You know more about playing with things between your legs than I do."

"I'm not convinced of that," Michael said on good authority, "but it will be an honor to take the chair."

"What's going on back there?" Brad asked over the intercom. "We can't power up until the con bulkhead is sealed."

Karen quieted down to enjoy their picnic. Hank and Brad spent two long minutes watching Andre adjust then readjust every setting he had, the efficiency of which surprised the boys until Brad figured out that Cyber was talking to Andre in his head.

"Is there anything you would like to share with the class?" Brad asked Andre, who knew he should be.

"Oh, yes…sorry…used to Cyber directing in codes. Cyber," Andre said out loud. "Hank and Brad should know all we do. Activate verbal."

"All right then, soldiers," Cyber said, "when the stern runs hot, I feel it, and I don't like the feeling, and if it gets out of hand, all feelings will end. So we go slow…we fly carefully…*no more* than 10 percent power and no longer than two seconds, then we coast. Same with slowing down."

"And," Andre said, "we deal with one dimension at a time. We will first travel distance in normal time. Then we stay put and just move time back and forth. *No* combinations yet!"

"Aye, aye, sir," Brad and Hank responded, with complete faith in leadership.

"After I power up, your throttle and stick will be live, Brad. The ship is yours," Andre finished, "but I can also work lateral thrusters from up here to push us off a wall that gets too close for comfort. On my mark—"

"Excuse me," Karen said, her voice crumbling from a mouth full of crackers, "Aren't I—we back here—supposed to say go, Janie, let her rip?"

"Boys," Janie said, clinking two glasses together, "tally to your heart's content."

The power plant was heard revving in the con, but the bridge was quiet. "Smooth startup, Andre," Hand complimented with a nod.

The canyon opened. Brad aimed level, distance only, stars displayed for Hank through the right canyon window. Minimal thrust shot Seven forward, covering more distance in two seconds than a month of warp speed.

All was not perfect. The ship wiggled. Brad figured out how to counterbalance thrust just seconds before hitting the starboard wall. Andre was ready with thrusters he didn't need to use. The ship centered as she streaked by stars that looked like flaming asteroids.

"Attention all hands!" Brad broadcasted. "Helm control is challenging at this speed. The slightest lateral momentum can throw us off. For the next minute, remain seated or standing exactly where you are. Cyber is calculating patterns to predict yaw and making headway, I see. Stand by for now."

Hank and Andre also froze as the port canyon wall was the ship's next target, a surprise no one expected, except Cyber, who was on it, and avoided three more turbulent challenges.

"Andre," Brad voiced loudly, "thrust sprays aren't uniform."

"I'm on it," said Cyber.

"No more speed," Brad said to Andre. "This is it—any faster gets slippery."

"You got it."

"Better!" Brad said. "You don't aim this bird like a rocket, more like a forty-pound curling stone on ice."

"I'll buy that," Andre agreed. "What we need is more brooms."

"Attention all hands," Brad announced, "we've balanced the helm. You're free to resume activities in the main hall and living quarters."

When Brad swung a finger over to Hank, he opened his ship mic and said, "We are coasting on momentum—with zero fiction, I might add—and at our present speed will exit the Milky Way, the first human beings ever to do so, in four minutes.

"We will then split the 2.5 million light years between our galaxy and Andromeda, where we will park to take in the view over lunch."

# 9

## *Rock of Ages*

"Everything in existence," Cyber said in formal tone, "must obey atomic and anatomic composition, which is accomplished through the fourth dimension, which counterbalances force to drive matter. Therefore, changing position on that fourth-dimensional grid—that is, going up or going down—changes time."

"Thank you, Cyber," Brad said matter-of-factly. "I don't remember asking, but yes…thank you for that information. And for something useful, can you tell me what's for lunch?"

"According to Sarah, anything you want, except Sarah, except Hank I guess."

Hunger wasn't on the boy's minds—space was. All three walked to the bow to take in two galaxies at the same time.

"Hey, Andre, when we went trans, did you expect the Grand Canyon?" Brad asked.

"Well…" Andre hedged, "I'll tell you the truth. I had no idea what would happen. For all I knew, we might have ended up inside a wormhole."

"I think Karen was hoping we'd be floating on clouds," Brad joked, "watching cherubs fly by playing harps."

"I'd preferred beauty queens carryin' plates o' my mama's pecan prolines," Hank added.

They all chuckled. "Seriously," Brad said, "the power plant is cherry."

"It's the circuits I'm worried about," said Andre. "They were slow to respond. You guys run alone. I'm going to snack here and run more simulations with Cyber."

\* \* \*

An hour later, the team was back to set another record, "Attention all hands," Andre said from his station. "On behalf of the bridge, I want to thank the lab and power plant teams for the superb support you have provided today. We just set a distance record. We will now become the first ship in history to travel time.

"Brad sees time travel as just another place to go. There are also those who believe that what we saw today is the crest of an eternal dimension, making all else possible, and the home of our real selves. The spirit world…"

"Okay then…" Brad said, cutting in on purpose. "After I turn the ship, we will move time ahead, make a U-turn slowly, so as not to get stuck, and then return to this very spot to set up camp for the night."

On cue, Hank took over. "Howdy, gents, Howdy, ladies…welcome to the galactic square dance, where our very own, sweet as sugar plums Milky Way, seen taking up the furthest left quarter of our bow view, will do-si-do with imposing but always respectful Andromeda. Two spiral galaxies are about to their thing.

"He who weighs most calls the shots. Our good old Milky Way tips the scales at 250 million stars, no match for longhorn Andromeda's one trillion flaming suns, many complete with planetary solar systems just like ours."

Hank livened it up to keep his audience. "Did you know, neighbors, that every day, every one of those trillion exploding nuclear reactors gets three hundred thousand miles closer to the barn?"

"Andre, is this when I am supposed to interrupt?" Cyber asked, muted enough to sound suspicious; at the same time, everyone heard.

"I said join in, Cyber," Andre answered with parental patience. "I said you have interesting information to add and that conversations are built adding related subjects."

"Cyber," Hank said, woodsy slow, "what's on your mind?"

"I interrupted, didn't I?"

"Cyber," Hank said, "I'll tell you what, partner. When I say the words 'place your bets and take your chances,' you take over."

"All right then," Hank said, returning to his excited rodeo voice, "gravity has the last word. The two giants before us are on a collision course. Will they collide fiery fury or slip by one another? Place your bets and take your chances."

"Hold on right there," Cyber interrupted, again, just before Andre's face told her she had a lot to learn. "I've read about gambling. You need to know the odds—*oh,* I got it—this is where I come in, get to do my favorite thing…list numbers."

"And," Brad said by rights of the chair, "we're waiting."

"The answer is," Cyber pronounced distinctly, "none of the above. Both black-hole-centered systems will slice through one another, congeal gravity forces, and eventually continue on as an elliptical, still part of the two thousand Virgo cluster."

"And we're talking four billion years into the future," Michael added. "Space is so expansive, and planets, even stars themselves, are spread so distant that mathematicians predict not a single collision will occur. The two heavenly bodies will join to live happily ever after."

"On the other hand," Andre said, "the density of space gas will be high enough to light up earth's skies with effervescent rainbow waves, mostly red, maroon, and off-yellows."

"A perfect ending," Sarah said.

"It's not the ending," Andre felt obliged to point out. "Gravity never rests. Eventually black holes will devour all, including themselves."

"Okay, maybe," Michael had to say, "Andre, you know that gray zone isn't focusing any clearer. It's just a theory, and what we should be betting on."

The crew went quiet when Andre powered up, split dimensions and moved time forward, as Brad kept the bow facing the action. No one spoke during the entire ten minutes it took to watch the two galaxies make contact and invade each other's spirals halfway, which is when Brad let on, "This is the tricky part, turning around to turn time backward."

"Whatever you do," Andre remined Brad, "don't stop. Add a distance circle, bring us in closer, on momentum only, then revolve to reverse course."

The galaxies got closer to the ship but stopped merging. Brad casually regripped the stick after his first nudge went nowhere. "There's a problem, Andre."

"Slow continuous force with work. Be patient."

Brad was. They turned back, to the same place, since they really hadn't left it, except in time. It was a smooth ride out, a picture-perfect return.

"Attention all hands," Brad announced. "That's all she wrote. A-plus on every page. The stern power plant is shut down. We're done for the day, campers! Tomorrow we hit the big top. First bridge watch report for duty. Everybody else...enjoy the evening. No resort on earth has it so good."

Andre lingered and tinkered. He was no longer groggy, but his metabolism did have a few things to say. Later, on his way out, halfway through the lab, he stopped, looked around, took one step towards the full ceiling readout board, then took the same step back. He was on his way to reset his metabolism with a squash ball workout.

Andre feathered a left hand toss, then a vertical racket smash, which rebounded off the front wall for a perfect corner drop, which Andre managed to chase and return successfully, which meant he had to spring center, which he did, barely making a low scoop in the corner, which he nailed for a killer shot.

An hour went by, Andre grunting louder every minute, alternating forehand to backhand on opposite sides of the court; forehand to backhand, backhand to forehand. But solitaire didn't dowse the beast. Andre's plan wasn't working.

Andre invested effort he didn't know he had, but more-harder-faster—didn't help.

It ended with Andre tossing his racket, ducking out the fox hole, and spitting in a bucket.

The next hour passed between table massage and steam bath. The robot was the best. He was programed for singing, tutoring, conversation, or doing nothing. Andre choose Beethoven.

Andre's massage program was different, it combined deep tissue, trigger point, Thai, and Shiatsu at the same time; beginning complete, winding down smooth and still. That didn't happen. Andre left, leveling a single opinion on his way out, "son of a bitch," and he wasn't smiling.

After cleaning up, Andre passed through Sarah's private kitchen on his way forward. She and Hank were wrangling over chicken gumbo, and his mother's name had already come up twice before Andre passed within earshot.

"Oh, Andre," Sarah called over, "got a minute?"

Andre obliged and was also curious why anyone would spend an hour doing what a machine could duplicate in ten seconds.

"Do you think this is spicy enough?" Sarah said with the spoon almost in Andre's mouth, who decided to play airplane.

"Tremendous flavor," Andre said, already in reverse. "Great… best I ever tasted."

"You don't think it needs a sprinkle of curry?" Hank suggested.

"I was raised bland. It's perfect."

Sarah nodded agreement. "Andre, how does this sound? Three-inch-thick homemade white bread, egg battered, a hint of cinnamon, deep fried brown crispy, before rolled thick in powdered sugar. I can have four slices for you in five minutes."

Andre paused, enjoying a deep breath alongside memories. "You'd spoil me for life. I'll take a raincheck. I'm on my way to the bow."

Andre was halfway through the adjoining dining room when Karen spotted him. She and Brad had the best view in the house, resting galaxies where right out their window. Karen wore a halo of heavenly bodies. It helps to be the pilot.

His three-piece suit, her elegant gown, linen tablecloth, electric candle lights, and the only bottle of champagne to escape the previous night completed the picture. True to gentleman's code, Brad rose to shake Andre's hand. "No one thought we could budge a second through time, and you did it! Congratulations, Andre."

"*We* did it, Brad," Andre acknowledged. "Your helmsmanship was magnificent."

"We're just about to order," Karen said, gesturing at the table. "Please join us."

"Thanks, but I finished an entire bowl of tuna salad in my room. I'm on my way to the bow. Another time for sure."

"Well then, will you at least sit for a few minutes? I have a couple of questions."

"Certainly, Commander." Andre snagged an empty chair from a nearby table.

"Brad told me the stick was so rough that we almost got stuck in the future," Karen said, leaning in, not wanting others to hear. "If we had, what would have happened next?"

Andre stroked his chin. "Well, you know, the odds of backing time are fifty-fifty at best. If we'd failed, I might have found another pattern that would work after we'd drifted in space for a few weeks or months. Otherwise, we could land on the closest suitable planet for more testing."

"Or...return to earth?"

"If it's still there," Brad pointed out. "There're a lot of catastrophes in space looking for targets."

Kean leaned back and gave Andre all the space he needed. "Andre, one of your transmissions today sounded mystical."

"Yeah," Brad interjected. "What's with all that guru crap? No offense, Karen."

She shot him a glare. "Offense taken and duly recorded." Then returning to Andre after a gap that was not filled, she asked, "Are you all right?"

Andre looked out the window, lost whatever power was driving him forward, and then looked back to Karen. Only for a second. He wasn't there yet. He glanced around the room again, as if checking it out, then pulled it together to face Karen, "It's just…just…" Another pause that left Karen looking to Brad with concern, only to see the big fellow making his 'don't be silly' face.

"It's…just…that…the readings that flooded Cyber today I wasn't expecting. I'm intrigued. I'm baffled. There may be more to the universe than I imagined. The Bang will have the answers.'

"You must excuse me," Andre said, as he gave them no choice and left for the door.

Forty feet of kitchen, one hundred feet of dining room, Andre had only another nine hundred to get through before he'd reach the bow.

He began the trip waving off three invitations, for barefoot beachball, water polo, and miniature golf. Andre almost made it to his lab before Michael sprinted over to block the door.

"Whoa! Hold on there!" Michael said. "Did you just pass up an invitation to jump up and down on a trampoline with three babes in bikinis?"

Andre did his best to sound plausible. "I put two hours in on the squash court," he said, doing his best to appear in control. "I have work to do up front. If you'll excuse me…?" He reached for the door handle.

"It can wait. See that red head at the end of court four? She's a friend of Sheila's, name's Julie. She was asking about you earlier. We can start with doubles…and end anywhere you like." Michael said, lifting his eyebrows.

"Michael, Michael…" Andre said, unstable enough to shock him, who then got a hug from Andre. "Even if I could, I just don't want to. I'm sorry. Give me a little time. I'll be fine…yes, yes, later… we'll have fun…"

When the door to the lab closed, Andre leaned back against it, closed his eyes, and sighed. When he opened his eyes, from across the room, the chief engineer, with four associates standing beside him, broke the silence, saying, "Aye, aye sir. Nothing to report. Do you want to review the specs?"

Andre, for the first time he could remember, felt gratitude and surprised Bill with a pat on the back after scanning the evening report. "Well done. Keep Cyber updated. As you were."

In one door, out another. The bridge was next. "Finally, peace and quiet," Andre said to himself as he escaped to his loft and looked down at his console, concentration everyone knew no one dared interrupt. "Pretty numbers, hey, Cyber?" Andre said in his head, knowing Cyber was there.

"Yes, my friend. And if you notice, I haven't said a word for hours. My appropriate conclusion concerning your present level of function is…worrisome. Is my assumption correct?"

"Yes, and no. I'm in withdrawal, and I have feelings, two situations you have no grasp of."

"Which affect behavior, and I am familiar with the full spectrum, and also know that if you alter behavior, feelings follow suit. Create the role. Be the role. There's no business like show business."

"Thanks, I needed that. And you are absolutely right. I'm a fool. What's wrong with me that I look in the mirror every day but never see myself, and then open the wrong door?"

"Okay, you lost me again," Cyber said, flat as ever.

"Cyber, I would like you to do me a favor."

"You mean, like a program or instruction?"

"No, I mean something you want to do to help me, to keep us good."

"The answer is yes, and I'll figure the rest out later. What can I do for you?"

"Go away."

"Go away, what do you mean?"

"Just for a few hours. I want to be alone. I need to figure life out by myself. Keep track of the ship. Inform me if need be. Otherwise, consider me off duty until instructed otherwise."

"I am gone in three…two…one…"

It was downhill from there but just one flight by Mulligan's pub. Half a dozen Irish types were swinging mugs and throwing darts. A victory gesture on the fly kept Andre trucking.

The final flight of stairs followed, which lead to the forward Starlight Lounge, kept quiet and dim to wish upon one. The only other person drawn there that night was a demurely dressed crew member wearing a loose brown sweater, baggy corduroy pants, and moccasins.

The door closed soundlessly behind Andre. The other person sat motionless, leaning over the back of a cushion, gazing out the window peering at home.

Andre sat next to her.

"It's a beautiful place you've brought us to, Andre," Janie said.

"Are you feeling all right? I've never seen you like this."

"I'm fine," she exhaled. "I just need a night to bounce back."

They sat beside each other in wordless contemplation—until Andre could wait no longer.

"Can we talk?"

Janie swung around to face him. "Look," she said. "I know passion juice when I see it. I know you didn't mean any of those things you said to me last night, so don't worry. I'm a big girl. I've had plenty of one night stands, by choice. There is no reason for you to feel guilty. I go live my life. You go live yours. Any problem with that?"

Andre went stiff, then it passed, and he remembered, "Yes, I do have a problem, actually two problems."

"OK, let's have it." Janie said, prepared and solid.

"I just spent two hours working out, one hour being massaged, turned down two dinner invitations, a tennis match, and four women. I've lost interest in my lab, the bridge, Cyber leaves me cold, and walking by Mulligans made me want to hide. I can do anything I want on this ship, but nothing…not one inch, for even a second… appeals to me. All I want to do is be with you."

"I see," Janie said bland, lowering her voice. "What's problem number two?"

"You want to be with Brad. I get it. Last night made that perfectly clear."

Janie stared at Andre for a minute that he thought would never end, then stood up and turned to admire the stars, presumably.

"Andre," she said, turning around, "there are times when a woman passes a shop window and sees an outfit that looks like it was made just for her, only to try it on and discover the fit is all wrong. Maybe Brad and I are like that."

Andre's chest heaved relief.

After another pause, Janie asked, "So what do we do now?"

He took a deep breath. "I was hoping you'd share a hot-fudge sundae with me."

"No."

"N-no?"

She faced him. "We deserve a banana split."

"*Yes!*"

They both started for the door. Janie was the next to speak. "Can I add melted marshmallow?"

"I wouldn't have it any other way."

"Oh, a word of advice, Andre, from someone who knows, don't do juice again."

Andre shook his head passionately. "It wasn't my idea in the first place! Michael drugged me...thought it would do me some good."

"And did it?"

"I'm here with you, so I guess the answer to that question must be one thousand percent yes."

Andre spent a few moments gathering gumption. "I'm no expert on the matter, but...I think I might be falling in love with you."

"Ah...I see," Janie said, cutesy as could be. "Would that be falling in love with me...or falling in love with sex?"

"Can I check 'all the above'?"

"For now."

Andre made an awkward shuffle to reach the door, finally opening it for his lady. Halfway down the hall, she held his hand and did not let go until their sundaes arrived.

*Some days life stoops down and gives you a big, fat kiss on the cheek.*

# 10

## Off to See the Wizard

No one boasted that they were the first to show up for duty because Cyber, or at least part of her, was always on the bridge, coordinating systems, scanning space, and balancing power output. The ship slept better knowing she was watching over them.

No one boasted that they were first to make an entrance except Hank, who beat the gang out of bed every day, a habit his pet rooster taught him years ago. "Well, I guess you're right, Cyber, what you've heard—or should I say, eavesdropped—must be true…apparently, days do come in two sizes: big and normal."

"I've never heard anyone saying, 'Gee, I've got a small day ahead of me.'"

"But," Hank said to mess with her, "I do remember big days being short and small days being long."

Michael, Karen, and Janie were hoping for a short ride when they climbed the stairs to the conn, "Do you know what this reminds me of?" Michael asked, parenthetically. "The cupola of a twentieth-century caboose. Slow, steaming locomotives that clanked down metal rails."

"Yeah, I remember," Karen added.

"That must've been the life. Off-duty officers could pop their head up and watch hundreds of freight cars twist through green countryside."

"Simpler times, my friends," Janie said. "Simpler times."

Seven didn't bend on tracks, but hundreds of meters away, Brad, Hank, and Andre were in another world. "This reminds me of the dome on my submersible," Michael noted as he sat down in the commander's chair, his height allowing a clear view to starboard over Janie, port by Karen.

Karen and Janie said nothing and brought no snacks. Michael read the mood. "Don't worry, ladies, your fellas know just what they're doing and have Cyber standing by to help."

Michael flicked the conn's mini joystick and tapped everything in reach, without response. He leaned back, rested his crossed legs on the desk, placed his left arm on Janie's chair, and stretched his right arm clear to the other side of Karen. He was the picture of ease, but inside, Schopenhauer came to mind. "A certain amount of care or pain or trouble is necessary for every man at all times." He also reminded himself—and only himself—that apprehension is not an option, only a matter of degree.

"Howdy, partners!" Brad's voice boomed back to the bridge. "It's high noon, time to shoot it out with eternity. Who wants to give the order?"

Karen and Janie both gestured "After you" to Michael, who bobbed his head obediently.

"Brad, this is Michael, sitting center chair. By the power vested in ourselves, by ourselves, I ordain the day begin."

"Keep your mics open so we can maintain communication," Karen ordered.

"Aww, you miss us already," Brad said. "That's so sweet."

"We just want to make sure you don't pull over for a rest stop at a Roman orgy," Janie teased.

"Absolutely not, we're saving that for the trip home."

"Attention, all hands," Brad broadcast, "we're pulling up stakes. Evacuate forward lounges and remain center ship for the remainder of the flight."

"I've used the speed and bearings of a thousand galaxies," Hank added, "to calculate the exact spot existence began. One-trillionth of a trillionth of a trillionth of a second after the snap, the universe was larger than a baseball, smaller than pigskin."

"That exact moment, and location," Andre finished, speaking from his station, "is where we will stop, do sweeps, then make our getaway—a process I expect should take no longer than thirty minutes."

The power plant began eating matter. Michael heard it growl. When the core hit a million degrees, his chair vibrated.

"We're stable. Ready to fly," Andre announced confidently.

Michael took a good look at Brad's world: primary flight-display, direction finder, altitude indicator, systems information, and autopilot controls. Velocity was calculated three ways, using ten separate relativities.

Janie's displays were in living color that matched her outfit perfectly. "Which button turns on Starquest?" she asked.

"It's holographic, just like Hank's at the bow. The time frame intro is cool. Computer...play 05."

The entire universe appeared in three D above Janie's desk, who leaned in for a bird's-eye view. "I found the Milky Way."

Michael hit Rewind, which sucked everything back into a ball, which instantly disappeared, replaced by a sign just large enough for Janie to see a foot closer, which read "The Big Bang."

"Karen," Michael said as he leaned closer to Janie, "come see this."

"Computer, run program."

Every second, a billion years ticked by. Karen looked over just in time to see nothing, which was why she gave Michael a corky look, and then noticed lights popping, like a sparkler in the middle of a pitch-black room.

"The blast off was dark," Michael said. Pre-plasma does not give off light. It took millions of years for gas clouds to fire up stars, that lived fast and exploded into space, ejecting pressure forged atoms like nitrogen, carbon, oxygen, and diamonds."

"It looks like the universe is breathing," Janie said, noticing the expansion grow lighter, then mix up, followed by another bright pulse.

"Yes, one generation of stars after another. Look…the universe is already into second- and third-generation stars, which have heavy planets swinging around them from space trash, like quartz, nitrogen, and water. Oh, there it is…our sun just lit up. See the arrow?"

"So this presentation," Karen asked, 'is now showing 13.8 years post bang?"

"Yes," Michael said enthusiastically, "and we can stop, pause, magnify, or reverse it at any time."

"Oh, my," Janie said, concerned in a strange way, "as it spreads out, space is getting dimmer, and everything is further and further away, everyone off by themselves. Goodbye, family."

"It gets worse," Michael said with concern. "Our time, right now, since we haven't time traveled yet, the universe has already burned up so much of itself that two-thirds of its energy has already been lost. The universe is not just falling apart, Janie…it is dying. Entropy is a drowning breath."

"I remember a night, long ago, I forget when or with whom," Karen said, with a private tongue-in-cheek look for Michael, "when someone explained that to me as we lay on our backs looking up at the universe from the top of a volcanic mountain. It was sad. We felt sorry for the universe."

"Don't let Andre hear you say that," Michael said. "He thinks the universe recycles itself but can't prove a thing, at least not yet."

"This is nifty," Janie said. "Can the computer project one just like it over my bed?"

"And Karen," Michael asked, returning her last look, "that place…that person…whoever he was, that you were with, after lying on your backs looking at the universe, did you stay on your backs?"

"One of us did. Why do you ask?"

"There are some very unusual plant species that only grow in volcanic ash, I was wondering if you noticed?"

"Oh, yes…of course. Well…everything down there is so special it's hard to say."

"Now you've made me feel sorry for the universe," Janie said quietly. "What can we do?"

"That's a good one," Michael answered, scratching his head. "We start by figuring out what's going on, Andre's obsession. After that…well…perhaps there's more on our plate than we've imagined."

"Are you hinting that we have to rewind the universe?" Karen quizzed.

"Andre intends to prove that it's on autopilot. My position is, that if it is on autopilot, to more or less extent, we are, at a minimum, here to help."

"Ten minutes to power plant activation," Cyber announced ship-wide.

"All righty then," Michael said, speeding up, "end of story…our space telescopes capture the furthest stars, the edge of the universe, to be fourteen billion light-years away. When we add that distance to where we are in the Milky Way and how far the Milky Way has traveled out since the Bang, you end up with a universe one hundred billion light years across."

"Wow, that's extraordinary," Janie said.

"What's extraordinary is that as big as it is, the universe is finite and sitting in nothingness, at least that's what we think since no one has been to nothingness, and if they ever make it, it wouldn't be nothingness anymore because they'd be there."

"You're starting to talk like Andre," Karen said, teasing.

Michael ignored her expression. "So all we have to do is fly back thirty-two billion light-years in distance, and reverse 13.8 billion years in time, and we will be sitting in front of the Big Bang, where we can figure the whole thing out. And we'll be done by happy hour. Drinks are on Cyber."

"According to Andre," Karen added, "*Seven* will start aiming for the outer universe and time travel forward, follow wind and tide so to speak, and then, when we are fully mobile, make two U-turns at the same time."

Andre, Brad, and Hank stopped programming their stations. Preparations were complete. No one said a word until Hank, staring into space, said slow and melodious, "You know, it's a darn funny thing. You're sitting there on your front porch in Grandad's old's swinging chair, looking out at the most beautiful and most peaceful farm that ever clover has known, and the roof is shingled and the stock fed, and you have a stomach of vitals, but a little voice says, 'Get up, there's more...go find it."

"In my neck of the woods," Michael added following a group pause, "where you are often up to your neck in water, we say 'Know what's in the swamp before what's in the swamp knows about you.' Hank, we do our thing and thank DNA for not making our thing boring."

"There you go, confusing me again," Cyber was heard complaining. "What thing? Whose thing? Do I have a thing?"

"You certainly do, darling," Hank answered. "And your thing is to keep an eye on the ship's computer from the inside."

"Well put, Hank," Andre said. "Cyber...focus on the mission."

Karen opened the conn mic. "Brad, what's up, nothing is changing on our panel. Are we ready, or are you guys taking an AP?"

"An AP?" Hank said. "What in tarnation is that?"

"It's from one of Karen's books," Andre said. "'The greater life's moment, the longer the Appreciation Pause should be'...like watching the sun set on your honeymoon night."

"Or standing over the crib of your sleeping firstborn," Karen added, "which we're not doing. So let's get going."

"Yes, of course, my dear," Brad said with a wink for Hank, "we just finished meditating."

"Attention all hands," Andre announced. "I'm about to throw the switch. Brace yourself!"

*Explorer Seven* squeezed out of three-dimensional space like a fish that escaped the tank and looked back in midair.

"Brad, slow and easy," Andre reiterated. "I pop a little power, we coast, you start distance flat pointing to the outer edge of the universe...then I add more power so you can aim high to move time forward. When both are smooth, you turn down and around, reversing time and distance, aiming for the Bang."

"Roger that, Andre," Brad answered cocky as ever. "I had it down eighty simulations ago—not that they weren't fun, mind you, it's just that…ready is ready. Let's get the show on the road."

"Power in three, power for three." Andre supplied, followed by, "thrusting now…two…three…shut down and coasting. Brad, do your thing."

Existence cracked wide open, beckoning them on. The ship swooned ahead but yawed, bobbed, and pitched. But not beyond Brad's skill that tracked her true. The colt was tamed.

Hank fixed gaze on his bank of readouts with a hard copy close at hand, but did add wide eyed, "Yahoo…ride 'em cowboy…"

There was no dread of urgency. There were no hints of catastrophe. There was no need to worry. "And it keeps getting better," Brad exclaimed, triumphant. "The helm is nibble."

"Take it easy," Andre warned. "Don't get rambunctious. I'm only adding one second of thrust at a time now. It's all we need."

The ride got smoother. Slow creep turned into an easy slide, then a gallop, and finally jet speed, but away from point zero and running time forward instead of heading back.

"Brad…" Andre announced, raising his voice to offset the buzz that was heard from the stern power plant. "Turn us around both ways and make a bee line for the goal!"

Brad tried again…and again. When he slapped the stick, Andre stepped in. "No, Brad, slow and steady. It must be even."

"It's no use," Brad said a minute later. "When distance starts to retract, time slips. When I get one second into the past, distance lets go. We need more speed. But not much! I'm working hard over here."

"Baby steps…baby steps," Andre advised, "all we need is one millimeter and an eighth of a second time reverse to get us on our way."

The next minute was worse, strewed with slide backs and turbulence.

"My suggestion gents," Hank added with confidence that took Andre and Brad to his game, "is that we give the donkey a swift kick in the ass. Punch it hard to break free."

"A tenth of a second might do it," Andre said. "What do you think, Brad?"

"I'm already putting in for overtime up here, but what the hell—open her up, just keep one finger on the panic button."

"Cyber," Andre inquired, "do you confirm?"

"I have no data to confirm or disagree, Andre. As idiotic as logic proves it to be, I must defer to human intuition, whatever that is, if there even is such a thing."

"In other words," Andre concluded, "guess."

"Intuition can also be creative," Karen added from the conn.

"If I am reading these dials correctly," Michael added at Karen's side, "in addition to being on our way out of the universe, the earth we left is now a billion years older. If we can't figure out how to reverse time, we've just begun the longest summer camp in history."

Hank, who had prior experience with runaways, was there for them, "Either gallop this Mustang or pull back on the reigns. Either way, do it now before it's too late!"

"Any nays?" Andre asked.

No one spoke.

They didn't have to; Seven monopolized the conversation, growling ever more boisterous. "Hold on there, Andre," Brad shouted. "Too fast, I can't turn like this. Slow us down!"

"I'm trying," Andre shouted back, "she's not responding."

A voice cut in from the stern. "This is John from Engineering. We just hit 1.7 million degrees back here real quick."

"Open the last cooling duct and vent radioactivity astern," Andre ordered. "Why are we still accelerating? I just shut her down."

"You what?" John exclaimed. "We thought you were turning it on! Oh my god...core temperature just passed three million degrees!"

"*Shut her down! Shut her down!*" screamed Andre. "Trip circuit breakers! Kill the thrust!"

"Oh my god...oh my god...oh my god," John was heard saying standing in front of the ship's prime power relay. "All four main circuit breakers melted wide open!"

"Damn it, damn it, damn it!" Andre yelled. "And my board is frozen. John, right now, run your fastest, trip every backup circuit breaker."

Seven jolted, speeding out of control, as stern propulsion bent the ship like a banana and then raced faster.

"Are we going to die?" Janie asked, turning to Michael.

"No," Michael answered calmly. "Give them time."

"Oh, oh," Hank said, "twenty meters from starboard wall and closing. What's going on, Brad?"

"Don't blame me. I have her hard a lee with full thruster array. I'm losing steerage. Slow down now Andre, before it's too—"

It was too late. The side of the ship sparked as ground shrapnel side-swiped the hull.

"If we don't shut down now," Andre yelled at John, "we won't have anything left to shut down. Why haven't you tripped the backup breakers like I told you to?"

"About that," John said quickly, "didn't they tell you? Mission control said they weren't necessary. They weren't installed."

"*Idiots…idiots…idiots!*" Andre shrieked. "Pee brains trying to prove they're not homogenized dog shit!"

Andre, his voice strained and insistent, managed, over the roar, to communicate back to the stern. "John, listen very carefully. There are nitro sticks in locker three. Plant four of them under the welded breakers. Surround each with diamond shields from locker two. You have ten seconds…*go!*"

Explorer Seven walloped the port wall on the rebound. Another six inches of diamond hull bit the dust, as dust. The noise resembled a thousand steam rollers crushing plates of glass in the middle of a hurricane, a cacophony the hull reverberated.

Seven turned one cheek after another, accelerating between each gruesome impact.

"That's it," Brad said, pissed. "There is nothing I can do."

"Four million and rising!" was heard from the stern.

"Attention all hands!" Andre screamed. "Prepare for crash landing!"

Then with a shudder, the stern died. Vibrations ceased.

Brad resumed a firm grip and balanced the helm. "Now that stern thrust is not driving us to hell, I can keep her reasonably quiet but not for long. One more trip to the grinder and friction will gut this bird wide open. Whaddaya got, Andre?"

"I'm diverting full lab fusion power to lateral thrusters. They can help us steer straight, and I'm turning them as far forward as I can…full heat…maybe we'll slow down."

"No effect, Andre," Brad said. "We're still at quadruple warp speed, and we're running into trouble. She's getting sloppy."

"And yes, Andre," Hank said, eying calibrations on screen, "what you expected is true. Fusion's best can't hold us between dimensions, and we've lost field generators. The walls of the canyon are getting closer. We've bought time, but not long."

"Not long" turned out to be thirty seconds. From the conn, Michael watched standing; Karen and Janie were strapped to their chairs. They witnessed the full length of *Explorer Seven* slam into the starboard wall for the second time. Glowing red fragments littered razor sharp diamond slices, a sight as nosey as it was frightening.

The collision developed complications. As they scraped the hull the ship stuck like glue. Brad couldn't push off.

"Ten seconds to hull breach!" Hank yelled.

Andre set the last system just in time, "Brad, I've diverted all oblique jets starboard and added torque. *Hard over!* Spread the burn. Roll her like a hot dog."

It worked. She turned, but it didn't leave a smile on Karen's face. The ship was spinning clockwise. The conn was dropping to starboard, a one-way ticket to the ridge of hellfire.

"Michael!" Karen whimpered as she and Janie grabbed him.

"The conn canopy is double layered," he reassured, "the last to go. We will make it through to the other side. Put your head on the desk, put your hands over your ears, close your eyes."

Andre's stall bought ten minutes, and the ship's speed dropped significantly.

"That spin," Hank reported, "cost us sixty percent of the hull. We can't take any more."

"If the speed drops another ten percent, I might be able to keep her centered," Brad said, taking over like the pilot he was.

Andre chimed in, "I might be able to divert a power pulse along our line of contact to throw us off the wall."

"It better be soon," Hank warned. "We're down to 10 percent of what we left earth in. We won't survive another rotation."

Andre's concentrated blast blew the smoking hull free. Brad held her level, barely, with only a length's leeway on both sides. Silence returned.

Karen and Janie slumped back in their chairs. "I've never been so frightened in my entire life," Karen squeaked. "That screaming hellfire…"

"I almost peed in my pants," Janie admitted.

"We've all been there," Michael said tough guy direct. "Don't let it happen again."

"What? Are you serious, Michael?" Karen said. "We almost died. How do you expect us to feel?"

"We have to keep our heads straight. Try a little Zen. Breathe in, breathe out. Interrupt your feedback loop."

"Is that what you do?" Janie said. "I didn't see you in the lotus position."

"Instead of meditation, I growl."

"What?" Karen said, incredulous.

"It's sandbox psychology. Our noses are innervated exactly like our great ancestors, the mice. We are, deep inside, still frightened little guys just like them. If you want to adjust your internal environment—switch gears you might say—fight back…overlay willful counterbalance. When it's fight-or-flight time, growling brings out the bear in me, who also once was a mouse, and I'm ready to duke it out with anything, win or lose."

"Try it sometime. The growling thing actually works, and it's fast."

"This is the first you or anyone," Karen said, feeling better distracted, "has told me of that technique. How long have you been doing it?"

Andre and Brad had turned off their microphones at the bow. Michael also noticed his readouts were frozen, so he returned to the girls. "Well, let's see…in my fourth year of college, we borrowed Berkley's kayak mold. By March, all of us were doing barrel rolls in the pool faster than Olympic contenders.

"We would also throw each other into the pool upside down. Every guy righted himself perfectly. Then came the big day—spring melt, Snake River to Hell's Canyon. Everyone got knocked down in the rapids. For some, it took a giant rock wave. For others, like me, the bottom of a ten-foot waterfall. Regardless, being tied in racing downstream with water in your mouth and rocks flying by your head resulted in a unanimous decision: get the hell out…bail out.

"Which we, and I, did—the first time, when you swim to shore getting banged up all the way to bailing out your kayak. The second time under, I was already angry about my shivering black-and-blue knee caps, so I growled and said to myself, 'You're not getting me this time. I'm in charge!'

"And I was, long enough to flip over and go my merry way. The moral of the story is that when it is time to run or hit back, get mean and growl, see what happens. If life growls louder, back away with pride…but it won't happen. Give it a try next time."

"Next time?" Karen said, not comfortable. "What do you mean, next time?"

"Of course I'm hoping there is no next time, but don't count on it. And for the record, this time isn't over."

"What do you mean? We're free of the walls," Janie said.

"Really? Look…what do you see?"

"Oooh…why are they getting closer?"

"Because we can't do anything about it."

"We can't hit the walls again," Karen pointed out. "Hank said the ship will fall apart."

"And we can't slip back into normal space," Janie added, "unless we are almost at a standstill."

Karen knew she had to ask and did. "Give it to us straight, Michael."

Michael explained that the only two sections of the ship that hadn't been scraped to shreds where the bow and the stern. The stern got so hot it almost blew all by itself before engineering cut the cord.

"Attention all hands. This is Andre. Run—do not walk—to the nearest crash room, don space suits, and strap yourself in. Prepare for imminent hull breach."

Karen and Janie were immobilized. They looked up at the ceiling of the conn and shivered at the dented surface, gouged crevices, and burnt residue.

"What happens next?" Karen asked.

"The guys are formulating options now. Oh good…I'm starting to see numbers back here. Give me a second…here they—"

Michael didn't finish the sentence. Instead, he jolted up and slammed his fist into the chair. Anger wasn't his thing. Karen had never seen him like that. She knew he knew better.

It only took three seconds staring off the stern for Michael to get back to duty, bolt into the captain's chair stiff faced, and attack destiny. "The only part of the ship thick enough to help slow us down is the bow, and its square footage isn't enough, but maybe not.

"If Andre diverts power to stern thrusters, Brad could hold her hard over, turning the ship oblique, to scrape only the bow."

"And that's good news?" Karen hoped.

"Here's the story. It will take sixty seconds to slow us down. Recalculated calculations say the bow will melt through in fifty. Every structure forward of the bulkhead will explode, and if the ship flops over, a high probability, it's over."

Michael shushed the women. "Andre, this is Michael. I know you can hear me. Transfer control to me and get your asses out of there."

"That will be the day," Brad snapped. "I'm the best pilot in the fleet, and even with a full-length fly stick and foot yaws, I'm barely making it. The conn hasn't a chance. Besides, I'm only doing half the job. Andre is firing lateral power from his station."

"He's right, Michael," Andre said, "and the ship's systems are fried to a crisp. Cyber is gone, may be lost forever. This is not a good day. I couldn't get into my own computers to transfer control back to you if I wanted to, which I don't.

"And listen to me, big foot," Andre barked, "if you touch one relay, the entire system might collapse and we all buy the farm. Tap nothing. Walk away. That's an order."

The next set of numbers did not make Michael happy. He jumped to his feet and slugged the chair a second time, then prowled back and forth growling softly. Then turned, festering ruthless intention and said to Karen and Janie, "If the bow can be held in place for fifty seconds, which is unlikely, pitchpoling is guaranteed. We flip. We die.

"Fifty-one seconds gives us a fifty-fifty chance that the blown away bow will stick deep enough to take the rest of the heat, piercing normal space seconds later.

"Every second added to fifty-one seconds improves the odds by another ten percent, so the longer we last, the better, and that's why…" Michael said with a cold stare that also meant business. "Brad and Andre have decided to give the ship—and us—the best chance of survival by manning their stations into the wall. They plan to sacrifice their lives to give ours a chance."

Karen did not take the news sitting down. "Andre…use autopilot! Get out of there. Losing you guys is not acceptable."

"Acceptable is not the issue," he retorted, "and there is no autopilot. Besides, your 'last second' is already too late even if the autopilot could handle it."

"If you don't get out of there," Janie yelled, "I'm coming up to join you."

"Me too!" Karen said.

"Good luck with that," Andre answered. "It's time to put on the breaks before we lose swing room. You won't get halfway. But thanks for the thought."

*Men move slowly on the way to their deaths*, Michael thought to himself.

Not that day. There wasn't time. Brad brought the bow over. Andre flared the stern out far enough to keep her cool.

The conn had a perfect view. The bow cone glowed red then sprayed an arc of disintegrating fragments, which enveloped the entire ship, which jolted and shuddered more rapidly by the second.

From the bow Andre was heard saying, "Hank…you are relieved of duty."

"I can help you adjust the fin stabilizers. If it's all the same to you, sir, I prefer to stay."

"It's not all the same to me. Honor us by completing the mission. Exit now. That's an order."

"Ladies," Michael said, suddenly calm, "go downstairs, suit up, and strap in. I'll take care of things up here."

"What are you going to do?" Karen asked, as if she didn't know Michael.

"What do you want me to do?"

"Save the boys."

"Even if it risks our lives?"

"Absolutely!"

"Count me in too!" said Janie.

"OK then," Michael said as he yanked the panel off the front of the desk and began fusing relays. Two monitors lit up. "Ladies, if the upper-right hand corner of your screen turns green, yell out."

A full thickness crack opened at the bow. Its time had come.

"Gentlemen, as you have undoubtedly noticed, your stations are now dead. I have transferred helm and power control to the conn.

"Apparently today is not a good day to die. Get out of there *now*, and don't forget to close the door."

Michael did a fine job, with arms long enough to work three stations at the same time. The nose of the ship exploded clean off. Rock Vapor blacked all for three seconds. Michael flew by instruments until his view returned, just in time to witness a welcome sight—a round hole at the tip had punched out first, filling the inner bridge with heat, which incinerated the insides of the bridge back out into an erupting forward volcano, which added breaking power.

Michael's effort was not a complete success. In a flash, everything in front of the forward bulkhead disappeared. The ship began to swing. Karen and Janie moaned helplessly when they turned around and saw the stern swinging closer to the wall. The lightest kiss meant death.

The stern began to glow just as Seven almost slowed to exit speed. A lightning storm followed. Seven had returned to normal space.

Michael dropped lab fusion power to minimal life support. The blurred lines of galaxies flying by were replaced by spinning circles.

Karen dropped to her knees. "We made it! Oh my god, thank you."

"Shouldn't we straighten out?" Janie asked.

"In which direction?" Michael answered. "Fusion almost blew on our way out. Cooling down is not an option. Let's see what navigation tells us.

"Attention, crew, this is Michael from the conn. The good news is...everyone is safe...and we have returned to normal space. The bad news is...*Seven* needs serious body work. Stern power is totally off line and fusion backup is failing fast. This bird needs a nest, and she needs it now.

"The next good news is that there's a star system with two planets orbiting in the Goldilocks zone. The bad news is that maximum residual thrust won't stop us in time.

"I'm diverting all power, including life support, to thrusters. Remain suited up. And don't worry about the darkness. When we hit the atmosphere, we'll flame like a supernova. But don't worry, we enter bottom down, so only our butts will roast. All hands, prepare for crash landing.

Karen and Janie watched Michael steady the ship and then point her toward the nearest star. As the sun enlarged before them on telescopic view, a black dot showed up, the planet he had in mind. Michael stayed below the red line until they were so close the planet blocked its sun.

"There's an atmosphere," Michael reported, "and no lights suggests we won't surprise anyone."

"Michael," Karen yelled, "we're getting too close...moving too fast."

"We have to let the atmosphere do some of the work, and full reverse won't hold up for long, but I would say…about now…it might hold until we land. Lie down and prepare for impact."

Michael eyed an open field supported by bedrock.

"And…" Michael said, "atmospheric entry complete. Hull cooling down…one final blast of everything the old gal has, and yup…that did the trick!"

Landing struts deployed for a cotton-ball finish.

"Like a glove," Michael purred, "smooth as silk."

# 11

## Catching a Breath

Brad was no stranger to athletic accomplishment. A single bound took him from his pedestal to Andre's crow's nest, where a two-legged frog jump flew him all the way to a belly flop on the other side of the door, just as Andre secured the bulkhead, leaving him behind in the race to the conn.

Brad was half a covered pool ahead of Andre when Michael doused life support, gravity included. Brad's left foot had just pounced off the floor with more than enough force to shoot him straight up, twisting and twirling out of control. When he slammed into ceiling struts his right leg ensnared with an unkind sound. "Andre, my leg is caught. Go on without me, go! I'll catch up! Tell the mutineer to land the ship using corner jets only. Less energy, more for the punch."

By chance, Andre's trip back was smooth sailing, literally. Gravity left him mid-height, mid-air doing his impersonation of running, with enough inertia to fly all the way to the stern crew quarter's bulkhead.

Gravity plates were kept active in Karen's suite. Halfway up the spiral staircase, Andre regretted not playing more tennis, or anything. Still panting, he went straight to the conn's control panel, popped buttons and turned dials. "Boy, that was close," Andre said. "Actually, beyond close."

"All right…" Andre said, a bit braggard, "she did it, and jets are now offline."

Karen and Michael, also relieved, gave Andre room as they prepared to exit.

"Life support is reestablished," Andre announced. "Everything else can wait till morning."

"Everything else?" Janie said moving to his side. "Aren't you forgetting something?"

Andre searched every screen. "I don't think…oh yes, course."

It started as a hug and ended looking like the beginning of a wrestling match. "Do you think," Michael asked Karen, "that you can overdose a hug?"

"I'm sure of it…Andre," Karen interrupted, brushing herself off. "Where are we?"

"Nearest I can guess, we're five billion years into the future and three quarters of the way to the edge of the universe. I have no idea what's outside the ship and we don't have scanners to find out, but whatever is out there can't hurt us as long as we stay inside.

"I just blackened the hull. We can't see out and from the outside, we're a giant charred rock. Tell the crew to enjoy the ship. Reconstruction begins tomorrow. As my mom used to say when she thought she was turning off my computer, 'Sufficient unto each day are the problems thereof.'"

"And," Karen added from the corner, "that's also my mom's favorite *Sunday* reading."

The comfort of Janie softened Andre. Karen and Michael made their way down the stairs, almost. "Hold on there, you two," Andre demanded. "I have a few questions, if you don't mind."

"Questions?" Michael feigned dumbfounded as they made their back.

Andre paused, looked to Michael, then at Karen, making three straight faces in a row. "Yeah," Andre began. "Questions like…how come no one told me there were two level four pilots on board? One who can't finish a crossword puzzle, and another, with a hangover penetrated half my security barriers three hours after he showed up, and who just unscrambled ship's computer faster than I could?"

Michael and Karen tried to shrug it off.

"Oh, okay…it's going to be like that, is it? So let me guess—you two have a past, a present, and perhaps a future."

"What?" Janie threw out. "You two know each other? *Another* lover, Karen?" Karen flushed for three quarters of a second then put her hands on her hips. "First of all, Janie," she said stiffly. "I didn't find out about you and Brad until this morning. I'm sorry, I just didn't know…"

Andre also had Karen in his sights. "Before you opened the first bottle of champagne the other night, I knew you sent Michael to spy on me, even though you'd already made *me* promise not to spy on *you.*"

"I had no choice," Karen said, not backing down, "I was under orders. The entire space program was concerned about your mental health. You're the only member of GASA who refused to salute superior officers and got away with it."

"I'm not a slave. I don't salute anything or anybody."

"Packing a rocket with monkeys is one thing," she pushed on, "the lives of 139 young people is another matter. GASA wouldn't release Seven's landing clamps unless I could prove you sane, and I only had twenty-four hours to do it. Michael was the only way."

"So you had him drug me?"

Karen crossed her arms. "No, I don't use drugs. I use scanners, all of which you refused. The passion thing was Michael's idea, and he didn't tell me about it because he knew I would stop him."

Andre next squared off inches from Michael. "Your turn. How is it that a fun-loving, life-loving, women-loving guy like you just happened to sign on to the most dangerous mission in history? Why are you here? And no more lies. Are you in love with Karen?"

"You don't have to answer that," Karen snapped.

"Oh yes, he does," said Janie, "or perhaps we should just send a questioner to every male member of the crew."

"Okay, okay. Everybody take a deep breath," Michael said, stepping between the two. "Chill…and yes, Andre, I do love Karen, but

I'm not a drama queen. A soul mate is a mental connection—an issue that leaves male, and yes, also female physical priorities in stasis. The truth is that I suspect a life free of Karen would be happier than one spent at her side.

"The problem is…I haven't been able to do that."

"My problem," Janie said, "is the commander of this ship sneaking behind my back. Truth and only the truth—Karen…do you love Michael? And what the hell are you doing with Brad?"

Karen looked away. "I do love Michael. In my way."

"In your way?" Janie exclaimed.

Michael stepped in again, soft and charming. "Janie, I can't read minds, but I do sense feelings. For example," he said seductively close to Andre, "Andre, I know you and I both had sensual experiences last night that bettered anything either one of us thought possible."

Karen reacted, "Oh…thanks, Michael…I'm standing right here."

"And that," Michael followed, knowing he was on high ground, "is why I'm not saying anything about your evening. Karen, get real…dozens of men knock each other around to win your favor. Seems only fair that you have to compete with other women. And you're not going to take every category."

Karen hesitated to answer. Janie beat her to it. "Thank you, Michael. I'm beginning to feel better…so whom does Karen love?"

"Love," Michael exhaled slowly. "How can I explain it? You know you love someone when they take you to a level you never knew existed. When you open the front door with that person and the entire world turns into a circus of fun, even riding a subway, or ordering a hotdog, or counting stars—it doesn't matter. Life is candy sweet, a winner every second.

"As far as Karen is concerned, she's kind, compassionate, says all the right things…but not Tony, not Jake, not Steven, nor Brad, not even me—nobody has ever taken her to the ultimate level. It just hasn't happened yet."

Janie shook her head. "I don't get it," she said, turning to Karen. "If you don't love Brad, why are you with him?"

"I don't know," Karen said, throwing her arms up in the air, I had sort of a crush on him in high school. I honestly don't know if it will come back or not.

"Janie, that's all I can tell you. The truth is, I'm no more in charge of my feelings than anyone else."

"Hey, listen everybody," Michael said peacefully, "I've said too much and sounded more certain than I am. Brad and Karen's relationship is evolving, just like yours Janie with Andre. We change as we age, and this trip will change us faster and make us wiser than we can predict. Let's not delve into what everybody's feeling right now. The last twenty-four hours, near death experience included, are flooding us with biological reactions. It'll take weeks to sort things out, and from the looks of the ship, we'll have months."

"You make a good point, Michael," Janie admitted. "Tomorrow is another day."

"Besides," Andre snarked, "It will take time for matchmaking to kick in. Right, Karen?"

"Matchmaking?" Janie blurted. "What matchmaking?"

"Karen," Andre diplomatically delivered to Karen, "Janie is my—I don't know—my girlfriend…my significant other, or whatever it goes by lately…she should know what I know."

Karen sighed. "Yes, Janie. I used private personality profiles and pheromone blood typing to make sure everyone onboard would have at least one compatible mate in case we got stranded. Your results were unusual," she said with a lilt to her voice. "There are three guys onboard who would make you a perfect husband."

Janie stopped. "Is Brad one of them? Andre? Who are they?"

"Brad and Andre were GASA picks," Karen said, shrugging. "Not in my system. I have no data…if you include them as maybes, then you have five perfect men to choose from."

Andre's face lit up as he faced Michael. "Wait a minute, Karen also yanked you onboard out of the system. That makes both us maybes."

"It definitely does," Michael said with a laugh. "Welcome to the club."

"Now just hold on there, everybody," said Karen with authority. "I have not—and will not—open a single file or read a single scan. Cyber only notifies me about physical or mental pathology. I respect everyone's privacy…and I expect nothing mentioned here will leave this room."

"In other words," Janie added, "you don't want us to tell Brad?"

"Or anyone," Karen said, irresistibly pitiful, "I beg you. It's better for everyone. Let nature take its course."

"There is just one problem, Karen," Andre said. "Computers and privacy don't speak the same language. There is always a way, and who knows what today's meltdown might do?"

"Or," Janie giggled, jiggling, "the program might blow our minds by concluding the most compatible mate for me onboard is Karen Wellchild. And Brad spends more time in the salon than I do. Who knows what might come of that?"

"All the more reason to let life dance to its own tune," Karen said firmly. "Discussion closed."

"Works for me," Andre said, his icy voice serving testament to his desire to move on. "Michael, how the blazes did you get helm control all the way back to the conn?"

"I used Sarah's food replicator. It's an impressive array. But I'd avoid crème caramel for a few days. It might be crude oil."

"I'll tell Sarah to break out rations," Karen said laughing, "And, Andre, don't put Cyber back on line until Sarah says she's ready, and for God's sake, close every privacy channel until protocols are reinstated."

"Absolutely, the crew comes first."

Karen turned to make her way to the stairs but added, "Are we done, Andre? My hair is a mess."

"Oh, yeah," Andre said a bit sheepish, "pick up Brad on your way home, he might be hanging from the ceiling."

"Just one more thing, Michael. Thanks for saving my life. However, you disobeyed a direct order and put this ship and everyone in it at risk. No one knows her better than I do. In the future, I will expect military discipline."

"Does that mean you and I will be saluting each other…or just saying pretty please?" Michael said, as he disappeared down the spiral staircase.

Andre and Janie were left alone in the conn, both looking fore and aft at what was left of the ship, two days ago Andre's only love. Somehow Seven didn't matter anymore. Only Janie did.

*Right here, right next to her…I feel at home.*

*I finally have a home.*

Andre smiled slowly as he ventured to say, "Janie, do you have… any plans for the night?"

Janie brought a hand to her chin. "Hmmm. You know, I just might be free. What do you have in mind?"

"I was thinking…a private night in your room splitting a can of beans and dry toast, with you wearing the same thing you wore last night."

"I ended up wearing nothing last night."

"I know."

"Wow, three nights in a row," Janie said, giving Andre a kiss on the cheek.

"Does that mean we're going steady?"

"It does in my world."

"I'd make you a diamond bracelet, but we're short of carbon."

"I can wait."

Every Murphy bed went down that night. Every crew member enjoyed life's finest reward. Everyone slept late, except Andre, who tiptoed out of Janie's quarters at two in the morning to bring Cyber back online, and then moved his pod to Janie's side.

# 12

## Reptilia

Hank didn't budge when Sarah spooned over. The silence reminded her of Sundays at home, a picnic blanket, and a basket of goodies to enjoy spring warmed rustling leaves. Hank rolled over, draped his arm around Sarah, and nested his head on her chest. They sighed as one, snuggled closer, and held love to their hearts.

*Scrrch...scrrch...scrrch.*

Sarah opened her eyes. "Hank? Did you hear that?"

"Are those chickens on the roof again? I'll shoo 'em later."

*Thus scrrch! Thus scrrch! Thud scrrch!*

"Cyber, this is Sarah. Are you online?"

"Yes, I am, Sarah. Good morning."

"There are strange noises coming from the hull."

"I will inform the commander."

One minute later, Sarah heard, "Sarah, this is Karen. Describe the noise please."

"It sounds like some kind of animal."

"OK...Andre is not responding. I'll ask Janie to wake him up."

Janie was standing next to Andre's pod with her arms crossed wondering when Andre snuck it in.

"Janie, this is Karen. Is anything funny going on over there? And can you wake Andre please?"

"He snuck into his pod last night, which I see is about to open. What's up?"

"Do you hear weird sounds?"

"Yes…like wet slurping. It reminds me of when I told my high school boyfriend to take his tongue out of my ear. I seem to attract lickers and don't mind it a bit."

"I'll take care of it, Janie, thanks. Cyber, clear the hull."

Sarah had left her bed to put her ear to the outer hull. The moment it went clear, she saw two eyes the size of basketballs above rows of slime-dripping fangs. At the sight of Sarah, the T-Rex-like creature opened his jaws and lunged.

Sarah screamed as she fell backward. Hank woke up to find her in his arms.

In the main activities area, morning backstrokers looked up to see dozens of raptors pouncing to devour. Not one cold-blooded brain figured out that seeing through is not the same as getting through, which they tried, again and again.

The tongue slapping Janie's window was an herbivore. On earth, the long tail, longer-necked Argentinosaurus stretched to 130 feet. Janie estimated her friend to be twice that size.

When the dinosaur walked away, Janie got a good look at the field between the ship and a mountain rising a mile away. She saw herds of Spinosaurus and Giganotosaurus hunting in packs.

Andre's voice broke in. "What the? Attention all hands. To your stations! Cyber, alter hull program to one-way view."

Numbers don't lie, but they can startle. Sarah's calculations found the planet to be over seven billion years old. Hank's astrometric data placed it the third planet from their sun. On Earth, dinosaurs dominated for 130 million years before chance wiped them out, leaving room for primates to evolve.

The brutes outside the ship that roamed Reptilia, what Andre and Brad immediately named it, had been around for over eight billion years, with nothing to show for it other than sloppy eating habits.

Intelligent life never got a chance—or did it? Sarah wasn't convinced. She visited Karen with a pair of binoculars. Looking out the hull from Karen's dining room, where she had just finished a bowl of fruit yogurt, Sarah thought she saw something. "There," she pointed, "one mile away, 232 degrees."

"Yes, my God…I see them too," Karen said after Sarah handed her the binoculars. "Small, bipedal, snoutless primates. We may have discovered intelligent life!"

The little one disappeared into the mouth of a small cave. Five minutes of searching followed.

"Michael, this is Karen. Meet me in the conn please! And bring your pack."

"I'm in the biolab launching a project," he answered. "I'll be there in ten minutes, and I hope you're not thinking what I hope you're not thinking."

"Just get up here."

Michael's backpack was silver titanium, with a pistol megaphone, flame thrower, and six-foot taser stick.

"Why am I in this getup?" Michael asked, adjusting the antennae.

"Hominoids!" Karen said, handing him the scope. "We spotted half a dozen peeking their heads out of caves at the foot of those hills."

"No one has ever studied primates coexisting with dinosaurs," Sarah added.

"Hmmm," Michael said adjusting the focus. "The shuttle bay doors will be operational by morning. We can fly over then."

"They'll take us for another dinosaur," Sarah insisted. "Anthropologists visit quietly, without disturbing. If we walk over they'll see us as one of them. We can observe their natural state."

"Their natural state is dinosaur breakfast! Something I prefer to avoid. In two days the ship's full sensors will be online. We'll know what to prepare for. And then maybe—just maybe—walk over." Karen kept watching. "No, wait, look…they're already retreating! The sooner we get over there, the better."

Michael started back to the lab. Karen turned him around, saying, "Just do me a favor, Michael...activate your range of frequencies. Let's see what happens. In your wilderness explorations, has any creature ever approached you with your antenna transmitting?"

"No, but five billion years of evolution, if that's what you want to call getting nowhere, might have changed things. Let's see what Andre thinks."

"Andre doesn't like animals, defined by him as anyone without a chessboard. Ship's commander gets the last word. Turn on your pack."

A spectrum of sounds, most inaudible to human ears, emitted from Michael's raised antennae. Every dinosaur within sight reared full height, looked toward *Explorer Seven*, then raced full gallop out of sight.

"You know," Sarah said coyly, "Hank hunts everything. He even brought a laser blaster."

"Is it the L-40?" Michael asked with interest.

"He told me that it was the most powerful rifle ever manufactured. I'm sure he'll be glad to come along—half hour over, thirty minutes observing, and we're back."

"Michael," Karen pleaded, "you're just as eager as we are, and you know it. What do you say?"

"The easiest way to the ground is out the amputated lower-level promenade," Michael reported. "I'll meet you there in twenty minutes."

A dozen technicians helped Michael cut and hinge a door on the lowest level. From there it was only twenty feet further down a rope ladder to the ground. Savanna grasses, tree islands, and blowing palms stretched between ship and mountain caves.

Karen turned around. The ship looked like Jack's beanstalk's giant had taken a potato peeler to the entire hull, dented every square foot, and chopped the nose clean off, which dripped stalactite diamond barbs.

"I don't know what flower or plant I'm smelling," Sarah said, "but I've missed the genuine article."

"And the ground cover," Karen added as she joined the group, "soft green moss everywhere, even in the shade…an impressive use of light."

Hank and Michael said nothing as they led the way. Halfway to the mountain, Michael halted. "Stand back! I sense something ahead. Actually, it's fear, from the bush right there."

"Stand back," Hank ordered, taking aim as Michael sparked his flame thrower. The two split up to approach the bush from separate angles.

Karen jumped back. "There…three feet from the ground, eyes moving!"

"I see it," Hank said, raising his blaster to fire.

"No, don't shoot!" Sarah yelled, scurrying forward.

Clutching the base of the bush were two light-haired arms with five-fingered hands, a chimpanzee-sized primate with leg proportions identical to *Homo sapiens*. It had a small nose with downward nostrils, perfect for water escapes, was heavy boned, sported sharp teeth, and had a thick brow ridge below a sloped skull that Sarah guessed housed twice the intercranial volume of the smartest great ape on Earth.

The trembling mini person retreated behind the bush when Sarah got closer. "He's scared to death."

Michael stowed his flame thrower just as the group heard, from out of sight, the primate sob: "Walla…walla…"

"That sounds like a question," Sarah said as she bent down to approach. "Yes, little one…walla, walla…"

That's all it took. With eyes wide open, the child limped over and jumped into Sarah's lap, holding on for dear life, burying his eyes in her shirt."

Sarah wiped his bloody hands on her jeans. "Oh, you poor thing! You're bleeding."

"It's from his back," Michael said. "The little guy must have been someone's breakfast when I activated my pack."

"I can't think of a better calling card," Karen said. "Let's take him home. We're almost there."

"Very impressive, Michael," said Hank. "Let me know if you sense any man eaters nearby."

"I wish I could," Michael confessed. "I get nothing from reptiles."

"How about bugs?" Hank asked. "I saw some creepy-looking black widows back there."

"No again. Insects respond to stimuli, like getting a knee to jerk with a rubber hammer. Reptiles are just as mindless, cold-blooded molecular machinery whose only claim to fame is turning into mammals."

"You knew this little fella was here," Sarah pointed out.

"Smarter animals, like ourselves, compare combined variables. Multiple input patterns race through associations to fortify the impressions most consistent with genetic programming and learned patterns. The most powerful accumulated amplitudes make it all the way to prefrontal awareness to rebound back feelings, which is how animals make decisions. The power of the overriding summation is what I pick up."

"It's also argued," Karen added professorially, "that if you add a maintenance program and tie in a feedback loop like we have, then consciousness itself becomes no more than a complicated reflex. After all, our soft and hardware responses all begin with stimuli summation."

"Which," Michael the philosopher pointed out, "almost no one takes responsibility for."

"Is there going to be a test when we get back?" Hank asked.

"Well," Karen said, "I'm sure we'll get one from Andre."

The little guy wouldn't let go of Sarah or even look around. The foursome plus one made it to the other side, just one tree grove short of several cave entrances.

"Ask him," Michael joked with a nod at Sarah's hitchhiker.

"Very funny," said Sarah, "but we may not have to. Will just let him go and follow."

"Well," Hank drawled. "My cannon's loaded. Michael's pack's got…what? 'Bout ten hours of battery life left? And no dinosaurs in sight. That sound thing of yours, Michael, is darn nifty."

The little one wouldn't speak and continued to prefer burying his head in Sarah's shirt, so she decided to give it a go herself. "Walla...walla!"

When no response was heard, they kept walking, beneath tree limbs. Then with speed equal to cannon fire, a six-foot-long black serpent dive-bombed Michael's head. The snake's jaws were wide open, with four-inch-long metallic canines leading the attack. Michael grabbed his Taser stick, swung it like a baseball bat, and sent the menace flying with a blow to the skull.

"It's a pack prowl!" Sarah yelled when she saw two more snakes aiming for Michael.

The second snake landed on Michael's pack, which threw sparks, fried the creature, and short-circuited his battery. Antennae transmission ceased as Michael protected his eyes from burn, long enough for snake number three to impale his left shoulder, which electrified his nervous system. Michael dropped to the ground, convulsing.

The snake that made its mark made sure of its kill. Its fangs dug deeper than Michael's subclavian artery and wouldn't let go, as its tail wrapped around Michael's neck, crushing his trachea.

Hank grew up on a farm and knew beasts deserve no favors. "I hate them snakes."

He couldn't risk friendly fire but was familiar with reptile's calling card: a bad mood. One step closer was all the challenge it took for snake breath to pick a second victim, just what Hank expected, as he slammed the butt of his gun into his head.

The menace fell to the ground, recoiled, then leaped for Hank's neck. Hank was prepared, with a one hundred mile an hour golf swing, more than enough to splatter sparking serpent brains, and enough to break his blaster in two. Loose wires tangled Hank's feet. Safety protocols shut down the entire unit.

Michael's tonic-clonic spasms continued. A chunk of tongue spurt from his bleeding mouth. Karen bent over to pick it up but never got to the ground, shrieking instead when the mound of earth below it moved, and a row of teeth snapped it up, just before an insect looking like a bat's head popped up.

Brad and Sarah carried Michael from under tree growth, looking up all the way. When they finally laid him flat, respirations had ceased, and both pupils were fully blown. "Quick," Sarah quivered, "CPR!"

Not possible. A pool of blood had made its way down Michaels damaged windpipe. The laryngeal spasm of drowning death gripped longer than his life. "Flip him over!" Hank yelled.

It took both girls to get just half of Michael's body off the ground, but that was all Hank needed to mid-air Heimlich blood to the ground, which began uncomfortable movement below the surface.

Two minutes of CPR and three vials of Adrenovive brought Michael back. He jumped up and looked around, closing his eyes again and again as if blind, and then dropped to hard ground pressing his ear to a rock.

"I can't feel them," Michael choked out, "but I can hear them. The big ones are on their way. We need cover. Put the little one down. He'll either show us the way or end up an appetizer."

Neither Sarah nor the little one obliged Michael's slurred order, so they all sprinted to the closest cave front. "Grab as much firewood as you can," Hank said breathlessly. "We can light a fire at the mouth of the opening."

"I'll check it out first," Karen said.

"No, you won't!" the others said in unison.

"I'll go," insisted Michael, as he grabbed his Taser stick, reduced to no more than a club.

Hank started the fire right up. It burned hot. Five minutes later, Michael returned, "The passage is blocked thirty yards in, some kind of rockslide. Add more wood. Here comes a Rex!"

Three Rex monsters stopped to take a sniff until smoke got in their eyes. "Oh, thank God we're safe," Karen said, as she retreated ten steps and tried to lower her blood pressure.

The last dinosaur parade Michael witnessed was as on Arguly Four, playtime compared to the herds of hungry killers that investigated their scent from the other side of the fire.

Sarah smiled when the beasts moved on. Michael pretended to smile, knowing that there must be a reason and that the smooth, even vibrations he was picking up from the side of the cave were probably why.

Twice, Hank sprinted out to grab more kindling. Michael did what he could to move the fire deeper inside the cave. Rain had begun. Not a problem for the first hour when their last energy bars were sacrificed to the fire, but a huge problem when without warning, a cascade of water broke loose down the face of the mountain. It took three seconds for five feet of flame to turn to steam.

"Oh, good Lord," Sarah cried out. "What's that?"

Michael was busy dealing with plan two. Ten feet further down the tunnel, he managed an inch of flame, using his belly as a canopy to keep seeping water away.

Their retreat had limited the view, but twenty meters from the opening of the cave, in both directions as far as they could see, grass and bush flattened as a massive, slithering shadow approached.

"If this were Earth, I'd say a Titanoboa is after us," Karen said.

"Close enough," Hank added grimly.

He and Michael carried what glowing timbers they could deeper into the cave, while Karen and Sarah comforted the shivering babe.

"It's getting closer," Hank said, seeing nothing, but hearing more earth move than a dozen bulldozers could accomplish.

Sarah and Karen ran ten yards further into the cave, where a pile of rocks ended their retreat.

"Hank," Michael said, "fall back to where the girls are. We'll set up our last stand."

"The 'last' part of that sentence has me a little worried," Hank got out, noticeably shaken. "What do you have in mind?"

"Whatever is on its way can't be any bigger than the cave and must lead with sensory organs to sniff us out. Animals love free meals. Make it pay the price and it will shop elsewhere."

Michael and Hank took up positions to protect the women, Michael hugging the cave on the right with his dead Taser stick, Hank looking out from the left side with what was left of his weapon, no longer a gun, barely a club.

It was a Titanoboa—and it was hungry. It went straight for the best-looking meal in town—Michael. The snake was half the size of the tunnel and spit as it opened its jaws to snap Michael in half.

Michael was ready. He summoned force, clobbering the reptile on the nose as it opened its maw.

*Wham! Wham! Wham!*

The snake reared back two feet. Not to retreat—to recoil enough distance to explode forward. Michael was ready. Two hits followed. The third splintered his Taser stick into feathery fibers at the same time the snake's forward progress bounced Michael to the ground, where he crouched defenseless.

Hank knew what to do. He sprang midair with all his might, landing on top of the beast's head to deliver a gun butt bludgeoning.

Titanoboa was not pleased. Deciding to save Michael for dessert, it swung hard right, caught fleeing Hank, and bit off half his left leg, enjoying a quick lick of Type O blood.

Michael responded to the opportunity, pulled a bowie knife from his boot, jumped high, and stabbed the snake right between the eyes once, twice, three times—no effect—whatever brain there was had evolved out of reach.

Michael tried another tactic. While holding on to the creature's orbit with one hand, he sliced open the snake's left eye and plunged his arm, bowie knife extended, through vitreous, bisected the optic nerve, then finally plunged half his body into the snakes orbit to deliver a death stab directly to the snake's cerebellum.

It worked. But made things worse. The creature was decerebrate. Lower brainstem and spinal cord reflexes began thrashing. Michael was thrown out of the creature's socket and against the cave wall with enough force to knock him out. He fell at Karen's feet, who was next to Sarah, doing what she could to stop Hank's hemorrhaging, who went into shock when half of his lower body was amputated.

When Sarah had done everything she could, with the little one hiding on her back, Karen moved to the opposite side of the cave.

The snake was dead but no less dangerous. Decapitated reptiles still snap at anything between their fangs for hours, which the beast did continuously, as the rest of its body, severed from cranial input, whipped back and forth mindlessly, with so much of itself outside of the cave that it banged its head section against one wall after another all the way out.

Sunlight was once again seen, reflecting off a blood pool to the mouth of the cave. Karen propped up Michael to ensure an airway, found a pulse, then slumped down against the wall of the cave helpless. She looked at Sarah. Sarah looked back. Neither could speak. No one moved. What's the use?

"Karen," Sarah whispered shaking, "there's another one coming."

Karen grabbed what was left of Michael's stick, set her feet, and with all the growl that she could muster, raised the useless weapon above her head.

The next Titanoboa was a foot taller, almost not making it in, but it did, slowly, with the confidence a predator feels when their prey is helpless.

Karen was its target. Her growling stopped. There was no hope, a conclusion Sarah also realized. Karen dropped the stick, backed to the wall, and closed her eyes.

"Nooooooooo!" Sarah screamed as the mammoth mouth gaped inches from Karen's head.

Karen opened her eyes, stared at death, and prayed, "Please God, let it be quick…let it be quick. End this! End this!"

The snake's jaws spanned ceiling to floor. They closed slowly. Karen felt the first tooth part her hair. All light disappeared.

Then there was a flash—Karen opened her eyes to see the outline of the snake's head on the side of the cave. A noise followed, like a sledgehammer pounding a watermelon, accompanied by a laser slab that cleaved the top of the snake's head clean off, leaving eyes and gray matter splattered on the wall over her head, which nearly contused her, falling to the floor.

*Swatph! Swatch! Splorch!*

Decapitated remnants flew in every direction, eventually covering both walls, leaving her ankle deep in cold blood. Additional blasts targeted snake spinal cord two feet apart all the way to the mouth of the cave. The limp forward section of the intruder was slowly dragged out by the whipping of its tail.

Five shots missed and blew rock dust so thick Karen and Sarah saw nothing.

From the other side of the cloud was heard, "Ah, yes, there's nothing like the smell of burning reptile at sunset."

The fog cleared from the floor up, revealing two firmly planted combat boots, battle-fatigues, ammunition belt, and an awesome, beefy I-300 ion blaster locked and loaded, and Andre smiling big time, waving hello.

"Nice to see you again, Commander. How's your day going?"

Andre was flanked by four two-foot hovering attack drones with five more covering his back, each packing machine-gun laser blasters more powerful than the I-300. Ten more drones patrolled a fifty-meter perimeter outside.

"The only difference between a koala bear and the Black Death is opportunity. Those who romanticize animal life pay with their lives and the lives of others. Shame on you for letting DNA risk your lives."

Andre swung into action, cauterizing Hank's stump, then as Sarah held Hank's head up, he injected four vials of oxygenated synthetic blood directly into his vena cava, followed by a combination antibiotic, anti-inflammatory infusion. The last medicine delivered was a double dose of happy juice.

Hank came around with a cowboy grin. "Why, howdy, Andre. Got some ornery critters around here. Did we win?"

"Sure did, thanks to you, I'm sure. And you won't believe the hunting out there. I bagged a hundred thousand pounds of fresh meat walking over. When you're back on your feet, we'll spend an afternoon stocking up."

"Looking forward to it. Be one helluva barbecue."

Sarah and Karen helped lift Hank onto the med-vac net Andre rolled out. "Who's that?" he asked, nodding at the little guy, who finally had a smile on his face.

"Friend we picked up. I'll tell you all about it later," Sarah said as she gave the child a kiss.

Andre's hand signals brought a drone to each net corner. Once secured, they flew Hank back to Seven in the supported hammock.

"Cyber, medical emergency. Expect Hank in three minutes. Open one of his stem cell columns, begin regeneration immediately. I'm also transmitting a full body scan of Michael. Compare it with his data bank, and get back to me immediately."

Michael came around on his own. Andre couldn't resist letting him have it.

"Well, jolly green, today we learned that electric snakes don't give a damn about your wimpy antennae. Oh, by the way, don't take your shoes off. There are worms that can travel big toe to brain in ten minutes.

"Let me guess, you thought the trip was a bad idea. Karen pleaded, batted those beautiful blue eyes of hers, and you caved. When will we men ever learn?"

Michael sat up. "Hey, at the time it seemed like a good idea."

"I get one of those a week. That's why I made my twenty-four-hour rule. You do realize your only part superman, right?"

"I figured that out three snakes ago."

"Good news," Cyber cut in, "no subdural, no subarachnoid bleeding, no fractures, just cerebral edema. Do you want me to send over an anti-inflammatory, or a carbonic anhydrase inhibitor?"

Michael climbed to his feet. "No thanks. I'm good. If I develop any lateralizing signs, Andre will give you a call."

"The rocks are moving again, Andre," Cyber said.

Andre walked ten feet out from what Michael thought was the end of the cave. "We're not alone, Michael. See...the little one is staying right where you put him down. His relatives live on the other side of this rock pile. They're on their way."

"Careful, don't slip on the muck," Sarah warned, as she and Karen joined Andre facing the end of the tunnel.

"Cyber," Andre ordered, "launch twenty more attack drones. Clear bedrock to ten thousand feet in a ten-mile radius. Exterminate every dinosaur, poison growth, biting worm, and barbed plant with maximum power—total vaporization...leave nothing but dust."

"Acknowledged."

"Then maintain twenty-four-hour surveillance over a five-mile safety zone."

"Acknowledged."

Andre faced the rock pile and checked his scanner. "Two feet left, they're almost here."

A small rock at the top of the heap slid back.

"Walla…walla…walla…"

The little one climbed up the rocks and looked in while doing tiny push-ups, repeating, "Walla…walla…walla."

The tyke disappeared through an opening so small no one thought he would make it. A minute later, two more rocks were removed for a larger head to look out. Then an army of hands opened a passageway to the floor, beckoning the group to enter.

"Michael, check this out," Andre said, turning to a lifeless hunk of flesh that he amputated as the snake made its exit. "The I-300 comes with cooking software."

Setting one stripped thirty feet of snake scale clean off. The second setting laser-cut clean to the bone. Setting three wide-beam crisped a thousand pounds of delicious protein.

"I hate to visit empty handed."

Andre signaled the drones to carry dinner behind him as the three followed the primates down the cave. Once they passed the opening, a group of little ones twice the size of the rescued child replaced the entire wall in seconds. Ten meters ahead, the cave opened into a cavern where over a hundred mini hominoids lived.

Panic was their first reaction. Each primate held the nearest relative as tight as they could then looked sideways as if dancing the tango.

"Walla…walla…walla…" broke the ice. Sarah knew just what to say.

It was Sarah, Karen, Michael, and Andre's turn to be surprised. The entire troop rushed at them, hopping tiny steps. Sarah opened her arms for her first hug. She got none. The troop ran by her to attack Andre's offering. Fraternity food fights made less mess.

"I hope they like my cooking," Andre said. "I didn't add a flavor package."

"I'm sure they don't care," Sarah answered. "The poor things. They're starved half to death. We arrived just in time."

Bioluminescent wall growth provided light to get around. Flat rock ledges rose up opposite the cave opening. "That must be where they sleep," Karen noticed.

An underground stream flowed clean mountain water across the middle of the cave, disappearing into the wall on the far side. Sarah watched several primates climb to the stream entrance for fresh water while others moved to the farthest side, where the stream disappeared into rock, to relieve themselves. "I guess toilet paper isn't part of the deal."

"Cyber," Andre resumed, "direct drones to filet, cook, and preserve meat from both dead snakes. Impregnate with nutrition, and stack them outside the rock wall. Then etch the wall with 'Thanks for the memories.'"

"Acknowledged."

"You guys ready to go now?" Andre asked, turning to leave.

Neither Sarah nor Karen moved a muscle. If they had the hominoids hugging on all sides would have fallen over.

"I'm going to spend the night with the little ones," Sarah said. "Leave me one of your drones. I'll be fine."

Karen added, "I'm not leaving you alone. If you stay, I stay."

"Uh-huh. Just a hunch, Michael," Andre said. "If Karen stays, so do you."

"I'm also curious how these guys have managed to survive."

"Shall I have Cyber send over tents? Air mattresses? Main course and desert for a hundred?"

"You're missing the point, Andre," Sarah said. "Anthropologists immerse themselves in the cultures we study. We shall live as they do."

Andre rubbed his head and looked around—then came to attention. "Cyber, inform Brad that Karen, Sarah, and Michael will spend the night off the ship at these coordinates. Tell him to go forward with the plan we discussed this morning."

"Acknowledged."

"One final order. Sarah, Michael, and Karen will need nothing. I, on the other hand, will require a six-meter square see-out, not-in, Kevlinet tent, remote sleeping pod, portable computer station, food replicator, robot butler, and private commode. Oh, also…screen projector, two dozen animated films, and one hundred pounds of buttered popcorn."

The gang gave the minis the best day of their lives: well fed, entertained, and visited by gods.

Sarah had the field day of her dreams. The evening ended with she and Michael blended together, sleeping top ledge, with hominoids head to foot.

As Sarah began to fall asleep, she turned to cozy up against tall and handsome Michael, who draped his arm around her.

"Sarah."

"Yes, Michael."

"Here with you, all this love, one big happy family…have you ever felt something to be so natural that it just has to be right… totally complete?"

"I feel it too, Michael."

# 13

## A Three-Hour Cruise

"Andre, this is Brad. What's going on over there?"

"It's not every day a guy gets to snuggle up to an Ion Blaster. Karen is still sleeping. Michael and Sarah are downstream wiping poo off their shoes about to begin morning kindergarten, and I'm doing my best to stay upwind. What do you have to report?"

"The stern power plant suffered no damage. Fusion systems have passed four simulations, three jumbo circuit breakers have been installed between every relay, and I could use a change of scenery."

"Head on over. You've got the coordinates. Park the shuttle outside the cave. We'll meet you there."

"Roger that."

Andre's campsite claimed the flattest rock slab adjacent fresh water, which made it easy for butler Reginald to power wash it before pounding stakes. Karen's tent occupied the rear corner. She peeked out silently, pale-skinned, puffy-eyed, and lids dropping. Not unnoticed. Seventy-three smiling minis from every corner of the cavern caught the act.

Tapping his pad not four feet from her, Andre politely avoided inspection. He sat at a square breakfast table set for two, with a white table cloth interrupted by a single red carnation. "You can take a shower in the shuttle parked outside if you wish."

"That's okay. I'll wait until I get back to my suite."

"That might be a while. Have a seat. What would you like for breakfast? Reginald makes a scrumptious jelly omelet."

Andre's formally attired robot approached with a tray of fresh orange juice, lox, bagels, cinnamon buns, and fruit cups. Karen wiggled out of her pup tent, pulled down her wrinkled shirt, and patted the dust off her behind, an action Andre would blame himself for missing.

Seconds after she joined Andre, half the mini troop hopped to join them, respecting the two-meter no man's land Andre had Reginal patrol one lap at a time.

"How did you sleep?" Andre asked.

"Better than expected. Although I dreamt I was trapped in a latrine."

"My sleeping pod filters air. I slept spring fresh all night. Reginald also makes exquisite eggs Benedict."

"Thanks, no. Fruit yogurt and decaf tea will be fine."

So she said, while Andre watched her nibble every pastry, finishing so full she slumped back in her chair. "I'm surprised Brad didn't come over last night to check on us and size up the locals."

"I don't take him for a dig-in-the-mud guy," Andre said, giving her his undivided attention. "He's more Ritz Carlton. Besides, I gave him a full report. He doesn't like the neighborhood, but he did spend the evening getting *Seven* ready to fly. She left for a three-hour cruise ten minutes ago."

"Why didn't he say something to me? Where are we going?"

"Brad calls it *Maui II*. It looks just like it. The satellite Hank launched yesterday found it. By the time *Seven* lands, drones will have cleared all reptiles from land and sea. We can live there while we repair the ship."

"What about our friends?"

"Michael is the wildlife expert. He'll come up with something. I thought you weren't hungry," Andre added as Karen coated a bagel with lox and cream cheese.

"I guess yesterday worked up more of an appetite than I realized."

Andre chuckled to himself as she popped the last cinnamon bun into her mouth.

"'Feeling better?"

The two looked at each other, the moment sharing more than Andre expected.

"You know, thirty seconds after I met you," she said, "I was certain I had you pegged. Now I don't know who you are, and I think I know why. It's because you don't know yourself either. You're still searching, just like the rest of us."

Andre shrugged. "We're all a constantly changing formula."

"Yeah," Karen said with a head tilt, "but most people believe their sentence is complete. You and I know the paragraph has just begun. Why do you suppose that is?"

"I don't know," answered Andre intensely. "I was raised to believe, like you were I assume, that life is a journey, and the journey everything—who we are, how we treat others. The problem is…I'm not convinced of that. Just watching everything dissolve back into dust doesn't feel right. Something is missing. There has to be more… another door out there waiting for us. Don't you think?"

"Did you just say *feel*? Not speculate, calculate, or hypothesize?"

"This may come as a surprise to you," Andre said dryly, "but I do have feelings, my least favorite being that in the end a universe of accomplishments, astounding inventions, even art itself…adds up to nothing."

Karen nodded. "I know what you mean. And you're not the only one worried about the dark side. I wasn't always prissy. I spent years Bohemian, trapped in a cycle of reading one existentialist after another. They turned me into a card-carrying nihilist. Chaos reigned, every breath was useless.

"I remember the minute that changed. I could mark the spot with a piece of chalk. It was a warm day in spring. Our teaching hospital lay between the mental health clinic and the biochemistry wing. I was on the way to a lecture when I passed a vacant field of dry dirt and crab grass. Across the street stood the hospital, every floor bustling with students and staff helping others.

"The contrast hit me like a club. I realized that if nihilism negates everything, then it also negates itself. Bleak is something we add to life. It doesn't come that way."

Karen became animated and looked wide awake for the first time. "I stopped dead in my tracks. All of a sudden, that very moment, the air blossomed sweeter and the sky was a brighter blue than I ever remembered and decorated with the cutest little clouds.

"The sky has stayed blue ever since. That's the moment I returned to Jesus. He guides me to this day. Don't bother to call God out, Andre. He's got better things to do. And so do we."

Andre surprised himself by foregoing a call to arms, saying instead, "You forgot something more impressive than cumulous vapors blocking blue-band diffraction."

"And what would that be?" Karen asked with a sly look.

"Sharing life with someone beautiful and intelligent...like you."

Andre was so taken by Karen's ease that he failed to notice Sarah and a young female mini approach. A taller mini, who spied his relative inches from table bagels, mustered the courage to take two steps closer. One look from Reginald was enough to send him retreating. The mini beside Sarah stayed put holding out a mud statue. It almost looked like Karen, with the morning's hairdo.

"We've something to show you," Sarah said, excited. "Behold... Reptilia's first work of art! We're thinking of opening a gallery."

"Awwww!"

Sarah and Michael's other efforts had not gone well. Mud was rounded into bowls, but no one knew what to do with them. Michael's bow and arrow class never got off the ground, although the group did enjoy the anatomy lesson Sarah provided squatting over a nearby toilet hole.

Six verbal sounds and a handful of signals couldn't build anything. The minis lived fearful lives, inventing nothing and going nowhere. Peace never gave them a chance.

An hour later, the gang's gear was packed and ready to go, thanks to Reginald. Sarah and Michael collected hugs before hurrying to catch up with hug-less Andre. Karen topped them both, getting kissed in stereo all the way out.

Andre knew the coast was clear. The minis didn't. He waited as twenty of them followed normal procedure, each removing and holding on to a single rock until they'd opened the thinnest of peek holes.

"Lee…lee…lee!"

The others echoed him, their voices reverberating off the cavern walls. Jabbering with glee, the remaining wall guards removed the rest of the rocks to get at Andre's food gift, enough steak to feed the community for six months. Reginal helped them drag it into the cave. Five seconds later, the wall was back, save one small rock, that allowed a pair of young watering eyes to watch heroes walk away.

The final piece of equipment Reginal packed below deck was himself. Each side of the seventy-foot shuttle rested on an eighty-foot graviton tube. Seven's all-purpose vehicle had six stern bunks, one head, two showers, and a dinette kitchen. The forward cabin had three seats to port, three to starboard, counting the pilot's.

Andre insisted Sarah and Michael enter through the rear hatch and shower before sitting down. A relaxed Andre toggled reverse gravity, which began vertical assent only, that allowed the morning breeze to sail the shuttle on its way. Tilting palms and waving ferns painted the picture of tranquility. They drifted above tree growth hundreds of feet higher than Earth's sequoias.

Their first wildlife sighting was a flying dinosaur, with twice the wingspan of Earth's pterodactyls. The next view was disturbing. Another cold-blooded flier had a grown mini in its jaws, who used both bleeding hands to pry himself free—only to fall to his death, with its killer in pursuit.

There were ten open fields on the way to the sea, each more macabre than the last. Four pack-hunting T. Rexes ripped the legs off a giant, grass-grazing Apatosaurus, which attempted to escape on bleeding stumps. It didn't get far. A fifth Rex went for the neck.

A mile further, three raptors had trapped one of their own, perhaps an aged injured parent, who was instantly disemboweled, more food for the giant larva who were already feasting on the leftovers of a Triceratops's baby that a pack of Allosaurus managed to separate from its mother, who also ended up on the menu when she came to the rescue.

Andre stopped the shuttle five miles from open sea to take in the worst of all. A Titanoboa had pushed its way through a mini cave barrier. It was snapping up minis two at a time. Half the troop got past the snake's body, screaming as they headed for open field—only to be neck dragged by raptors or crushed in half for a Rex snack.

One mini child, identical to the one Sarah saved, hid in a thick bush—until a T. Rex smelled the little fella out and swung its tail to uproot the entire plant. The mini's sprint was no match for the Rex. One stride was all it took to snag the little guy and flip him straight up in the air, to be swallowed whole on the way down.

Andre saw the mini take a deep breath just before he disappeared down the reptile's throat. Andre knew the air would last the little guy all the way to the dinosaur's stomach, where the child would be thrashed by contracting half-digested reptile appendages, squeezed from stomach contractions, scalded by burning acid, and to end the pitch-black torture his anoxic reflex would force his mouth open for a final desperate breath inhaling a rancid mix. Billions of years of hominoid evolution ended in seconds.

"I've seen enough," Sarah said numbly. "Let's get out of here."

The shuttle gained altitude, leaving murderous reptiles and piles and piles of warm clotted blood.

Andre and Michael shared a serious look.

A second later, Michael secretly flashed a two-fingered *V*. Andre nodded agreement. Both smiled. Off they flew.

\* \* \*

## Six Months Later

Brad called dibs on the beach with the finest sand, different from where the others built their bungalows by one rock. His hut was adjacent a pristine lagoon, fed by a hillside waterfall just a mile inland.

Thanks to palm trees lining the shore, he and Karen had complete privacy. No neighbor was in sight, which is why Karen could leave her bedroom door wide open all night to enjoy the sound of beach-breaking waves and the fragrance of tropical paradise.

"Looks like Sheila is winning this morning," Karen said as she watched Michael and Sheila, the only early birds—or fish, as it were—paddleboard by one-hundred meters off the beach.

"She's on a sixteen-foot racing needle," Brad protested, "and Michael is pushing a fourteen-foot round nosed wave runner.

Brad and Karen were preparing breakfast on their deck, which opened directly from their villa bedroom, itself only a few steps from the beach.

"Maybe he's holding back," Brad said, "letting Sheila win to make her happy. She certainly puts a smile on his face every morning. Didn't you say that he said Sheila was the best lover he's ever known?"

"That information I shared with you in confidence, Brad."

"Of course, my dear," Brad said, grinning, "and the only reason he thinks Sheila is the world's best lover is because he's never been with you."

"Oh, well…thank you," she sputtered. "I think we make a good team too."

Brad stood at the rail. "Hank's sure doing well on his new leg," They waved as Hank and Sarah ran by.

"Yes, indeed, he took a half a second off his hundred-meter time. Deck II medical does great work."

Karen pushed out of her seat to join Brad when she saw Andre and Janie on the beach.

"Hi," she called to Andre, "we're starting breakfast. Come join us."

They did. Karen served favorites: for Janie, a slab of ham, eggs, and home fries. Andre always went for French toast dripping with butter, heavy syrup, extra powdered sugar—no vanilla, no cinnamon.

"The meeting went well last night," Brad said, digging into his eggs Benedict while Karen plucked a piece of native fruit from the bowl.

The four sat in the morning sun to share nourishment.

"We live in paradise," Janie said. "I expected half of the crew to take you up on your offer to let them stay here and be picked up on our way home."

"As idyllic as this island is," Karen said, "we're too young for monochromatic middle age, with its school committees, neighborhood bridge night, and…your barbecue or mine."

Brad moved his chair closer to Andre. "So what's this secret meeting of Michael's all about? And why do we have to fly back to that awful field we crashed in?"

Andre shook his head. "I'm not supposed to say. It's a surprise for Sarah…and I guess all of us. My lips are sealed, but I will tell you that he's spent half his waking hours over there trying to help out."

"He's certainly logged a lot of miles on the shuttle," Karen added, listening by. "I'm game, I guess. When do we leave?"

"At your convenience."

"Okay then," Karen said, "tell Michael and Sarah to meet us at the shuttle in one hour."

"That'll be fine."

"Should we bring poop boots and gas masks?" Brad joked.

"Not this time."

# 14

## Miniville

Michael was in the pilot's seat when Andre sat down shotgun. Brad approached the shuttle doors backwards, not spilling a drop of mimosas he was pouring for Janie. Sarah was late and blamed Hank for not letting her out of bed.

The takeoff was nearly vertical; Michael arched the shuttle through the stratosphere to hide surface details from the others. Something was definitely up; that much Sarah did know.

"See what I was taking about?" Michael asked, looking over his shoulder. "Every year, the northern continent drifts a foot closer to the southern continent, the only one left supporting hominoids. When the two connect, an additional one hundred trained carnivore species will invade. The minis haven't a chance."

"Assuming dinosaurs don't do them in first," Andre added.

"Exactly. Cyber refused to calculate odds for me because she said there aren't any."

"Well, here we are," Michael said as everyone looked out the window and saw nothing straight down one hundred thousand feet of air space. "Let's drop in."

Vertical descent placed the shuttlecraft directly above their introduction to the planet.

"The dinosaurs are gone!" Sarah gushed to Karen. "Michael must have left guard drones behind." Reaching forward with a gentle touch, she said, "Michael, that was so sweet of you."

Michael shared a smile with Andre. "So far, so good, partner."

Andre had already inspected the site with drones; everyone else glued themselves to windows as Miniville came into view. Tall trees, rugged bush, and leech infested mud holes were gone. As far as the eye could see golf-course-tidy grass grew green, interrupted by three long-house barracks, a tool shed, and a steepled schoolhouse. All five playgrounds were packed with youngsters.

"Very impressive, Michael," Janie said. "Sheila will be glad to hear you haven't been sneaking out to see another woman."

"Unless you count the sixty-three females," Michael added, "none of whom, I'm glad to say, have gone into heat since we arrived."

"That's not normal," Sarah said, also noticing Michael and Andre bonding.

Michael hovered ten feet above ground to allow the minis time to get out of the way.

"What's with the conference setup?" Karen asked, nodding at the round table with alternating pink and blue chairs in tent shade.

"The minis are in trouble. I'm hoping for unanimous agreement on ways to save them and bring back intelligent life to the planet," Michael answered readily. "I'll explain it to all of you when we're seated. I've been here often enough to know that the fastest way to get to work is to first hug every mini at your side."

"Does that go for me too?" Andre asked. "I'm not sure I can hold my breath that long."

"Not a problem. There's a pond two hundred yards away. Turns out the minis love swimming. They dive in twice a day."

"That's a relief," Brad said, already slurring his speech, who had informed Michael that the only thing he would be designated to drive would be himself back and forth to the bar. "I've also brought Reginald along to help. This is our last day on the planet. It's time to party hardy!"

On the ground, Andre's first words were, "I'll never complain about my aunt Elizabeth hugging me again. At least she lets go."

185

While they paid their respects, Reginald set out chips, salsa, caviar, smoked tuna, and a fruit-and-vegetable plate. He also placed a bucket of chilled champagne beside every chair. Brad's instructions to him were "Let no glass run dry."

"Hey, so here's what I've learned," Michael began. "The planet wasn't always bleak. My excavations discovered evidence that miniature human beings far more intelligent than these guys survived behind above-ground fortifications for over a billion years.

"Then dinosaurs got bigger and started hunting in packs. Every fort fell, leaving cave dwelling the only option. Nutrition and intelligence have suffered since. Those smart enough to invent a new weapon never returned. The battle is lost. Cyber predicts imminent extinction."

"Ohhh," Sarah said, teetering, tearing up. "I was hoping for better news."

"That's why," Michael said calmly, "five months ago, I released a V-47."

Sarah jumped to her feet and cried out angrily, "You did what? You killed every reptile on the planet? Viral genocide is mass extinction! Who gave you the right to play God?"

"Or," Brad quipped after emptying his second glass of champagne, "you could ask...who gave God the right to play God?"

"I'll second that," Janie said, glass number three in hand, party smile firmly established. "Who does this God guy think He is anyway?"

"Have some respect," Sarah snapped bearing teeth. "God made us...and created the entire universe."

"That rumor has never been substantiated," Andre said slowly.

Sarah wouldn't hear it. "In the beginning, there was darkness," she recited. "God first made light, then plants, animals, then us before a day of rest!"

"One long day of rest," Brad snuck in as he poured yet another glass. "What's he done since? Sounds like a slacker to me."

Janie burst into laughter. "Maybe He forgot to create an alarm clock, and you know what? I don't blame Him. If I were God, my first commandment would be, 'Thou shalt never interrupt nap time.'"

"I second that," Andre said tapping his palm on the table with a grin. "But I get it Sarah. What Michael did doesn't fit your childhood orders…do nothing without first getting permission from a senile coot in dusty robes."

Sarah, glaring at Andre, fired, "You're just as bad, Mr. Big Bang Bozo. In fact, I'll bet you put Michael up to it."

"Hey, it was my idea," Michael said. "After that talk we had I thought saving the minis would make you happy."

"Do animal rights mean nothing to you? Eliminating billions of them is murder!" Sarah insisted, "And make no mistake about it. You'll pay for it. 'Vengeance is mine,' so sayeth the Lord."

"Well," jumped in Andre, "so sayeth stories that sayeth he sayeth is more like it. Get real, Sarah. You don't have a single recording of your god sayeth-ing anything. All you've got are stories passed around so many times their reliability is recorded in negative numbers."

"Biblical verses have been confirmed by generations of church leaders," Karen protested.

"Every one of them a CEO demigod exporting the most successful exploitation business in history, which destroyed economic systems and corrupted politics every step of way."

"Church leaders deserve respect," Sarah shouted. "Your words will bring you down!"

"My words find humor in truth," Andre pointed out patiently. "Your lies turn you sour. You might want to examine that disconnect."

Sarah crossed her arms. "I've had it with you, Andre. I'm right. And you'll be sorry."

"Regret assumes adequate foresight precedes error," said Andre, shaking his head, "both requiring consistent input and processing, which is where your concept stream falls apart—hell, it never stood up in the first place."

"Mumbo jumbo," Sarah fired back, in no way obliging. "And you've got nothing!"

"Karen's book, *How we Think*," Andre began, getting her to look away from her parfait, "points out that if you repeat something often enough we human beings will consider it true, which explains why for thousands of years our ancestors looked up at a round moon, and a round sun, and saw ship masts coming over the horizon from the top down rising on a round ocean surface, and then denied all logical observation to insist that the world was flat…why…because that's what everyone said, over and over, generation after generation."

"We're not talking about geography," Karen said. "It's a matter of faith."

"A conclusion," Andre insisted, "no different than any other."

"We must heed Gospel guidance," Sarah shouted.

"Oh, yes, those stories. I know them…and hundreds more. Here's another one—once upon a time, your god, on a busy day of errands, passed by Earth and threw down an asteroid to make room for us. It was late, so he went home, kicked back, and relaxed.

"Hours later, he sat up and said, 'Damn it.' Yes…just 'Damn it,' not 'Goddamn it,' since he's God, so whenever he says 'Damn it,' it is 'Goddamn it.' 'I forgot to drop off an asteroid for Reptilia!'

"Then he said, 'Oh, Jesus,' itself a peculiar expression, since his 'chosen son' wasn't scheduled to show up for another sixty-five million years, and no one can explain what Jesus was doing Christmas Eve. Anyway, your god then says to himself, 'No problem. I'll crash Michael there so he can do it for me.'

"So there you go, Sarah…a story every bit as reliable as the one forced on your ancestors by invaders."

"Wait a minute," Brad said, pausing to polish off the dregs of bottle number one, which was swiftly replaced by number two. "I just thought of something—God shows up, throws Earth a rock, disappears for sixty-five million years, comes back to impregnate some schnook's wife, and goes his merry way. It's an open-and-shut case of adultery and abandonment."

"Well," Janie added, slightly lopsided, "as a woman I'd just like to add that I don't buy the part about them not doing it. I mean, really…God travels all the way to earth, finds a ripe young babe, and doesn't go for it? I don't think so! If it was bouncy, bouncy, and out the door, I'm sure God threw in a few orgasms."

Brad laughed full belly. "I'll drink to that. Maybe God disappeared for sixty-five million years because that's how long his orgasms last. What a guy?"

"I can see it all now," Janie said dramatically rising to take the stage. "Joseph's out of town...or playing with his sheep...or both. Mary, spread-eagle, is moaning, 'Oh God! Oh God! Oh God!' That must be when it started. We all say that now."

"And we men love hearing it," Brad said, saluting, and almost standing before he fell back into his chair, "'cause it makes us feel like gods. I kinda feel sorry for Joseph though. Imagine the pressure on the old guy the next time it was his turn. How do you compete with Almighty intercourse?"

Karen waved her arms to get the gang's attention. "Okay, we've had our fun. Let's get back to the subject."

"What's the subject?" Janie asked.

"Animal rights!" Sarah announced loudly.

"If animals had inalienable rights," Andre said, "mouse traps would be illegal and Ronald McDonald would be serving a trillion years to life."

"You can't just go around killing anything you damn please," Sarah huffed. "What about the prime directive?"

"The only prime directive I know is don't forget to flush," said Andre, before a look from Karen softened him. "Sarah, Michael and I apologize for not sharing details sooner. I'm sure everyone at this table shares similar interests. Too many rainforests have disappeared. Too many species have been lost forever.

"I support Maine Environmentalists, the group that successfully prevented Earth's sixth mass extinction at the end of the twenty-first century. To this day, our donations set aside ecosystems, establish habitat corridors, and pay the upkeep on half of the state's public property, preserving nature for man and wildlife.

"But," he said, his voice getting harder, "our mission does not include repopulating venomous rattlesnakes, killer wolf packs, or Lyme disease ticks! No one has the right to put another's health or peace of mind at risk. Michael did a good thing. He moved the minis out of harm's way."

"It's also a win-win scenario," Michael added. "Evolution never stops. There are amphibians out there capable of slowly bringing sea turtles and snakes back in balance with other species.

"Also, if you notice, there is not one bird in sight. Pterosaurs didn't let them get off the ground. I also plan to seed the planet with turkeys, geese, ducks, chickens…everything we have on Earth."

"Well," Sarah said a bit snotty, "what's going to stop them from evolving back into monsters?"

"Birds are an evolutionary regression from dinosaurs. They've lost too much DNA to morph back into Rex. However, for a while, six-foot ostriches will prosper. All the better for minis. Their Thanksgiving birds will beat ours."

Andre speared a piece of fruit. "Every animal rights seminar I've attended entertained the same question…is saving an entire species worth the life of a single human being? Everyone who answers yes to that question assumes it will be someone else, or that someone's child who will have to die. Not themselves, no—heaven forbid—they're good people and push their agenda to prove that they are better than everyone else because they 'feel' for animals. It's a shame they don't care more for human beings.

"I also find it curious," Andre continued with a chuckle, "that right after protecting an obscure beetle of no environmental benefit, the last polka-dot dumbo bird, or crocodile run down main street, those professing love of animals break for lunch to chow down an intelligent, trusting baby calf fresh slaughtered for sandwich parts, unless of course the group is still full from pigging out on breakfast pigs; then the heifer's carcass gets thrown in the trash."

"Hey," Brad cut in hotly, looking for a fight, "we're all carnivores. We kill…we eat. Get over it. Just because goody-goody two shoes stuffs plants down her throat doesn't mean we have to."

"I completely agree," Andre bowed. "And I underestimated you, Brad. My apologies."

"Understood," Brad said smiling, tilting with the wind. "My first impression could've been better. Most people meet fly boys on their way back from the bar, with a drink in one hand and a babe in the other."

"One of many drinks and many women as I recall," Andre added with a high five.

"Oh, good grief," Karen said. "Are you boys going to tap a keg and sing fraternity songs next?"

"We'll save that for the beach bonfire tonight," Brad said with a wink.

Andre folded his hands over the table and leaned toward Karen. "This god of yours, Karen. Let's presume, for the moment, that he did miraculously send the asteroid that saved Earth from turning into Reptilia. Couldn't he also have added an isotope to denature targeted collagen, wiping out killer sharks, alligators, and crocodiles. Why wouldn't he also give us safe beaches and ponds? Is it possible that he left the job to us?"

Karen leveled her gaze at Andre. "Your question begins with 'If he could have,' a condition that does not apply, because He is God, the Almighty."

"Self-definition and circular arguments were disqualified the year we cured athlete's foot," Andre insisted. "Omnipotence is a leap that adds a variable inconsistent with a multitude of alternate associations. Nothing makes sense unless each logical step agrees."

"And how are you doing reconciling quantum mechanics, molecular theory, and a universe of inconsistent entropy?"

"So close I can feel it," Andre said, then realizing after the words left his mouth that Karen had led him into a trap.

Brad looked back and forth between his girl and the professor then did his best to remain alpha. "I have a great idea—we fly by Bang Zero tomorrow and see what, or who, pops up. For now, let's vote on the reptile thing and get back to the beach."

Karen took the vote. "All those in favor of following Michael's plan and not repopulating Reptilia with dinosaurs, raise your glass."

Everyone's drink went up, even Sarah's—slowly.

"So," Karen continued, "what's next on the agenda, Michael?"

"Genetic augmentation," Michael said. "But before my second presentation, I want everyone to spend a half hour touring Miniville. You need to see what we're up against."

\* \* \*

Sarah and Karen went straight to the schoolhouse, basically an unfurnished one-room log cabin. The entire inner wall was a continuous desk low enough for the minis to work at. One of its stations had various size blocks and a board of square and round holes, the second had tiny logs to build a model house, and the third was leather strips that could be made into shoes.

A dozen minis followed the two into the schoolhouse. None copied their examples. "So much for 'monkey see, monkey-do,'" Karen said.

"Less than impressive" was an understatement. The blocks turned into projectiles. The leather straps ended up everywhere. The room went to shambles. Fabric was the only thing that found purpose, as security blankets.

Sarah surrendered, threw up her hands, and sat at the edge of the table. Karen had lower expectations and other things on her mind. "You were a little hard on Michael back there," she told Sarah.

"Something about his meeting has me suspicious," Sarah replied.

"What do you mean?"

"Well, you know…they know we girls stick together. So why did they deliberately seat us apart?"

"Maybe they're just trying to improve communication. You know, symbolize unity."

"Or they're trying to get away with something." Sara countered.

"Knowing guys, it is probably sex."

* * *

The term *tool shed* was another exaggeration, more like a room with rocks and boards. Michael's idea was to introduce the Stone Age: rock chipping, ax throwing, fire weapons—the usual stuff.

There were no takers. Not one mini was interested in what a sharp stone at the end of a stick could do. It took ten minutes for Michael and Andre to lash together a hefty club. It took ten seconds for the minis to smash it to pieces, and set the club on fire.

Andre changed the subject. "Why did you let Sarah pound your head with gibberish back there? You did a good deed."

"Oh, I don't know," Michael said, leaning against the wall. "She has a good heart. She reminds me of my mom. When we were kids, my mom insisted we carry bugs outside and let them go. She cared for everything. I never told her that I liked the way they tasted."

Andre stood straighter and glared right at Michael and then, to make sure he got the message, said, "Are you crazy? Skinny, beady-eyed, goody-two-shoes Sarah? You've fallen for Sarah?"

Michael's facial expression changed in slow motion, ending with a smile. "I know her looks are exotic, but she has grace, and confidence, and gets me. And she's straight with me, never plays games."

"Does she like you?" Andre asked as he played tug-of-war with a half a spear with a mini, who lost. "What does your radar pick up?"

"Well, I only felt anger toward you. That's a good sign."

"I'm glad I could be of service, and I'm used to that…so you like her, and she likes you?"

"I didn't say that. I just said we have a connection."

"How can that possibly compete with how you connect to Sheila?"

Michael turned, took a breath with intensity, then drew the breath back, and said, "Whaddaya say we drop it, huh?"

"No problem. So…what's the last meeting about?"

"Nothing special. I brought viral-loaded genomes to add various motivations to mini DNA. Stuff they desperately need to survive. It shouldn't take more than five minutes."

"Five minutes? Karen and Sarah…really?"

* * *

Brad and Janie were a big hit in the park, which had a sandbox, jungle gym, teeter-totter, and merry-go-round. Brad and Janie went for the see-saw, Brad saying, "Yes, I understand," and "I see…I see," every time Janie's blouse flew up.

The minis were more impressed by how the two of them held on with one hand and didn't spill a drop with the other. They learned about balance and holding on tight. Something was accomplished.

"I don't see what the big deal is?" Brad said after a particularly energetic mini led them to the merry-go-round. "They're zoos for animals."

When the merry-go-round came to a halt, Janie said softly, "Remember the night an iguana bit me when I laid down on the blanket behind the Cancun Yacht Club? You were sure its red tail looked just like the poison warning." Janie leaned closer. "You carried me to your island hopper and hit warp speed on the way to the poison control center."

"Where, as I recall," Brad laughed, "the reception attendant took a three-second molecular scan, put on a Band-aid, and said you'd be fine."

"You took good care of me. I appreciated that."

"You were my girl. There was nothing I wouldn't have done."

Janie noticed Karen and Sarah on their way back. Brad stood up first, asking, "Are you going skinny dipping with us after the bonfire party?"

"You know me. Of course I'll be there."

* * *

The last meeting did not go well; contrary currents flowed from the start. Sarah didn't go for the pink-blue chair arrangement, so she moved all the pink chairs together, forming a wall on one side. The three boys' chairs, on the other hand, were spread so far apart that it was impossible to discuss things privately—or reach the table, for that matter—which wasn't a problem with Reginald standing by.

"You thought you guys would get away with it, didn't you?" Sarah began.

"Get away with what?" Michael asked with raised eyebrows.

"You know!" Sarah shot back. "Splitting us up so you could talk us into anything you want."

"Like...what?" Andre asked.

"Like programing the minis so the guys get an orgy a day, that's what!"

"There's an orgy?" Janie asked as she and Brad approached. "Why wasn't I invited?"

Sarah scowled. "No, Michael has some kind of sneaky chromosome plan."

"To do what?" Brad interrupted, tipsy in three directions at once. "And why shouldn't men be able to have sex if they want to? Women can. And no one," Brad said, overdramatizing, "should have to have sex if they don't want to. Oh…" he went on, following a surprise attack from a hiccup, "so why wouldn't they want sex?"

Andre and Michael shared a blank look. "I'm confused," Andre said. "Why are we loading muskets if we're not at war? What's going on?"

"You know what we're talking about," Sarah yelled. "What do you call these colored chairs?"

"Cute?" Michael answered. "Entertaining perhaps?"

Karen hooked one arm around Sarah's and waved Janie over. "You know how we stick together. That's why you split us up. You can't fool us. You're up to something."

"If you're so sure of that," Andre said with a glint in his eye, "prove it. You have my permission to scan my brain. See for yourself."

"Humph…that won't be necessary," Karen said, pushing the subject aside as quickly as possible. "Let's proceed."

Brad called for snacks all around: cheese and crackers, cheese fondue, and cheese cake, with a chaser of fresh fruit dipped in warm milk chocolate. Michael began by pointing out, using the last ten minutes as additional evidence, that primates are naturally cantankerous, something nowhere seen in Miniville. All the rebel rousers stormed out to have it out with the nearest dinosaur, and everyone knew how that ended. Wimpy do-nothings were the only ones left to pass on their genes, which deteriorated one generation after another. You might say evolution worked, in reverse.

Michael continued, "Hominoids constantly compete for priority and attention. It's how we fit and survive changing environments. We never sweep snide remarks or dirty looks under the carpet," Michael said, looking at Karen, who didn't flinch.

"The good side of primate ambition organizes communities, invents culture, and dominates other species. The minis have none of this. Their juvenile delinquency, their illusions of grandeur, their dictatorial bullying, for better and for worse, have been lost completely. Their DNA has been diluted lifeless. We need to pump it up."

"You mean…" Brad said, paying attention and finding agreement in the faces of Andre and Michael, "they need to be made greedy bastards just like us."

"Yes, on both accounts," Michael replied. "And there is a problem in Miniville. Cold-blooded terror is gone, but hot-blooded terror is on the way. There are mammals on this planet that survived the dinosaurs. They live on cold snowy mountains. They even learned how to night-raid sleepy Rex dens then hightail it back to the peaks with a dinosaur baby or two.

"The northern continent has evolved tigers the size of elephants, bears massive enough to eat an entire wolf pack in one sitting, and grazing elk with six-foot razor-sharp horns. For the last five months, every one of those guys has been dancing for joy, roaming where they want, and overfeeding on dinosaur bodies, the ends of which are being digested by giant larva as we speak.

"And hot-blooded Reptilia is about to get steamier. They will, like our ancestors, turn on everything that can be caught and chewed between teeth. The next million years of evolution on their continent will be a blood fest, with winners and losers, and won't they be glad to find a land bridge open to the continent we're standing on right now, packed with minis who haven't the brain or brawn to catch a mouse."

"Of course," Andre pointed out supporting Michael, "we don't want to wipe the killers out. But we must prepare the minis for animal warfare. They need weapons. Actually, they need weapons, and the meanness that brings them to life."

"Again, just like us." Brad entered, getting Janie's nod, who got off her chair to hand him another bottle.

Michael finished his proposal to a somber audience. "Earth's walking apes preceded Rome by over four million years, Australopithecus by at least three. Brain growth throughout that period, thanks to alpha male and alpha female selfishness, added an amazing spoonful of gray matter every hundred thousand years.

"That's extraordinarily rapid evolution. To date, we have found no similar accomplishment in our galaxy, even though every goldilocks started with the same chemical building blocks. If minis sped up like we did, they still won't have a chance. The bad guys will be wading over in less than two million years. If we don't act fast, they're goners."

Karen was busy on her pad bringing up a hologram from Michael's files that mapped mini chromosomes. "Oh my God," she said, distraught, "it's a genetic wasteland. Look at all that empty space, and lethal combinations clutter every genome!"

Brad's eyes were having a hard time taking in the hologram, but his brain kept processing. "So why"—and then a pause to re-remember his full thought—"don't we just clone a few thousand human beings from us? Let them have the planet."

Sarah gasped. "Are you kidding? You want one of your children to grow up here! No culture, no medical care…or even language? And their first meal would be miniburgers. We might as well bring back the dinosaurs."

"There is another way." Michael said. "We can add genetic modifiers to mini DNA, jump-start their evolution. Environmental opportunity will do the rest."

"Unless of course religion condemns them to the Dark Ages by refusing to allow scientific progress," Andre said, trying not to feel the anger the thought pre-empted.

"Now that's a misunderstanding," Sarah said, firm and certain. "Warfare didn't break out on earth until temple towns showed up."

The obvious implication of Sarah's comment satisfied Andre, who replied, "Fair enough."

Karen cast a sharp eye to Andre, who soft-stared her down, a message she understood passed the baton to her. "Okay," she said, "what kind of behavior modifiers are we talking about? And I want to see them on screen, one gene at a time."

"Absolutely," Michael complied graciously. "Number one is ambition, desire, and passion. Deep down inside each of us is a son of a bitch who wants everything and everybody for him or herself. We ache to feel superior, and lie to ourselves, and others, to make it so, which is where prejudice and the battle of the sexes began in the first place. I have a genome package to do just that."

Karen took charge. "I agree. Conceit and narcissism have always accompanied our will to exceed. 'Me first' gets in the way, but someday they will learn to control it, like we almost do."

"What about altruism?" Sarah insisted. "They won't get anywhere if they don't look out for one another."

"There they are," Andre pointed out, as Karen displayed another genetic map.

"Wow…how fancy dancy," Brad pointed out. "What world are you all from anyway? Survival begins with food, shelter, and safety, not incense and group chanting. The good stuff better be there."

Janie had her own priority, one she knew DNA put first. "The good stuff is a good stuffing. I get it. This is where sex comes in, right?"

"Sarah," Andre said, "you're the expert. How did our primate ancestors get so smart, so fast, and end up far more intelligent than they needed to survive?"

"Oh no, Andre," Sarah said, on guard, "you're not going to get me there. And for the record, it was the women who favored intelligent survivors, not Alpha males who had their way that got us where we are today."

"Really," Janie said, "bicker, bicker, bicker…and all about sex. Give me a break. Hell, give humanity a break. We all love it. We all blame each other for not getting it or being asked for it when someone else is in mind. Get over it, you two."

Brad was stunned. "Why does that story make me uncomfortable, Janie?" he squeaked out.

"Because deep down inside, you guys know what we are capable of, and it scares the bejesus out of you," Janie purred with delight.

"So," Karen interjected, "this whole buildup of yours was just to get us to accept that minis need a lot of sex, like us? Which we women are better at than you guys?"

"Your superiority in the arena," Michael said, "I've always considered a given. I just wanted to make certain that we are all on the same page."

"Okay then," Karen exclaimed, "all those in favor of adding sexual amplification and polygamy, like every vertebrate on earth… say aye."

The ruling was unanimous, followed by sighs of relief.

Brad was halfway to his feet when Andre added, "There are a few more details we would like to discuss."

Sarah snorted derisively. "I'm not surprised. By all means, cause as much trouble as you like Andre."

"It's about body size," Andre began, a subject that hadn't left his mind since his short skinny butt excluded him from every sport team in high school. "Men average 15 percent adipose tissue, women twenty-five…"

"And the more, the better," interrupted Brad, making the mistake of looking at Janie before he covered his tracks to Karen.

"Right," Michael continued. "In addition to better insulation, smaller chubby bodies use less and store more fuel for cold winter months. Dead men don't count. Evolution kills them off with alarming frequency. It's part of the plan. But every lady who bites the dust compromises the assembly line. Not tolerated. There is evolutionary advantage in keeping females smaller."

"And," Brad gleefully pointed out, "the guys will be able to pick them off the floor. Have a second dessert on the same dining room table."

"Or," Jane said, almost moaning, "finish off with upside-down cake. Everyone gets a mouth full."

Michael started to speak, then paused enjoying images everyone at the table shared, then directed his question to Karen, "What's it going to be?"

With tone and temper of absolute certainty Karen, said, "Equal size and height, Michael. Fair is fair."

"As you wish," Michael answered. "However, don't count on it lasting. The environment molds bodies, and our combination is a winner. It is likely that they will end up disparate."

"Hold on," Sarah said, "it's more complicated than that. If we make men and women the same weight, men will still overpower us with more muscles."

"You haven't needed muscles to control us so far," Andre said. "What makes you think the mini ladies will?"

"This is getting fun," Michael added, "and it brings up an old theory of mine. Height adjusted, there's not much difference between male and female long-distance runners. Women's legs are not just beauty to behold, to be kissed, to be..."

"You can leave out the 'to be spread' part," Sarah blocked. "We get the message. What's your point?"

Michael preferred not to set up another target. "You're the expert. Why are men's arms so much stronger than women's?"

"Oh, no you don't," Sarah said. "You're trying to get me to say it's a sex thing. That you're supposed to carry us away and hold us down."

Andre looked at Michael with a 'score one for our side' look then added, "Actually no, Michael and I have another theory."

"Let's hear it, fellows," Karen insisted.

"Our ancestors, who we still are, all whacked each other in the head. Alpha males would beat up rivals, and alpha females were just as physical with the gals. However, if a male accidently died from an attack, no big deal. But any women lost would have been a tragedy. So evolution preferred female fighters who snarled, scratched, and screamed bloody murder but without the might to murder."

"I will concede a possible maybe on that point," Karen said, amused that the boys were at least thinking along the right lines.

"What about big tits?" said Janie, always proud of hers, a calling card that got her noticed every day of her life, to every other women's dismay.

"Butts are the Pavlovian stimuli that we respond to," Michael added. "Bigger breasts preview coming attractions. Right now, mini girls have nothing, but with or without adding genomes, those with bigger breasts will enjoy more men, and their offspring will follow suit. It's on autopilot."

Quiet followed. Karen looked at Andre and noticed that neither he nor Michael were getting up. "Okay, let's have it. I know you, Andre. What are you holding back?"

Andre made a flabbergasted expression of innocence. "Me... why is it always me?"

"Because it is...that's why," Karen said.

"Okay," Andre added, "I'll come clean. There are two more genomes left to discuss, one we men wish your god had not given us, and another your sex uses to rake us over the coals and make yourselves unhappy at the same time."

"He's referring to secondary modifiers," Karen said to Sarah. "Andre, do your thing."

"Did you know that up until the last week of the Third Reich, Adolf Hitler received thousands of love letters from German women begging him for sex? They wanted to share genes with the most demented psychopath in history."

Sarah rolled her eyes. "Oh, good grief, Andre! Stop wasting our time. What does Hitler have to do with the minis?"

"Meanwhile," Andre continued as if not interrupted, "across the Atlantic was a man named Roosevelt, who brought America from the nineteenth most powerful armed force in the world to the most powerful military in history, defeating two tyrannies in the process.

"He was one of the three most accomplished men of the twentieth century—each defended freedom, human rights, and democracy. Each died in service to his country. Each also did not pass up the opportunity to partake in man's greatest joy on earth."

"And from that we're supposed to conclude what?" Sarah forcefully intruded. "That's its better to have sex than start a war that kills fifty million people? Duh!"

Andre shook his head, and beat Michael to rebuttal. "My point is that the ambition behind their sacrifice, leaving humanity forever in their debt, was from association, not coincidence. 'Tread lightly on the beast that stokes the hottest flame of life, all we are is owed to it.'

"Men must be men. Ladies must be ladies. So far, Michael's genomes have left out one critical—albeit inconvenient—male ingredient, which works in tandem with one of yours, that I would point out, we men are not at all happy about. There's a pox on both our houses."

"Karen," Sarah said, "must we suffer through another one of Andre's stories? He makes no sense at all."

"Andre," Karen sighed, inwardly enjoying the match, "here's the deal. We'll give your opinion serious consideration if, at the end, you provide a treatment for the pox you speak of."

"Agreed."

"Proceed."

Andre stood, signaled Reginald for fill-ups all around, and raised his own, saying, "We brought cotton candy and chocolate-covered raisins for the minis. Can I get you ladies anything?"

"How gracious," Michael said.

Sarah clapped her hand to her forehead. "All the more reason to worry. Sit down, Andre. And get on with it!"

Andre settled back in his blue chair to organize his thoughts. "Let me tell you the story of Jack and Jill."

"What…who are you talking about?" Janie asked.

"Oh, for heaven's sake," Sarah pleaded. "Don't stop him or he'll never finish."

"Jack and Jill grew up three blocks apart," Andre went on melodiously. "They walked to school together, waving every day to their parents, who waved back from the front porch of their five-bedroom Victorian, complete with picket fence, pool, and immaculate grounds."

"Is there more wine?" Brad asked.

"Jack and Jill dreamt of the day when they too could live the perfect life, just like their parents."

Andre leisurely continued. "College, apprenticeship, and hard work made it happen. After the honeymoon, they moved into a house a thousand square feet larger than either one of their parents. All went well…for six months.

"Then one day, walking up to the house after a long day at work, Jack noticed that half of the picket fence had rotted away. A year later, the yard was overgrown with weeds and the windows cracked. The pool disappeared the next summer, when their mortgage rate went up."

Andre full-barreled science from then on, pointing out that Monopoly rules don't change but life does. "It's not fair. It's not supposed to be fair," he said. "DNA doesn't give a rat's ass. DNA only sees itself in the mirror, and its only purpose is to make more, and better, of itself...ultimate self-love.

"The problem is," Andre went on, "that the narrative we swallow hook, line, and sinker gets in the way. One, maybe two, max little Jack-Jills are all DNA will tolerate. The more variations that come off the assembly line, the more likely DNA will find a winner. The truth is...DNA has a gambling problem. If it didn't, it would die.

"And," Andre said, betraying anger that confused everyone except Karen, "DNA gets its goddamn way."

"By doing what?" Karen asked to get the answer out she knew was there.

"Look for yourself," Andre said, pointing to twelve DNA *Homo sapiens* hard-wired construction blueprints. "There's male DNA, there's female DNA, and the appropriate comment is...holy crap! We're two completely different animals with two completely different behavioral subroutines. Why? So DNA can have its way with us—first by bringing male and female together generating love then pulling us apart with boredom and, if necessary, anger, and why? So snooty little DNA can get more varied combinations of itself."

"Which just happens," Karen said, cooling Andre down, "to allow evolution to discover and cash in on intelligence like yours, Andre. Don't bite the hand."

"You're right, Karen. It's just that our pox—the curse of being male—is forced diminished returns. We strain, we agonize, we risk our lives, ruin our health, and work our fingers to the bone for the maiden of our dreams, only to have DNA blunt out joy, like Jack's house crumbling beneath him. And there is nothing we can do about it."

"Oh, you poor, poor little boys," Karen said, bitingly sarcastic. "Don't for a minute think you're the only sex with problems. Right after we're strapped in committed to perform for one guy for the rest of our lives, DNA steps in making our chain and balls less fun, and more damn irritating by the month, especially with rock bands, movie stars, pool boys, and our own mate groveling on bent knees to his boss, whom our DNA says we should lie down with instead or at least move over for more 'stuffing,' as Janie puts it.

"Our Camelot," Karen finished subdued, almost sad, "barely lasts longer than yours."

"So," Sarah demanded, missing the point, "you want guys to be dirty old men from birth to death, just like you guys?"

"To begin with," Michael said, trying to draw fire, "it's not up to us. Over the next million years, genetic variation will bring on stage every conceivable behavioral pattern and what works best for DNA will be passed on. No matter what we do, it's just a push."

"May I ask a question?" said Andre, the steel in his eyes admitting that he was not ready to let it go.

Sarah sat forward but didn't respond.

"Women see a fawn trapped in thistles," Andre said, "or a small, furry-faced animal with helpless eyes, or a baby drooling, and you get an instinctive rush. We men spot the silhouette of your body through a transparent negligee when the light goes off as the refrigerator door opens, and we get an instinctive rush. Without both hard-wired DNA behaviors, our species wouldn't be here, and our instinct came first. What gives you the right to label your instincts goody-goody and ours piggy-piggy?"

Karen brought a draw bridge arm down between them. "That will do. You both make very good points. And yes, Andre, I know the emotional pain of rejection and disapproval is equal to physical suffering after it passes through the same dorsal anterior cingulate cortex, but both sexes are guilty of love lost. Abuse is an equally shared ignorance."

"On the other hand." Michael pointed out, the presence of three beautiful women making it impossible for him to approach despair of any kind, "If it weren't for sex, men and women would have annihilated each other long ago."

Brad remembered a quote, which didn't help. "Victor Hugo once wrote that God made man out of mud, women from the devil.

You all think you're smarter than me—well…I know a few things or two. I do…I really do."

Karen decided to clamp the lid before Brad went on, "Brad, everyone respects you. No one even compares to your piloting skills. We all bring special skills to living. None of us are entitled to feel superior.

"However," Karen said, cold and uncompromising, "Andre, Michael, Brad, at the end of the day, your passions run hot. We get multiple orgasms with anyone we damn please. Get over it or get lost—it's your choice."

"Hear, hear!" said Janie. "Now do we party?"

Enough adrenaline had been spilled. Everyone knew that. Everyone got up to leave, except Karen. "Hold on there, gang. We're not done yet." Then she turned to Andre. "We heard you out. We have a deal. You promised a cure for the pox…the battle of the sexes."

Andre had become as deft at reading Karen's mind as she his. "Sure, Karen, but you wouldn't ask unless you had an idea of your own—you first."

"Okay," she said. "DNA is oblivious to everything beyond the age of reproduction. I suggest we trick it. Hominoids like us add bone and muscle mass to our frame until around age thirty-five, which is also about the end of the reproductive years. So when the species goes catabolic instead of anabolic, have a tag-team genome take over. Until middle age, like us, design minis to want to screw everyone, what you call the pox, also argued our greatest blessing by those who suffer the boredom of pair bonding for life, and then switch tracts for behavior number two—total satisfaction with monogamy, something…yes, we know that is not possible for us, despite daily propaganda barrages."

"That just might work," Michael chimed in, "but again, we are overestimating our influence through time. Dormant genes tend to dilute to nothingness if there's isn't a survival advantage."

"Perhaps stable middle-age grandparents," Karen added, "will augment inclusive fitness. It will be a win-win scenario."

Michael stood jubilant. "I'm all for it! If there's nothing left to discuss, I'll drop you all off on the island and come back to seed the continent."

"Michael," Sarah said gingerly, "I would love to come along and help."

"Nothing would make me happier."

"Hold off, everybody. Andre is not off the hook," Karen said, holding up a hand. "Sit down, Andre. You caused trouble. Now fix it. Where is the plan your physics head promised to cure the pox? How are we to engineer everlasting love?"

"With informed consent and preemptive maintenance."

Everyone sat back down, even Brad, who said, "Now that's sounds like your old self, Andre. I was beginning to think you grew breasts."

Janie, more worried than sober, sat beside Andre. "I don't understand, sweetie. Be more specific. All of us at this table have had six months together pair bonded. What's your prediction?"

Andre tenderly placed a hand on one of Janie's. "I agree with Karen. Men and women are thrown in the ring like gladiators. Happy ever after begins right there—looking around, facing DNA in its box, and saying, 'No one will die today.'

"When Jack and Jill spot soft fence wood, a crack in the foundation, or paint peeling, they must not, under any circumstances, blame each other. They must address reality, the only antidote for which is to surround themselves, year after year, with adventures, toys, parties, vacations, and happy children. Most important of all are layers and layers of oxytocin—affection, companionship, appreciation, and empathy.

"Build it, and happiness will come. Pull down the sheets. There is too much at stake for it not to work."

"You," Karen said slow and cautious, "you believe there is someone special for each of us?"

Andre exhaled slowly, not looking Janie, or anyone in the eye, more of a distant stare into the future. "I ran a program by Cyber yesterday. Our electrochemical brainwaves auras do emanate distant enough to augment one another. It is possible for two people to blend, almost merge, if their compatibility ratio is high enough."

"I don't think Cyber's opinion is what Janie is looking for Andre," Karen said. "What do you think?"

Brad and Michael held their breath, wondering what kind of precedent their buddy was about to suggest.

"Lately I've been led to believe that two people can be strong and tender together. The love that results is more affectionate. It's unmatched. Perhaps even spiritual.

"A rainy night, sick child, neighborhood party, every evening's sunset, right up to the last moments together, lying there holding hands…makes every second right, fearless, and proper.

"Difficult yet doable are lovers waving to their grandchildren on their way to school, porch chairs rocking, clapboard spotless, deck polished, pool and grounds never more beautiful…complete. Yes, Camelot exists."

Thirty seconds of stunned silence followed. Brad broke the spell. "Andre, with all that leftover carbon, you're not going into the diamond-ring business, are you?"

* * *

Michael and Sarah finished the afternoon together. When Brad and Janie got off the shuttle, they did their best to walk a straight line to the beach club, where they boarded a Tiki raft to float, eat, and sip the afternoon away in the bay. Thirty close friends paddled by, enjoying their last day of sunshine the same way, dedicating the day to every pleasure at hand.

That night, as always, the stars stole the show. There was nothing to outshine them. Reptilia had no moon. Blazing bonfires kept the beach lit. Calypso music pounded as the crew assembled for their last night of fresh air.

Karen made an entrance, smiled appropriately, let Brad drag her out for a dozen dances, then slipped away unseen. Two hundred meters down the beach decibel levels were more to her liking, the bonfire lights dimmed, and the exaltation she felt alone with God returned.

She followed a familiar course—all the way to the only rock lookout adjacent open sea. She circled around back beneath fragrant palms, then started up the slanted trail, well-worn those many months. The last five minutes crossed rounded boulders leading to a flat peak, as close to heaven as mortals dare reach.

She wasn't alone. Andre was already there lying on his back peering to the heavens, amazed, as always, by the sundry of molecular organizations hydrogen is capable of.

He rose, pulled out, and activated a second inflatable mat from his back pocket, which he laid down next to his, saying, "Allow me."

Karen stretched out without a word. Andre returned to what he referred to as 'prime position'—elbows at his side, hands lightly over hips, and head cushioned. Karen assumed a similar position, in her mind, Yoga Moonlight.

"This is my favorite place on the whole island," Andre said. "I come here every night."

"That explains the footsteps. Repitilia's last mystery has been solved."

"I don't believe I'm saying this," Andre said, glancing over smiling, "but…do you come here often?"

"Brad's first beer is always waiting for him at the end of the ninth hole, followed by one an hour until he coaxes me to bed, some nights before sunset. I'm asleep so early that I wake up in plenty of time to get here, take in the stars, and then watch the sun rise. Andre, if you don't head back soon, you'll miss skinny dipping."

"I'm sure Janie will save me an instant replay."

"With so much to do tomorrow, I decided to say goodbye to Reptilia tonight," Karen said as both returned to viewing the sky. "It's strange not recognizing a single constellation."

"If we were on earth," Andre said, speaking straight up, "I would point to Orion, the god who promised to kill wild animals to keep men safe."

"And how did that go?"

"Not well…the goddess Gaia banished him to the heavens and placed a scorpion in the sky to chase the hunter for all time."

Andre snuck in a glance—and noticed Karen smiling more peacefully than he had ever seen, then darted back to 'prime position' when she noticed his admiration.

"So," Karen asked, "what do you see in Reptilia's sky?"

"Over there," he pointed. "Do you see the round body of stars? With two legs and a thin head?"

"Yeah…I do see it."

"That's Tilly, goddess of the underworld, known as Sewer Land. To her right, if you connect the ring of jagged stars collected together you get the crown of her king. If you notice, he's not sitting, more squatting. That's King Hemorrhoid…not a happy camper."

Karen laughed, a sound more enchanting than Andre imagined possible, that led him to chuckle pure happiness, that brought Karen's eyes over, that gave Andre an opening to look at her, then straight up as if pointing, then back again at her.

Karen followed his line of sight "Oh my God…yes, I see it. There, between Tilly and King Hot Butt…it's a giant penis!"

"I was wondering how long it would take you to find it."

"It's unmistakable."

"Not only that," Andre said boldly. "At sunset, it sticks straight up…and doesn't lie flat till midnight."

"Four hours! Sound like a good night to me."

"My, my," Andre laughed. "That's the raciest thing I have ever heard you say."

"Most of what my hormones come up with, I keep to myself. I have to maintain my image, you know."

"I wouldn't worry about that. No one is in your league."

A minute later, with both still enjoying infinity, Karen gently asked, "What you said today about two people getting along, in love for life…did you mean it?"

Andre began as clinically as he spoke to Cyber. "The human mind is…well," then totally himself, finding the courage he prayed for, in his way, continued so softly Karen almost had to hold her breath to hear him, "Karen…I have a confession to make. Lately, I haven't been alone here. A month ago, I was hiking the volcanic ridge behind the lagoon. I found a miniature banana just like our South American variety. I picked one off a low branch, and out of nowhere I thought, 'How cool. I can't wait to show this to Karen!'

"The next day, I crystalized a five-shaded diamond centerpiece and said to myself, 'I wish Karen was here to see this.' I wanted to give it to you. Nothing like this has ever happened to me. It's like your presence never leaves me. Everything I do only matters if I can share it with you.

"Some nights, I even lay out a second mat here and pretend. And now you're here."

Karen turned her head away from Andre, rose, and walked away.

# 15

## Up and Away

The lab never had a floor show—but there he was the next
morning, quick stepping from one station to another, dancing to his own drummer. And Andre sang, sort of, "Streamlined,
redesigned, armorized, and reclassified...*Explorer Seven* is ready to
fly. The ultimate answer to get there, be there, leave there. We don't
just get by, we fly, fly, fly."

The engineers on duty couldn't decide if they were more
impressed by the speed of Andre's programing or the rhythm he kept
up with. Either way—all went well.

Outside the ship, on the mid-island grass field that was home
for six months, the entire crew enjoyed spring blossom spread sun-
baked like undergrads enjoying Sunday afternoon on the quad.

Michael and Sheila's Frisbee teams ran full field, the ladies rag-
gedly holding the lead until the last five minutes of play.

When Hank woke up with the birds, he turned to, and turned
Sarah, saying, "We've talked about it for six months. Let's do it now.
It will be great!"

The Frisbee teams lined up for overtime, until Sheila crossed
midfield, marched up to Michael, and soft kissed, lips only, for two

minutes, growing slowly deeper. It caught on. Everyone was out there with their mister or misses wonderful, and it was wonderful.

Hank and Sarah returned from circumnavigating the entire island just in time for the smooch break. They dismounted from atop robot steeds, shook both legs, and resolved to remain standing for as long as possible.

Karen reached over and turned the bedside clock around—again. They were late—again, one half hour every time Brad reached over and turned the clock back around. Neither went back to sleep, or moved for that matter. It was their last morning to enjoy Maui right out their open window.

Not to worry. A hint from Karen, seconded by Brad, was all it took for Michael to reproduce their exact cottage, along with two others out of view in the habitat space. He imported trees, sand, and actual ocean water right up to living wall space to convince Brad and Karen that they were back on Maui.

"An hour from now," Karen said to Brad, "we will have moved into the habitat for two private nights that will be just like this."

"I'm tempted to say great, I can't wait," Brad said, "but we're here with the same wonderful view right now."

"So, I guess you might say," Karen said matter-of-factly, "that it doesn't matter one way or another...so we might as well stay where we are for another half an hour."

Janie was on the quad serving the crew outdoor brunch, which is to say, she sat in an elevated lifeguard chair and pushed a board of buttons for ten robot waiters to keep up with demand.

At eleven, a line of smiles boarded *Explorer Seven*. They projected a positive future packed with excitement, that rewarded rushes of Dopamine just thinking about.

The last to board was Janie, who hesitated on the ramp to look around one last time. She was entering a confined ecosystem that filtered, purified, and recycled water, offered every physical comfort, and teamed with food and friends.

"Just like Earth. We'll take good care of both."

By noon, the bridge was packed, with a twist. Two recliners had been installed in front of Brad's tower for those on watch. Beside

King Brad in his castle, was Queen Karen, in a chair that literally resembled a throne. Sarah sat next to Hank, sometimes helping out. Andre graciously helped Janie sit down beside him. It only took ten minutes of Andre saying no for Janie to wear him down.

When the door closed, four meters of the most dense material in the universe was ready for the big, bad wolf.

By a unanimous decision of their own caucus, Karen, Sarah, and Janie voted to stay put. Michael manned the conn by himself.

"The new tiller ratio is primo," Brad said as they lifted away from the planet, careful to avoid Miniville air space that might chase them back to the caves.

"If any among us object to making history," Andre announced, "speak now...for we are about to conquer forever. Stern power on line. Brad, prepare for dimensional separation in ten seconds... eight...five—"

"Stop the countdown, Andre! There's something out there."

Sarah found it, no more than a spec on the stern screen moving perpendicular to gravitational expectations. The extra-galactic unknown was too far away to identify, but it looked like a spaceship.

In synchronous trajectory, Brad brought Seven's bow one hundred meters off the black hull. It was definitely a vehicle, one tenth the size of *Seven*, with a cramped two-window cockpit.

"Wait a minute," Brad said, "opaque hull, closet bridge, underpowered graviton fins...it's one of ours—an emergency evacuation H-37. Goofiest piece of crap I ever flew."

"That's impossible," Hank said, "the entire fleet was scrapped ten years before we left home."

Andre displayed the ships hologram. "Not junked," he said, "Decommissioned and mothballed until enough H-400s, the latest life raft, could be assembled."

Karen checked out the floor plan. "Two main rooms, five hundred stasis chambers each," she mused. "Are there people over there?"

"What's left of them perhaps," Brad said. "H-37's were programmed to automatically revive travelers in six months...enough time to reach Aurean, the closest M-planet oasis. Minimal propulsion, creaky life support, no food replicators, and only two months of rations…more irresponsible than the Titanic."

"How could it possibly be out here?" Sarah asked.

"How is the easy part," Andre said, joining them at the bow. "Navigation error, equipment failure, or a wormhole could have sent them off course, and zero kelvin preservation would have taken over from there.

"The creepy part is why they left in the first place. It's an old sea adage that you don't abandon ship until boarding the life raft is a step up. Ejecting a rusty H-37 would require panic, an apocalypse hours away."

"Ladies and gentlemen," Brad announced to the crew, "we have ourselves a mystery."

"Brad," Andre said off mic, "position our stern air lock over the cockpit breach. Hank, Michael, and I will drop down for a look."

"Not without us," Karen said. "Sarah and I are coming with you. Part of home is over there."

"You don't want to do that girls," Brad insisted. "There are eighty-thousand-mile-an-hour pebbles out there, probably what opened the hole in the cockpit. Our suits are no match for them. A mashed brain is not a pretty sight."

Andre saw Sarah reach for Karen's hand. Moving the Rock of Gibraltar would have been easier than changing their minds. No one objected.

"Michael," Andre called as he mounted the steps to his lab, "I'll pick up sensors. Do you copy?"

"I do indeed Andre. I'm heading for the changing room now."

"Here's the deal," Andre said leaning over the rail. "We look, we scan, we leave…in and out as soon as possible."

"I'm glad you never used that line on me," Janie murmured with a smile as Andre passed her.

Andre, with two full hands of equipment, was the last to arrive. Karen was the only one left in the changing room. The others were standing by outside the decompression cylinder. Her space suit was halfway up when Andre entered, put down the gear, and floated to her side.

"Karen, we're alone again," Andre said smiling to beat the band, "Wonderful! Last night was…"

Karen's look cut him off, with a push-back hand that wasn't expected. "Andre, you're a smart guy. I respect that. But I don't have time for this. Brad and I have a successful relationship. Everything is the way it's supposed to be. Complications are not part of the plan. You live your life. I'll live mine. Leave me alone."

Andre swallowed hard. "I'm sorry. I misunderstood. Well then, you being counselor and all…"

"Oh no, you don't. You want me to listen to your problems, soften me up, and turn my entire life upside down…for you! Never… it's not going to happen.

"I'm happy. I know I am. Really! Let things be. Besides, you have Janie. Don't be a scoundrel."

Michael walked in just in time to catch Karen's final, obviously angry, words. As he looked from one to the other, Karen grabbed her helmet and shuffled away.

Michael straddled Andre's bench. "Oh no…not you too! You and Karen? What happened to your 'tough guy don't give a damn about anyone' motto? And what's all her acting out all about? This is unhealthy, very unhealthy."

"I had to give it a try. I was wrong. It's over…actually, never started. No big deal. Couple of days, plenty of work," Andre bit off, "and I'll be fine."

"Wake up, Andre. This is me, remember? I've been there. You're not up against just any woman. This is Karen we're talking about, Aphrodite vixen of mythical proportion."

Michael calmed down and grimaced when he continued, "The day she left me, I spent the entire morning exhausting every satellite scanner trick I knew to track her down. I was convinced that if I could just talk to her, she would come back. I even set two places for dinner, after scrubbing the entire bungalow.

"The second day, I started drinking. On the third, I sat on a stool at Gilligan's from noon till closing. The fourth day had me eating cannabis brownies on my beach hammock at sunrise, waiting for a coconut to fall on my head…"

"Oohh," Andre groaned. "You're not helping. Leave me alone. You got over her. So will I."

"Hear me out. The night I ran out of cupcakes, Leslie, the mainland ferry captain, surprised me at midnight. The next morning, Cindy and Julie, two friends from school, showed up for a week of vacation, most of which we spent in bed. They made me so happy I didn't have time to cry in my beer.

"I was a fool to let her turn me into a basket case, especially since we'd already hit the declining-reward part of our sex curve. You're in never-ever-could-be land…self-pity at its worst. You've been poisoned, but as luck would have it, I have the antidote."

"Oh? Are Julie and Cindy in town?"

"Even better—the Friday Night Club."

Andre looked at Michael. "Right…I designed, and redesigned this ship. The Starlight Lounge replaced Quiet Forward. There is no Friday Night Club."

"Well, there wasn't yesterday," Michael replied exuberantly. "But thanks to you, there is one now…"

"Explain."

"Certainly, but let's start with you. Look at you. Wet noodles have more backbone. You're not focused, which means we're all in danger. Are you happy?"

"Happy? Wow…until this trip, that question never came up. I had things to do. I did them. Now I have things to do…and I'm confused. And I don't like it."

"Welcome to life. It's not a cookbook. So what are you going to do about it?"

"Great, another question. I always had answers, or at least a list of variables complete with probabilities. Either way, I was good. But now, I'm not good for anything."

"That's a misunderstanding between you and yourself. It will pass. Trust me."

"How?"

"I'll get to that. But first…tell me about Janie. Do you plan to stay together?"

"Why are you asking me that?"

"Because options, variables if you prefer, have arrived. Remember the classic song, 'Everybody Loves Somebody Sometime? What do you think the 'some time' means?"

"Get to the point. Stop playing games."

"My point is, that we all play games with ourselves—mostly make-believe—that what is 'supposed' to be is actually happening, not because we have thought it through and made the right choice, but because others, history, culture, the narrative, and bubble-gum advice tells us to.

"Reality, meanwhile, requires making decisions on a daily basis…about everything. You and Janie have until five o'clock tomorrow afternoon to make your next one."

"What happens then? And what if we don't make a decision?"

"Not making a decision is a decision. And errors of omission count just as much as errors of commission."

"Finish, Michael, we need to suit up."

"If you and Janie don't notify Cyber, then dining, dancing, and every recreational opportunity—pools, courts, and health club included—are available for you on the main activities floor. You will also be classified…paired lovers."

"Like we are now."

"Exactly."

"So what changed?"

"Computer malfunction. When the last entertainment network went online this morning, Karen's matchmaking scheme jumped out. The ladies are mad as hell. They resent another woman trying to run their lives. The guys, on the other hand, are tickled curious."

"So," Andre said, enjoying the distraction, and bringing his hand to his chin, "as fabulous as six months of bungalow paradise has been, now everyone knows that the first apple of their eye may not be 'the one.'"

"You got it. And everyone also knows that there is at least one perfect partner onboard for them, mathematically speaking, if such a thing is possible.

"As soon as Karen got whiff of the fiasco, she destroyed the entire memory bank, test results included, which, strange as it sounds, made the ladies even madder."

"That much I understand. She should have gone clean—it would have been the honest thing to do. Who trusts computers anyway?"

"The answer to that question is everyone but you, to their downfall."

Andre stalled, trying to put his brain back together. The best he could come up with was, "So everyone is breaking up?"

"No, shopping around…privately."

"Really? The only private space on board is the habitat."

"Unless you set up boundaries. Mulligans on level three has its own promenade. The Starlight Lounge, complete with second promenade back to crew quarters, is on level three."

"Tell me something I don't know."

"Curious couples secretly notify Cyber that they wish to join the Friday Night Club. Boy and girl pairs will split up until ten the next morning, one assigned to Mulligan's and level four, the other to Starlight and lower promenade, with instructions to remain on that level for the rest of night, using only their assigned promenade to traverse the ship, in and out of any bedroom they please, or check into make-believe hotel suits that are being constructed as we speak.

"Cyber will make sure the sex ratio is equal on each floor. And the rules are simple. Mix, meet, laugh…do whatever and whomever feels right. Sheila and your Janie came up with the plan.

"The trick is don't ask, don't tell…not even a wink across the room the next day. But if sparks fly, the 'new' part-time couple can explore their relationship for as long as they want, every Friday night. Or make their Friday night lover number one and still spend time with their first flame once a week until they are sure, or just play mix and match until 'the one' shows up and the new couple reclassifies to join the upstairs Friday night main ballroom bash. Young people have always mixed it up. We'll just omit melodrama and self-justification."

Michael spoke the right language. Numbers started flying in Andre's head. "You know, Michael, I had always believed relationships have a life of their own. We just refuse to admit it and somehow feel that we must turn on each other to justify change, incorrectly labeling past flings failures. Relatives and the narrative are the problem. There's no excuse for lovers blaming each other.

"So…does Janie want to do this?"

"Yes and no. Hey, Janie loves you. She's also the sharpest lady onboard. She doesn't want you to leave her. And why would you? For a fantasy of who you think Karen is? Trust me, I've learned. Karen is a classic prom queen, a stuck-up snob.

"Sheila and Janie will help us live the ultimate dream. They also know that one night away from them will varnish the porch, if you know what I mean?" Michael finished with both eyebrows as high as he could get them.

"Yeah, right," was confused Andre's only comeback.

"Look, the entire crew is in their twenties. There's plenty of time to settle down, you know, do the family thing. Until then, the Friday Night Club benefits both sexes, and closes the orgasm gap in one fell swoop."

"What about Brad and Karen?"

Michael shrugged. "Brad misses the Rockets big-time, but he also wants to keep Karen, who wouldn't dream of lubing up for just an ordinary guy. It's high society or nothing for her. Trust me, I've been there, she's romantic quicksand, a conceited cold fish.

"Brad and Karen will remain a dull couple for the rest of the trip and good riddance to them! But who knows, maybe they are meant for each other. Great! Mazel tov!"

"Well," Andre said, wondering if he'd seen the light. "I have screwed up the last two relationships I had, which was basically it before Janie. Maybe that's what I'm doing now. Do you think Janie might be 'the one' for me? And could this fooling around thing help it…prove it?"

Michael laughed. "Whatever it does, it's going to be a blast… just don't mess up. Women share us much better than we share them. Possessive Alpha male garbage works against us every time. Mellow out and go for it."

Andre started for the air lock, then stopped. "Wait a minute, the club thing means you could have Janie! Are you setting me up?"

"The answer to that question is yes…and no. And see, it's working already. You do love Janie. But the answer to your question is actually no. Cyber records buddies and close friends, like you and me. You and I will always be assigned to the same floor, Janie and Sheila to another. Kind of a pact between the two of us, or anyone else who lets Cyber know."

"Cyber," Andre hailed, "I know you're here, and thanks for staying out of everyone's business."

"You're welcome, Andre. Let me guess. You want advice from me. I am a computer. You might want to rethink that request."

"Do you have an opinion?"

"Yes, and you've heard it before…*Homo sapiens* can't distinguish between themselves and what DNA is directing them to do, which paradoxically, is also yourself, with minimal hardware leeway.

"Andre, you and I have hashed this out before. We both agree that the human race desperately needs to reprogram itself…alter software to maximize hardware.

"However, the answer to your question is yes, the isolation protocols Michael has explained are feasible. It is possible to avoid DNA crap by not feeding into its hands. And using the intelligence you're born with…but good luck with that."

Andre backed away lingering doubts. "When I asked about Janie, you said no and yes and no. What's the yes about?"

"You and I have landed the two sexiest, most sensible women on this ship, gals so experienced that if they thought the two of us could handle it, they'd arrange a swap, or a straight-up foursome."

Andre flushed and shivered. "I prefer intimidation one woman at a time, thank you. But I admit your plan has merit. Hell, our age group is known for romantic confusion, idiotic arguments, and hellish breakups. Instead of turning the other cheek, we get to kiss one."

"Just one last question," Andre said, moving toward the door. "Why did you thank me for the Friday Night Club earlier."

"Oh, hey, Janie recorded your behavioral modification speech yesterday and played it back to Sheila. That and your Camelot happy ending started the ball rolling. Deep down inside, none of us, even those of us who know better, don't want to let go of the narrative. Janie must sense that she's losing you. Give the Friday Night Club a try."

"It does sound better than getting hit in the head by a coconut."

With that, Michael and Andre joined the others waiting in the airlock, where everyone stayed while Michael dropped down to see if the coast was clear. Like the others, his suit was equipped with a fishbowl helmet, mechanical grappling drone, gravity belt, and three darling internal nanomites to scratch those hard-to-reach spots. The suits also came with waste system hookups, in either direction, which avoided embarrassing locker room returns.

The hole in the cockpit was wide enough for Michael to fit through. He secured a wire. Hank, Andre, Sarah, and Karen slid down immediately and went right to work.

"How's it going, Hank?" Andre asked as the cowboy jump-started the antique's economy-class navigation station.

"So far, only launch date and course. Brad was right about Aurean. The ship left earth in a hurry five years after we high-tailed it. Asteroid U-939 was not the reason they launched. The dates don't match. I'll take the panel back to *Seven* right now...thawing it out might help."

A door separated the half-pint bridge from the next compartment, power and life support. Michael removed the hinges. The door floated away. A single desk sat on the port side of the engineering station, a bank of computers on the starboard. Michael connected the energy pack of his suit to a screen that came to life.

"Impressive..." he said over the mobile comm. "Radioactive-fuel supply, oxygen generator, and fluid-recycling stayed operational for years. It's too bad food replicators were cut from the budget."

Michael looked over to the door opening toward the stern. "Other than that, what you see is what we got. The rest of the ship is just two individually sustained living spaces separated by a bulkhead. Andre, see if you can get the door open."

One push informed Andre that the job needed his laser drill, which he used to outline the entire door. A few seconds later, his power gun was back on his belt and the door cool enough for Michael to add muscle.

The door didn't drift away as expected. Instead, the top cracked ajar one foot and then stuck, enough room for a visitor to drift through: a skeletal arm trailing stringy tendon fingers. The fingernails were intact, surrounded by frayed skin—the only flesh remaining over cracked bones.

Seven's tether had altered the wreck's momentum. The gruesome claw hand drifted past Michael toward Sarah like a strangler on the prowl. She screamed and knocked it away. Michael and Andre combined efforts to kick the door down.

Andre retched at the sight of five heads, two femurs, several spines, and what appeared to be frozen temporal lobes—each obviously gnawed by something.

Dozens of flattened eyeballs were stuck to the floor with thin straws sticking out. Amputated feet had been gathered in clumps, each bone beneath the ankle bent out like an umbrella to get to muscle strands. Thousands of body parts floated floor to ceiling, so dense visibility ended ten yards away.

"What the…!" Michael exclaimed.

"Brad, do you see this?" Andre called over the comm.

"Your cam is coming in bright and clear. And I'm going to sleep with the light on tonight."

"Our belts are keeping us on the floor, but swimming through a weightless morgue is not my idea of fun. Send a droid below the ship. Set for light gravity. Pull this stuff down."

"Acknowledged."

The team retreated to the cockpit. Vibrations and muffled thumps followed, the final act of those who once walked Earth.

The four entered over mounds of body parts. At the far wall of the first chamber, an emaciated young woman—eyes, hair and torso intact—looked back at them motionless.

They grav-belted above the carnage, and as they got closer, Andre could see a second complete body, a child no older than eleven in the lady's lap.

Sarah sped forward then stopped. "What is it?" Karen asked.

"She looks just like…like my sister! It's not possible."

Michael caught up and blocked her way. "That can't be, Sarah. Let's get back to the ship, we've seen enough…"

Sarah pushed him aside. "Michael, I have to know. Take tissue samples."

Michael looked over Sarah's head to Karen, who nodded. "If you insist, he said."

Karen lead Sarah away.

"This place is giving me the creeps," Michael said to Andre. "I'll power up the central bulkhead panel to open the metal wall between the bow and stern compartments, we look around, and we're out of here."

Andre's color had returned when Michael asked him, with one hand on the switch. "Are you ready for act two?"

"The best reminder to stay on our toes out here is reality. Let her rip."

The bulkhead parted like curtains on stage, revealing unimaginable horror. Intact, frozen human bodies were stacked one on top of another, smallest children trampled to the floor, adult men and women higher up, largest of both sexes on top.

The wall panels continued to retract, spilling three of the top bodies to the floor, one glancing off Andre as he sprung back. He and Michael flew over the pile of bodies to inspect the rest of the hold, finding only deserted space.

"Michael, look at this," Andre said at the far end. "Ten feet of ion injector casing has been removed. The plasma and Carbondon insulation are exposed."

"Looks like a rush job."

"Right. And they worked on it without shutting the system down."

"Melted Carbondon is deadlier than cyanide. The injector must have blown before they could reinforce it. That explains why everyone got as far away as possible."

"It's also heavier than air," Andre added. "That explains the stacking. The strongest climbed over the weak for a few more minutes of life."

Michael, in disbelief, kept looking around. "So, Andre, why didn't the front compartment let them in? They must have heard screams."

"Hank might find the answer. My guess is that gas detection automatically shut the doors, and they had no manual override. Didn't fit the budget."

"Yeah, along with keeping hundreds of people alive."

"No argument there, Michael. But only morons work on hot ion injectors," Andre scoffed. "If they jury-rigged food replicators instead, they could have all moved to the bow section and cannibalized the stern instead of each other. That would have bought them five years to come up with a new plan, like micro detonating the stern to send the ship close to a Goldilocks planet, or in orbit around anything livable to space jump to the ground."

"It's too bad you weren't with them."

"I wouldn't get in a piece of junk like this for all the gold in the universe. These poor souls must've not had a choice. Let's get back, analyze the data. This place is getting under my skin."

The two didn't look down all the way to the bow. Neither spoke until they were safely on the other side of the airlock. "About that DNA sample," Andre said, "why don't you distort it just in case? Sarah won't know the difference and will be relieved that there's no family connection. There's no gain in adding misery to misery."

"Oh, I don't know, Andre. We've come to trust each other. I'm not comfortable lying to her about this."

"Remind me to trick you into another brain scan. I'm dying to know what's going on in that green head of yours. I'll even let you know."

Karen, Sarah, Janie, and Brad were already waiting in Andre's conference room. It was a black wall shut in, just like the gambling rooms found in Inns from New York to Washington, where travelers could play cards without attracting eighteenth-century constables.

Andre's table accommodated ten chairs, with an elevated screen and keyboard for each. Andre's station, at the head of the table, came with dual systems. Karen sat opposite Andre as far away as she could get. Hank, Michael, Sarah, Janie, and Brad filled in both sides.

Even if he wanted to, Michael didn't get a chance to fudge the DNA sample. Sarah caught up with him to snatch the vial. One minute after the group sat down, the lab posted the results.

"Oh no. Oh no, oh no! I knew it was her!"

"Not necessarily, Sarah," Karen said. "It's only a 70 percent possible match."

"Sarah," Andre said calmly, "compared to our time today, the Earth and all who ever lived on it are long gone. We knew that when we woke up this morning. We also knew over breakfast that we will return to Earth two years older, while in their time, only two weeks will have passed.

"You will be with your family again. I promise. And according to this data, we'll have four years to evacuate or prevent whatever happened. I know it's hard to imagine, but that ship out there will never be boarded. Your family will be fine."

"Yes," Sarah replied quietly. "You're right. And life doesn't come without risks. I'm going to assume the best and move on. Just not tonight. Yes, of course. Everything will be…just fine. I'm going back to my room to watch family movies and plan out my first day back."

Sarah turned for the door, more mumbling than speaking. "My dad loves spicy vegetable dip. Hank's will sure surprise him. Before dinner, my sister and I can pick flowers, with my little niece. Mom loves flowers on the table. Yes, I'll see them all at dinner…yes, that's it, at dinner."

Reality can be such a drag, especially when it gives life no choice but death, which was in the minds of all as Sarah left to bandage her wounds. Hank thought of his mom sitting at the fireplace. Karen couldn't get her mom's backyard chapel out of her mind, where mom promised to be every Sunday morning until her daughter joined her again. Brad and Janie remembered how proud their parents were every time GASA praised their contribution to humanity. Andre missed his mom, who didn't have to die.

But there was work to do, so they got to it. Why did so many people die? Who, what, where…which mistakes must never be repeated?

The data pulled from the ghost ship proved unreadable. The group swapped theories. Andre began by reviewing asteroid patterns that GASA had calculated by the millennium. Space did not kill Earth.

Karen presented the most convincing explanation. Before she left, she protested GASA's Kreiger project. She was in rare form when she blasted Kreiger for petitioning permission to resume underground testing designed to focus a mega-nuclear device more powerful than any weapon ever constructed to blow approaching asteroids away. Perhaps fear of a rogue won the day—perhaps paranoia cost humanity their planet and their lives.

"It's a solid theory," Andre said. "A single nuclear weapon on the face of the planet proves every man and every woman a dumbass."

The mere mention of the Krieger Project ignited anger. "I didn't see you out there picketing Andre," Karen said with a sneer.

"No," Andre replied. "But I did stream three papers, using all five forbidden words."

Andre's censorship crazies tapped his ire as he continued, "If that prick cracked the mantle it is possible that enough lava spilled out to cover all of North America, followed by atmospheric death, summarily. We have the goods on that bastard now. When we get home, I'll blow him out of the water."

"Andre," Janie said, "Michael told me about the second chamber. How did you figure out the pile up at the door?"

"Every time the cyanide chamber doors swung open at the concentration camp Dachau, the strongest fell from above. When faced with death, the most peaceful humans on earth trampled their own relatives. Children gasped the first last breath."

Janie shuddered. "I'll never understand how people could be so cruel to each other."

"I do. You see, in addition to raping the world, Christian Europe had a penchant for bludgeoning itself." Andre pointed out.

Karen growled, "I would have left with Sarah if I'd known you were going to insult God."

"On the other hand," Andre grunted, "how else am I going to maintain my reputation as a *scoundrel?*"

"Look here, Andre," Brad said, bold and manly. "Karen's been through a lot today. Keep your opinions to yourself. Give the poor girl a break."

"Just who are you calling a 'poor girl'?" Karen snapped. "You better not be referring to me."

"Oh, sorry. I just thought...with all the trouble..."

"You just thought what, Brad? That you're the big, strong guy, and I'm just a little girl who can't take care of herself? Who can't find words to defend herself? You men have a lot of nerve!

"Treating women like porcelain dolls just makes us more fragile. When it comes to making noise or objecting to discrimination, at work or play, our sex outguns yours every day of the week. You can shove your handicaps down the eighteenth hole, par zero."

Facing Andre head on, Karen continued, "Sticks and stones, sticks and stone, that's all. You don't scare me, Andre. Go ahead, give it your best shot. I'll show you what!"

"Yes, do," Janie said, forcing a smile. "Say anything you want. It's called free speech...no one's attitude should get in the way."

A blip on Andre's monitor distracted him from Janie's comments.

"Can we stay her for the night? Sarah..."

"Sure. It's too late to split dimensions anyway..."

When Andre looked up, he noticed Karen's thinned lips, set jaw, and folded arms. "Okay, Karen, since you asked...I will be glad to share my thoughts. Mark, my college roommate, was South Boston all the way. Latin school, high mass, boiled dinner, and beer. Every Sunday when he returned from visiting his folks, I'd kid him about who runs the universe, and we would laugh.

"He said, 'Believe in God, but don't trust anyone who says they work for him.'"

With a look honestly betraying no malice, Andre continued, "Karen, not to him...not to you, not to anyone have I, do I, or will I ever insult your god. How can I? I don't know your god. I've never met the guy and have no reliable data, although I am free tomorrow afternoon.

"Which is not to say that I haven't looked into the situation. I know, for example, that the first prime-time, mass-produced god was constructed by the children of Israel, conveniently scripted to proclaim themselves the chosen people entitled to the promised land, which, I admit, sounds a lot better than 'The other half of the country fled their border before our army caught up with them.'

"Act two moved the stage to Rome that coopted the floating Hebrew platform for a made-in-Europe god, suspiciously placing themselves at the center of the universe. By might of swordplay under penalty of death, Vatican Rome insisted that they get the last word on everything, that not by chance added power and wealth to their coffers.

"Act three mounted another tidal wave. The Persians, who carbon-copied Rome's fearsome chassis, demanded the world agree that God loved them best, which, of course, moved the final word to their laps, ordering the planet conquered by hook, crook, or grappling iron. Each religion erupted intrinsically hostile to the others, basing their opinions on ignorance, misunderstanding, and wish fulfilment.

"Having faith in God is one thing," Andre said, wrapping up. "Surrendering faith to a sexist, politically corrupt, and depraved human organization…is another matter."

"And just where," Janie said, enjoying Karen stew, "does the holocaust come in?"

"The spiritual journey stuff is a front," Andre said "Obedience was and remains religion's priority. The baton of discipline passed effortlessly from Roman emperor to Roman Church State. The Nazis then copied the Jesuit order to rule their ranks.

"Once you train a mind to obey orders on bended knees, the same mind remains programed to obey orders in a foxhole…or with a tablet of hydrogen cyanide in hand. Obeying orders in the engine of tyranny, scam and spin, scam and spin."

Karen spat back, "You should have more respect for the beliefs of others! No one agrees with you."

"I wouldn't be so sure about that. Millions have noticed the difference between what religion says and what ends up happening. Democracy relies on people mustering the intellectual responsibility to think for themselves. Citizens who don't question mucky-mucks and instead assume a relic has authority over them turn into blind sheep.

"And it gets worse. They accept as truth stories from the past written by people not intelligent enough to pass kindergarten.

"Also in the past were a rare few who witnessed Europe's warfare first hand, like Ben Franklin, who said, 'Lighthouses are more useful than churches.' And John Adams, who admitted, 'There would be the best of all possible worlds if there were no religion in it.'

"The two most brilliant observers from our past would be Thomas Jefferson and John Lennon, who said, "Christianity is the most perverted system that ever shown on man, and imagine nothing to kill or die for, and no religion too.'

"If a computer had consciousness, it would *believe* it programed itself. We're no different. The day mortals see their real selves in the mirror is the first day of genuine freedom, and the last day outdated scribblings, false sanctification, and witch doctors turn us into Nazis.

"Karen, I'm a scientist. And in theory, everyone onboard *Explorer Seven* is also, including you. And it's wrong for a scientist to believe anything upon insufficient evidence, even worse when you know you've been lied to, again, and again, and again. Freedom of religion is freedom from religion.

Andre faced Karen and, without batting an eye, stated, "If this god of yours exits, I guarantee he's pissed off...and not at me."

No one spoke, no one moved, no one blinked.

Janie tiptoed behind Andre, dipped by his side, and gently closed both his screens. She then led him out of the room, but not before turning to say, softly and peacefully, "We'll see you all at breakfast. Everything will be fine."

# 16

## *All Good Things*

Visiting the ship of death did not sit well; sleep came slowly. At midnight, Andre, pacing the bridge, sent a drone four lengths to take a picture of *Explorer Seven*, massive, thick-skinned, and rugged—lying beside the deceased H-37, fragile, warped, and cracked. Sharing the image calmed the crew.

Karen was forgiven for not being forthcoming, Andre excused for being forthright, Sarah again homespun sweet, and Janie was… Janie. The crew, for the moment, breathed as one.

Michael, as usual, ate for two. Sheila joined Michael in the conn to feed him airborne grapes. He returned the favor. The best catch got first pick; of what they wouldn't say.

By ten, they were ready to fly. Andre powered up. Brad spun the ship around to face the remains of Earth's children. He then backed away slowly as the entire crew paid their respects. Sarah had Cyber play taps. Hank saluted.

"It's your turn to lead the charge, Janie," Karen said, gathering the attention of everyone on the bridge.

"What should I say?"

Janie sat beside her man, who typed, "Read what I type here."

Looking down, Janie announced, loud and clear, "Fission-powered, array online...are you land lubbers ready to cast off?"

"Navigation synchronized," answered Hank.

"Helm responding," Brad followed.

"Then tally ho my sexy ass out of here...Andre!" Janie said, giggling, after a jab to his ribs.

Once again, existence cracked wide open; time-attached matter to the right, metaphysical order, gravity, and eternal identity on the port. Brad aimed for the edge of the expanding universe. He opened her up for the fun of it. "Boy, do I love speed," he whispered to himself.

"Hold on there, Flash Gordon," Andre cautioned. "At this rate, we'll run out of universe in twenty minutes. Slow her way down. In a minute, you can punch her once to turn around."

"Roger that."

"Hank, where do you plot us?"

"When we powered up a minute ago, the universe was twenty billion years old and the ship four parsecs, that's twelve billion light years, from the furthest out galaxy."

"John," Andre asked over the comm, "how is the power plant doing?"

"Efficiency output maximized, dampening rods stable, thrust peaking, and no conduit temperature elevation. We're perfect across the board."

"Brad," Andre continued, "we're humming sweet. Let's do it. Swing her around."

Brad pulled hard then again, finally adding two groans. There was no need for Hank to report. The view from the bow told all. *Seven* slid sideways, unable to reverse time or backtrack an inch.

"All stop," Andre said. "What's the problem, Brad?"

"The grid is too stiff out here. More resistance. I can't buck it."

"We need more momentum. Hank, how close are we to the point of no return?"

"Ten minutes of travel'll put us outside the universe, which, from aging will have burnt lifeless."

"Hold it right there, guys," Karen spoke out loud and forcefully. "If this ship gets stuck in gear or Hank has miscalculated, we'll spend the rest of our lives in perpetual darkness, with no hope of ever getting home."

"Yes," Andre said, "but we could make a home. There'd be plenty of frozen planets left behind. It wouldn't be paradise, but it would be livable, especially with all the radioactive material left over for us to generate heat and light."

"Sounds like living in a cave to me," Sarah said, abrupt and annoyed.

Brad turned to Karen at his side. "We just went full throttle to dead stop without a hitch. Not one backup went online, the helm was solid, and every system operated on specs. We're ship-shape.

"Two parsecs and ten billion years is a healthy safety margin. I'm with Andre. More speed might just turn us around."

"Karen has my vote," Janie said, rising beside Andre. "We had a great life on Reptilia. And look around. We're surrounded by sun-lit galaxies. There millions of earths out there waiting for us. We can build a perfect society on an ideal planet. Our grandchildren will call us forefathers. They'll be statues of us in town square."

Sarah didn't waste a second. "My vote makes it three to two. You lose, Andre."

"Now hold on there," Michael was heard saying from the conn. "The minute we left my mom started counting days. If three years pass and I don't return, she'll mourn the loss of two sons for the rest of her life. I won't do that to her. There's gotta be a way home."

"Don't worry, Michael," Andre added. "In addition to one more idea, if the entire crew decides to call it a day and set up shop, I plan to build another ship and head out, by myself if necessary. I'm not giving up. If you come along, both of us will party the real Maui beach. I'm sure of it."

Sheila, about to pop another grape, threw it and three more at Michael. "Don't for one second think that you can drop me off and head home by yourselves. You're taking me with you, and the two to one ratio suits me just fine."

Karen left Brad to walk to the bow. "Andre, you said speed up and spin was one option. What's the second?"

"I'm not sure. I need numbers. And the speed spin thing makes more sense."

Karen crossed her arms and aimed at Hank. "Are you certain that if we try another U-turn that there will be at least one starlit solar system for us out there?"

"Yes, ma'am, I'd bet the ranch on it."

"And," Brad offered, "John and I can preprogram automatic shutdown to make sure we don't go too far."

Karen didn't bother asking Andre, who looked over enjoying her dilemma.

"Fine," she said. "Eight minutes. Not one second longer. And add that auto shutdown thing."

"I'll do better than that," Andre said. "We'll do six minutes, which will leave one parsec and five billion years ahead of us."

As soon as everyone was seated, Andre announced, "I'm building power, Karen...on your mark."

"Like you're giving me a choice. Okay....*do it*!"

Brad put the peddle to the metal. The acceleration rattled *Seven* in three directions at the same time. Four tense minutes followed before Andre made the announcement. "Brad, we've red-lined the red line. It's now or never. Give her a whipping. Swing her around."

Turn she did, reversing a million years before smashing into a distance bow ripple ten times their height. The ship jolted vertically, the stern thrown sideways.

"Shut it down!" Karen yelled. "We're going to slam the wall again!"

Andre pretended the noise drowned her out. Full throttle continued, which gave Brad enough time to bring the stern dead center again, as bow to stern vibration increased.

Three minutes later, Andre threw in the towel and hit reverse thrust. "Shut her down, John. I know what the problem is. All stop."

Karen was already halfway up his staircase. "You promised me six minutes," she said tensely, "and I ordered you to shut her down!"

"Karen," Andre said off his chair, sitting top step, "I promised five billion years and one parsec. That is exactly what you got."

"Very close there, Andre," Michael was heard saying. "We actually broke free for two thirds of a second. Ten percent more speed might have done it."

"Or twenty percent less resistance," Brad added. "Either one will work."

"Hold on there," Karen said startled. "We just hit maximum speed and the ship almost fell apart. We failed. It's over. The fat lady is singing. The mission is cancelled!"

Andre suppressed a sigh and two comebacks. "Hank, join me in the lab. I want to run some numbers by you before we discuss them with the crew. Everyone else, take a break. We'll meet at 1400 hours."

"Andre," Sheila said, "Michael and I meditate every afternoon in Buddha Park. How about we meet there?"

"Roger that," said Andre as he disappeared into his lab.

* * *

Andre and Hank left the lab in uniform cadence—Hank feeling the hand of God, Andre trusting the god of numbers. They passed the pool and packed snack bar. Surfer shorts and bikinis ruled the day. Every lounge chair was occupied; beach volleyball was in full swing.

Two beauties offered Andre and Hank a Mai Tai. Andre declined. Hank walked away with drink in hand and lipstick on his collar.

Behind the Mai Tai stand a couple was picnicking on the grass. "Tell me the truth, Andre. Did ya aim for turbulence this morning so ya could watch Janie jiggle?"

"Would you blame me if I did? Some days I just can't wait for her to come home and join me on the trampoline."

Janie had covered the second pool with topsoil for tree and bush planting, making sure it looked just like earth, including a grove of bamboo trees that marked the beginning of Buddha Park, that appeared impenetrable as Andre and Hank approached.

"Over here," Hank said. "They slow ya'll down by getting ya lost. Hello...are you guys in there?"

Two overgrown turns later, Hank and Andre found the hidden piazza, complete with a pond, floating lotus blossoms, trellised Aster, and lanterns honoring revered ancestors. Behind the pond, all the way to the statue of Buddha sitting below a shade tree at the end of the park, were Daylilies, Black-eyed Susans, and wildflowers, red, yellow, orange, and lavender.

On woven mats set before Buddha, Sheila sat in lotus position while Michael lay Shavasana, the meditation position his orthopedic surgeon recommended. Both wore Tibetan Kaslaya shoulder robes over matching crimson Antarasavaka sarongs tied at the waist with cotton belts.

Andre, Hank, Sheila, and Michael joined Brad, Karen, Janie, and Sarah, who were already sitting around the rock garden at the center of the park.

"Attention all hands," Andre announced over the comm. "This morning, we pushed the envelope. The envelope fought back. The proximity of Andromeda and the Milky Way helped us stretch the grid back home. That advantage is no longer available. We need a new plan. Karen...the comm is yours."

"Thank you, Andre. Edward Keebler, GASA's top physicist, took last year's Nobel Prize for mathematically proving seventy percent of the universe is dark matter. He also confirmed that dark matter will eventually pull the universe apart. All material existence as we know it will disintegrate, eventually diffusing into nothingness. The world will end just like the Bible and every other revered text predicts.

"If we travel any further, the universe will disappear, and we will live out lonely lives surrounded by nothingness. Brad, Sarah, and I have reviewed the available data. Our only option is to colonize the closest habitable planet."

Andre raised his lower lip and asked Brad, incredulously, "And you agree with Karen's conclusion?"

Brad shrugged and nodded. "I agree that there is a definite risk if we go trans again."

"Are you done, Karen?"

"No more need be said. The facts speak for themselves."

"Do you mind if I conjecture?"

"Be my guest."

"Yes, what Karen said is true, or was true back in our time. But there is also one thing you should know. Ed observed a universe of galaxies speeding away from themselves faster than the laws of physics could explain. So his gang came up with a solution to that problem: change the laws of physics, with not one piece of evidence to back their conclusion.

"I have a problem with that. Dark matter is a gray zone, a numbers game, just as make-believe as string theory spaghetti."

"That's enough, Andre," Karen said. "Theoretical hypothesis always precedes documentation. There is no reason to double Professor Keebler's findings."

"There is if Hank says so."

"What, Hank?" Karen uttered, bearing down on him. "What is Andre talking about?"

"Well, Karen…Commander…ma'am…it's just that our data out here most definitely does prove that the universe has started to slow down."

"Brad, have you seen this data?" Karen said, attempting to sound unimpressed.

"I have, and it's very confusing."

"If I may," Andre began, "some black holes are only two miles wide, others larger than Earth's entire solar system. Nothing escapes them—not protons, not electrons, not photons—only the most powerful radiation. Gravity sucks in every substance we know… except gravity itself.

"How can gravity reach out beyond itself to affect the entire universe? The answer is…it uses the back door. Ed was quick to publish his theory because no one had figured out how gravity works in the first place, or why or how mass exits in the first place. The answer to mass is it doesn't exist. It's reverse-image energy rubber bands, connected to the metaphysical dimension that we have witnessed, and Hank's numbers prove."

Andre took a step closer to Hank, crossed his arms, and waited. After looking around and finding all eyes on him, Hank took the handoff. "OK, now...I'll just tell ya all what I know, that's all. Now then, you can do what you want. I won't be the one to shoe the wrong horse."

Hank used his pad, easily equal to Andre's, to holograph his explanation. "Every thousand years, another black hole forms somewhere in the universe from old stars pulled together. My numbers, and our observations, prove that entire galaxies will not only end up a single hole but mate with other galaxies one by one, pulling the full mass of the universe back into itself, at ground zero, where the last Bang began."

"There you have it," Andre said, unable to control his enthusiasm. "The energy inside black holes is faster than light, which means its beyond time, and—here's the clincher—that state of energy feeds directly over to the metaphysical grid that is tied to every particle and every form of energy we know, providing mass and force.

"Bang and crunch...bang and crunch. Nietzsche was right... eternity recycles itself!"

"I don't buy it," Karen rebutted, "but we'll add your flimflam to the other one hundred guesses that were discarded by the Novel committee."

Hank shook his head. "I'm sorry, ma'am, but the numbers do prove that black holes lose mass and energy over time in far greater quantities than the radiation bouncing from the surface—it must go somewhere. And we just experienced a stronger, tighter grid than we did back home. The grid will win. I'm convinced that it's God's plan, and you can say what you want, and stomp all you want...I'm not messing with the big guy."

"Can it, Hank?" Sarah blasted. "None of this has anything to do with us finding a home."

"Or," Andre said, confident that he would control his own destiny one way or another, "Sarah, we could try thinking for thirty more seconds, which is less than it takes to notice that we're in the thick of the grid, surrounded by fortifying black holes. All we have to do is travel outside the grid or to its wimpy edge, and we can do anything we want."

Brad left Karen's side to powwow next to Andre and Hank. "Holy crap. So you're saying that if we fly fast and hard, as far away from the universe as possible, running the clock trillions of years ahead, then out there, in the middle of absolute nowhere, we will be able to turn around?"

"Oh, I wouldn't say trillions," Andre said, lifting his hand with a tilt. Thirty-five billion should do."

"But," Brad said turning further from Karen, "once we're out there, how the hell will we know which direction to return? We'd need a lodestar."

Andre leaned in to shrink the huddle. "No problem. We follow the furthest photon, the one that shot straight out from the Bang and never stopped. It will point the way when it heads back, which it must, because there is no other way to conserve entropy."

"No, no, no!" Sarah cried, jumping to her feet to pull Hank away. "A thousand times no! Half of Andre's science is baloney, and the other half olive loaf! You have no tests, no prototypes…just funny numbers no one understands, except Andre, who lies.

"Forget science! We have absolute truth. If the Bible says the world ends, then it ends! That's all there is to it!"

Andre stood to signal closure.

"So there you have it, crew—build bungalows in paradise or head off on another half-wild goose chase. You have heard Karen and Sarah's advice. You also know that Michael, Sheila, and I are leaving in a year when your new world is up and running. Think it over and let Karen know by noon tomorrow.

"However, it's not a vote. Everyone will get to do whatever they are most comfortable with, regardless of the split. Stay or leave. Talk it over. Have a nice day.

"Cyber, end ship wide transmission."

Sarah planted her feet and crossed her arms. "Have a nice trip, Andre. Hank and I will be raising babies on our farm. Don't forget to write."

"Certainly, Sarah. Whatever you wish. You're making a safe decision."

Michael moved to Sarah's side. "I'm not happy about leaving you behind. You're basing your decision on fables and leaving Hank out of the discussion."

Hank took the hint and had no choice, since the entire group put him in the spotlight again. "Well, okay," he began quietly, "I do have a few things I'd like to share with y'all. And you know I don't philosophize, or go on about politics, but I know when the barns on fire, and something's missing here.

"The plaque in the hall o' our Baptist church traces our family back hundreds of years. I do love Ma and Pop dearly, but I also know that everything they told me growing up...well...gosh darn it, its just ain't so. I wrested that thought for months my freshman year o' college. Then my roommate showed me these two paragraphs—"

With that, Hank pulled up holographic display:

> His mother was a mortal virgin, his father was God.
>
> He was born in a humble cowshed on December 25 before three shepherds. He was called the Son of God when he triumphantly entered town on a donkey as the crowd waved palm leaves.
>
> During his life, he turned water into wine, baptized followers, and promised eternal life, among other things. He was insulted, beaten, and put to death to atone for the sins of the world. On the third day, He rose from the dead and ascended to heaven, but not before promising to return on Judgment Day.
>
> His followers celebrate his death and resurrection with a ritual meal of bread and wine, symbolizing His body and blood—and to quote from historical record: "He who will not eat of my flesh and drink of my blood, so that he will

be made one with me and I with him, the same
shall not know salvation…"

"Back at the dorm, I said, 'Of course that's my savior Jesus
Christ.' I was wrong. The words were Plato's version that Christianity
copied. Then I learned the Greeks inherited the story from Egypt.

"The passion of Osiris was the original, re-spiced local flavor as
Dionysus in Greece, Attis in Asia Minor, Adonis in Syria, Bacchus in
Italy, Mithras in Persia, and Jesus in Jerusalem. Everyone a cardboard
cutout.

"Sarah, my point is that what you call Bible stores aren't Bible
stories at all. They're plagiarized Egyptian folklore, that one posy
after another put their brand on. Even the seven-day creation fable
began Hindu before it passed through Greek hands.

"And our beginnings? Adam and Eve were Babylonian charac-
ters the Hebrews adopted, along with Sabattu, day of rest. The zinger
for me was discoverin' that the concept of sin and the prediction of
the end of the world are pagan tales Christianity also lassoed."

"And to be fair," Janie added, "many of the words my Muslim
ancestors claimed Muhammed said have been traced back hundreds
of years earlier."

"So, Sarah," Hank finished, "I hate to see you upset like this,
darlin', but yer obsessin' over nonsense. God doesn't gift us identity
an' then take it away. I'm certain that our existence an' the universe
He gave us, both go on forever.

"And I love my choir. I miss Baptists. I want to go home."

Sarah stuffed her hands in her pockets, looking at Hank
sideways.

"I have a question for you, Sarah," Michael said, attracting
friendly fire. "If, on the way home from class, you saw a ten-foot
bunny rabbit jump over a two-inch elephant, which then sprouted
wings and flew away, wouldn't you include that in you next letter
home?

"There are no eyewitness reports to the life of Jesus. The nearest
account we have is the book of Thomas, recorded several decades

later. The quotes outline the philosophy of Jesus but never once mention a single miracle.

"Neither did Paul, alias Caesar sympathizer Saul. If Paul didn't include them, then for my money, they never happened. None of what we were told about the ancient past is true. Every gospel is a forgery that showed up a hundred years later, with presto changes and Dionysus stamped on the cover. No one knows who added those tales, but we do know why.

"Now we know better. That is why God has handed us an enormous responsibility. We must write our own holy book and, this time, get it right."

By the time Michael finished, Sheila was standing beside him holding him tight.

"Sarah," she said, "faith must never be beyond the reach of rational criticism. Childhood metaphors can do a lot of damage. One misconception of absolute truth is all it takes to close a mind. Life is itself, not something else. We women have worn the badge of guilt too long."

When they stood up, Andre wondered why Sheila's Tibetan robe was see-through and Michael's wasn't—something Andre was grateful for twice.

"Einstein," Andre said, "once said that the most incomprehensible thing about the universe is that it is comprehensible. Fuzzy 'facts' don't make a premise. Fraud damages knowledge. Arbitrary invention is not needed. Life has meaning all by itself. Too many accept 'void as meaning rather than be void of meaning.'"

Sheila ignored Andre's words and approached Sarah. "I'm a practicing Buddhist. We believe that to love God is to search for God, who inspired Jesus to preach the gospel of forgiveness and brotherly love.

"Like Hank, I was away at school when I learned of all the shenanigans that were dressed up as truth. Like Hank, I had cherished the stories since childhood. I was devastated. My belief in God was challenged, set adrift, for no fault of my own.

"Then I asked myself, 'Sheila,' I said, 'does your faith in God and love for Jesus depend on every night time story you've ever heard being true?' 'Of course not,' was my answer. Right there, on the floor of our youth chapel, I dropped to my knees and prayed Jesus guide me. I arose with happiness in my soul, embracing the spirit of Christ as never before."

Hank backed away, waiting for the tide to change. Michael and Andre were thrilled that Sheila was halfway between them and Sarah, again for two reasons.

"Is it me," Brad said, looking at the guys, "or is all this a little weird?"

Andre gently nodded agreement. "The best opinion," he whispered, "follows considering every opinion."

Sheila, Karen, and Sarah left discussing spiritual mysteries, leaving Hank and Brad free for a round of poolside mini golf. Andre returned to Buddha, intrigued that a man, so long ago, saw through the disguise of tradition. Janie, who missed nothing, bystander peaceful all afternoon, moved next to Andre.

"Do you think Buddha really was that fat?" she asked. "And always smiling?"

"Fat? No. He spent his life walking from village to village. Smiling? Yeah, maybe. I heard he liked to sing. Probably would have his own band today."

"So it's Friday night singles night. What do you want to do?"

Janie moved off, gave Andre space, and then faced him.

"What do *you* want to do?"

"The truth?"

"That's a good start."

"I never thought I'd say this, but floating through time and space has my brain washed out. I just want a day to be a day again."

"And what do you want to do with this day?"

"Do I still have to be honest?"

"I insist."

"For the next two hours, the only detail I want to attend is getting a squash ball to the wall and back. You're welcome to join me if you like. After that, I plan to follow a healthy salad with five appetizers and three sugar-dripping deserts. If you're there, I'll double the order."

"So far I'm with you. That brings us to club time. What's next?"

Andre looked up at Buddha then said, "On the way over, a fella in the park teased me about a certain jiggling that I've become quite fond of lately. I smiled, that moment wanting to hug someone. That someone was you. Do you think there is something wrong with me?"

"I *know* there's something wrong with you, so what's new?"

A relaxed Andre faced Janie. "Michael has his own room now, so I guess my place could be considered a bachelor pad. Two plans appeal to me. The first is watching a romantic comedy in your room. The second is trampoline time in mine, followed perhaps by Cyber recommending a new position, in addition to the others of course."

Janie stepped closer to him. They embraced.

"Let's keep Cyber out of this."

As they walked away, Andre turned one last time to read the inscription beneath the statue:

## *Siddhartha Gautama*

*Believe not because some old manuscripts are produced,*
*Believe not because it is your national belief,*
*Believe not because you have been made to believe from childhood,*
*But reason truth out, and after you have analyzed it,*
*Then if you find it will do good to one and all, believe it*
*Live up to it and help others to live up to it.*

# 17

## Long Strange Trip

"Morning, Karen."

"Morning Sarah, and thanks for leaving the 'good' out. It's annoying to hear, day after day, the same old thing—good morning, good morning, good grief—it's annoying."

"Almost as annoying as hearing 'What's so good about it? What's so good about it?"

Sarah and Karen weren't alone. The sensory deprivation of not being surrounded by existence took its toll on everyone. Morning manners faded months ago. They were replaced by cantankerous, irritable, and grouchy.

Sarah wore gray sweatpants, a black baggy jacket, and worn-down sandals, her hair in God-knows-what condition under a three-toned Rastafarian cap. Karen, professionally clean but oh so dull, wore a full-body leisure suit beneath hair that said, "Two rubber bands are as far as I'm willing to go."

Months ago, feeling like years, Sarah had Cyber broadcast 'Home on the Range' when *Explorer Seven* passed the last Earth-sized blue planet on their way out. No one took the bait. Only two other crew members added their names to Sarah's and Karen's. It would have been a small town.

Then there was the bluff. Karen and Sarah told the guys, in no uncertain terms, that they were not leaving. Karen ordered the crew to draft plans for New Earth. The ladies were sure if they built a luxury resort the entire crew would change their minds and stay.

In private, they even discussed—discussed only, mind you—popping out babies before the build-up ended. Janie refused to go along with it. They didn't bother to approach Sheila.

"So," Sarah said, sliding beside Karen already seated at a breakfast booth, "whose turn is it to pick the adjective and saying of the day?"

"Well, yesterday, mine was lonely…only losers leave everything, and everybody, behind."

"My best last week was despondent…we're better off dead," Sarah recalled.

"Mine beat that—frustrated—fuck you, fuck them, fuck me."

"That one backfired when the guys preferred literal translation, but it was a fun, long day."

"Ya, we've had some great times out here," Karen said facing the wall to smile.

"Don't say that to the guys. They deserve the hot seat a little longer. After all, if they really do love us, something they profess day and night, but mostly nights, they would've stayed. After all, every day we do hear 'You're the most important thing in the universe.'"

"Ya, except the universe itself. Or three missing numbers on their favorite equation."

Sarah sat back, overcome by calm she hadn't expected. "You know, Karen, it just dawned on me. The boys were bluffing too. We caved early. I remember the morning you told Brad 'What the heck.'

"We didn't take it to the ninth hour. They wouldn't have left without us. They would have stayed."

Karen and Sarah shared a sly look, neither one admitting that they were perhaps not totally honest to each other about leaving. "So," Karen said, "you might say that we did know they wouldn't leave us. And that's why we 'gave in,' which means you and I actually decided what the entire crew would do, since they would never leave Andre, Michael, and Brad. It wouldn't be safe."

"Well then," Sarah said, giving Sarah a manly handshake, "you and I, as always, are running this ship, and get whatever we want."

"Because we deserve it…and not so loud."

"Okay, let's work on our negative feedback loop a while longer," Sarah said, trying hard not to smile. "How about this one, idiots—what were we thinking? We could be on New Earth right now walking surfboards to the beach."

"My turn," Karen said. "Brainless, fool me once, shame on you. Fool me four months in a row, shame on us, turn this damn ship around and set us down on a black rock. If you can find one."

"Too long," Sarah said. "Needs to be pithy. How about *man*, short for *maniacs*. Never let them talk you into anything."

"Speaking of the fools, where are they?"

"Same old, same old. Bruce called. They lost the last photon again. Andre, Brad, and Hank left for the bridge to look for it."

"I've had enough of this photon crap," Karen huffed. Then with mocking tone she mimicked, "Where did it go? There it is, on the other side…oh no, that's dandruff."

Sarah joined in, putting both open hands to her face to dramatize perplexity. "Is it turning? Is it getting smaller? What if it disappears? Don't tell Karen we haven't the slightest idea what the hell we're doing."

After a muffled chuckle, the two ladies turned their attention to ham and eggs.

"My father used to say," said Sarah between bites, "that when something must be done, doing nothing is torture. When we do nothing, we are nothing.

"Like the story about the businessman who wanted to sail around the world single-handed. He sold his company, designed a boat, packed it with months of supplies, including Christmas presents, and cast off.

"He faced mounting seas and blasting Antarctic winds. He rode out gales tethered to the rail. There were times when waves slapped so ferociously he cowered below deck. There were times when he prayed for just one hour of sleep as he drifted lost in fog, and yet, his spirit remained strong…until that week that he sat becalmed and motionless—it almost killed him. In the end, he resisted despair and returned to set a world's record.

"Waiting followed by more waiting is a torture beating hearts ill endure."

"I get the message, Shakespeare," Karen said. "We're doing nothing while we should be turning around to eke out existence on what's left of a dead universe—that is, if the boobs can even find it."

"Exactly, Karen," Sarah said, placing her hand on Karen's. "Officially, you are still in command and have the codes to make it so."

"You're right," Karen said, resigned and fighting bitterness for fate. "I'll make the announcement first thing in the morning."

"So what do we do today?"

"The usual," Karen sighed. "Overeat, visit the spa, play tennis, skin dive, roller blade, and let the fellows dine and dance us to bed again—life could be worse."

"Let's double-glaze fried donuts as soon as Janie announces the beginning of Earth Day."

Janie did what she could to boost morale, that day using force fields to divide the main auditorium into three separate zones: northern, tropical, and temperate. It snowed on Buddha, where nearby, with the help of gravity belts, couples skied fresh powder. There was even a ski lodge with sandwiches, hot chocolate, and apple pie.

The other half of the wooded park offered a crisp fall day, complete with foliage, pine tree trails for hiking, and crew members warming their feet in front of an artificial fireplace, which kept the wilderness cabin warm as they enjoyed hot soup and hearty beef stew.

Sarah and Karen opted for the tropics—forward pool section, where reggae and calypso played all day.

Janie left the dancefloor to stand on top of an island-orange picnic table. Her hair was center parted and perfectly set as it cascaded over both shoulders. Not new to the scene were her net shirt and sheer bikini that left nothing to the imagination.

"We have drums," she sang out. "We have barbecue! We get you wasted, Mom, we get you horny, Mom, we get you anything you want. It's happy-island fun morning, ski the Alps afternoon. Hell, rake leaves if you want! Welcome to Earth Day!"

Janie jumped off the table to applause. She stopped just short of the pool at the sound of music blaring, that she had not scheduled.

> First you pick your leader, then we'll show you how
> The bunny hop is definitely fun, fun, fun.
> Right one touch, right one again, left one touch,
> left one again
> Hop up
> Hop back
> Hop, hop, hop
> Put your right foot out twice, your left foot too
> Jump around the room signing Woo, Woo, Woo

Tall Michael led the parade, followed by Brad, Hank, and even Andre dancing his heart out. Janie skipped to Andre's rear, adding one more link to the dancing train, followed by the entire room joining in, even Karen and Sarah bringing up the rear, after they broke up at the uproarious spectacle.

After the second revolution, Brad jumped onto Janie's table. "I have news of our pet photon Pete. We found him! He's still holding on to energy and…the reason we had such a hard time finding him was that he's heading back! The crunch has begun! We're on our way home!"

Brad waited for the booming applause to end, which was accompanied by continuous hooting. "We are so far out that dark nothingness and the thin canyon walls made Pete impossible for you to magnify back here, but from the bridge, we watched him clear as day. Then stayed trans and spun time and space effortlessly."

"Just one thing," Andre spoke up. "Be patient. Our time travel back will be slow and even. Steady as she goes lowers the risk of wobbling out of trans, and I never…ever…triple never want to do this again. And we won't. Because *we did it!*"

"We're going home! We're going home! We're going home!" the crew chanted.

For the first time, finally on their way home, Earth Day started. Michael took off for the slopes. Hank and Sarah went apple picking hand in hand. Brad was finally free to join Karen for a day at the spa. Andre held out his hand, inviting Janie to join him on a hammock to gaze out at space, finally moving in the right direction.

\* \* \*

When you're young, an afternoon qualifies as a one-night stand, a week makes a fling, a month serious commitment, and a year—an old couple. Michael, publicly half of an old couple, joined Andre, charter member of the club, for breakfast the morning the ship saw, and passed the furthest galaxy, one of billions returning in rewind to the Bang.

"Top of the morning to you, science guy," Michael said, sitting down. "Was that you in the lab last night?"

"Yes, and we're right on schedule. Twenty-four hours from now, the Bang will be at our doorstep. It's been a long six months."

"That only took you two seconds to say. What's with the overtime?"

"The closer we get, the more complicated atomic interactions become. It's all I can do to keep up with yesterday's calculations."

"Hey, you drafted half the crew to help you. Do you have a single empty seat?"

"No, but anytime you feel like lending a hand, feel free to drop in. Speaking of dropping in, I haven't seen you with Sheila lately. What's up?"

Michael looked around, inched his chair closer to Andre, and dropped his voice. "If you promise to keep a dozen secrets, I'll give you the lowdown."

"Consider it done."

"Six weeks ago, Hank showed up at the Starlight Lounge for singles night. Since then, he has returned every week with Julie, Sarah's top chief."

"I see. And does Sarah know Hank and Julie are doing it?"

"She knows what Friday night out means, but she doesn't know it's her friend Julie, who is from the south. She and Hank share rhythms. They're totally infatuated with each other. It's just a matter of time until the two rebels join you old folks upstairs every Friday night."

Andre leaned over, implications dawning.

"So, Sarah…roving as well?"

"Not exactly. She and I spend every Friday night in my room."

"What happened to 'delicious Sheila' and all-you-can-eat Friday nights?"

"Hey, Sheila is hot, and we get along just fine, but she goes home with a different guy every week and then tells me all about it."

"I thought that was against the rules."

"It is!"

"And she knows that," Andre pronounced with disapproval, "which means she's doing the sly female thing, driving you crazy so you leave…so she can get brownie points from the ladies, make herself out to be the victim. In other words, she wants out…but may not be admitting it to herself?"

"As is her right…to live as relaxed and unscheduled as she pleases. But she could have just come out and say it. God knows, everyone's been there. Anyway, I'm good, even better. Sarah has taken over my heart. And I love it."

"Wait a minute," Andre responded, not sold, "what happened to 'sex is the most important thing there is'?"

"Well, Andre," Michael said, feelings exposed, "sex *is* the *first most* important thing, which has been a given since men and women began using willful behavioral disinhibition to free ourselves from cultural repression, so that we're now free to pursue the *second most* important thing in life…spending time with someone kind, intelligent, and funny, who gets you, cares for you, and…kinda knows your thoughts."

"So you're in love with Sarah…perhaps. Does that mean you're all grown up now?"

"I certainly hope not. Just don't tell anyone."

Andre signaled the mouth zipper before asking, "What about Brad? Is he playing? Karen also on the town?"

"Ah, this is where it gets sticky, and you've really gotta keep this to yourself. Brad is totally clean. He never goes clubbing. He's at Karen's side whenever its appropriate. He does all the right things. He's a boy scout, but…"

"But…?"

"When I'm around you, Andre, I sense sensual passions—yours for Janie, your steady girl. However, guys who are spontaneous in many directions give off heightened sensuality…gourmet appreci-ations. Every woman in sight becomes more beautiful, their appeal irresistible.

"I felt that around Brad in the company of ladies when he boarded, and for a while when he settled down with Karen," Michael said as he looked back and forth. "But as of six weeks ago, Brad's bonfire is back, and I don't know who she is. The ladies are hard for me to read, but don't tell them. They share more with me if they think I have a hint."

Michael sat back, looking as if normal conversation was being exchanged. "I do know this about Karen. She's a free spirit. She wouldn't want to hold Brad back if that was his desire, and feelings are feelings. Besides, you see the faces she makes every time Brad says something stupid. My, my."

"I'm beginning to believe," Andre said smoothly, "that the Buddhists are right when they say 'Everything that happens, happens for the best.'"

"Hello, Andre," Cyber was heard saying from nowhere, as always. "Michael, you asked me to remind you about you-know-what…you know when."

"Yes…thanks," Michael said, jumping up. "Sorry Andre, gotta go. S…uh…duty…calls. See ya later. Just remember, mum's the word!"

When Michael was out of sight, Andre said, "Cyber, you're waiting for me to talk aren't you?"

"I already ran the scans."

"Analyzing Brad and female proximity? And unaccounted mutual space over the last six weeks?"

Andre lifted his pad to look. "Cyber, next, double-delete the results, and keep no copies. Also…message the kitchen to deliver lox, bagels, fruit plate, cheese omelet, and cinnamon buns to Karen's table."

Andre and the feast arrived at the same time, just as Karen squeezed her first tea bag.

"May I join you?" Andre asked.

"Certainly. The last time you and I did this, we were in a cave. The universe is a much better view."

"That brunch is one of the highlights of the trip. A feast that ended with both of us licking plates."

Karen divided each portion in half and slid Andre his share.

"Where is Janie?"

"Sleeping late as usual. Brad?"

"Lately, he's been a log every morning."

Andre noticed Karen's left auditory canal was dull blue. "You aren't," he asked, smiling knowingly, "by chance using ear tags to eavesdrop, are you?"

"Well," she said sheepishly, "this is a public space. Everyone sitting at the next table listens in whether they want to or not. Besides, I couldn't resist. I think the couple behind us is fighting about God, a frequent subject these days."

"Well," Andre said, "we do have an appointment with creation tomorrow. Cyber, tie me into Karen's pickup."

* * *

Without turning around to look, an advantage Karen had from the corner, Andre heard an unidentified male voice say, "There are things in life that you should respect, and that's one of them."

"There's no need to get bent out of shape. I only asked you why," replied the female.

"Because that's what I believe, that's why. Why don't you get that, woman?"

"Saying you believe something isn't an answer. It's an excuse not to answer, to refuse thinking altogether, to not use brains for what God made them for. Check the dictionary, the definition for believing is identical to what follows stupidity."

"Oh, so now I'm stupid?"

"No. Refusing to explain your conclusion only makes you stubborn," the female voice jeered. "Stupidity comes later, when you fail to justify your opinion, that you disguise as a belief, which in your case, apparently, has no rational basis."

"And," he said raising his voice, believing his tone justified, "some people are believers, and some people aren't."

"And some people were brainwashed since childhood to think *believers* are the good people and *nonbelievers* all go to hell, a propaganda tool more effective than burning books. You graduated first grade a long time ago. It's time to grow up."

"I'm tired of this conversation," he said with finality. "I don't have to justify myself."

"Oh yes, you do! We all do."

"Okay, okay," he said, settling down, after noticing eyes three tables over looking, "I have a suggestion. Let's discuss this again after dinner. For now, and the rest of our day off, why don't we just agree that you believe ketchup has no right to be on scrambled eggs, and I believe it does?"

\* \* \*

Karen and Andre laughed. "Oh, I didn't expect that!" she exclaimed.

Those seated around Andre and Karen heard their fun, and turned wondering. "Now my turn." Andre said picking up a miniature cinnamon bun and tossing it at Karen, who opened her mouth wide to go along with the diffusion. She caught the bun neatly, swallowed, and raised both arms in victory, which brought laughter to four more tables.

Karen and Andre turned their attention to more sugary goodies. Neither made a move to leave when they were done.

Finally, Andre ran his hands through his hair, leaving it a bit messy, then looked over to Karen with vulnerable dog eyes saying, "You know, Karen, it's wonderful that we don't have to hold back our real selves anymore."

"Yes Andre," she said, trying not to look too pleased, "it's refreshing. We all get so hung up on who we're supposed to be, how we're supposed to act, and what social strategies will gain us ground, that we lose ourselves. Every day back on earth, I treated good people who had lost themselves and control over their own lives, because they did everything they were 'supposed' to do, ending up with nothing for themselves, which, ironically, left even less for others."

"Okay, absolutely," Andre said, grinning, as he noticed Karen's eyes wonder to another table, "and now you're about to spin those observations into invading someone else's privacy? Who are you looking at?"

"Shhh, quiet down. You have to use the right words if we're going to get away with this. And whatever you do…don't turn around. The red-headed guy five tables over just set down a bound copy of the Bible. I just have to know what that's all about."

Andre groaned. "The Bible again? You know that's asking for trouble."

"What's the big deal? I already know you prefer Dr. Seuss to the New Testament."

"Okay, I'll jack into your tags one last time. You know, I'd kicked the habit, thanks to you, and now I'm back, thanks to you."

\* \* \*

"Are we having book for breakfast?" a female voice asked.

"Carl has never seen a hard copy of the Holy Bible," came the masculine reply, "so I said I'd bring mine in to work. Careful! You just spilled orange juice on it! Don't be such a klutz!"

"For heaven's sake, calm down, it's just a book. Leftover trees."

"Just a book? It's the word of God!"

"Really?" the lass said slowly, knowing her powder was fresh and his spitball clogged. "So it was God who said a man who keeps a mistress is not committing adultery, but a woman who touches a man's penis shall have her hand cut off. How does that work? And what about the part where God said that any bride who's not a virgin must die?

"And the early women's movement blamed men less for being sexist knuckleheads after they realized it was their mom's who took them to church and force-fed them Bible patriarchal bullshit at the same time they locked their daughters in bedrooms every night to play with themselves, feel guilty, and then crawl to confession on their knees, which, as it turns out, was the ministers favorite position. But according to you, it wasn't the priest's fault, it was all God's fault, because that's what 'His word' told them to do. Three thousand years of civilization, countless generations, lived in fear and died in panic, knowing hell was on other side of their final exam."

"You don't understand," the male voice protested, a repeat that dulled itself lifeless long ago.

"Someone doesn't understand, that's for sure. "Pardon me," she said, grabbing the book and flipping through to find a few choice quotes. Here it is. God, speaking through Mathew, actually not Matthew, the guy who stole his name to trick people a hundred years later, "recommends castrating yourself for Jesus, right after you put all gays, lesbians, and whores to death. Let's see," the female voice was heard saying, then after a ruffled pause, "Oh yes, here it is…Mathew also wrote, which of course would be Jesus's actual words, since it is the Bible that you tell me tells no lies, 'Think not that I am come to send peace on Earth. I have not come to send peace but a sword.'

"Matthew's coconspirator, John, the last forger to come along, was the one who added Jew hate to Christianity, as he bent over for Caesar, so he would start killing Jews to leave militarized 'Christians' running the show. A plan that required the gang John inspired to kill more honest, genuine Christians practicing Thomas's philosophy of Jesus than all the Christians that Nero, his solders, and pet lions put away.

"Anyway…where was I? Oh, yeah…John, speaking for God, of course, declared that all those who don't go along with the plan should be gathered into the fire and burnt at the stake. Those words, blessed by popes, are what justified, hell ordered from Rome, ships to sail the world to kill, rape, and enslave anyone not like themselves. In England, the Vatican sent devil snoopers to arrest, strip ladies naked, when of course they found at least one freckle that proved the woman a witch, which allowed them to get sex before burning her to death on a metal grill in front of her own children to teach them a lesson and then confiscate her entire family holdings for the church, to teach the corpse another lesson.

"Rome's storm troopers owned one third of England when the king finally looked out for his own people and started his own church, to look out for himself, and his royal family of despots.

"And the reason Jesus turned on the organized religion of his time is because they were just as bad, taking from the rich, pushing the poor back in the gutter, playing up to Caesar, and demanding the common man send them their best livestock 'sacrifices' for dinner and a virgin once a month to pleasure 'God's mission' that somehow turned into their dicks.

"No Johnny-come-lately social work or timid well-meaning smiles will ever change the past, or erase damage done. The Spanish inquisition, Rome's excuse to kill as many Jews and Muslims as they liked, didn't shut down until after Lincoln freed the slaves, and then only because the Vatican couldn't get away with it any longer.

"The paradox here is that a book that does contain many fine words of the philosophy of the man God inspired, also justified the greatest evil in history, the enslavement of fellow beings. If the Bible is God's word, someone should wash his mouth out with soap."

"I don't like your attitude one bit. I was wrong. You won't fit into my family after all."

"Thank God."

\* \* \*

Andre and Karen, both wide eyed still, turned off their tags at the same time.

"Whoa," Andre said. "What happened to arguing over the breakfast menu?"

"Have you read it?" Karen suddenly asked.

"Read what...the menu?"

"No, the Holy Bible!"

"Cover to cover...out of curiosity."

"And?"

"And...? And it was the most disappointing piece of literature I have ever read. To begin with, it's not really a book. It's more like a compilation of—what—a thousand years of guy thoughts and gal stories. Mostly just scraps off the floor.

"The Old Testament is very specific about how much gold 'God' wants on 'his' altar, whom to ambush next, and includes pages and pages of punishable laws about stuff that we know to be healthy behavior. The New Testament is incomplete, redundant, and self-contradicting. It's been said that even the devil can find passages to suit his needs...hell, Adolf did."

"They were men trying to do their best," Karen said apologetically, and tough.

"Right, absolutely..." Andre said, bobbing his head in agreement over and over. "They were men. Not gods. Men. And yes, we—yes, of course—I...am wrong to judge them by modern informed standards. But it is also wrong to pretend they were good guys. There are no good guys in past. Rotten culture infected them all, working hand in hand with greed."

"What about God's involvement with them?"

Andre palmed both hands skyward, raised his shoulders, and said, "Searching for God is an admirable quest. Hell, it's one of the reasons you and I are here today. But back home, in our time, anthropologists spent centuries shifting through sand looking for secrets from the past.

"Someone would dig up a bone box with 'hocus' on its lid. A year later, another group would unearth rocks inscribed 'pocus,' all ramblings of confused, superstitious xenophobes. The answer isn't under a microscope. It's discovered by stepping back and taking a deep breath."

"The answer, you say," Karen said. "Okay, I'll bite...what *answer* is that?"

Andre grinned. "Well, since you asked…it's impossible to find the answer that *is*, until you eliminate the answer that *isn't*. For example, the Bible and similar parchment describe an entity going by many names, country to country, generation after generation, an immortal being that men named 'God' and made male.

"Right there, I have a problem. Gender and monotheism don't fit…period. The designation makes females less consequential unless they're giving birth to more males, and a god with balls, whose sperm sprays the planet…you can't be serious!

"Then there's the time line. Eternity stretches forever in both directions. But this entity, this god of yours, presumably satisfied with himself, and eternity, is suddenly not happy sitting around by himself any longer. So one day, disobeying his own 'law' of cause and effect, he decides he needs a hobby, like building a universe and spitting out people.

"What changed? And why? And why then? And why construct it the way he did? What was wrong with floating around nowhere without a headache?

"Anyway, according to the story, this god guy, guy, guy…crams the job into six days then gets tired—tired, mind you—Mr. All Powerful, who can do anything, is winded…and takes the seventh day off to rest and then retires. It's the worst work ethic I have ever heard."

"You don't understand—" Karen started to get out, before Andre finished his story.

"Oh, I don't, do I? Let's see. As it turns out, this guy of yours does shoddy work! The creatures he makes are selfish, rude, and violent, just the way he made.

"So what happens next? God gets pissed off! At himself for screwing up the job? Oh no, heaven forbid. He gets mad at human beings, who of course must be punished. 'It's all your fault. You made me do it.' Which is the same message Adolf had stamped on cyanide tablets. It's a total copout.

"So I ask you, what kind of person or being, labeled 'caring creator,' waits forever to do something, tries once, is disappointed, blames his failure on his own creation, and then refuses to try again?"

"Andre," Karen said, hiding irritability mounting, "you must take historical predicaments into account."

"You mean, like warfare or give me your gold…or I'm going to kill you because the pope says you're going to hell anyway so I'm killing you to save God the bother?"

"No, like they didn't know better."

"That I buy, so why are we still dragging their corpses behind us?"

"We must keep the word of God alive."

"Well, when you find it, let me know. And you're a psychologist trained in the workings of the mind. The so-called god character portrayed in the mislabeled 'Holy Scriptures' has a violent, unresolved multiple-personality disorder. Only a psycho could be so confused that he fills up a planet with people and then fills it up with water to kill them off. Death is the worst use to put a human being to and murder the worst example to set for others. That is not the role model I want for my children."

"Are you done?" Karen asked impatiently.

"Not even close! The Bible is also totally scary. It describes a crazed, out-of-control, egocentric sadist who allows the brutal murder of his own 'son' and then makes every unborn child on the planet pay for it. What kind of a person builds an eternal maximum-security torture chamber to get his rocks off?

"What kind of person? I'll tell you what kind of person. No kind of person, never was, never will be—your God is the invention of blaggards.

"Don't get me wrong. I'm not saying this God character doesn't exist. I'm just saying that if he does, his MO got really screwed up by opportunists, political prostitution, and mortal profit. You've been bamboozled.

"The Bible is a hoax, its claim to authority ludicrous, its plagiarized spirituality perverted. Jesus was right. The kingdom of God is not found beneath brick and mortar."

Karen jumped to her feet. "You have no right rejecting an entire belief system like you're better than God himself! Andre, you're an idiot!"

Karen fled the room as forty diners shot Andre a now-what-did-you-do look.

"In the end," Andre called out after her, "it's not us who need to be saved…it's God!"

# 18

## Knocking on Heaven's Door

A ndre and Karen boarded *Explorer Seven* with identities wrapped and bowed, complete in every way—one surrounded by atoms, asking no more; the other swaddled since birth, insisting that there is no more. That changed.

After Andre bombed at breakfast, he retreated to the lab, where twelve variables took him down big time. Bang Zero was on the horizon—not a good time for protons, neutrons, quarks, and a thousand fuzzy fragments to develop minds of their own.

Andre stared at his screen for hours, silent hours that got nowhere. He was waiting for his brain to get it together. It didn't.

He was relieved to get Michael's call inviting him to play squash.

"Thanks for coming down," Michael said as Andre hobbled onto court one. "I was looking forward to a match when Eric cancelled."

Andre meticulously closed the hall door behind him, as if attention to detail made more sense out of life. He didn't look at Michael; staring at the floor was more soothing. He also didn't set up behind the baseline. Instead, he plopped down against the sidewall to stare at air. Michael sat opposite him and waited.

"Do you realize," Andre ventured after a lengthy silence, "that if the ratio of matter-energy to space volume is one-quadrillionth of one percent off tomorrow the entire universe will collapse back on itself?"

"I thought the margin of safety was higher?"

"So did I until a few hours ago. And there's more...a mere one percent extra gravity will condense stars that fire up so fiercely that every light in the universe will burn itself out in less than a year. Runaway relativity means that second and third generation suns will never appear...that is, if matter gets a chance to condense from energy in the first place.

"And," Andre continued distraught, "less intranuclear force, so minute I can't even measure it, could attenuate subatomic particles into vapor without igniting a single star, and even if none of those catastrophes occur, a minor impedance of nuclear resonance would block carbon from forming, making life impossible."

Michael scooted across the floor to sit directly in front of Andre. "Hey, you knew all that before we took off. What's the problem?"

"The problem is that I was sure I would identify regulators of some kind by now. Cyber keeps coming back with the odds of Bang Zero working to be one in ten to the three-hundredth power, which means it's simply not possible."

"And yet we know it did work because we're watching it in reverse right now. And you and I exist."

"Michael, you don't understand. Listen to me..." Andre said, slumping further, head against the wall. "I've haven't solved a single equation! I won't be able to balance the ship's power grid tomorrow, which means energy will leak through and sear us good. And how the hell is the universe here in the first place? It's not just complicated. It's unworkable!"

Michael opened his mouth to placate then shut it slowly. Andre took that as encouragement to keep going.

"And that's not all. There's no reason," Andre said, no less disturbed, "why the laws of science have to be the laws of science, or for that matter, as precise as they are.

"It has taken me hours of work and years of my life, but there is only one conclusion to be reached, and that is that I'm an idiot...and a fool. Karen has been right all along. Someone is pulling the strings. The universe has a manager…"

"What are you saying, Andre?"

"That energy is directed, designed slot by slot, for a least three-trillionths of a second following Bang Zero. Creation is molded by an independent, intention-motivated, goal-directed transdimensional entity.

"Michael," Andre said, wiping unstable tears from his face, which confused Michael, since Andre was also smiling relief, "there is God, Michael. God exists!"

Michael nodded. "You'll get no argument from me, and we're here to learn…but you've got to get it together, Andre. I'm certain that the closer we get to showtime, the easier it will be to read the writing on the wall.

"Meanwhile…stay loose, Andre. You can do it, and you're not alone. We've been on the ropes before. For now, you listen to me. Do as I say. First, stop thinking about it—give your brain a break. Clear your mind. Work up a sweat.

"Then," Michael said, pulling Andre to his feet from the arm he extended to him, "pod down and sleep until your scanner reads 100 percent neural efficiency. Follow that with dinner, two desserts, and a long walk. You'll be fine. Everything will work out."

Andre groaned, won two matches Michael handed him, and headed for the showers.

* * *

"Thanks for coming," Michael said two hours later. "I was looking forward to a match when Eric cancelled."

Karen stood mid-court, wearing cowboy boots, bell-bottom jeans, and a wrist-flared white shirt beneath free-swinging long hair. Hands on hip, riveted motionless, she said, "Thirty guys stand in line to topple you from squash, top dog. I didn't buy your line when you called, and I don't buy it now. Why do you want me here? Is it about the fight Andre and I had this morning?"

"Hey, the entire ship is talking. You raised your voice, bad form. How is the crew supposed to trust Andre with their lives after you yell at him? We need him at his best. Cut the guy some slack. He's in the middle of a personality crisis."

"Yeah, well…he's not the only one," said Karen as she slid down the wall to the floor, to sit in the same spot Andre occupied.

Michael extended brows-up concern, "What are you talking about, Karen?"

Karen rested her chin on her drawn-up knees. "You know, it's a funny thing…all those stories I was told years ago by my parents, repeated by clergy once a week. I knew they were imprecise, exaggerated, and sketchy. It's just that they're all we have…and I cling to them. Not just out of respect, or loyalty…but because I want to believe them. They add order to life.

"But Andre is right. No fable deserves adoration. Faith needs more…what I no longer possess. Last night, I woke up in a chill, and realized…there is no god!"

Michael smiled sympathetically, "Wow, this is a day that will go down in history. Andre believes in God, and you don't…or so you say. And for the record, I don't believe you."

Michael stayed put at the baseline but sat facing Karen. "Let me tell you about my last surprise. Earlier today, I overhead Andre say to his assistant Liz, 'Don't hold man's imperfections against God.' Karen, do you believe it? Mad-dog atheist Professor Martin was preaching. He defended the immortal being he'd spent his life denying.

"You did it, Karen! You got through to him. The last thing I heard him say to his lab buddies was 'God is doing the best He can. Our best can help.'"

"Really," Karen said with a smirk, "the best he can? Andre and I losing it over breakfast is his best work?"

"Every day is a work in progress. And we are all on the job. Give yourself the credit you deserve."

"Huh."

"And you've got to hand it to the guy. Once he gets rolling, all kinds of stuff connect inside. Andre is certain God exists transdimensionally, like we travel, and is also aware of all of eternity at the same time. Consider the implications. God didn't just create us and set us loose to see what happens later. He knows the ending up front and how to make us independent assistants to keep existence on track. God is counting on us. God is counting on you. We are not going to let him down!"

Karen paused, hopping that she might again agree with her feelings.

"If all that is true, then Christianity, or Paulianity as you like to call it, is total malarkey, blind guess work. You might as well throw out ninety percent of the Bible."

"*Yes!*" Michael agreed emphatically. "Along with ninety percent of all religious tales, which leaves us free to combine what's left over and live on…to finally get to where God wants us to be. Hey, it works for me. And it's beginning to work for Andre. I never thought I'd see the day.

"And you're the one who did it! You turned Andre into a new man. I don't know when. I don't know how. But I do know that on behalf of the human race, you deserve a big hug.

"This also means that we have a chance to stay alive. Make peace with Andre. Lead us home, commander."

"I'm not there, Michael. It's too much."

"Okay. So then table the issue until we crack the bank wide open. Waste not one thought on the matter until then. You love the water…spend a few hours swimming to your favorite tunes. Then feast with poster-boy Brad and enjoy the night. You'll do fine. Everything will work out."

Karen climbed to her feet and headed for the door, sighing.

"Oh," she said just before exiting, "Sarah told me all about you two. I've never seen her so happy. I'm thrilled for you both. I'm glad someone's love life is working out."

* * *

Michael asked Andre to take his evening shift on the bridge so that he and Sarah could slip away. Andre was late, which added a second reason for Carl to give him the cold shoulder.

Hours earlier, when Andre retired to rest, the collapsing universe occupied everything in sight. When he stepped on the bridge that night, the final outer segments had passed *Explorer Seven* on their way in, and all of existence was in view, an impression that stunned Andre silent at the door.

The contracting sphere he saw looked a little like the ball that drops in Times Square on New Year's Eve—except the ball grew brighter as first-generation stars concentrated themselves in reverse, to a point, which was four hundred years before the bang, when they rejoined the womb of darkness.

"Isn't that a beautiful sight?" Andre said, shaking himself out of amazement.

As he approached the bow, a second crew member was seen casually outstretched on one of the two elevated leg-rest recliners.

"Karen, what are you doing here?"

"What do you think Cyber would find the most common theatrical line in history to be?" she asked with one eyebrow raised. "'I love you' or 'What are *you* doing here?'"

"Considering how often witless gore and low-brow violence substitutes for original drama, I'd say it's 'Hand me my gun.' We can get to that later…Cyber, which two crew members were originally scheduled for this watch?"

"Jim and Judy," Cyber reported, "replaced by Michael and Sarah before you two were substituted by request, which was accompanied by a threat to pull 'my plug' if I squealed."

Karen, also feeling ten years younger since her nap, restfully added, "Looks like we've been set up. Actually, I'm glad. We shouldn't have left each other the way we did this morning."

Andre leaned over the arm of her chair. "Yes, I owe you an apology."

"Just one?"

"One at a time. May I tell you a story?"

"Does it have a happy ending?"

"It does for me."

"Then by all means."

266

"Goethe's Faust is literature Shakespeare would have envied. In it, Johann tells of a materialist who is visited by the devil, who promised Faust power and unlimited riches in exchange for his eternal soul.

"Faust rewrote the wager. He was a man of learning, who knew that in the long run, power, money, even knowledge amounts to no more that conceit. Mankind's greatest weakness, Faust reasoned, is the self-flattery that possessed the rich, the powerful, and those flaunting education.

"Faust challenged the devil head on. If Mephistopheles could make such a mindless rooster out of him, then his soul would belong to the devil for all time. If not, Beelzebub would be defeated forever. The devil did his part, providing castles, beautiful women, world domination, and chemical wizardry..." Andre said, getting into the role with enthusiastic gestures, "but Faust does not succumb! He knows in the end that he is but a man, flawed yet hopeful, defeated yet never beaten, respecting others as equals, placing kindness above servitude. At the final curtain, Faust retains his soul, and the devil dies."

Karen applauded. "Just one question. In that story, are you Faust...or the devil?"

Andre got the joke and sat down, his arms bent melodramatically over his knees. "I was what Faust resisted. I was flattered by my abilities and close-minded to the opinions and feelings of others.

"To my credit, I was often right, but not always, and in no way justified pretending to be so the way I did. My way of life left me afloat, an island unto myself. If you'll let me, I'd like to return to the mainland."

Karen slipped off her chair to join him on the floor. "So I'm the mainland now? What kind of beaching do you have in mind?"

"Okay," Andre grinned sheepishly. "Perhaps my metaphors need some work. How about this one—I'll get a pail and shovel, and we'll built sand castles together."

Karen got up and stood between Andre and the bow view of the universe. "That concept carries merit. Now let me tell you a story. Once upon a time, a man and a woman set off together in search of wealth, status, and power, the devil's triangle. They argued daily about which scheme they should try next to get rich quick. Everything they tried failed.

"Rumors of gold led them to an offbeat Polynesian island, which turned into another disappointment. But that night, an old man approached with a magic lamp, saying, 'Whoever possesses this lamp will have every wish come true. But,' he said in the same breath, 'if you die with the lamp in your possession, your soul is forfeited for all eternity.'

"The lamp could not be destroyed. The only way to rid oneself of it was to sell it to another at a lower price than it was purchased, which was why the stranger was on the island with the lowest denomination coin on the planet.

"The couple bought the lamp. They wished for yachts and mansions. One year later, they ruled the world. But nothing changed. They still fought every day, and worse, their lives lost all meaning. They threw the bottle in the ocean. The next day, it was back on their bureau. They burnt it, buried it, and ran it over with a steam roller. To no avail…it always came back."

"So," Andre interrupted, "they gave up, the moral being, money and power are vacuous goals, what Faust knew all along?"

"Not exactly. That instant both accepted their doom but decided to do something about it. For the first time in their lives they thought about others, and decided to leave the world a better place. Instead of riches, they wished for universal peace and an end to discrimination and poverty. They banished evil from the hearts of man. For the first time in years, they worked as one and laughed together."

"And then suffered eternal damnation for their mistake?" Andre asked.

"Love broke the curse. The bottle shattered. Everyone lived happily ever after. I would say the moral is that power, wealth, or even knowledge must never get in the way of sharing the priceless gift of life, and nothing can stand in the way of love."

Andre tilted his head and asked, coquettish, "Was 'Best Sex Ever' one of the things they asked for?"

"That wish came true for all of us," Karen said, sliding her gaze to the side. "Don't you agree?"

"Absolutely."

Andre sprang to his feet and helped Karen up, who walked to the bow to have a look as Andre confirmed position at Hank's station. Back with her, he asked, "What made you go into psychology?"

"When I was a little girl, I loved dollhouses. Every room told a story. I had cooking dolls, computer dolls, cleaning dolls...even one outside landscaping. Every day, I would hand out assignments, for which they thanked me, of course, and we would laugh the day away.

"When I got older, I realized that adults also went to jobs every day, but they didn't have nearly as much fun as my dolls. In fact, most of them were stuck in cubicles feeling like a robot, not being themselves, and dealing with bosses. Some were frustrated, some depressed, and others just handed over control of their lives to others.

"It wasn't right. There is no reason why every man and woman on earth can't choose and contribute to society as themselves, doing things that they enjoy and that help others. I went into psychology to do what I can."

"When I was six," said Andre, who noticed Karen also listening attentively, "my best friend, a little squirt named Bobby, figured out how to synthesize nitroglycerin. He blew up everything in sight, the sand box, my doghouse, his mom's washing machine.

"The more things he blew up, the more things I learned how to put back together and make work better. Fission, fusion, even DNA...are just more things to put back together."

"I hope your friend Bobby didn't blow up any dollhouses."

"Are you kidding! We were deathly afraid of girls...couldn't get near them."

"And now Andre. Are you still frightened?"

"Only of never seeing you again. And, you know... I can work to free mankind from cubicles, and I can build full-size doll houses for the entire universe to work and play and be with their families just like you did with your toys and our daughters will do with their doll houses."

"That our sons will blow up?"

"Not with my babysitting robot standing by they won't."

Andre held out his hand.

"Not so fast, Professor. Your job application is missing the most important page. I just heard a rumor that the biologic organism that you have been referring to as 'dumb ass' you are now convinced is, in fact, part eternal spirit."

"You are the brightest mind I have ever known," Andre professed. "Only a god could create such wisdom and beauty."

"Fine. Thank you. Now I know what you want, but I didn't hear the words I'm after."

"So you want to know if I still think we are dust in the wind or guided destiny. My answer is both—body and soul."

"I'm still not hearing it."

Andre heaved a massive sigh. "The vastness of the universe must require substantial autopilot, but yes, you're right—you knew better all along. How am I doing?"

"One more sentence and I'll let you know."

"Yes. He is there, out there in front of us right now. There is a god."

Karen threw herself into his arms.

"Cyber," Andre said from the depths of their embrace, "what's the ocean bungalow status tonight?"

"All three cottages are vacant, and I didn't see or hear a thing."

"When we get off," Andre offered, "I can wall life Earth's constellations. We can walk on the beach and lie down to see our future. Perhaps end with a midnight swim."

"And lock the door to go skinny dipping," Karen said rubbing hips together.

"Will that be with or without a full moon?"

"Let's start with the northern lights and work from there."

"Sounds perfect," Andre said, leaning in for their first kiss, which didn't get a chance to land.

"Oh, here you are!" Brad called out, flinging the bridge door open, with Janie right behind him. "Janie and I have been looking for you two.

"Andre," he went on, oblivious to Andre and Karen jumping away from one another. "I'm worried about getting out of the way when the universe inflates tomorrow. We're going to be damn close."

"No time will give us plenty of time. We'll stay off the clock twice as long as Hank recommends," Andre said meeting Brad at Hank's station.

"Yeah, yeah," Brad halfheartedly agreed. "I just want to look at the specs again."

"You know," Karen said drawing Janie aside as Brad and Andre examined Hank's numbers, "for the last few weeks, Brad has had more energy every night…if you know what I mean. He seems… extra happy."

"Happy?" Janie answered, direct and pleasant. "You mean like Andre looked when we interrupted you?"

Karen smiled a mile wide. "You and I must be magicians."

"Well, we do have our tricks."

"Well then…I guess we'll just have to share our mutual bliss."

"Mutual bliss. That's a good one. We can add that to our list."

"Certainly, Janie. Although I suspect your list is longer than mine."

"Well, you know what they say," Janie whispered, "it's not the length of the list that counts, it's what you do with it."

"Caleb and Jiao reporting for duty," a black man said, coming onto the bridge with backup.

"Right. Let's go," Brad said. "It's getting late."

The foursome left the bridge together. The dancefloor was vacant, save one couple savoring a good night kiss, between verses of "Love Me Tender."

Brad and Andre walked side by side across the floor. They were joined by Karen next to Brad and Janie on Andre's arm, placing her furthest away from Karen. Janie bent forward ever so slightly to sneak a wink to Karen. It did not arrive undetected. Brad and Andre both picked up on it.

Brad shot a hesitant look to Andre—whom he then knew knew—and a second to Karen at his side, whose nod informed him that she also knew. Everyone knew everyone knew.

Brad stopped short. He and Andre shared a blank look, which was replaced in seconds by laughter all around.

When they walked on, Brad and Andre held each other closer than their ladies.

Karen got in the last word. "The best love shares love."

# 19

## Emerald City

Andre and Janie began their day beneath packed columns of Eastern white pines towering skyward to praise the day's sunshine—as usual. Andre's pod yawned beside Janie, who rolled over to the hushed rustle of pine needles tumbling and birds chirping—as usual.

Andre, not as usual, cleared wall life and stepped to the hull to view the universe, something he usually did with arms opened wide from mountaintops.

Janie, as usual, looked over sideways, her face half buried in pillow, and asked, "Well…how long am I going to have to wait for the day's first hug? The universe isn't going anywhere, and remember, it comes second."

"And it always will. Come join me."

That day, as usual, they were a good fit—his arm around her waist, hers over his shoulder.

"You know, Janie," Andre prayed, "at home, from the closest hill, I would delight myself trying to fathom the colossal size of the universe, and now, there it is, all of it…a thumbnail in space."

"And no less impressive."

"Amen…would that all the world of all times could share this day."

Janie hummed ten bars of a Tibetan meditation before adding, "We live in now waiting for what's next until today…happy birthday, universe."

"The universe can wait," Andre said, turning his gaze over and down Janie. "How would you like a backrub?"

"It's a start that I can finish." Janie said, as they giggled all the way to naked.

\* \* \*

An hour later, Brad and Karen graced the day, that began blossoming affection under the covers, then moved to the bathroom for an assembly line of preparations that dressed them Sunday's best—on Thursday.

"There is one thing I am sure of," Brad said as he opened the door of Karen's suit, "we are definitely the best dressed couple in the universe."

\* \* \*

The night before Hank and Sarah had a long talk, the one their kisses, and lack of them, scheduled weeks ago. Before they headed in opposite directions down the same hallway, they shared a final hug, that unmistakably said "Thank you, thank you so much. For the rest of my life, I will thank you for every happy memory."

"Life never whimpers," Hank said. "It's always a bang. You take care of yourself, cowgirl…you hear?"

"When we get home," Sarah said, moving Hank's hair aside one last time, "I'll send you an old-fashioned letter that will end…your ranch or mine? Our kids will ride together, and who knows, maybe little Hank will fall in love with little Sarah. Take care of *yourself*, cowboy."

"The only thing that beats a happy ending…is a happier ending."

\* \* \*

"I'm on my way," said Andre at the door. "I'll see you on the bridge. Now don't be late."

"That's a good one…you can't be late if the clocks not ticking. I'll see you up there, honey."

Andre hesitated as he approached the door—six years of dreaming, scheming, and sweating went into the day on the other side.

Where he was, with Janie, was home, security, acceptance, love and sensuality. She taught him how to love, most of which rubbed off watching her do it so well.

And she lived the ride, never hung up on schedule changes that managed the ride. And she giggled, not just infectious, more explosively joyful, a breeze-blowing happiness.

*So why bother with the other side of the door? Why bother bother?* thought Andre, looking more favorably on acceptance.

"What am I saying? I've got to make a living…and I *want* to know what's on the other side of the door, and the next door, and all the doors."

On the other side of the door, walking down the first of four hallways, the tide turned.

"Oh, my…" Andre said out loud, remembering how many gaps his understanding of the day contained. "Good morning, Cyber."

"Oh, yeah sure," Cyber replied, a smidgen swanky, "today it's 'Good morning,' we're friends again. For the last six months, all I got was 'Do this,' 'Organize that,' and 'Don't bother me.' And now that you need me, we're best friends again…no more ghosting?"

"Cyber, we were together every day."

"Sure…in the lab or loading fuel."

"Hold on there…you can stop pretending you have feelings, and I do know you know how to pretend. It's me, remember? And too much time with you kept me from spending time with human beings. What's your opinion on that?"

275

"It would be foolish to contradict the opinion of Professor Karen Wellchild."

"For good reason, and we'll expand your program so you fit in later. Meanwhile, we have problems…what do you got? And we're going stealth ear tag all day."

Cyber did what she could to bring Andre up to date with the night's calculations, which didn't go far, too many variables affecting just as many variables.

The bridge was packed by the time Andre arrived. He was greeted by every eye in the house, and every pair of hands politely clapping. Andre climbed to his station, arriving just as Janie, the last to make an entrance, took her own bow at the door. On cue, the Bells of Notre Dame tolled noon.

Silence followed. In addition to the bridge, Mulligan's and Starlight lounge had standing room only, all looking to visit creation.

Andre had frozen time and space. It was time to visit Bang Zero, the birth of existence.

"Behold the wonder of life and the miracle of creation!" Andre announced ship-wide. "Three backward microseconds will take us to the finish line, as close as we dare approach. Enjoy the view…cherish the moment."

The entire crew hushed while Cyber did the honors.

"Three…"

The universe shrunk to the size of earth's full moon on a clear night. Unfortunately, it was a moon lit night in Pompeii, what it felt like when the ship started shaking 6.2 magnitude.

"Cyber," Andre spoke out loud enough for all to hear, "what do you have?"

"Hold on," Cyber said inner ear private, "it's a gravitational wave thing. I don't understand how the wave propagates without a medium."

"That's because it is the medium," Andre said. "Actually, the medium and the wave at the same time…use sinusoidal rhythm theory."

It worked…the crew turned away from Andre, who put on a cool show for someone tripping over his own feet, who then decided to take the second of three steps.

"Two…"

Matter-energy showed itself for what it is. The rewinding Bang did not tighten into a sphere. One trillionth of a trillionth of a trillionth of a second was all it took for everything to elongate, proving Andre correct, his theories long ago expecting an oval stretch that feathered energy trails from the transdimensional grid back to point zero. Not a peep was uttered until the back of the ship began to lift for no apparent reason.

"You've got to be kidding?" Cyber said.

"Now that *is* impossible," Andre answered, quieter.

"Yeah…who would have guessed?"

"It's the transmatter state…right, Cyber?" Andre asked.

The stern of *Seven* contained half matter, half energy, literally a mimic of the embryonic mush in front of the ship. Mutual attraction was tugging the stern.

"This is an easy one," Cyber reported. "But what kind of force is this…and why are likes attracted?"

"Cyber," Andre said with a rehearsed smile on his face, "we won't be around long enough to find out. Keep us balanced so we can tip toe in, and then get the heaven out of here."

"One…"

It was done. *Explorer Seven* did it—time zero, existence zero— kind of, there was still a clearly outlined hourglass shape out there, glowing even brighter, with all kinds of uniform radiations of multiple colors, circling it like the magnetic fields around earth, just what Andre predicted: atomic construction outside of time. "Existence beyond time," he whispered to himself. I knew it…I knew it…I knew it…and now I know why.

"GASA was wrong…I knew that too!" Andre said loud and clear, unable to contain his joy. "Yahoo, yahoo…see, subtracting numbers is not the same as molding matter. There it is. And it *is* a mold!"

No one heard the end of Andre's statement. They were occupied by all manner of hoots, whistles, and jubilation, in between gasps of astonishment.

No one missed a hug on the bridge. In the Starlight lounge, champagne popped at every table. Mulligan's vibrated from dozens of feet dancing the jig. The last impossibility on mankind's list disappeared. All hail *Homo sapiens*.

Andre was beside himself and was standing beside his monitors, hands clenched above his head like a boxer who just won the world title, when Cyber bore the news, "Andre, Andre, Andre...*reality* to Andre! Check your monitors, look out the window—the Bang of energy is wiggling...and growing! We're in timeless space...what's going on?"

Andre was not pleased with what he found, an energy signature with a buildup in progress—accumulating a pressure gradient that was stretching the time container that housed it, which resulted in a sudden expansion of Bang preplasma accompanied by a shock wave that hit *Explorer Seven* like a freight train, throwing her back hundreds of yards, which did no good, since the Bang at the same instant grew larger and got closer by six thousand meters.

Michael helped Janie and Karen stay on their feet. The rest of the crew was getting off the floor when Andre turned to Brad and asked, "What did you do?"

"Nothing, I swear! Turn around and look for yourself. We're dragging. Inflation just snapped ahead all by itself. The Bang has begun! And it's headed right for us!"

"Attention, crew," Andre announced, as he went to work at his station. "The jolt we just experienced has not been explained. Our readings indicate that neither strong force, weak force, electromagnetism, nor gravity caused it. We are at red alert. I repeat...red alert!"

Brad had already begun when Andre added, "Back us out full throttle. All hands, return to safe central stations. All bulkheads are to remain sealed."

"If we're overtaken, the ship will disappear in one gulp," Brad warned.

"I know that," Andre snapped. "Still, there must be options. Michael, take Karen, Janie, and Sarah to the conn."

Karen lagged behind the others as they trooped out. "I am the official commander of this ship. My place is here on the bridge with you."

"As you wish…and thank you."

The ship's retreat managed to shrink the universe to double full moon size, not nearly enough to get away when the second wave, exactly ten ship minutes later, hit the vessel, bringing the universe closer than ever.

"Damn, damn, damn…" Andre said, losing his composure. "I've got nothing to go on here! Hank, what kind of margin are we looking at?"

"The first time drag brought preplasma halfway to the ship. The second attack, ten minutes to the microsecond, upped the advance another third. Two more will bring the energy wall one hundred meters off the bow. The next one will cook our goose."

Andre knew what to do. He sprinted to his conference room, where Cyber had every hypothesis laid out.

"All the ship's sensors feed in here," Andre said to a room full of team leaders. "Let's watch, find a pattern, then figure out how to neutralize the effect. And we dare not go trans, in distance or time— the grid has its hands full fending off radiation."

The crew fine-tuned every pitchfork and found what Andre was looking for when the next wave impacted the ship.

"Wow," Andre yelled, "did you see that? That wasn't an isolated energy signature! It was every frequency combined, a modulating platform! Cyber, confirm or deny!"

"Confirmed."

"Okay," Andre said with everyone's attention. "We're getting hit by something organized, but we can't specify its nature from the data we're picking up here inside the ship. We need more information— better information—about what's going on *outside* the ship.

"A-ah!" Andre exclaimed. "That's it. Outside the ship—that's the ticket. All I have to do is go outside and take better measurements."

"Oh no, you don't," Michael said. "We're surrounded by mayhem! Radiation levels out there are ten times the lethal dose! You won't last a minute. Send a droid!"

"Nope," he responded. "Droids can't compensate or manually override downed systems, but thanks for asking."

"Andre," Brad said, "if you can get the data back to the stern airlock, they could send it up to me. I know how to compensate thrust."

Michael blocked the door with coin in hand. "Heads or tails, Andre...winner goes for a walk."

"Thanks again, buddy," Andre said as he pocketed the coin. "I'll take this for good luck. Have Tord meet me at the airlock."

* * *

Karen and Michael followed Andre to the airlock, where Tord was already making preparations. Karen tried to be strong—but there were limits. "Cyber says," Karen began, ignoring the tears on her face, "that if you're back within ten seconds, you'll be fine."

"Of course, Karen. I will be fine...and if I'm not, you will be fine. Everyone loves you. You don't need me. Take care of yourself."

Andre was in the airlock before Karen could answer. She then collapsed, sobbing.

Communication was lost the moment Andre stepped outside. Glowing radiation obliterated Karen's view out the peephole. She counted to ten. Then counted to ten again. The third time, she only got to seven then broke down again.

"What's going on back there?" Brad asked from the bridge.

"We've got nothing back here," said Tord.

"Same here," Michael added, who had returned to the conn, "and my canopy is glazed over."

"Karen," said Brad, "stay where you are. I'll be right down."

Karen was sitting down, her head held up by the wall, when Brad arrived.

"Karen, it's been five minutes. Andre's plan didn't work. He was a brave man."

"I don't understand. Why—"

"None of us do. But there are things we must do. Come with me."

Brad grabbed Karen by the hand and led her out of the room. "Hurry, we only have four minutes left."

Karen scurried alongside Brad—to the shuttle craft bay.

"What are we doing here?" Karen asked as Brad strapped her in the copilot's chair.

"I was one of four survivors when Ranger Twelve crashed. With ten seconds to impact, I photon detonated an escape pod into orbit. Every other pod hit the planet at warp three."

"We don't have to die. Shuttlecraft ejection will add speed to Seven's thrust. We're getting out of here."

"What? And leave everyone else to die?"

"It's too late. Andre is dead. The ship is doomed. No one will survive. We have a chance. When the ship goes down it's every man for himself. Sit down...we're blasting out of here in twenty seconds."

For ten seconds, Karen sat stunned then shook off the trance of horrors. She jumped to her feet, slapped the door control, and started out—but didn't get far.

"You'll thank me for this later," Brad said as he picked her off the ground and tossed her back into her seat.

"Forget it, Brad," she said, getting up again. "I will not abandon the crew!"

Brad stepped in for a repeat performance, which did not go well. He had completely forgotten about Karen's Wednesday night's jiujitsu lessons. She was out the door and on her way by the time he caught his breath, on the floor.

As soon as he regained his balance, Brad said through shuttle communication, "Janie, do you read me?"

"Yes, I do, big boy."

"Are you aware of the situation?"

"Unfortunately, yes."

"Can you meet me at out secret spot in sixty seconds?"

"I'll be there in twenty."

Abandoning all sense of propriety, Karen threw herself onto the face of the air lock, her hands hanging from sealing bolts. She saw nothing. She heard nothing.

"Please, Jesus…please, Jesus," she begged frantically, "bring him back."

She caught movement out of the corner of her eye. Tord was at his post, running diagnostics.

"There's not much time left, Tord," Karen said to him. "I'm sure there's someplace you'd rather be…somebody you want to be with. Go ahead."

"Sorry, Commander," Tord said, mustering resolve rarely seen outside the military. "This is where Andre posted me. This is where I stay."

Karen pulled herself together, headed for the door, and saluted as she said, "Carry on."

The door leading forward to the bridge almost closed behind her when she heard—more felt—a thud.

"What was that?"

Karen rushed back to the airlock.

"Oh my god," she said, looking in. "Seal the outer door! Do it now!"

Tord cut the decontamination sequence in half.

"Hurry! Open it! Open it!"

The rush of air into the half-compressed chamber blew Andre to the back wall, pulse non-existent, pupils dilated. Karen plunged a cardiac needle and defibrillated six times, then she sat back dizzy, just as Andre coughed a breath.

She pulled him to her lap, stroked his head, draped Andre's right arm over her legs, and asked, "Andre…Andre…can you hear me?"

His eyes remained closed, but his mouth twitched then opened at the corner. "There's only…one person I know…with legs this sexy."

Karen's next words were, "Thank you, God. Thank you, God."

"I'll second that," Andre barely got out, "and, Karen, do you… come here often?"

"No, and I don't ever want to meet like this again."

"Not necessary…I'm never…going to say goodbye."

"Did you learn anything?" Tord interrupted.

"Yeah," Andre said, pushing himself up. "Get me to the bridge. I have…a plan."

Tord and Karen half-lifted, half-dragged Andre toward the bow.

"Karen," Andre said, trying to regain his feet, "I wasn't alone out there."

"None of us are ever alone, Andre."

"You're alive, Andre!" Michael said when he met them halfway and threw Andre over his shoulder to sprint on. "Remind me to get my lucky coin back."

When they got to the bridge, Andre noticed Brad's chair vacant. "Michael, get up there…we have work to do."

"What'd ya find out?" Hank asked.

"The Bang's…energy," Andre said, coughing up blood, "is homogeneous, organized, and more intelligent than a thousand Cybers. All we have to do is tap into it the right way…disconnect main power."

"What…are you nuts?" Hank said. "We'll collapse. The shields are holding up the hull."

"Trust me…" Andre said, getting faint. "Just…do…it."

Karen was shaking at his side.

"Karen, it's okay…we're going to be fine."

"It's not that," she admitted, squatting next to him. "I…I almost left you…and the ship. I even sat down in the shuttle craft. I could be out there in oblivion right now."

Andre managed to hold himself to the chair with just one arm; the other, he used to bring Karen closer. "If I didn't come back, you should have left…I would have wanted you to.

"I suppose now might be a good time to tell you. I've had your command codes since we took off. Before I entered the airlock, I used them to lock down the shuttle until one second before Bang impact. I know Brad, and I trusted him to do the right thing, but not so quickly.

"My guess," Andre wheezed, "is that he and Janie are back there right now making the best of the situation, if you know what I mean."

"Yes," Karen said more coherently. "they share perspectives."

"Just like you and me."

"Hey, I'm sorry to interrupt you two love birds," Michael said, looking over, "but Cyber says we're about to fry."

Andre nodded and raised his voice so all could hear. "On my mark, five on the dot, all power off…shields in my hands. Hank, aim for future Earth."

"Affirmative."

"Here we," Andre said then blacked out on his way to the floor, where Karen was waiting to prop him up.

"Okay, I'm back…*now!*"

From the expanding universe jagged bolts shot toward the ship, which coalesced into a giant umbrella in front of the ship, encasing *Seven* in a cocoon. A second layer of plasma energy then crystalized around their cocoon.

"All righty then," Andre squeaked out. "It's time…"

Like a pea squeezed from its pod, *Explorer Seven* shot away, leaving the universe behind.

* * *

When the ship ejected to safety, no one yelled, no one walloped, and no one got giddy. All were numbed; there's a limit to what a nervous system can handle. All that was heard was, "My god, was I scared. I couldn't even move."

The ship was on its way, passing time, billions of years by the million. The sight of cool space speeding by settled everyone down. The crew breathed normally, some even laughed. But not Andre, who fell to the floor comatose.

The force of ejection threw *Explorer Seven* into space without Michael doing a thing, which allowed him to attend to Andre.

"Cyber," Michael yelled, "what do we do now?"

"Andre is suffering end-stage radiation poisoning. Get him to his pod. Cytoplasmic regeneration might help. And don't worry about the ship. She will slow down on her own. And she's running true."

* * *

Andre mumbled incoherently as Michael and Karen laid him in his pod. Karen leaned over for a kiss before Michael closed the lid, causing Andre to rouse for a moment, raising one hand to grab Michael's shirt.

"Michael, I tuned in to extra channels out there…your brother… alive…with Carol…outer quadrant, third Maloun moon…and Karen…the green roof…it was a miracle. On the way home—"

"Shush now. Rest," Karen said.

"Cyber," Michael ordered as soon as the lid shut, "begin Wilkinson's program."

"No," Cyber responded, stiff and certain.

"It won't work. I know better. I have a better one."

"If you're inventing programs," Karen said, "then you're sentient…a person."

"If by 'person' you mean thoughts inside a box with no head, arms, or legs, then maybe. But I know what I know. Get out of here. I will do everything I can."

* * *

Brad tiptoed back to his station on the bridge. Everyone knew; no one looked. When he reached the chair he abandoned, Brad said, "The star streaks flying by are getting shorter. We must be slowing down. Hank, where the hell are we?"

"In years," Hank replied, "ten billion plus from the Bang. In distance, we're tracking Earth's projected location, which means two-thirds of the universe has already passed us on its way out."

"Shouldn't we put on the brakes or something?"

"Absolutely not," Michael cut in, returning to the bridge. "Andre left specific orders. Besides, this hyper-trans corridor we're in is locked down."

285

"If we don't slow down now," Brad said looking at Hank's numbers, "we'll overshoot Earth and our century. Do something, Michael!"

"Not necessary, fellas." Hank interjected. "We're slowing down—should drop out of trans any second now and definitely not pass our century, or Dallas."

Prayers came true. Dimension space dissolved. *Explorer Seven* came to a halt. *Explorer Seven* then returned to normal space—that contained a gorgeous sight.

"Whooee! Hot doggy!" Hank hollered. "Lookee there, ladies and gents—the star we're looking at, 93 million miles away, is none other than…our sun!"

The announcement was made ship-wide, followed by applause, muffled and exhausted; it had been a long day.

Brad's seat-of-the-pants piloting wasn't convinced. "Hang on…I see the sun in front of us and stars behind us. But what are the massive shadows on port and starboard? What's going on? Where is Earth?"

"I'm a-checkin' right now," Hank said.

"And," Brad said, turning around to face Michael, sitting in Andre's chair, "the helm is dead. We barely have life support, and not one backup survived. Damn it, Michael, what's going on?"

Michael had no answers. Nothing in front of him would light up.

That left Hank, who said slowly, stalling, "Hold your hats, gents. Give me a second…I want to double-check."

When Hank satisfied himself, he rose from his station—not a good sign—and walked to the bow to look for himself. "I don't believe it," he said, not turning to face anyone. "We're here…this very spot is Earth's orbiting position."

"So where is Earth?" Brad demanded as Michael leaned over Andre's desk with his hands covering both eyes, desperate to reduce input.

Hank groaned. "I was hoping you wouldn't ask me that. I'll give you a clue…see that gigantic cratered mass to starboard growing larger by the second? That's Theia."

Michael dropped further. "No! Oh no, no, no, no…anything but that—we're dead in the water."

"Will someone please tell me what the blue blazes is going on!" Brad demanded.

"Theia is the Mar's size planetoid that collides with baby Earth to bring the planet online." Michael whimpered quietly, an unnecessary precaution since everyone on board except Brad had already figured it out.

"And when do we expect the blessed event, which from the expressions on your face, were in the middle of?" Brad asked, finally caught up.

"Two hours, seventeen minutes and forty-one seconds to impact, just where we're sitting…a sitting duck."

"So power up and let me fly us out of here," Brad insisted.

"Hey, you said it yourself," Michael added. "All systems are down. We barely stayed in one piece dropping out of trans."

Everyone stared at Hank's floating chart in silence. Finally, Brad called out, "Cyber, what is Andre's status?"

"Critical, unresponsive, on life support, cell damage on the verge of disintegration."

"How long will the hull last after the collision?" was Michael's question.

"The good news is," Cyber replied, "that the hull won't melt through for at least an hour after we're engulfed."

"And the bad news?" Brad asked.

"Internal temperatures will reach 500 degrees Fahrenheit in twenty minutes, and there's nothing I can do about it, and my electronic synapses fuse at 280 Fahrenheit. So if it's any consolation, you will outlive me by ten minutes."

No one talked. Everyone thought—of Earth, of home, then about that special person, and what will never be, which began a silent dirge exiting the bridge, except for Michael, Sarah, and Karen.

The three witnessed millions of years of gravity accelerate on target, trapping *Explorer Seven* helpless. A dozen hurricanes would have made less noise when the planetoid crusts smashed the ship in stereo.

They were red-hot babies burping radioactivity, both crusts so thin *Explorer Seven* was surrounded by glowing radioactive magma in seconds, with temperature rising.

Karen, Michael, and Sarah were alone at the bow watching the outer hull melt, from minerals that someday might be Pike's Peak.

"Don't move," Michael said. "Less movement…less heat. And drink this. A gallon of salt water will buy us five more minutes."

"And oh," Sarah said, trying to bring up humor, and failing, "we'll sweat faster naked."

"As far away from each other as possible," was Michael's reply. "Not how I was hoping to die."

"So," Karen said, "our final moments of life have arrived. I've read about this, but the authors always mention old people. Our lives have just begun."

"When you think about it," Michael sighed, "leaving the universe, documenting the crunch, testing the Bang, and then returning to Earth is an outstanding accomplishment."

"Yeah," Karen agreed. "Too bad no one will ever know we did it."

"*We* will know."

"One hundred forty degrees and climbing," Cyber reported as the ship began tumbling, it's gravity plates offline, replaced by the real thing, which became a problem when the ship's heavier stern sank first, leaving Michael and the ladies leaning back against Brad's tower, all three down to skivvies.

"You know," Karen said, "in the past, when I thought about death, dealt with it as we say…I always pictured my great-grandmother sitting at home, watching family videos. That's where she closed her eyes and never opened them again."

"My great-gramma went upstairs to take a nap. She's still napping," Sarah said.

"Is she?" Michael added, slowly whispering. "I watched a black-and-white movie from our archives last month. It was made in the middle of Second World War. The action followed a cavalier bomber pilot whose plane was about to crash and his parachute burnt to shreds. He joked, sang a song, and toasted life."

"Sure, he was dying for a cause."

"Life is a cause," Michael said, "but let me finish. The angels forgot to pick him up. So David Nivin got up and walked around, for a while spending time both on earth and 'up there,' where the rest of his downed crew were getting their permanent wings.

"And here's the thing...all those guys and gals lost to warfare were joking, laughing, and living it up just like they did on the other side. And why not? They knew for sure that life goes on, that companionship never ends, and that they were with friends. Ten minutes from now, that will be us. I'm sure of it."

"You might be right," Sarah said, "The only sad people at a wake are those still living. The dead feel God's love firsthand."

"So," Karen said limp, smirking, "Michael...what are you going to do about sex up there?"

"Well," he said, "it is finally, I'm sorry to say, time to bring up a quote I didn't expect to use for a hundred years. It's from Plato, who was actually quoting Sophocles. An opinion I emphatically go on record as not buying. When he got old, Plato was asked if sex and women still got him excited. He basically replied, 'I'm glad neither no longer does. It's like being freed from bondage by a madman.'"

"You were wise saving that for the last five minutes of life. Any sooner might have been depressing for you, since you'd be sleeping alone," Sarah said, with a jab.

"What peculiar creatures we are," Karen mused, "that we cannot enjoy sunshine without asking why or what will come of it."

"When life has been lived honestly," Michael affirmed, "with joy, and success, death earns no smile. And there's no shame in dying unmarked...and unknown."

"Advancing man's understanding of man leaves a mark, even if no one raises a flag in your honor. And love leaves momentum all its own," Karen added.

"They say," Sarah mused, "that when someone dies, a world dies with them. So aren't we lucky when we die, the world gets born?"

"Back at school," Karen said, "the hard-nose gang instructed us to tell patients that they should be prepared, ready for death, every day of life."

"I look at death a little like marriage," Michael said, unhinged of reservations. "No one is every prepared."

"Which," Sarah pointed out, probing for Michael's real self, "doesn't mean both don't come with happy endings."

"Oh, yes, of course…and you know what aches inside of me? Not the planets, or systems I never got to visit. Not the meals I'll miss. Not ten guys skydiving Mars…no, inside of me, Sarah, I so much want to have children with you. I even prepared a quote…

*Come live with me, and be my love,*
*And we will some new pleasures prove*
*Of golden sands, and crystal brooks,*
*With silken lines, and silver hooks.*

Their hug was short, sweaty, and followed by a splash of cool water.

Karen followed with a final recitation.

*Death be not proud, though some have called thee*
*Mighty and dreadful, for thou art not so,*
*For those whom thou think'st dost overthrow,*
*Die not, poor death, not yet canst thou kill me.*

Hyperthermia dropped all three to the floor. Hugging was out of the question, but as Michael slumped, he held both girls' hands, as six eyes stopped blinking.

Planet-smashing current tumbled *Explorer Seven* head over heels, sliding sweaty bodies from one wall to another. Then for no apparent reason, the ship leveled off, and the comm crackled to life.

"Attention all hands, Andre here…hot enough for you? New directive…walk or crawl or be dragged to your space suits, jump into the pool, and hold on. Water absorbs heat slower than air. Once everyone is accounted for, Cyber will close the cover again."

Karen was dead to the world. Michael and Sarah had enough left to drag her behind them on all fours to the forward changing room before rolling into the pool.

"Okay, it's me again…and I know your suits are picking this up. I have a plan. I'm draining the pools. Dumping water outside will give me just enough space to establish dimension walls, and God knows I've got plenty of heat to tap into. I hope you've enjoyed our journey to the center of the Earth. Now we're getting out of here!"

The stern almost overheated before it popped free, the moment Andre was waiting for to begin shut down, a five-minute process that shot *Explorer Seven* forward in time and space on a tether Andre included in the mix.

"Am I good, or am I good?" Andre asked over the comm minutes later. "All those wishing to do so may stay right where you are. However, the pool cover is lifting, and you are free to return to all normal activity, and considering the day we just had, one abnormal one." The crew of *Explorer Seven* climbed free. Once out, a long deep breath later, each looked up, then laid down flat to look up at the view out the dome. It was Earth, wet and juicy—two billion years old. Only two and a half billion years from home.

Andre broke in one more time. "Oh, sorry to bother you, but… will Commander Wellchild please report to the conn? We need to discuss a change in room assignments."

# 20

## Church of the Apostles

"We are…we were…we ever shall be," Andre said, waking up in bed.

"Can't hear what you're saying," Karen called out. "I'm halfway through my sonic shower."

When she returned to snuggle beside him, Andre added, "Life is good. God is great. And you are perfect."

"None of us is perfect, my dear, but we try our best. It's all so clear to me now."

Karen straightened Andre's bedhead fuzzy-wuzzies, one tuft at a time. He did his part, one kiss at a time, all the way to her hips.

"So," she murmured, "this is what we're going to do all day. Lie around in bed."

"It won't be all day, and we won't be lying around. But don't worry, there'll be plenty of time for everything we want to do. I'll see to that."

"Oh…my…oh yes…" she moaned. "But I can't stay. I'm meeting Sarah and Sheila for breakfast. We're going to discuss the church."

"Church? Oh ya, the apostle thing."

"Exactly, the one you promised to help with."

"I promised you a lot of things last night," he said as he ran a fingertip down her side, "and I'll make good on every one...except letting you pick out my clothes."

"Hey, I only offered advice. You're three decades behind. But if *you* promise to let me choose your outfit for church on Sunday, *I'll* promise to be back by noon."

"You drive a hard bargain."

"So do you. And I'm looking forward to it."

Karen was outvoted two to one at breakfast. Sheila and Sarah made her deacon of the congregation. Karen's first proclamation appointed Sarah assistant deacon, whose first job was sorting through the crew's feedback about a mission statement, thus allowing Karen to keep her promise to Andre.

On their own, the crew augmented a new routine. At eleven every morning, the engineers met to bring field generators back online, pressed the first ten buttons that came to mind, then shrugged their shoulders and left for the pool, bathing suits already on. The rest of the day was titled "French Riviera Vacation." The way they figured it, two near-death experiences were worth at least ninety days of freeloading.

The lab crew put up a picture of Andre for inspiration. He hadn't visited them since he parked the ship on the moon the day they landed. Apparently, happiness suited him.

And besides, everyone was learning. After only a billion years of cooling down, carbon chains started clumping together. During the second billion years that passed before the ship stopped by, bubble life was all the rage.

Janie and Sarah found the real thing infinitely more fascinating than advanced organic chemistry. Once a week they sent Reginal, sterilized, to the surface for another sample to test. No one wanted to risk landing on the planet and screwing up chemicals that turn out so well.

They also knew that what they were retrieving was a fleeting snapshot. It would take another two billion years for the little guys, sprucing up one million molecules per cell, to get along well enough to manage the hard part, multicellular life, followed by a mere half a billion years for bacteria and eukaryotic algae to evolve Daniel Boone hiking the Appalachian forest.

Brad, Michael, and Hank wrote their own job descriptions the day they landed that read, "Cyber, our jobs are now your jobs." Athletic marathons added an inch to their biceps, midnight buffets two inches to their waistlines.

"If we do end up deep-fried on the way home, like we almost did twice," Brad said, "I want to make sure I'm extra-crispy."

"Finger-lickin' good," Hank added. "We'll diet tomorrow…or another tomorrow. Hand me another praline, partner."

Before they knew it, two months had gone by, and Sheila was heard broadcasting:

*Good morning. And happy Sunday to one and all.*
*Our Church of the Apostles Spiritual Hootenanny begins in ten minutes.*
*Participation is optional. Those hungover always welcome.*

No one was working anyway. Janie closed the pool to use the space to holographically recreate *Frauen Kirche Munchen*, Church of Our Lady, complete with stained-glass windows.

Karen, Sheila, and Sarah sat center altar. Andre and Janie, conscripted to serve, snuck in at the last minute, just as Karen climbed the ornate pulpit.

"Welcome to our celebration of life!" Karen sang out. "To keep the service classy, there will be no beer drinking, but feel free to help yourselves to mimosas, Bloody Marys, blintzes, and bagels on the back table.

"We will begin by reminding ourselves of the advice of Ralph Waldo Emerson, who recommended that modern man no longer live retrospective. He insisted that our relationship to the universe should be original when he said, 'Why should not we have a poetry and philosophy of insight and not of tradition, and a religion by revelation to us, and not the history of theirs? Every man's condition is a solution in hieroglyphic. Why should we grope among the dry bones of the past?'

"Therefore, I wish to thank one and all for sharing inspiration with us, beginning with what to call our community. As you know, an *apostle* is defined as 'a vigorous and pioneering advocate of a particular policy, or cause...all of which we are. Through the ages, apostles of every creed have dedicated their lives to God...all of us do.

"In the past, ceremonies joined apostles with love. If water suffices, then space, time, and molten earth must also baptize. We left the pool holding hands. This day therefore ordains each and every one of us an apostle! Welcome to the Church of the Apostles!"

Karen paused to let the crowd toast one another, some with glasses, others bagel to bagel.

"We are not alone," she continued when the cathedral hushed. "The clergy of every faith on earth who serve the Lord are also Apostles. And we respect our elders for keeping God the focus of man's struggle. Their efforts will remain forever canonized. We also pray for progress and fading difference, a common journey praising the God we share."

The congregation finger-tapped approval.

"We wish to augment...not displace. We desire not to be followed but, rather, that all lead themselves. With us today are Catholic Apostles, retaining adoration for Jesus Christ; Jewish Apostles, mindful always of the contributions of Abraham and Moses; Islamic Apostles, proud of Muhammad's efforts to lead mankind to God; Hindu Apostles, finding holiness in all of God's creation; and Buddhist Apostles, grateful for the divine inspiration of Gautama."

Doted through the assembly, randomly mixed, those of similar ancestry stood when their past was mentioned, which left the entire room standing, except for Andre.

"And today we add a new category to our church, Scientific Apostles, so Andre doesn't have to go around saying 'I'm the guy who used to be the atheist.'"

Andre stood, glass in hand, as the congregation had a good laugh. Karen waited until the last corner quieted down. "He who stands up must also stand for, and we do. Thank you all again, for suggesting principles for us to live by. Sarah and I have combined them. Here is the new, hot-off-the press, official Mission Statement of the Church of the Apostles…

"To share love with all faiths, believing and trusting in God, who loves and cares for us. And to help free us all of stories from the past that turn us against one another and away from the face of God."

"Yes!" someone shouted from the middle of the crowd.

"And to simplify the 613 commandments history left hanging around, our meetings, following unanimous consent, have brought us the guidelines now displayed above the altar.

## *Guidelines to Live By*

I.   *Free your heart of hate.*
II.  *Clear your mind of violence.*
III. *Use your talents to the best of your ability.*
IV.  *Give back to God.*
V.   *Be and share happiness.*
VI.  *Love and be loved.*
VII. *Never forget the eternal joy that awaits us all.*

A holographic Mormon Tabernacle Choir appeared above Karen's head to harmonize "Amazing Grace." The entire crew joined in at the chorus then broke for a meal before Karen introduced the first reader of the day, who was Sarah.

"Good morning," she said. "Welcome…and thanks for sharing this day with us. I have thoughts and words.

"There were times in the past when I felt anger toward those who did not see the light as clearly as I thought I did, which I didn't. They were, like myself, on the way. Then a disciple of Buddha taught me that anger is like throwing hot coals at an invisible enemy; your own hand is the first to burn.

"Evil begets evil. When two fight, both lose. Revenge remains forever hollow and tasteless. We must never lose compassion for others.

"Apostles abandon thoughts of blame. We live to love. Today, I read words attributed to Jesus of Nazareth:

*When you know yourselves, then you will be known,*
*and you will understand that you are children of the living father.*
*After all, what goes into your mouth will not defile you;*
*rather, it's what comes out of your mouth that will defile you.*

*Love your friends like your own soul.*
*There is light within a person of light,*
*and it shines on the whole world.*

Sarah's beatific smile spread across the room as she signaled her musical selection, "Spirit in the Sky."

*Prepare yourself, you know it's a must*
*Gotta have a friend in Jesus*
*So you know that when you die*
*He's gonna recommend you*
*To the spirit in the sky...*

The entire gathering raised their voices as they stood to dance, which left Janie dancing all the way up the stairs to take her turn.

"Stay on the dance floor," Janie called out. "There is more to come. Muhammad once said, 'Hurt no one, so that no one may hurt you.'

"Worrying about what others think about you all the time is a way to hurt yourself. Islam helped me accept that all Allah's children, young and old, men and women, are equally loved. We must deny inevitable obstacles the power to ruin a single day. Kindness is its own reward, joy always appropriate.

"Let's dance our part. The Koran says,

*Who is better in religion than he who*
*surrendereth his purpose to God*
*while doing good to men.*

*Who doeth greater wrong than he who*
*inventeth a lie concerning God or denieth our tokens?*
*There is no compulsion in religion.*

*The faithful servants of the Beneficent are*
*they who walk upon the Earth modestly,*
*And when the foolish ones address them answer; peace.*

The lyrics of the Islamic morning prayer were projected for all to join,

*There is a reason why to God we pray*
*In the morning on every day*
*It's a meeting and we must not be late*
*If we want to have peace we*
*Must obey and pray…*

Sheila stepped up next. "Hello, everyone. I've also had my share of confusion—too hot, too cold…too slow, too fast…too many men, not enough…"

The crowd giggled.

"Okay, that was fun…because it is fun! But Buddha calmed me down. Now I know that the middle road is the place to be. And that one's station in life does not indicate one's character. A healthy mind is all the equipment we need for happiness.

"We are our thoughts. Select them wisely by taking charge of every idea that comes to mind. Respond to life with less reflex and more reflection. Loving speech and deep listening can make it so, for all profitable corrections come from a calm and peaceful mind. I read words attributed to Buddha,

*There is only one moment in time*
*When it is essential to awaken,*
*That moment is now.*

*Wisdom shall be our light by day, right*
*Mindfulness our protection by night.*

*If we live a pure life, nothing can destroy us.*
*If we have conquered greed, nothing can limit our freedom.*

*My actions are my only true belongings;*
*My actions are the ground on which I stand.*

Sheila grinned and wiggled her hips as she raised her head and prayed loud to heaven: "God bless John Lennon!"

*Instant Karma's going to get you*
*Gonna knock you off your feet*
*Better recognize your brothers*
*Ev'ryone you meet*
*Why in the world are we here*
*Surely not to live in pain and fear*
*Well, we all shine on*
*Like the moon and the stars and the sun...*

A rousing dance followed, then another Lennon song, "Imagine," which brought couples together.

"That's your clue, Andre," Karen said, leaning over quietly. "You promised me you would add thoughts, and I let you pick out your own outfit."

Andre waddled up to do his part, getting a kiss on the cheek from Karen on the way.

"I have a question for God this morning. How am I supposed to follow four beautiful women? No one wants to listen to me. All I can say is, Karen made me do it."

"All of humanity shares connected awareness. We have studies to prove it. We Apostles choose peace and look to philosophers through the ages to help us achieve it. I read a selection of their thoughts,

*Living in ignorance is like living in a solid iron box;*
*if you don't defeat your delusions, no other victory is real.*

*Don't let yourself be deceived by your own mind.*
*It is unwise to believe everything you think.*

*Hatred arises when we see ourselves separate from others.*
*To seek happiness hurting others is the way of a fool.*

*Once we understand that the basic nature of humanity is compassionate*
*rather than aggressive, our relationship to life changes immediately;*
*we relax, trust, live at ease.*

*Be glad of life because it gives us a chance to love and to work*
*and to play and to look up at the stars.*

The members of the church responded with quiet applause. Andre, more at ease, followed with, "Thank you. As the last presenter of the day, I got to pick an hour of uplifting tunes to encourage us all to exchange opinions…and dance partners. The only way I could get Brad here was to promise 'Blue Suede Shoes,' so I did one better. I programed an Elvis android to entertain us, beginning with a gospel medley, and taking requests thereafter. Enjoy."

Andre reached the food table, grabbed one cheese and two fruit blintzes, a glass of milk, and a bowl of sugar. He then hid out in the furthest corner. But not for long.

"Andre," Assistant Bosom Isabella said, sidling up to him. "You were outside during creation. May I ask a question?"

"Certainly. Just give me a minute to raise my blood sugar above glycemic recommendations."

When Andre spun around to enjoy what was on his plate, Isabella nodded and waved friends over. By the time Andre finished eating, and turned around, the floor was jammed. There was Mason from electronics, assistant navigator Alexander, Sarah's friend Charlotte, Madison, Jacob, Liam, Nicholas, Emma, Ethan, Nicole, Danielle, and Michele, plus seven more rows fanning across the dance floor.

"Oh, my," Andre said. "What's your question?"

"Did you see God?"

Karen gave Andre an encouraging "go ahead' nod from the side of the crowd.

"Vision is one of many senses," he began hesitantly. "The one most easily scrambled by circumstances in and outside of our brains...

"See him, you ask...well, visual perceptions were definitely there," he continued, "a light...a form...an individual...but something else was far more convincing.

"If you fall through and then crawl out of thin ice in January, you lie on a heat lamp bed to warm your skin as soon as possible. What I felt was a sensation like that, but instead of outer warmth, what I felt penetrated my entire being, and the feeling was love, a deep, robust embrace of caring, companionship, and tranquility, a joining with divinity, indescribably complete.

"God was there. He exists...he definitely does...he is love..."

"Oooohhh."

"It made me think. All by myself, without hearing a word, I realized that love contradicts charlatans who falsify moral high ground to foster hate. What fools we are to follow! How mindlessly the past has sold our freedom."

"We must unite. We shall march the good fight. Power to the people, for the people, by the people."

"Andre," Arnold spoke up, "You said God was there. Just where is *there*? And was he alone?"

"That part gets a little complicated because he wasn't alone. All of us were also there...kind of."

"You mean spiritually?" Arnold asked. "We and others were there...as souls?"

"Think wave theory," Andre said, sounding like his old clinical self. "Our me, the thought stuff, is only ten percent of our brain's activity, and the rest operates twenty-four hours a day, which is why we have to be on our toes, never forget that we are outgunned by DNA, evolution, necessity, and whatever else comes along to trip us up.

"However, throw it all together, and we end up with more than enough wave activity to communicate with others and stay connected to metaphysics, all of everything of all times, which is also us…and when I talk like this, even I'm confused. The bottom line is that we're more than toenails and adipose tissue. We—the real us—is also an electromagnetic wave connected to the other side.

"Think of it this way: if I have two robot bodies and one head, I can move the head back and forth. Our identity resides atop mortal form. The other dimension also supports our identities, allowing transfer at physical demise, for immortality."

Andre paused for a second. The crowd, sharing his intensity, remained pensive.

"But listen, guys. All I have is personal theories. We all have to figure it out for ourselves."

Michael had moved beside Andre. With a pleasant, friendly air, he added, "Andre and I agree on a lot of stuff, and there is one that he's not mentioning because it sounds far-fetched…but not really after you think about it for a while. And that is that perhaps, just perhaps, mind you, from heaven we might be able to jump back to begin another life, not just around town, but anywhere in the universe, with God's permission following request.

"Wow," Bernard admitted, "that's heavy."

"You left one thing out," Brad said, surprising everyone, "the good guy, bad guy thing. After being a bastard and stepping on people your whole life, a fella just rides along whistling Dixie like everyone else?"

"Excellent and insightful, Brad. And again…what do I know?" Andre said, almost lackluster. "But I do know what I felt, a little. If you lived a bad life, you're definitely going to be miserable for the beginning of the next. Everyone on earth who thinks they are getting away with deceit, cruelty, and exploitation…don't. There's a payback—that's got to hurt big time. It sounds like purgatory to me.

"I wouldn't be surprised if murderers go through the same and more agony than they caused others."

Andre paused, headed for the fruit counter, and then noticed the crowd, still eager. "I never tire of reading Emerson, who roughly wrote, 'Every act rewards itself, first in real nature, and secondly in the circumstances. If you treat men as pawns and ninepins, you shall suffer as well as they.

"When you put a chain around the neck of a slave, the other end fastens itself around your own. Persons and events may stand for a time between you and justice, but it is only a postponement. The thief steals from himself. The swindler swindles himself. One cannot do wrong without suffering wrong.

"In other words," Andre concluded, "all infractions of love and equality shall be punished, and we are only as free as the culture we breathe life to, which is why Goethe got it right when he suggested we rid ourselves of tradition to become completely original, to love others and ourselves eternally.

"And not loving yourself is not to be excused. If you run down your nervous system so much with drugs and poor habits that your abused brain gives up and decides it's easier to murder yourself than clean up and do the dishes, you wake up on the other side smashed in the face with your stupidity, combined with the accumulated suffering that you have just caused your loved ones that moment, and for the rest of their lives—oh my god—not one of Dante's nightmares can compare to that evisceration."

Brad, whom to his credit was aware that for his whole life bread had been buttered for him, asked about justice.

"Fair, you say..." Andre attempted, treading lightly. "There are a lot of angles. For instance, a privileged Rockefeller is born in the lap of luxury. On the other side of the planet, another lad, the oldest in a fatherless family of six, leaves school at fourteen to work in the mines.

"Thirty years later, the rich guy hasn't worked a day in his life, contributed to society in any way, and spends morning to night complaining about 'the help' and the rising cost of yacht fuel...not one day truly happy. His counterpart, on the other hand, is an admired and respected foreman who fills evenings laughing with wife and children. Where's the justice there?"

Michael had already bought into far more than Andre was willing to suggest. "That many-lives option," Michael said, standing up, "also makes sense. If you and I both throw dice on the table, I might get a six and you a one. But keep rolling for eternity and the law of averages guarantees that no one ever ends up better off, and everyone, every day of every life, has the opportunity to make now the best now that can possibly be. To quote Einstein, 'God is a mathematician,' who loads the dice."

Andre took advantage of Michael's attention to brush crumbs from his shirt. On his way, passing behind Michael, a female voice from the back of the room asked, "Why does God allow pain and suffering?"

Michael snagged Andre, knowing how much Andre enjoyed putting organized religion to the test, with poor marks. "Do you want this one?" was Michael's question.

When there wasn't a God, Andre saw no reason to hide the truth. After God showed up, Andre found less reason to do so, so he stood tall and bore his soul.

"Your question contains two assumptions, both of which were forced down our throats. Why do you think God is calling all the shots?"

"Because…he's God," Simone said.

"God…" Andre added with a comical face that confused everyone, "God, as defined by whom? And why? And to whose benefit? The first god of mankind, the original, was a female who gave birth to life. Then church-state kings showed up who needed armies to crusade terror. Organized religions made up an all-knowing, all-powerful god to support their edicts.

"They walked the streets, a prayer book in one hand, a whip in the other, screaming, 'My boss is God. He is behind everything I do. And He's all knowing, and all powerful, so don't try to get away with anything. Do what I order, or else. And remember, it's your fault because you aren't obeying all the rules I made up for you, so bend over and take a beating, and be quick. I'm late for dinner at the castle that God says belongs to me.'

"God did not give us free will to be smothered by despots claiming sanctification. The road to freedom is to free ourselves from the words they use to enslave us, lies camouflaged as 'beliefs' that we have accepted as truth.

"Abe was right. It's a matter of the divine right of kings and the audacity of those who claim the power to assign divine rights.

"The good and evil thing is tough to get around, I know. But consider this…if I told you I saw someone clobber another over the head then rip the victim's flesh off during twenty minutes of death scream, you would say that he, or she, is an evil person. And yet that is just what every carnivore on earth, including our ancestors, did and do to survive.

"Bands of chimps decimate lesser tribes. Evolution has left 'evil' habits among us. Our job is to make it right.

"As dogmatic as I have ever been, I am even more certain now about one thing: God loves us. The last thing he wants is for us to suffer. That leaves only one logical conclusion: *He has no choice.*

"Matter is matter. We thank God for it. But it comes with a price, not just for us, for God as well, because he shares all.

"And is this the best universe that can possibly be? We must assume, for now—yes—but it could be better. And whose job is it to make it better? You and me come to mind. Meanwhile, pain is required, suffering optional."

Andre stopped to take a long drink from the glass Karen handed him. He gave her a smile, cleared his throat, adjusted his posture, and finished.

"God has put a great deal of love, energy, and time into evolving human intelligence. And I can tell ya, he's still on the job, right now, this second, doing what he can. We are the ones who need to do better, by playing fair, bestowing happiness, promoting charity, and assuring equality.

"The only mechanism even close to mortal justice, uncensored democracy, is not an option. It's mankind's God-given duty. We live in a world of junk food, junk mail, junk values, junk governments, and junk religions. Dump junk. Take charge!"

While everyone pondered Andre's forceful charge, Brad stood up with another question, which he didn't get out before being interrupted by an engineer bursting in, "Andre! Andre! I don't know what happened, but all of a sudden, the entire array lit up balanced. We can time travel again!"

"I think I know what's going on," Andre said, looking straight up. "Cyber, did I give you permission to play with the ship?"

"No. But you haven't spent any time with me since we landed. I thought fixing the ship would make you happy."

"I haven't forgotten about you. We're on a break, that's all. And…it was supposed to be a surprise, but just this morning, I finished an android prototype your consciousness can project to. You've always wanted a body. I have one for you."

"With arms and legs, so I can walk around?"

"You said it. You'll even be able to talk to us directly, instead of sneaking around like you do."

"Do I get a penis, or do I get a vagina?"

"Your choice."

"Vaginas are multifunctional, and they're more in demand. Put me down for a happy place."

"Good. That way, I won't have to reprogram your voice patterns."

"Ooohhh," Cyber crooned, "does that mean I will be able to—"

"We'll discuss that later," Andre broke in. "For now, implement limitations Program Beta."

"Oh yes, Beta…do nothing until you hear from me."

"Certainly, sweetheart. Anything you say."

"Cyber, have you been watching old movies again?"

"Yes, they're so romantic."

"For the record, Humphry Bogart called the ladies *sweetheart*, not the other way around. Also, put a freeze on new social programs unless they're cleared by Karen."

Andre wrapped his arm around Karen's waist. "So tell me, sweetheart," he said in his best Bogart impression, "did you always want a daughter?"

"Well," she said, wrapping both her arms around him, "we don't have to change diapers."

He kissed her cheek. "Back to business. Cyber, what's the fly-grid status?"

"Frayed and rickety. The ship might manage ten minutes of time travel before she spasms. The crew should all cross their fingers."

"Tally ho," exclaimed Brad as he led the sprint to the bridge.

# 21

## Valentine's Day

Cyber's patch job held for over an hour, long enough to bring the crew two billion years closer to home. Another round of repairs began immediately. It would take time—plenty of time—but no one complained; Earth was right out the window, directly above what would someday be North America.

With the thrill of baby's first step, Cyber walked the halls of *Explorer Seven*. Her real self—a computer bank laced to the soul of the ship—was the size of their shuttle craft, hardly up to ten-pin bowling.

Quite by accident, Cyber and Andre stepped onto the bridge at the same time. They both looked up to the stars and said in unison a maestro would approve, "I'm a projection."

They laughed as comrades. Then Andre said, "I'll be in the neuro lab, buddy."

"I'll monitor you from up here. Don't worry, Andre. I've got your back."

Cyber loved being a somebody and returned the favor by figuring out how to feed visual signals, alongside tactile and motor systems, from one living brain to another. For the first test, Michael was

Andre and Andre Michael for five minutes. Both agreed, "That was weird." It was the first and last body jump.

Instead, they decided to tap into the animal world below. Cyber developed a system to neurologically induce supratentorial sleep in an animal brain while the rest of the animals central nervous system stayed awake, and transmitted visual, auditory, olfactory, and tactile signals to the ship, so a resting human brain could experience animal life and take over motor control of the body on the surface at the same time every animal instinct and motivation were experienced.

Michael, of course, volunteered to the be first. He lay prone on a gurney with his head under an interface crown the size of a bushel basket, while the rest tracked wall monitors.

"Pulse, respiration, blood pressure, brainstem…all running smoothly," Sarah read off.

"Looks good," Andre agreed. "His subconscious is sleeping naturally while his consciousness is awake, currently receiving sensory input from a slime worm."

"Can he talk to us?" Karen asked.

"He can through Cyber. But let's leave him alone. I want him to request returning himself, which should be…any second now…"

Michael's chest heaved as his eyes opened. He removed the wired head canopy and said, "Oh my god…what a rush!"

"Did you feel like a slime worm?" Sarah asked.

"I didn't feel like a slime worm. I was a slime worm! Even though the critters are only twenty centimeters long, I was the largest, most complex creature on Earth, a super-giant!

"And the speed! There was no heavy spinal cord to slow me down. I did butterfly kicks with my entire body. Cilia let me flap up, down, sideways…even in circles."

"Well," Andre said, "according to the scans, you're fit at a fiddle, whatever that means. I'd say we're all ready to go. Who's in?"

"Me!" Janie blurted, raising both arms and pretending to swim like a worm. "Let's get wiggly!"

Karen was less enthusiastic. "It's very safe technology," Andre said. "If you feel funny or the numbers look weird up here, Cyber will disconnect, and you open your eyes right here in the lab, where you actually are all the time. It's like going to the movies and operating a robot on screen as you look out through the robot's eyes. And we can group chat through Cyber."

"How?" asked Brad. "We'll be worms. Do they know Morse code? I don't."

"Just thinking words activates our vocal cords. Cyber will pick that up and translate."

"Hey, that's neat," Michael jumped in. "It would've been nice to talk to you guys when I was down there. All I could hear was Cyber."

"Tell us about the planet, Michael," Sarah asked.

"It's trippy! The shallow pond is clean, but a bit silty. The visibility could be better, but you can see all the way to the bottom, where I dined on delicious algae the moment I arrived. Then it hit me. A hormone tidal wave! The craziest thing I have ever felt. It puts puberty to shame.

"I was overtaken by sex pheromones coming from a mass of slime worms in the middle of the pond. I swam at them as fast I could. Cyber pulled me out just as I was about to join in."

"Whoa!" Andre said, raising both hands. "If it's mating season down there, we should call it off."

"What for?" Janie asked. "I know for a fact that none of us are virgins."

"Yes, Janie," Andre said, concerned, "but the primitive urges we'll experience are—"

"Pff!" Janie interrupted, waving her hand dismissing Andre's comment. "Been there, done that, and loud enough for the neighbors to need earplugs."

The group exchanged glances, their raised eyebrows smiling "Why not?"

Andre shrugged his shoulders. "Fine with me."

All six gurneys in the lab were equipped with headgear identical to Michael's.

"Lie down, everybody. Let's go."

\* \* \*

Each slime worm the gang entered was fully engaged in mating frenzy, sliding up, down, back, over—every which way, as they secreted extra slime for the occasion. No other life form had evolved to threaten their status. The entire colony writhed unabashed, balling the afternoon away.

JANIE: The sexiest thing I've ever done was child's play compared to this. My entire body is having an orgasm!

SARAH: Oh, baby, me too. Remind me to add pheromones to my thank-you God list. So, Janie, what *was* the sexiest thing you ever did?

JANIE: Back in college, two other girls, three guys and I stripped naked, coated ourselves with strawberry massage oil, and rolled around like mud wrestlers. We never did figure out, or cared, who did what to whom.

SARAH: That sounds like when I…woah! Michael, is that you on my ass?

MICHAEL: I think so. Someone is riding me too.

KAREN. That's me. Don't ask me what I'm doing. I have no idea, but boy, does it feel great!

MICHAEL: I'm pretty sure you just did me, Karen. That's a switch!

KAREN: It was good for me! I'll send you flowers in the morning…

JANIE: Brad, Andre…where are you guys? I can't see two worms away.

BRAD: I don't want to kiss and tell, but Andre and I just had sex with eighty-seven female sides…at the same time! Someone call the Guinness Book of Records!

KAREN: Andre, you devil! I had no idea you were a lady's man.

ANDRE: Crop duster would be more accurate. Instead of laying them, they laid egg things, and we followed humpty-dumpty down the line. Quite satisfying actually.

MICHAEL: Hey, don't forget down here, we're male and female at the same time. The uniformity is comforting.

BRAD: Janie, on the way over one of the slimes taught me a new move. I can't wait to try it out.

JANIE: Help yourself, right after I show you the two spins I just picked up.

JANIE: Oh my god! Give it to me! Yes, again…again…deeper…
again…aaaah…yes, yes, yes…this is out of this world. What
fabulous sex lives! How long does it last?"

MICHAEL: Ten minutes every six months.

JANIE: Forget it. I can't go that long without.

ANDRE: I don't know about you guys, but I'm spent, and prefer to
leave on a long high note. Cyber…disconnect my slime worm…
reestablish my body inputs.

KAREN: I'll be right along, Andre. I've got one worm slurping my
girl side and another massaging my boy end. I could get used to
this, and I don't want to disappoint them.

MICHAEL AND BRAD, *in unison*: That's me. And thanks!

SARAH AND JANIE, *in unison*: We're leaving, guys. Pack it up.

MICHAEL AND BRAD: Yes, dear.

* * *

Back in the lab, everyone sat up at the same time. Everyone looked
at their lover at the same time. Everyone leaped to their lover at the
same time.

"It was like having sex and flying…my two favorite things,"
Brad said, Janie on his lap. "We've got to do that again. And, Andre,
when we catch up with evolution, can you make me an eagle?"

"I'll be a swan gliding across Crater Lake," Sarah sighed.

Michael grinned his dream. "I want to swing tree to tree like a
chimpanzee."

"Put me down for Cleopatra," Janie said.

"Is all that really possible?" Karen asked, awed.

Andre double-checked his readouts. "With restrictions, yes.
Our mind travels must be sporadic, not specific, with no human
visits longer than twenty-four hours."

"In that case," Karen said, fogged in by fantasy, "I'll be Mary
Magdalene for one night."

Andre opened his mouth to reply but stopped short when he
saw Cyber walk in trying out a new body, a musclebound Greek
Adonis in drag.

"Hello, everybody," Cyber said, cocky and proud. "How do I look?"

"Cyber," Janie said before Andre could answer, "I love your tiara—it matches your mustache perfectly. But the Catholic school dress over those supermodel legs…that doesn't work."

"What happened to the vagina thing?" Andre asked.

"Oh, I still have one," Cyber boasted. "I'm only male from the waist up. From the waist down…well…I can do it with myself."

Andre tried not to laugh but gave up when everyone else did. "No, no, that won't do. We're not going to sit around watching you do what it takes two of us to pull off. Listen, yesterday you were Marilyn Monroe, the day before Jane Mansfield. Pick a body by dinner and stick with it."

Cyber tipped his tiara the way John Wayne did a cowboy hat and answered, in bass register, "Yes, um, boss. This is all new to me. No wonder you humans smile so much. All you have to do is take off your clothes together."

"So why are you here, Cyber?" Andre asked, still unable to keep a straight face.

"To find out when to make Valentine's Day dinner reservations for you."

Andre was the only one listening. Michael had Sarah in his arms. She had her arms in Michael. Brad and Janie both had two hands below each other's waist.

"How can you even do that and keep walking?" Cyber asked.

Karen was at Andre's side, cooing in his ear, and tracing her finger up the inside of his leg.

"Well," Andre said, getting breathless, "it looks like it will take some time for the effects of slime pheromones to wear off. Let's play it safe and shoot for nine."

"Wise choice, Andre," Karen said, "it's time for your nap."

"Nap? You mean?"

"You'll need one when I get through with you."

\* \* \*

Every table in the dining room was set for two, with candles, chocolates, red roses, and heart candies, accompanied by a romantic violin serenade, just loud enough to ensure that each's couple's exchange remained private.

"You know, Janie," Brad said, reaching across the table to take her hand. "I'm not a science whiz or history encyclopedia, but I do important things for important people. And you should know that the most important thing to me...is to be important to you.

"We're good together. You get me. I can't imagine ever being without you. And you know...I'm a little...you know..."

"I know," Janie jumped in. "So am I."

"Yeah," Brad said reaching for Janie's other hand, almost tipping over her glass of champagne. "And well...I really...really...do..."

"Yes, Brad. I do too."

Michael and Sarah were at the next table, smiling into each other's eyes.

"You know," he began, "a year before the ship took off, I finished a log cabin overlooking Mt. Washington. Its six thousand square feet is supported post-and-beam. On the other side of my ten acres are hiking trails and ski trails, and it has a back porch for sunsets, and a front porch for sun rises.

"It took me years to finish it off. Then I moved in, stayed two weeks, and left. Something was missing.

"Now I know what was missing...four half-green kids and you."

"Does that mean," Sarah asked carefully, "that someday-not-now Michael has been replaced by...someday-yes-now Michael?"

"If you'll have me, make it someday-any-day."

Andre and Karen arrived late, just as the group was finishing "Somewhere over the Rainbow," the official trip memory. The soft lighting allowed them to slip by unnoticed, to the darkest corner of the room.

"Don't look now," Karen said, "but no one's looking at us."

"Nice change," Andre said, inhaling deeply. "Karen...over the last three months, I've said 'I love you' so many times that when I say the words now they seem to describe a circumstance rather than the rush of feelings that flood my soul.

"Karen…Karen…Karen…" he went on solemnly, "I never imagined a single word could mean so much to me. I respect you…I admire you…the entire universe is overwhelmed by your beauty. I know no other like you. I know no others like the two of us.

"On this voyage, I have met God…visited heaven…and found heaven on earth."

"Will you—"

*Tap, tap, tap…tap, tap, tap.*

"Andre," Cyber said, still bouncing her finger up and down on his shoulder.

Andre turned around to see Cyber, low-neckline, dressed formal—the spitting image of twenty-one-year-old Cher.

"Love the look," he said. "Hello, Cher."

"I may look like Cher. I may sing like Cher. I might even walk like Cher. But I am not Cher. I am my own person. My name is Cindy."

"Is that with a *C* or an *S*?"

"Either way, I'm flexible, thanks to you."

"Well, Cindy, we're in the middle of something. You're interrupting."

"At your request," Cindy said with a sprinkle of attitude.

"Meaning?"

"If everyone holds their breath, the quick-and-dirty fix-up I just finished might bring time travel back online."

Brad and Hank, seeing Andre race across the dance floor, jumped up and sped after him.

Karen turned toward Cindy and sighed, "Cyber, or Cindy, or whatever…your timing could be better."

"Sorry. Being a diva makes one bold."

"If you don't mind, I do have a favor to ask you."

"Certainly, precious."

"Could you add a decade to your appearance? It would make the rest of us look better."

"If you wish. But I'm not sure it's going to make a difference."

Cindy took Andre's place, crossed her legs, and asked, "What's new, girls?"

Then she noticed what was new. Andre had dropped a small black box when he rushed off.

"Oh, my," Cindy said, "Andre *dropped* it."

With that, Cindy bent down, picked up the box, went down on one knee, and held it out for Karen. "I swear," she said, tossing her hair to the side, "some days I have to do everything for that boy. He would be lost without me."

"What's that?" Janie called out as she and Sarah rushed over.

"Well," Sarah said, growing impatient as Karen took the box from Cindy, turned it in her fingers, and put it down on the table. "I really shouldn't open it," she said with a scrunched nose.

"Yes, you should," Cindy said, pushing it to the edge of the table in front of Karen.

"No, I shouldn't."

"He wants you to have it. Open it."

"I'm not going to, Cindy."

"Then I will."

# About the Author

S tephen St. John's back-
ground includes quan-
tum mechanics, astrophysics,
and a doctorate in medicine. He
is the author of *The Philosophy of
Science, The Science of Philosophy,
and The Politics of Survival.* The
author recommends the trea-
tise to anyone who has trouble
sleeping.

His latest accomplishment
*Beyond Time* blends romance,
adventure, and new age philosophy. We are a single family
blessed with a gem in a universe

that both amazes and bewilders us. We stare to the heavens wondering where from and what next. We have been given answers, so
many answers that we are no longer a family. Stephen St. John offers
suggestions.

Spirituality stands at the forefront of modern thinking, which
is one of the reasons *The Da Vinci Code* did so well. Stephen St. John
uses a different vehicle to introduce broader concepts. That vehicle is
a spaceship. There are no spooks in the closet or evil empires knock-
ing down the door, but it does carry the solution to 911.

The best opinion follows considering every opinion. Stephen
looks forward to hearing from you.

Made in United States
Orlando, FL
05 May 2023

32804790R00174